CORPSE
de Ballet

CORPSE
de Ballet

A Nine Muses Mystery:

Terpsichore

E L L E N P A L L

ST. MARTIN'S MINOTAUR
NEW YORK

www.minotaurbooks.com

Designed by Lorelle Graffeo

Library of Congress
Cataloging-in-Publication Data

Pall, Ellen
    Corpse de ballet : a nine muses
mystery : Terpsichore / Ellen Pall.—1st
ed.
        p. cm.
ISBN 0-312-28033-5
    1. Ballet companies—Fiction. 2.
Women novelists—Fiction. 3. New
York (N.Y.)—Fiction. I. Title.

PS3566.A463 C67 2001
813'.54—dc21
                            2001019174
First Edition: June 2001

10 9 8 7 6 5 4 3 2 1

for Billy

CORPSE
de Ballet

c h a p t e r

ONE

Like many marriages and most divorces, murder is more attractive on paper than it is in practice.

Who among us has not whiled away a happy hour planning the discreet dispatch of a superfluous colleague, or plotting the deft removal of a relative gone stale? In the quiet groves of thought, we may fondle harmlessly the garotte, the razor, even the bear trap. Smothering, poisoning, rabies, an opportune train, a gentle nudge—in soothing revery, all are ours to ponder.

Yet with murder, as Mark Twain once observed of life in general, it is easier to stay out than to get out. What begins with high hopes is apt to end in sorrow, in a welter of ugly details and frightening consequences. Or so, at least, thought Juliet Bodine, when in after-years she reflected on what she came to think of as the Summer of Too Great Expectations.

There was a curious gracefulness in the action of the hands that held the trim little hammer. Up and down it went, up and down, always precisely, always with a certain delicate care.

Beneath the silvery head, the cake of eyeshadow first cracked, then broke into a dozen tiny shards. The neat hands swept the remains together and resumed the process of gentle pulverization.

Eyeshadow had been only one of a number of possibilities. Cinnamon, nutmeg, cloves, Nesquik might also have done the trick. But after some experimentation, eyeshadow had won. It was simple and effective, the perfect solution for such a perfectly simple means of assault.

When at last the cosmetic had been crushed to a satisfactory fineness, a fork was introduced to mix in an equal amount of a snowy white powder. Then, a crisp page of paper was slipped beneath the resulting mound, curled into a funnel and raised to pour the compound into a small plastic jar. The screw-on cap closed with an easy twist.

There. The jar tumbled into the warmth of a pocket. Perhaps circumstances would fall out in such a way that it need never be used after all.

Or perhaps not.

It was a warm Tuesday evening in early July, and Juliet Bodine had decided to serve dinner to her old friend, Ruth Renswick, on the terrace of her apartment on Riverside Drive. Soft, brackish air drifted up to them off the Hudson, mingling with the fumes from the West Side Highway, the charcoal of the grilled shrimp before them, and the faint fragrance of roses in planters all around the terrace walls. Juliet, regretfully setting her fork down, sniffed cautiously at this New York potpourri and was flooded with memories of summers past. The sun had set, the dusk was gathering swiftly, and a mild coolness crept into the quickening breeze. Ruth gathered a black shawl up from behind her and pulled it over her bare shoulders.

The women had been talking about art and morality, which Juliet thought were completely unrelated and Ruth insisted had to be linked in some way. They started with Wagner and whether one might enjoy his music despite his historical legacy, then moved on through T. S. Eliot and Ezra Pound to the reflexive xenophobia of the great

English mystery writers of the 1930s. From there, they drifted to D'Annunzio, then Hergé, the Belgian author of the witty, delightfully drawn "Tintin" children's books and an enthusiastic Nazi collaborator.

At last, "Talent and ethics have exactly the same relationship as talent and height," Juliet declared. "Which is to say, none. A tall man can be a dreadful poet and a short man can be a towering poet. A good man can be a terrible poet and a terrible man a wonderful poet. Coleridge was an opium addict who deserted his wife. Rod McKuen's probably a saint."

When Ruth had no answer, Juliet at first imagined her adversary had conceded the argument. The silence went on for some moments, with Juliet feeling comfortably triumphant and Ruth apparently interested in a dust mote about three feet away from her in the darkening air. But suddenly, she dropped her head into her hands and groaned. After a moment, Juliet realized she was crying.

In the twenty or so years she had known Ruth Renswick, Juliet had never seen her cry. Scream, yes. Bully, threaten, rage, fume, sulk, manipulate—but weep? It was disconcerting, like seeing a cat out of breath.

"What is it?"

"Sorry," Ruth muttered. Hurriedly, she dashed away the tears spilling onto her cheeks. "It's this goddam ballet, this goddam *Great Expectations*. Damn *Great Expectations* anyway. I think this project is cursed."

Ruth lifted her face to look bleakly at the other, then dropped it again so that her graying bangs flopped into the remains of her salad.

"Today," she went on, addressing her place mat, "I spent six hours choreographing a pas de deux for Act One. And it's all wrong. I think everything I've done is wrong. And now the Jansch has decided to have it performed at the gala that opens the season, for Chrissake." She started to sniffle again. "Oh, shut up, Ruth," she snapped at herself. "Damn. Hell!"

Juliet studied the top of her friend's head. When they had met in college some fifteen or twenty years before, Ruth had had no friends at all. She was a wiry, sallow girl—dark, broody, sullen, and nearly mute. It wasn't until Juliet took a modern dance class (thus fulfilling a dreaded Phys Ed requirement) that she realized Ruth would reward attention. Juliet, small, round, and blond, a compulsive smiler with a misleading little-girl voice and a peaches-and-cream complexion, was astonished to see this human anchovy transformed by movement into a kaleidoscope of passion. Intrigued, she gently cultivated a friendship, advancing the intimacy by slow degrees until she came to see that Ruth, though she had the manners of a child reared by Siberian wolves, was, inside, a sterling person driven entirely by a need to dance. Through their twenties and into their thirties, Juliet had watched without surprise as Ruth rose steadily in the contemporary dance world, first as a performer, then (after two operations on her left knee and one on her right foot) as a choreographer. In spite of Ruth's lengthy wanderings in Europe and California, they had stayed close, drawn together as much by a mutual, rather amused appreciation of the extreme differences between them as by the bond of trust they had established in school.

Now, as they sat across from each other in the gathering summer night, the women seemed mildly drawn caricatures of the girls they had been when they met. Juliet was still soft and fair, with round blue eyes and a short, pale halo of curling blond hair; if anything, in fact, she appeared softer and even less worldly than she had in college, and when she spoke, her breathy, childish voice suggested something approaching simplemindedness. For her part, Ruth had grown only more angular and unsmiling. Her short hair was streaked with silver, but her body had the same forbidding tenseness of old. If Juliet had been introduced to her now, at a party or on the street, she would have assumed something awful had just happened to her, a catastrophic medical diagnosis, perhaps, or a deep, sudden betrayal. On the rare occasions when she introduced friends to Ruth, she always warned them to expect her to be abrupt, distrait, or worse.

Ruth, Juliet had been forced to admit as the years went by, was a bit of an acquired taste.

On the other hand, when Juliet's marriage had gone to hell some years ago, it had been Ruth who kept her sane. Ruth canceled her own plans to listen hour after hour while Juliet sniveled on the phone or in a café or a bar. Ruth pulled her out of her apartment and dragged her to concerts and movies. Ruth even had the kindness to sleep in Juliet's spare room a couple of nights, until Juliet got brave enough to face the apartment alone. In her fierce, wolfy way, Ruth loved Juliet. And she loved Ruth. So it was not merely rhetorically that Juliet asked now, "Is there anything I can do?"

Ruth looked up and blew her nose in her napkin. "Make me smarter?" she suggested. "Turn back the hands of time?" The unsettling tears started again to her eyes. "I'm not sure anything can be done. I'm not sure I can pull this off. Entre nous, I'm so scared I puked on my way to the studio this morning. And I only have eight more weeks to finish."

Unsure whether to make light of her fears or give them their full due, Juliet settled for more information. "How did this happen?"

Ruth rubbed the tears away again. "Now, that's the easy part. I made a mistake. When I wrote the synopsis, I assumed people knew the basic story of *Great Expectations*. But they don't, as I now have learned. Some of the dancers never even heard of it. One of them identified it as the name of a male escort service."

"So—change the synopsis?"

Ruth made a rude noise indicative of scorn. "The music was composed exactly according to my directions, Juliet," she said. "I gave the composer a scene-by-scene breakdown and he followed it to the second. Two-minute duet for Pip and Estella, thirty-second transition for the corps, seventy-five-second solo for Miss Havisham. Et cetera, et cetera. Now it can only be changed in the most minuscule details. I left myself no space to establish the characters, even to convey the narrative. So how do I do it? I can't use mime, it's antediluvian. I can't make things vague and impressionistic, because the Jansch is counting on a real story ballet to pull kids in, to sell tickets to families. And this stupid pas de deux today, which I thought would be so great . . ."

Ruth subsided into frustrated silence and sat staring off into the deepening dark. For a moment, Juliet feared she was going to start to cry again. But a few seconds later, she suddenly straightened and spoke as if deeply struck.

"You know, Juliet, maybe you could help me," she said. "As a matter of fact, I really think you are the very person who could."

Juliet raised her pale eyebrows till they disappeared briefly under her curly hair. "Ruth, dear, you saw me dance in Miss Lewis's class. I haven't improved. I really don't think—"

"Of course I don't want you to dance," Ruth said, with a contemptuous snort of laughter that Juliet tried to welcome as a sign of returning confidence. "I mean you could help with the storytelling, the characters, the synopsis. Why not? That's what you do best. And you must know *Great Ex* backwards and forwards."

"Oh!"

For a moment, Juliet seemed to lose the power of speech. It was true that she was good at storytelling. The very shrimp they were digesting had been bought with the proceeds of the dozen historical novels she had written under the pen name Angelica Kestrel-Haven, not to mention the Spode dish they sat in, the hand-painted table on which the dish was placed, and the wraparound terrace sixteen stories above the Hudson River that supported the table, herself, and Ruth. No one had been more surprised by the success of Angelica Kestrel-Haven than A K-H herself. Her works were historical novels, drawing-room comedies set in the English Regency era, gentle, literate farragoes of love and misunderstanding that owed much to the romance writer Georgette Heyer. When she had written the first one (*A Dandy Out of Fashion*, it was called), Juliet had been a full professor at Barnard, teaching English literature with a feminist slant. Sheer loathing of academia, combined with a low liking for genre fiction and a rainy summer misspent ten years ago in a rented cottage on Prince Edward Island, had inspired her to try (as they said in the Regency) her pen. To her astonishment, that first effort sold promptly and for a good sum. She invested it all in Microsoft (then trading at two dollars a share) and, six novels later, thanks to a series of similar forays into the stock market, smilingly declined Barnard's offer of tenure review.

Since then, there had been translations, book club sales, and several television movie options. Miss Kestrel-Haven was regularly asked to speak to groups of Anglophiles and futurophobes, aspiring writers and Societies for the Preservation of the English Regency. There was even a Kestrel-Haven Fan Club, complete with Web site and quarterly newsletter. Juliet seldom met a soul in Manhattan who had read or even heard of her, unless it was somebody's mother visiting from out of state, yet somehow the thirst for escape to the world of Jane Austen so greatly afflicted the nation that book after book could not slake it. She purchased a duplex penthouse on Riverside Drive and hired a personal assistant. To share the wealth, she agreed to chair a committee at the Authors Guild, recorded books for the blind, and donated a healthy slice of her earnings to various causes and cultural institutions.

The abrupt explosion of a car alarm on the street far below coincided exactly with Ruth's next words, so that Juliet had to ask her to repeat them.

"I said, will you come in tomorrow?"

Ruth's tone was briskly impatient (for her, the nearest thing to imploring), yet Juliet hesitated. She herself could not have said why. Most days, she would jump at an excuse to escape her desk for a few hours. That very morning, she had reordered her sock drawer, written four thank-you notes, and alphabetized her "future ideas" file rather than get to work on *London Quadrille,* her current novel. Writing was interesting, but it was never easy, and Juliet now knew herself to be one of those many writers who will do almost anything rather than sit down to the terrifying, blank sheet of paper: run errands, make phone calls, pay bills, polish silver, chop vegetables, even scrub the floor.

At first, being Angelica had been illicit fun, a quasi-decadent escape from her real-life job as a professor. But as Angelica had become her professional identity, writing had begun to feel like work. It was the difference between an affair and a marriage. Now, whole months sometimes went by without Juliet writing a page, months when the thought of whipping up even a dollop of literary froth made her want to go to sleep. At such times, almost anything seemed pleasant and easy by comparison. While avoiding *Duke's Delight*, she had picked up a working knowledge of spoken Chinese. *Present Love*, one of Angelica K-H's earlier novels, provided an occasion to learn how to sight-sing. Juliet felt guilty and furtive about these apparent detours, but she preferred not to term them writer's "blocks"—an ugly word, she thought. Instead, she tried to see them as necessary bends in the circuitous, mysterious road to achievement. And, as she often argued to herself, she did almost always find inspiration in her absences, as if invention were a pot that could not boil while watched. She worried—worried constantly—about meeting her deadlines. Yet, somehow, she always did. Writing down a hundred thousand words did not take very long in and of itself, she sometimes observed. It was choosing the words that was time-consuming.

She squinted at the translucent shrimp tails on her plate and tried to block out the racket of the car alarm. It was the kind that sounds like a German klaxon alternating with a fire siren, and she had been a little depressed to notice a few months ago that she'd gotten so used to the pattern, she'd almost come to enjoy it. Surely a visit to the Jansch studios would be rather fun?

Besides, it was Juliet Bodine's general policy to help friends in need immediately and without stint. Her mother having died when Juliet was three, friends had become her family. She had no siblings. Her father was a freewheeling, high-flying, mercurial cad who probably ought never to have married in the first place. Always successful in business, Ted Bodine had provided his small daughter with a capable nanny, a plush room in a handsome apartment over Park Avenue, and the best private schooling available. But he had given her little in the way of personal contact. For personal contact, Ted Bodine preferred a series of women in their twenties. Juliet grew up feeling herself a cross between Sara Crewe and Eloise, with a soupçon of Christie Hefner thrown in for irony. Her father still lived across town, and they met for dinner now and then. But for her, the Upper East Side of Manhattan was a haunted place. The alley formed by the tall buildings along Park Avenue was her Valley of the Shadow of Death, and the very epaulets on the doormen threw a cold chill into her heart.

But as a grown-up, nesting in her own roomy, airy place on the Upper West Side—a region she considered a different city from the Upper East Side—Juliet had collected a family of her own. Her agent, Kimmy Lauer, her neighbors June Corelli and Suzy Eisenman, her dear e-mail correspondent and fellow connoisseur of unfamiliar words (naumachia, anarthria), Simon Leff, her writers' group, her former classmates (Ruth being one) and academic colleagues, as well as various others formed the core of a virtual cult of friendship by which she lived. The world, she believed, was cold and hard; the least friends could do was work to be kind to each other.

And yet, petitioned by Ruth for aid—Ruth, who would have chewed off her own paw if Juliet had needed help—she hesitated. She had a funny feeling, a notion that going into the Jansch would mean crossing a boundary into a world that was . . . that was what? She couldn't possibly think ballet was dangerous?

Her hesitation lasted only a few seconds, and she hoped it had not troubled her friend. With a smile at her own ridiculousness, she shook herself mentally, looked up, and said, "Absolutely. Don't worry. We'll fix you up in two little shakes."

At exactly 11:55 on the morning of the next day, Juliet stepped out of the elevator and into the sleek little lobby of the Jansch Repertory Ballet Troupe headquarters. After some thought, she had decided not to change out of her habitual jeans and T-shirt for this visit. But as she gave the receptionist her name, she regretted the decision. She felt out of place in this stylish bandbox of chrome and leather and hoped the receptionist—Gayle Remson, according to the nameplate sitting on her desk—would wave her on at once. But alas, instead of pointing her straight to Ruth, Ms. Remson (petite, fortyish, dressed in a neat summer sheath and crowned with a shining helmet of apricot-colored hair) asked her to sit down, then told an intercom, "Miss Bodine is here."

Eight seconds later, Max Devijian, executive director of the Jansch, sailed down the hall and into the lobby, his arms raised, his carefully tended hands stretched before him, as if Juliet's head were a particularly gorgeous hat he could not wait to try on. Juliet, familiar with his habits, attempted to turn away strategically, so that he could salute only one cheek. But, as was his way, he seized her skull regardless and soundly bussed her left and right.

Max Devijian was a slender, compact man with huge, dark eyes, a receding hairline, and that effusive, embracing sort of energy which can neither be fully resisted nor entirely trusted. As executive director of the Jansch, it was his job to kiss and cozy up to people like Juliet, New Yorkers with money who were well disposed to the lively arts. And he was very good at his job. In the four or five years since his arrival at the Jansch, he had transformed it from a large, shabby, second-rate company—a company with excellent dancers but a musty repertory that had barely changed since the late Florence Jansch founded the group in 1934—into a large, revitalized, increasingly first-rate troupe. Like all good fund-raisers, he took it as a given that people wanted to hand their money over to someone; they just didn't know who. In his former post, at Lincoln Center, he had been known for efficiency, zeal and—his only weakness, perhaps—a certain impatience with those whose good opinion he did not need. Since that included the company's artistic director, support staff, rehearsal pianists, ballet mistress and masters, even most of the dancers, Devijian was a more popular man outside than inside the organization he served.

"Miss Bodine," he now pronounced, his tone implying that it was a tremendous satisfaction to him simply to say her name. He had an odd, distinctively raspy voice, a little high for a man. He released her head, but took hold of her arm as he drew her toward a nearby sofa.

Juliet stiffened involuntarily. She had cut her work short to be here today. Of course, it was lovely to be out of her office and in such an unfamiliar setting—an unearned release, like cutting high school or getting out of jury duty early. But now that she was here, she was eager to go in to Ruth, not sit and have her favor curried.

But Max was adamant. "When Ruth mentioned you were coming, I insisted on having a moment with you. I must fill you in on our new season," he said firmly.

Juliet tried to make herself relax. She had known Max for some years now, ever since she volunteered some money to rescue a failing arts-in-the-schools program he had initiated. Once he had made up his mind to "fill you in" on something, nothing stopped him.

"It's going to be marvelous," he declared. "Best ever." He then presented a flowing summary of each planned production, oozing on about this dancer and that set designer. He crowed about grants he had managed to get, then backtracked to make sure she knew the Jansch could still use more funding. He asked what she was writing, whether she planned to travel this summer, how she knew Ruth. *Great Expectations*, he said, would not only open the season, it would be the centerpiece of the Jansch's year, the focus of all possible attention.

"The music is splendid, you know," he added. "Have you heard it?"

Juliet shook her head. She knew that the composer was Ken Parisi, an Englishman known mainly for composing the music for various Masterpiece Theatre productions. Ruth had been dubious about his ability to write for dancers, but it turned out he had experience in that area as well, and in fact the music pleased and excited her very much.

Inevitably, Max burst out in a string of superlatives describing Parisi's music, ignoring, as he went on, a youthful man who had hesitated as he entered the reception area, then come to within a few steps of Juliet. Here he stood, clearly waiting to have a word with her. He was slight and graceful, about thirty-five years old, with a long face, small blue eyes, and a short, thick mass of kinky red hair. Juliet recognized him as Ruth's assistant, Patrick Wegweiser, whom she had met at performances of Ruth's work once or twice before. With a dancer's poise, but something also of a human being's impatience, he stood listening quietly to Devijian's vague description of music he himself, as Ruth's aide-de-camp, had been listening to and discussing for the past six months. When at last Max paused for breath, Juliet hopped up from the sofa and firmly took Patrick's arm. An instant later, Max also jumped up suddenly, as if at a pleasant surprise—as if Patrick had been invisible until Juliet touched him. With a faint feeling of disgust, she finally extricated herself from Devijian's chatter, said good-bye, and turned to follow Patrick down a corridor into the mazy studios.

The Jansch troupe was headquartered in three floors of a former upholsterer's warehouse on Amsterdam Avenue, on the Upper West Side of Manhattan. South lay Lincoln Center and Carnegie Hall, north the great food emporia of Fairway, Citarella, and Zabar. From the polished uppermost floor, where the lobby and executive offices were located, spindly metal staircases at either end of the building spiraled down into the grimier works of the place. A dancers' lounge, small offices, and rehearsal rooms occupied the middle story; on the lowest floor were the company's big rehearsal studios and the dancers' locker rooms.

Though the architects would seem to have had plenty of space to start with, the various rooms on all three stories felt jumbled and crammed in, as if they had been modeled on dice spilled at random. Dim, narrow corridors ran at peculiar angles among them, and the staircases seemed to Juliet, as she descended first one, then the next, in Patrick's wake, unnecessarily slender and rickety.

Devijian had so delayed her that now, as Patrick explained, the first hour of rehearsal was in full swing. (The dancers' mornings were devoted to warm-ups and classes.) Piano music drifted from behind doors along the hallways as she and Patrick reached the first floor, bits of *Sleeping Beauty* and *Giselle*, but the windows in the closed doors were too high and small for Juliet to see through without stopping.

"Ruth's in Studio Three," Patrick murmured, pointing her to the left as they came to a four-way intersection of halls. A dancer apparently dressed in rags leaned against a wall here, her eyes closed, her slim right leg extended, foot severely pointed before her. Juliet hurried by, all of a sudden acutely aware of the comfortable cellulite pouches on her either side of her own thighs. She was relieved when Patrick interrupted her thoughts.

"I'm really glad you're here," he said. "Ruth's kind of been losing momentum, and I'm afraid it's infecting the dancers."

As she replied, Juliet noticed, not for the first time, that there was something about Patrick that made him a natural helper, some quality in him that seemed to want to set aside his own agenda in favor of another person's. He was a happy server. She was soon to learn that this quality of being able to lend oneself, physically, emotionally, and intellectually, to another's purpose was exactly what a choreographer needed in a dancer.

Aware that he had worked for Ruth for years, "Have you ever seen her flounder this way on a new project?" she asked.

He shrugged. "Anything new is a challenge," he allowed, "but—no, not like this. She's really rat— Oh, excuse me—" He stopped walking suddenly, raised a cautioning hand, turned his face away from Juliet, then sneezed explosively. "Sorry," he said, over Juliet's automatic blessing. "I have a summer cold. We all do, it's germ warfare in there. I was about to say, she's really rattled."

Put off by the prospect of an hour in a studio full of cold

germs—Juliet hated colds, and what was it about "summer" colds that seemed to make people think they were charming?—she nevertheless said gamely, "Well, I stayed up all night rereading *Great Expectations*, if that's any help."

"I'm sure it will be."

Patrick smiled again. He had stopped before yet another closed door and now peeked in through the window. A piano rendition of a spiky melody Juliet did not recognize could be heard in the corridor, its notes muffled by the door. After a moment, Patrick moved back and beckoned to her to take his place. She peered in. Ruth was inside, working with a very tall, lithe dancer Juliet recognized as Lily Bediant. She had been a Jansch principal for years, perhaps decades, Juliet thought. She wondered if it were possible Bediant could still be taking leading roles. Margot Fonteyn, she knew, had danced through her forties, but that was hardly the rule, and Bediant must be forty at least.

A second dancer, a tall, icy blonde Juliet did not recognize, stood nearby, watching carefully each move Ruth and Lily made. "That's Kirsten Ahlswede," Patrick whispered suddenly in her ear. He had come forward so quietly that she had not even sensed him. Now he peered in over her shoulder. "You must know Lily."

Juliet nodded.

"We'll just wait until she reaches a little pause," said Patrick, the "she" clearly referring to Ruth. Indeed, every time he mentioned Ruth, there was something almost reverential in his tone, as if were saying "the admiral" or even "her Grace." "Kirsten is Estella in the first cast," he added. "Lily is the first Miss Havisham."

"There's a second Miss Havisham?"

"There's a second everyone. Eventually, in fact, there will be three casts. What they're working on now," he added, "is a pas de deux where Miss Havisham teaches Estella a dance to enchant men but also to keep them at arm's length. That little tune is Estella's motif. We've been working on it for days."

Ruth had taken hold of Lily Bediant's graceful arm and was

moving it up and down, in and out, apparently trying to convey the trajectory of a gesture she envisioned, as well as the degree of anger it was to carry. It was quite angry, and when Lily tried it a moment later, Ruth shook her head and showed her again what she wanted, demonstrating this time with a slash of what seemed authentic fury.

"What's the difference between the casts?" Juliet asked.

"The first cast dances on opening night and Saturday nights, and probably most of the other performances. The second will dance too, but probably mostly matinees. The third cast is really more like understudies, in case of injuries. Normally, a choreographer only works with the first cast while the dance is being created, but Ruth likes to take ideas from everyone. That's why Elektra Andreades and Mary Christie are there. See them? That small, dark woman who looks like you imagine Cleopatra must have looked—Cleopatra during a famine, anyway—that's Elektra Andreades. She's the second Estella. Mary, the lady with the pigtails next to her, is her Miss Havisham."

Juliet glanced at the women. "And who is the first Pip?"

She scanned the studio for likely candidates. Some four dozen dancers were ranged around the vast room, which was mirrored on three walls and windowed on the fourth. Long barres were attached to the walls on either end of the room. The floor was of dark, battered linoleum; fluorescent lights glared unsteadily from above. The windows, Juliet could see even from this distance, were extremely dirty, admitting only a dim, unwholesome glow. They faced north, with a view of a solid brick wall a few feet away.

Patrick drew back a bit from the door, and his voice went up a couple of keys. "Ruth didn't tell you?"

Juliet shook her head.

"Anton Mohr. You know, the German dancer? Greg Fleetwood just managed to sign him last year. He's only nineteen. He is quite amazing."

"I've seen him. Not with the Jansch yet, but he danced with the Royal Ballet a few years ago, didn't he?"

"Yes. What did you see, *Billy the Kid*?"

"*Petrushka.*" Juliet looked back in through the window, trying to match one of the dancers inside with the blaze of glorious energy she recalled from that evening.

"Lucky you," said Patrick from behind her, as her gaze finally came to rest on a young man lying on the floor near the piano, knees bent, one hand under the small of his back, engaged in raising and lowering first one, then the other, extraordinary leg. Like all the other dancers, he was dressed in tatters—it seemed to be de rigueur—but even his faded brown T-shirt and threadbare black tights could not disguise the tall, magnificent body inside them. From this curious angle, with Mohr lying down and facing away from the door, Juliet could see only the top of his head and a sliver of face; but it was enough. His lush hair fell in thick, honey-blond waves; his taut skin was creamy, his forehead smooth, his nose straight, his lips full. As she watched, he relaxed his legs, withdrew his hand and lifted his head. With an effortless, articulated elegance, he arched his back and turned to look at what she would later find was a clock over the door. His heavily lidded eyes were jade green and huge, his gaze sleepy and sensuous. No wonder Patrick sounded faintly orgasmic.

"Mm," Juliet agreed. "Who's the second Pip?"

Patrick's tone lost its dreaminess. "Oh, Hart Hayden, of course. Elektra's partner. They've been dancing together since they were teenagers at North Carolina School of the Arts."

"Hart Hayden?" echoed Juliet, who had seen him dance several times. "But didn't he dance Romeo on opening night last year? Why would he be the second Pip? He was wonderful."

She tried to pick him out among the dancers inside as Patrick answered, "Oh, yes, Hart's great. Ruth worked with him here a few years ago, when they mounted a revival of her one-act, *Cycles*. But his style is totally different than Anton's. Hart's very balletic, you know, very up in the air and youthful and effortless, that kind of classic ballet thing. Wonderful precision, really breathtaking. He was terrific in *Cycles*. But for this, Ruth wants a more athletic, muscular movement. Which Anton has."

"But isn't he a principal? And Elektra Andreades?" asked Juliet, still puzzled. She thought she had located Hayden, sitting under a barre between a woman tapping a busy rhythm on her bony knees and another who seemed to be clipping her toenails with a kitchen shears. His back was very straight, his arms stretched up to the wooden rod above him. He was very short and slight—considerably shorter and slighter than he appeared on the stage—but she recognized his fine, shingled, extremely pale hair and the long, narrow, handsome face it framed. For a dancer, he looked unusually intellectual, Juliet thought; the bones of his face were sharp, and intelligence shone from the light-colored eyes beneath his pale eyebrows. She could easily have taken him for a State Department policy analyst had he not been wearing burgundy tights and a faded black T-shirt with "Ballet Rio" printed on it in white. Now that she looked at him, she realized she knew Elektra Andreades too—knew her to see her on stage, anyway. She looked Andreades over again, this time taking in more clearly the heavy dark hair and ivory skin, the clear, slightly tilted brown eyes, the delicate, idiosyncratic lift of the head as she stood, hardly five feet tall, absorbed in watching the choreographer. Certainly she had been Hayden's partner in last year's *Romeo and Juliet*, but without her costume and stage makeup, she looked a dozen years older than the love-struck adolescent she had played. Juliet supposed that meant Hayden was also thirty or so by now, since the two had met in ballet school.

"Oh, you bet," Patrick answered. "In fact, they've pretty much been the brightest lights of the company for years. But—" He fell silent abruptly, drew himself straighter, and gently turned the knob, pushing in at the door. "She's stopping now," he whispered. "Let's go in."

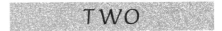
The first thing Juliet noticed as she entered the studio was the heat. It was warm outside—it was July, after all—but the studio was so hot and the air so damp that a cloud of outrushing steam seemed to roll over her as she followed Patrick in. It was like walking into the tropical glasshouse at a botanical garden—or rather, she corrected, as the smell assaulted her, at the zoo. She had already gotten a hint of this odor in the corridors, but here it was a Phil Spector–style Wall of Smell: sweat, perfume, sweat, cologne, more sweat, deodorant, powder, yet more sweat.

Juliet Bodine was afflicted with hyperosmia, a highly abnormal sense of smell. Her nose was sensitive to a degree that was freakish. Moreover, like a person who can't filter out background noise, she experienced all odors in her vicinity with equal immediacy. Scents flooded up to her from every corner of whatever place she walked into, so that the fragrance of a vase of flowers on the mantelpiece at the distant end of a long living room slammed into her with no less force than the reek of a glass of Scotch on the coffee table at her elbow. The roses on her terrace, which she kept for their visual beauty, had been chosen for their near lack of aroma. She was the only person she knew who smoked tobacco for medical reasons: A handful of cigarettes a day dulled her nose just enough to make New York tolerable.

She crept in behind Patrick hoping to make as little stir as possible. But she soon realized her efforts to be unobtrusive were needless. While they were in motion, the dancers kept their eyes diligently glued to the mirror, apparently lost in a world of literal self-reflection. When at rest (except for a few of the most junior members of the corps), they were far too well trained in maintaining their dignity to look at her, or at least to be seen looking at her.

Ruth, by contrast, came anxiously to meet her, kissing her on the cheek and urging her to make herself comfortable on one of the three or four chairs ranged along the east wall, by the door. She was wearing a much-washed green sweatshirt with the sleeves cut off, long enough so it struck her white tights mid-thigh. Ruth had not gained an ounce since college. She fit right in among the stick-thin, wisp-waisted ballerinas around her. Juliet, on the other hand, felt as if she were waddling across the floor, even though her softly rounded, familiar little body was normally quite comfortable to her. While the subject of body weight generally bored her silly, she could not help but notice the almost anorexic faces on several of the dancers, Elektra Andreades especially. Her fair skin, made to seem even fairer by her fine, dark eyes and the dark hair that fell to her shoulders, seemed almost too scarce to cover her sharp jaw and delicate nose; her collarbones and shoulders poked up like spiky pebbles from under her leotard, as did a row of bumps down the center of her sternum and the "outie" bellybutton on the tiny dome of her tummy. Lily Bediant was bone-thin, lean in a hard, sharp way that was almost scary. Her large eyes—could they really be violet?—had a cold, predatory look, and with her crinkly, almost platinum mane of hair, she reminded Juliet of a rather feral Australian Shepherd. The men looked less likely to blow away in a good breeze, but even they were generally more slender than they appeared on stage. All the dancers held themselves with a self-conscious poise that struck Juliet as almost smug, as if being encased in their bodies were a particularly great honor. In fact, thought

Juliet, every one of them looked as if his or her coronation were just about to begin.

Wishing herself invisible, she schlumped into a chair as far from them as possible. Ruth knelt down at her side.

"Thank you," she whispered.

"Don't be silly. You know I'd pay money to get out of writing."

"Did Patrick explain to you what we've been doing?"

Juliet nodded.

"I want this duet to encompass all the malevolence of Miss Havisham, but also the way she can't see Estella as a separate individual—her narcissism, you know?" Ruth explained. "And I want to make it clear that Estella is completely dependent on her, and always has been. She's like an abused child, she doesn't know anything else."

Ruth murmured on for some while, referring eventually to the synopsis, a copy of which she had faxed to Juliet late the night before. The pas de deux came early in the first act, which Ruth felt was necessary both dramatically (you had to show your prima ballerina before too much time went by, after all) and for clarity. But it felt static to her, she now realized, and this was the stumbling block that had been driving her to despair.

"It's a set piece," Juliet diagnosed. "It doesn't advance the narrative."

"That's right," Ruth exclaimed, as if much struck. "It is. It's free-standing. It doesn't flow from what precedes it and it doesn't lead anywhere."

This apparently dismal epiphany seemed to have the paradoxical effect of allowing Ruth to find her solution.

"It needs to have Pip watching," she exclaimed, and visibly breathed easier. She sprang to her feet, then began to move, by herself at first, then with Patrick, whom she grabbed and forced to act as her Estella. Juliet, who had never seen Ruth actually create, watched in astonishment as a new set of steps seemed to flow out of her.

"Anton, I need you to stand there," she said, after three or four minutes of twirling and hopping and gliding on various angles with Patrick. She pointed to a spot off to the side from where she had been working. "You're not going to do much, but you must watch intently, as if you were peeking into a house through a French door. Luis, start from measure twenty-four," she added, calling to the pianist, who had been hidden from Juliet when she peered in, but who she now saw was a small, paper-dry, middle-aged man with thick glasses and large liver spots on his face and hands, as well as under his thinning gray hair. Even with his nimble hands on the keyboard, he had an air of fussiness; his clothes were crisp and spotless and much more formal than those of anyone around him, and he moved his head pedantically at the start of each new measure.

"Andante," Ruth added, as she felt her way tentatively into the new idea, barking now and again at Patrick, "Try a rond de jambe there. Come around this way. No, fall back against me."

Anton, meanwhile, rose as bidden and went to a low wooden box, like a small sandbox, near one of the windows. Into this he dipped each of his feet, rubbing them briefly against whatever was inside. He then spread his arms, leapt from one foot to the other and executed a swift, experimental spin before going to the place Ruth had indicated. He watched her work with Patrick for a moment, then chose to crouch as if looking into the house from behind a bit of hedge. His face took on a look of intense curiosity, and the very rise and fall of his broad shoulders and chest with each breath were somehow expressive of his interest. Immediately, Juliet saw that Ruth had been right; with the innocent Pip looking on, Miss Havisham's lesson acquired a tension and forward thrust it had not had before.

At the end of each sequence of steps, Ruth would ask, "Did somebody get that?" and look to Lily Bediant or Kirsten Ahlswede, both of whom stood watching her, then trying slowly to replicate what she had done. Hart Hayden had stood up and positioned himself vis-à-vis Lily and Kirsten in a spot corresponding to the one Anton had taken. He did not crouch, however. Instead, after a moment of reflection, he hovered sidewise, as if concealed by one side of the frame of the French door. Though his face showed only the effort of professional concentration, the excitement of the secret watcher trembled in each elegant limb.

A few yards toward the back of the room, Elektra Andreades and the pigtailed, sinewy Mary Christie also echoed Ruth and Patrick's movements, though even more hesitantly. How all these dancers could possibly catch and remember such a fluid series of movements as Ruth was whirling through, Juliet had no idea, but they did. She supposed they were trained to do it, like actors who must remember improvised lines.

As Ruth worked on, going back again and again to start at measure twenty-four, Juliet allowed her attention to wander away to the only other person in the room seated in a chair. This was an elderly, slim, extremely erect woman dressed all in black: black tights and leotard, and a short, flaring black skirt tied around her waist. That she had once been a dancer was apparent not only from her clothes but her carriage and even her smoothly scraped-back hair, which, though silver, was long and twisted behind her into a bun. She sat with a clipboard on her lap and a pencil in her slender right hand, her handsome dark eyes fixed with minute attention on Ruth and the movements she was making. From time to time, she removed her authoritative gaze from the choreographer to make a little note on the paper clipped to her clipboard. Patrick would later identify her as Victorine Vaillancourt, once the star of the Paris Opera Ballet. For many, many years now, Mlle. Vaillancourt had been senior ballet mistress at the Jansch, overseeing the little cadre of masters and mistresses who gave the daily classes and rehearsed the dancers in the Jansch's repertory. Lily Bediant had been her particular protégée, Patrick added, and Victorine was concerned to ensure that none of the modern movements Ruth might require would unduly strain and injure her now decidedly mature pet—or, of course, the other dancers in her care. Ruth planned to keep her ballerinas in pointe shoes, a footgear not always convenient when dancing in her style.

Her initial spurt of invention over, Ruth at last dispensed with Patrick and was starting to work directly with Kirsten and Lily when Victorine stood up. Juliet, who was still looking in her direction, saw that she rose very slowly, and that her lips and jaw tightened briefly with effort or pain. However, she moved quite confidently toward Patrick, who had squatted to make a few notes in a notebook of his own and was again carefully watching Ruth. The moment Victorine caught his attention, she raised her eyebrows meaningfully. Patrick turned quickly to look at the clock above the door, then back to Ruth. He gave a respectful cough, which she ignored, then reluctantly went close enough to lay a hand on her arm.

She looked up angrily, but when Patrick again turned his eyes toward the clock, her expression changed. As Juliet later learned, the all-important, union-decreed break was upon them, indeed overdue. With a sullen frown, Ruth grudgingly dismissed the dancers for fifteen minutes. All around the room, company members took advantage of the pause to stand, stretch, gossip, wander about the unbearably stuffy studio, or flee it, take a swallow from a bottle of Evian tucked into their dance bags or nibble the smaller end of a baby carrot. Most of all, as it seemed to Juliet, they blew their noses. The ballerinas blew them delicately, the male dancers mightily, but they all seemed to need to clear them, and Juliet made a mental note to take zinc and buy stock in whoever made Sudafed. The place was a bacterium sanctuary, she thought, watching the dancers cross and crisscross the room, faces buried in Kleenex. Apart from everything else, they seemed to touch one another constantly, not only when dancing (as of course they must) but while walking or making plans or greeting each other or saying good-bye. Kisses, caresses, massages, tweaks, squeezes, all varieties of flesh-to-flesh contact were the rule. Juliet, dreading contagion, unconsciously folded her arms and tucked her hands under her armpits.

She had thought Ruth would want to confer with her again, but in fact, the choreographer worked on, pressing poor Patrick into servitude even during this piano-less general intermission. Hart

Hayden also came forward and resumed his sidelong position as Pip, an act of generosity Ruth seemed to appreciate, for she stared at him between bursts of steps as if the mystery of where to go next were contained in his face. He did not appear to mind being treated as an object in this way. His expression was alert but quite impassive, as if he were an artist's model Ruth was painting. Yet, after a few minutes, as Ruth experimented with a section in which Patrick, as Estella, seemed to fall under Miss Havisham's spell, moving as if in dreamy hypnosis, Hayden slowly broke his pose, took a few steps backward and also began to perform the same steps and gestures, foreshadowing the power Miss Havisham would ultimately wield over Pip.

"I like that, Hart," Ruth said, panting by now after half an hour or more of constant exertion. "That's good. Patrick, look at him. Keep that."

Glancing at Hayden's face, Juliet thought she caught just the ghost of a smile pulling at the habitual, nobly indifferent set of his mouth. A moment later, Anton returned from a visit to some place outside the studio door and Ruth asked Hart to show him the new steps. Meantime, Ruth herself sat down on the floor, flopped over so that her forehead approached her shins and gasped in the direction of her knees. She might be in excellent shape for her age, but a life in dance takes its toll on the body. Juliet gave her a minute, then approached, intending to take her leave. On the whole, it had not been such a difficult favor to do—in fact, it had been rather interesting and fun, she thought. But she really ought to get back to her own work. It was not yet two o'clock. If she went home immediately, she could still confer with her assistant, Ames, about the text for her lecture (on "Revery and Reading") before the Association of University Departments of Folklore and Mythology meeting in Boston next month, then get in another three or four pages before knocking off for the day. She crouched near Ruth.

"Thank God you're here," Ruth breathed at her. "That went so much better. Thank you. Now, when they all come back, I'm going to go back to the corps' first scene. They're villagers, of course, and I want you to see what they could be doing that's a little less literal than what I have. I'm afraid it looks like a rock musical."

"Ruth—"

"It can't look like a rock musical. Greg Fleetwood would kill me."

Gregory Fleetwood, Juliet knew, was the artistic director of the Jansch, a former star of the ballet world who still wielded considerable influence.

"It was criminal of me to let the corps sit all that session," Ruth was going on. "Do you know how much that costs? I was just so flummoxed until you came. Honey, I'm going to owe you bigtime."

"Ruth, I don't think you need me to stay any longer, do you?" Juliet finally managed to say.

Ruth looked up, her dark, sulky face a mask of horror. "You're not going to leave me!" she more or less snarled. "Juliet, you just got here."

"But you've solved your stumbling bl—"

"But it's all stumbling blocks! You can't go!"

Juliet opened her mouth to suggest Ruth could at least try to work on her own from here, but closed it again as she recalled the summer of her divorce. Ruth had been there for her, not just for a quick cheering-up or two, but over many weeks. She supposed she could just dust off the lecture she'd given to the Cyberomantics in Santa Fe last year and spruce it up a bit for Boston. And she wasn't too far behind on her schedule for London Quadrille. Yet.

Meanwhile, a tide of dancers began to sweep through the open door and settle on the fringes of the room, washing Juliet away from Ruth. Victorine Vaillancourt entered arm in arm with Lily Bediant. Behind them came a woman who looked strangely like an older, taller, slightly distorted version of Elektra Andreades. Then a little crowd of dancers came in all at once, a knot of men and women including Elektra herself. A moment later, a tall, muscular young man with thick black hair and rough, handsome features entered and hurried after her.

With a strong, surprisingly elegant hand, he caught at Elektra's elbow and pulled her away from the little crowd she'd been with. The man's eyebrows were very dark and the eyes they surmounted looked both angry and cold at once. He was a strikingly good-looking man—most of them were, come to that—but there was a ferociousness about him, a lack of ordinary, civilized restraint in his movements, that Juliet found disturbing. However, he did not seem to trouble Elektra. She regarded him with serene detachment as he raised one heavy eyebrow and said, quite audibly, "We have to talk." Then she ignored him as he turned abruptly away and strode off toward one of the barres.

"Who's that?" Juliet asked Patrick, who had materialized by her side after enjoying a break of some two or three minutes, during most of which time he had attended to his own overflowing nose.

"Ryder Kensington. Mr. Elektra Andreades."

"They're married?"

Patrick nodded.

"Is he a principal?"

He shook his head. "Never made it out of the corps. They were both in the corps when they married, I think. But Ruth likes him. She cast him as Magwitch. He's quite good."

"I see," Juliet said thoughtfully. "And who's the woman who looks so much like Elektra Andreades?"

"Olympia Andreades." He smiled. "Elektra's big sister."

"Oh! Is she in the corps, too?"

"Yep."

"Hmm."

Intrigued and a bit unsettled by the anger she had seen in his face, Juliet sought out Ryder Kensington again, locating him as he finally reached a corner at the farthest end of the room. Once there, he cleared a bit of a space and began to practice a powerful kind of leap Juliet could not name; it was short and quick and involved a little kick and turn before a landing on bent knee. Even from across the room, Juliet could see the thick, hard muscle tense on his thigh as he landed. His expression severe, he performed the maneuver perhaps half a dozen times before Ruth clapped and brought the room back to order. Uneasily, Juliet resumed her chair and prepared to observe for another hour.

Some ten minutes into the session, Gregory Fleetwood stole noiselessly into Studio Three. To Juliet's surprise, he came directly to her, seated himself in the chair beside hers, put out his hand and, with a sort of noblesse oblige, murmured his name.

"Juliet Bodine," she whispered back. After a moment of inward debate, "We've met," she added.

Fleetwood's thin, angled eyebrows shot up skeptically, but the rest of his aristocratic features gathered in an expression that implied the mere possibility delighted him. Before Max Devijian managed to sign him on as the Jansch's artistic director, Gregory Fleetwood had danced with most major American companies and quite a few European ones. Even now, in his early fifties, he carried with him a powerful aura of artistic authority. He was tall, with sharp, hawklike features and an arrogant bearing that trumped even the accomplished arrogance of the company's foremost current performers. As the new artistic director, he had torn into the Jansch, sweeping away every vestige of quaintness and signing up principals from leading companies all over the world. While maintaining the traditional repertory, he invited contemporary composers and cutting-edge choreographers in to experiment with the Jansch's classically trained dancers. It was typical of Fleetwood that he was backstage with Ruth Renswick on the very night her triumphant one-act *Wuthering Heig, .s,* choreographed on the Los Angeles Ballet, premiered. As the curtain fell, he offered her a commission to create a full-length story ballet for the JRBT, and in the ecstasy of the moment, the normally cautious Renswick shrieked, "Yes!"

Now Juliet gazed into his thin, bird-of-prey face, which was surrounded by a corona of Little Prince–style, spiky yellow hair. She clearly remembered seeing him perform a number of times. He had danced with extraordinary beauty and éclat, and she certainly had not realized until that meeting last year that one of his eyes was blue, one brown. He also had a sizable scar, the type left by a bad burn, that spread across his upper-right cheek. From the look of it, he had had it since childhood. Yet he had been exquisite, flawless on stage. Amazing, how dance could transform a man.

"About a year and a half ago," she went on. "We sat at the same table at a library fund-raiser."

"Oh, of course!" Fleetwood gave a small smile and she suddenly understood that Max had told him she was a potential donor and sent him in here to give her a thrill. Fleetwood was one of those people who consider their own presence a noteworthy event. He moved through the world in a cloud of ego so thick he could hardly make out the separate identities of mere mortals, let alone remember them individually. It would be like expecting a monarch to name the people he'd graciously waved at. Juliet had met others like him, people who live not to see but to be seen. She doubted whether he even recalled the evening at the library. If she had asserted that they went to elementary school together, he would have replied with the same, "Oh, of course!"

Nevertheless, doggedly, "We discussed ginkgo trees, male and female ginkgos," she went on.

"Indeed we did," he agreed, casting a lightning glance into the mirror behind her before meeting her gaze.

Juliet recalled that the conversation had gone from there into a discussion of male and female pipe fittings and thence even further afield. It had been, to her mind, a peculiar and memorable discussion. But she was sure she was the only one who remembered it.

Fleetwood had unconsciously allowed his voice to grow a bit louder, and since the music had suddenly ended, Ruth turned suddenly to glare at him and Juliet. Fleetwood's eyebrows rose again, and with an amused smile and a graceful hand raised in salute to Juliet, he stood and hurriedly stole back out of the room.

"That's better," muttered Ruth tartly, as the door closed behind him. Only a few of the principals dared to smile openly at this bit of insubordination, Juliet noticed, while the rest of the ensemble confined themselves to meaningful glances at one another. She also noticed that Ruth remained entirely unaware of the little stir her quite audible remark had caused. Ruth Renswick, Juliet had to concede, was low on what are sometimes called "people" skills. She was not really a "people" person.

Juliet forced herself to pay attention as her friend struggled on with the villagers' first appearance. Like the book, the ballet started with Pip in the graveyard, meeting the terrifying, escaped convict, Abel Magwitch. But the corps soon appeared, some as Christmas diners at Pip's home, some as soldiers in search of the fleeing convict. Ruth had devised some mildly comic bits of business in an effort to convey the rough, grudging treatment Pip receives at home from his sister, Mrs. Joe, and Juliet began to suspect it was these that were throwing her off. There was a fancy piece of nonsense in which the other diners, dancing on and around the table, distributed half a dozen oranges between them but just prevented Pip from quite getting hold of his. The troupe performed this bit of jugglery nimbly, especially the Pips (who had the difficult job of appearing to catch at the oranges without actually disrupting their trajectories) but most of the other humor somehow didn't work. It was too broad, too Dickensian, not Renswickian enough. Ruth would have to learn to be less respectful of her co-librettist, Juliet decided. After reaching this insight, she considered herself at liberty to turn her thoughts to her own problems (books did *not* write themselves, she reminded herself stern ,), and so she spent the rest of the hour mulling over how Lady Porter could engineer a marriage between her niece and the Earl of Suffield.

She had no opportunity to share her thoughts with Ruth during the next union-required break, for the company publicist—a fanatically groomed woman in her middle fifties—sailed into the studio the instant Ruth dismissed the dancers and carried the choreographer off, peppering her even as they went with questions about an imminent press release on *Great Ex*. When Juliet turned around, she found Hart Hayden standing by her chair, an unexpectedly warm smile on his handsome, rather ascetic face. Along with the other principals, he had had little to do in the last hour, as Ruth focused on the corps and soloists, so his breathing was relaxed and he did not seem very tired. Looking at him now, Juliet could see that his complexion was badly pocked, no doubt by acne in his teens.

Instinctively, she stood.

"No, don't," he said. She ignored him, discovering as she did so that she stood a disconcerting two or three inches taller than he. "I hope you don't mind my introducing myself."

He did so. Juliet reciprocated.

"I couldn't help wondering who you were," Hayden continued. His voice was surprisingly resonant and deep, his accent slow and Southern. "People are taking bets, you know. Some of the dancers think you're on the board, some that you're a reporter doing a story on the company. And some say you're the lighting designer."

There was something inviting in his manner that prompted Juliet to ask, "And what's your theory?"

Hayden grinned and leaned over—and up—to speak into her ear. "Oh, I think you're Ruth's lover."

Juliet was too startled to answer at once. To the best of her knowledge, at least, Ruth was not and never had been gay. Nor was she.

"Well, it's a theory, anyway," she said at last.

"Obviously a wrong one," he observed contritely, stepping back. "Who are you?"

Juliet gave her credentials.

"Oh, really? Do you have a pen name?"

"Angelica Kestrel-Haven," said Juliet, experiencing the quiver of silliness the admission always gave her.

She was relieved when Hayden replied admiringly, "Good choice. I was born George Washington."

Juliet laughed before she could stop herself. "Oh, dear," she said.

For a minute or so, they stood in companionable silence, gazing around the room. The studio was once more full of dancers blowing their noses. Several of the women stood stretching their thigh muscles, one leg bent and held by the foot behind them, like cranes. Kirsten Ahlswede sat near the front mirror, dexterously sewing a ribbon onto a pink pointe shoe, her long, slim body curled, her shiny blond head bent, her cold, beautiful, sharply cut features completely blank. Her partner, Anton Mohr, had resumed his supine position and was once more pumping his legs in the air with fierce concentration, a plastic bottle of Coke by his side.

"What is he doing?" asked Juliet, indicating Mohr with a discreet thrust of her chin.

"Strengthening his abs. He hurt his back a few months ago," Hayden said. "A lot of dancers rely on their backs too much and let their abs get weak. Then when they—"

He cut himself off abruptly as Ruth reentered, clapping as she came. The studio sprang to attention. Waves of chatter stopped abruptly; laughter died mid-giggle. Several of the ballerinas went to the low wooden box and dipped their feet in as Mohr had done.

"What is that b—?" Juliet began.

But Hart Hayden, she found, had left her and was already on his way to the middle of the room, where he took a place facing Ruth and stood quite still, clearly composing himself both physically and mentally. Juliet felt better for her conversation with him; it was nice ⌐ feel she had a friend (or at least a friendly face to seek out) in the room.

With one notable exception, the rest of the session was lackluster, devoted to a few measures of transitional music that tied the recapture of Magwitch to the pas de deux (now a pas de trois) in which Miss Havisham instructed Estella. All the dancers except Pip had to be gotten off the stage, and Miss Havisham and Estella brought on, a bit of mechanical work akin to what Juliet, when she was writing, thought of as furniture-moving. She did not see what good her presence could possibly be doing for Ruth, and the welcome exoticness of the studio had already begun to wear off. Finally, her head filling unbidden with voices, she brought out the little notebook she always carried and began to write snippets of dialogue for Lord Suffield and Lady Porter. She realized, as she looked up between sentences, that those dancers who thought her a reporter now considered their hypothesis confirmed. Several of them allowed themselves to look sidelong at her for a moment or two, and she read even in their well-trained faces the yearning to be singled out.

The session's one note of excitement came shortly after two-thirty, when Ruth decided she wanted to see the "Peeping Pip" pas de trois (as it soon came to be called) performed by Lily, Kirsten, and Anton. The corps sat down to rest as the three principals assembled at the front of the room. Luis Fortunato struck the now familiar first notes and Lily and Kirsten, coached by Patrick, repeated as best they could the steps Ruth had devised earlier that day. Ruth watched the sequence from under lowered eyebrows, making furious notes on index cards and signaling her skepticism about various moments to Patrick. Juliet thought she was concerned only to see her own handi-work, not about the quality of the performances. So she was startled when Ruth suddenly clapped twice in manifest displeasure.

The music came to a halt at once, as did the dancers. The heads of the entire ensemble swiveled to face front.

"Not like that," Ruth muttered fiercely, walking around behind Lily Bediant and seizing her by the waist. She laid her own front flat along Lily's back, took one hand of the ballerina's in each of her own and began to perform a sort of warding-off gesture in which Miss Havisham's head bent low and her hands and arms stretched before her. "You are *middle-aged*," she said, forcing Lily's body to twist crookedly under her own. "Middle-aged. Remember it. You are dancing much too fluidly." She added, with vehemence, "Stop being a ballerina."

When she let go, Lily straightened immediately, anger radiating from her rigid spine, her almost trembling shoulders. "Miss Renswick—" she began.

"Lily!"

Victorine Vaillancourt had come forward in her chair and her low voice thrilled with warning. Juliet saw her protégée's eyes meet hers, hold their defiance an instant longer, then drop in automatic deference. All the same, Juliet would not have liked to be near Lily Bediant just at that moment. Fury told in her limbs and her narrow, stiffly held torso. Her slender, white hands were clenched into fists. When she raised her violet eyes and trained them again on Ruth, her face was set, her gaze burning. Victorine got carefully to her feet and went to the choreographer. Into Ruth's ear, she murmured a few inaudible words.

Ruth turned back to Lily. "I meant that Miss Havisham is middle-aged, of course," she said, her tone (alas) more annoyed than apologetic.

Lily's gaunt cheeks drew in more sharply than ever at this explanation, which Juliet felt she must certainly take as a further indignity; but she only bowed slightly to Ruth—a very measured, very noble bow—and said nothing. The session proceeded, with the villagers reassembled to polish the transition. By the time Greg Fleetwood slipped quietly back in, tossing a smile to Juliet, murmuring a word in the ears of several dancers around the room, then departing with a quick, wry salute in Ruth's direction, the tension had dissipated substantially. Promptly at three, Ruth curtly thanked the dancers and dismissed them.

An immediate tumult ensued as they prepared to hare off, most of them to lunch (generally ingested, with great self-consciousness, in the dancers' lounge on the second floor), a few of the soloists and principals to concentrated sessions with Victorine Vaillancourt or other instructors. Most had bags in which they carried shoes, bottles of water, morsels of nutritive matter, cold pills and the like. These had been left all around the perimeter of the room, and the dancers now hurried to them. They crouched to shove them full of wadded tissues and other detritus. Several of the women pulled out shawls or sweatshirts and wrapped them around their bony hips or shoulders before venturing from the steamy studio into the merely baking corridors. Elektra Andreades, who had settled herself with Hart Hayden near the sandbox (or whatever it was) through the last part of the session, slipped her legs into a pair of bright pink leg-warmers. Hayden, after a certain amount of gathering this and that into his bag (he seemed to have spread himself out liberally over the floor around them), fed her a tiny morsel—a cornflake? a sunflower seed?—kissed her casually on the side of the neck and rose to join the crowd streaming out the door. He threw a farewell smile to Juliet as he passed her.

At the same time, Ryder Kensington bore down on his wife from across the studio. He crouched and initiated a brief, murmured conversation. Thirty seconds later, he strode off again to leave the studio, looking to Juliet somewhat less angry than before.

On the other side of the wooden box, meanwhile, Lily Bediant listened as Mlle. Vaillancourt spoke softly to her. Mlle. Vaillancourt had remained standing throughout the end of the session, and Juliet wondered if getting up from a chair was so difficult for her that she avoided it. Her attitude was gentle but earnest as her words to her protégée flowed on; Lily, still stiff-backed but calmer, nodded occasionally, her face a careful, impassive mask. When Patrick Wegweiser crossed the room to join them, Juliet was sure it was to make apologies for his employer.

If so, Lily was not interested. She turned her head away as he arrived, avoided his eyes while he spoke, and for answer only glared at him briefly in silence. Mlle. Vaillancourt, clearly disapproving of this lapse in good breeding, put her arm on Patrick's and drew him away with her toward the front of the room. Lily then knelt by the dance bag she had left near the wooden box and, with the utmost dignity, blew her long nose one quivering nostril at a time.

Across the box, looking not at all ruffled by her conversation with her husband, Elektra Andreades was refastening a pigtail for Mary Christie. Mary turned and said something to Elektra that made her laugh as she gathered up the rest of her things. Then, dance bags slung over their shoulders, arms twined around each other's waists, dark, graceful heads tilted together as if Petipa had so arranged them, they left the room together.

Gradually, the vast, echoing studio emptied out. One of the last to leave was a blond, apple-cheeked, round-faced girl of nineteen or twenty whom Juliet had vaguely noticed hovering uncertainly some yards away from her. At last she darted up.

Apologetically, "Did I hear someone say you're Angelica Kestrel-Haven?" she asked. Her voice was wispy and small, her brown eyes bright.

Juliet nodded.

"Oh, I love your books!" The girl dropped what little she had of the dancer's hauteur and gushed with adolescent eagerness, "I'm Teri Malone. I'm in the corps. Oh, would you talk to me some time about writing? I love to write."

Inevitably (and despite the fact that, in her experience, most people who loved to write were not doing it correctly), Juliet said it would be a pleasure. The ballerina bobbed what Juliet realized, after a moment's thought, was a curtsey before glancing at the clock, squeaking, "Oh, God!" and dashing away again. Watching her vanish, it occurred to Juliet that the world of ballet and the world of historical romance were probably adjacent at several points.

Ruth, meanwhile, had been assailed again by the fiercely groomed publicist (her name was Gretchen Manning, Juliet later learned), who had clicked in on her pristine high heels with a freshly revised draft of the press release for the choreographer to look over. Ruth turned helplessly to Juliet, shook her head apologetically and allowed herself to be corraled.

"I'll get this out of the way and shower and we can go have lunch," she said, as Manning waited impatiently in the open doorway. "Stay here; I won't be ten minutes. Anton, you won't mind if Juliet stays and watches you work on your solo," she rather informed than asked that splendid young man.

Juliet had not even noticed it, but Mohr had remained in the studio as the others left, stationing himself by a barre, where he was practicing something jumpy. He now favored her with a languid glance of consent in which she read a world of sensual awareness.

"Patrick," Ruth instructed finally, leaving in Manning's wake, "look after Juliet."

Ruth's assistant dutifully gave Juliet a smile, made a gesture of welcome, then turned his attention to Anton. They were by now the only three people in the room. The pianist had left, but Patrick had a boom box on a small table and half a dozen tape cassettes of various bits of music. He was looking through them, frowning at the labels, when Mohr began an experimental series of turning glides into the middle of the studio floor. He jolted to a stop.

"Please, you must have the floor mopped," he said. It was the first time Juliet had heard him speak. He had a slow, reedy voice and a thick German accent. His tone was severe.

"Oh, hell!" Patrick shook himself as if he had been criminally remiss and darted out the door.

Left suddenly alone with the unfamiliar, thoroughly physical Mohr, Juliet experienced an unsettling flash of girlish awkwardness and had to force herself not to stare at her knees. The dancer came nearer to her. His green, heavily lidded eyes flickered over her face. At the same time as his easy self-assurance irritated her, she was amused to notice her own breath quicken. Really, she thought, how on earth could such people work professionally with each other?

How could anyone maintain a businesslike demeanor around a creature such as this?

"You like ballet?" asked Anton Mohr.

"Very much," she answered.

"I also like ballet, but not so much. I prefer dance, modern, contemporary. Ballet is very tedious for a man."

"Is it?"

He smiled, revealing strong, perfect, gleaming teeth. "Pick her up, put her down. Go here. Pick her up, put her down. Go there. And always noble." He struck a pose, a parody of nobility that made Juliet laugh. "But with Ruth, this is better. She gives me the opportunity to make something." He put his hand, which was long and slender, on his heart. "I move how *I* move."

He said *moof*, not *move*, Juliet noticed, as he took a few steps closer to her.

"You dance?" he asked.

She shook her head.

"But—what would you say, socially, you dance?"

"Oh, of course."

"So." He put his hand out as if to invite her onto a dance floor, a gesture so unexpected and charming in the deserted studio that Juliet exploded into laughter. It was clearly no more than the reflex of a man who enjoyed flirting, enjoyed playing with the notion of seduction. This was a trait that both attracted and repelled Juliet, no doubt (the mere thought made her sigh inwardly) because her father was that way. And, in quite a different style (yet not so very different, of course) her ex-husband, Rob, had also been easily, playfully, meaninglessly seductive.

Well, usually meaninglessly.

She turned at the sound of the door opening and was relieved to see Patrick returning with a portly man in overalls, who set to work at once on the floor, swabbing it with a long mop and a lot of elbow grease. The man's expertise was such that, within a few minutes, all but the farthest reaches of the room were finished and darkly glossy. As Patrick thanked and excused him, Mohr once again went to the low wooden box. Juliet had realized by now it had something to do with traction, and she watched without surprise as the German dipped in first one strong, graceful foot, then the other.

Then he spread his powerful arms, raised himself on one leg and began the same, swift little leap and spin Juliet had noticed before. But this time, the instant he shifted his weight, he seemed to become abruptly diagonal, a blaze of muscle hurtling down a disastrous slant toward the gleaming linoleum. There was a long, sickening moment in which he tried but failed to recover his balance. Then, like an animal felled by a bullet, he crashed to the floor.

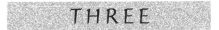
Human wickedness feeds upon a splendid rainbow of ills, but its manifestations are not, as a rule, very colorful. Certainly there was nothing specially vivid in the scene that greeted Ruth when she returned to the studio after her shower—no spectacular glare to set it apart from the dozens of injuries bound to occur each season, nothing sensational to flag it as the fruit of an evil deed. An anxious trio huddled around the choreographer's leading Pip: Patrick cradled Anton's shoulders and head while Victorine Vaillancourt carefully experimented with one after another part of his left leg. Juliet stood hovering over them, cell phone at the ready, wincing in sympathy each time the ballet mistress moved to another site.

Yet, though obviously in pain, the patient himself looked serious rather than anguished, as if a certain detachment prevailed between him and his body. He and Victorine kept up a murmured inventory, checking various muscles and tendons to see whether this or that movement hurt and what the pain might mean. It reminded Juliet of an acquaintance who managed a rather large money fund. She had been with him when word came one autumn afternoon of a sudden swoop in the market. She expected him to rush off to a phone in terror, or in anger, at least. Instead, he had been calm, methodical, concerned only to get the facts straight. He was a professional—and so was Anton Mohr. First he had to know what had happened to his body, which was to say, his business. Later there would be time for suffering, rage, or regret.

It was Juliet who had been sent to fetch Victorine, while Patrick stayed behind. Mademoiselle had leapt with surprising speed from behind her desk in a second-floor cubicle, where she had been transcribing notes. Then, like Miss Clavell on the night when something was not quite right, she had flown through the corridors and downstairs to her charge, muttering darkly all the way in French.

Now Ruth let the heavy studio door slam shut behind her and demanded, "What happened?" Her short hair was still wet from her shower and she had changed into stylish street clothes. Neither Victorine nor Anton looked up.

Patrick said quietly, "He slipped."

These seemed to be fighting words to Anton, who did look up now and corrected, with dignity, "I did not slip. Something slipped me."

Juliet caught the skeptical glance this provoked between Ruth and her assistant.

"How was the floor?" asked Ruth.

"It was sticky when you left," said Patrick. "So we had it mopped."

"But I used the rosin box," Anton put in hotly. "As always."

Rosin! That was the weird, turpentiny smell that had been teasing Juliet's nose.

"It wasn't something in the choreography that threw you?" Ruth ventured reluctantly.

The dancer shook his head. "We did not even yet begin. I was making myself ready."

Ruth sighed her relief. From the beginning of this project, as she had explained to Juliet, she had worried about injuring the JRBT dancers by forcing them to perform modern movements for which they had not been trained. She and Greg had discussed the matter several times, and she had promised to give it special attention. So far, she had heard nothing worse than that the physical therapists who routinely worked on the dancers had noticed an upsurge in sore arms in the women, the result of contemporary dance's greater demands on upper-body strength. Kirsten, Lily, and Elektra, she knew, had all begun strengthening programs for their upper arms.

Another minute or so passed as Victorine continued to probe. Finally she sat back and patted Mohr on the shoulder. "You have twisted your ankle, but I do not think it is serious. Thank God, I believe you have not reinjured your back. We will take you to Dr. Keller."

The company, Juliet later learned, kept an orthopedist on retainer, with the understanding that when an injured dancer came in, he or she would receive immediate attention.

"I can call a car for him," offered Juliet, who had an account with a local company. She waved her cell phone. "They'll be here in two minutes."

Mademoiselle looked offended. "We are able to call a car, thank you. Patrick, if you will be so kind . . . ?"

Juliet held out her phone to Patrick. But it seemed she was not to be allowed to help in any way. Under Mademoiselle's severe gaze, he hurried from the room. Ruth knelt to take his place, and Juliet began to wander around the studio.

Mohr's turn of phrase, "something slipped me," had joggled a dim awareness of something she had noticed in the last little while, some condition in the studio. The shiny floor was the obvious candidate, but since it didn't seem to worry the others, she supposed it couldn't have caused the accident. She ambled toward the east wall, her sneakers making irritating squeaks and thuds, her softly rounded body suddenly feeling like a stuffed animal's as she moved into the dancers' territory. Her blue eyes squinted now and then, and she wrinkled her small, unimpressive nose like a hamster uncertain of his surroundings. Something, something. . . .

Along with her abnormal sense of smell, Juliet Bodine had an eye for the odd detail, a habit of taking note of what most people regarded as marginal and making it the central focus of her attention.

It was a trick that had served her well as a novelist, and once or twice in the past, it had even proved to have a practical value in the world. Not always. Not usually. Most of the time, in fact, her tendency to set aside what others found most striking (a person's clothes, or age, or the fact that he was missing an ear) and focus instead on some minor trait was a source of embarrassment or worse.

"Did you meet that man who kept saying, 'Righty-right' instead of, 'Uh-huh'?" she was apt to ask when leaving a party with a friend.

This would initiate a series of puzzled rejoinders that finally ended along the lines of: "You mean the guy in the wheelchair?"

Yet just occasionally, this same peculiarity had helped to turn up a missing set of keys or track down the source of a misremembered quotation, or even provide a landmark that pointed the right way back to the road.

Now she was sure that some inconsistency, some incongruity she had half observed, was tapping at the door of her consciousness. She circled the room, peering questioningly at the floor, the mirrors, the lights, the windows, the piano. At last, by the rosin box, the elusive detail rocketed to the top of her brain, where she could get at it.

That smell.

She dropped to her knees (instantly regretting it as they banged against the vinyl-covered floor) and stared into the box. It contained a sort of bulky gravel made up of translucent brown lumps. Juliet was vaguely aware of movement behind her—the door opening and closing, a stir of activity as Anton, no doubt, was helped from the room—while she scrutinized this, but she was too interested in the rosin to turn and look. Tentatively, she reached a hand into the box and rubbed a pinch between her fingers. She held some to her nose and sniffed. Then, after a little hesitation, she took a handful and, standing awkwardly, stuffed it into the pocket of her jeans.

Only Ruth was left in the room, she found upon turning away from the box. Her friend had slumped down on to the floor and was leaning exhaustedly against the front mirror, looking more like *Bleak House* than *Great Expectations*. In the studio next door, a pianist was playing a tragic phrase from *Giselle* over and over. The music, swollen and distorted by its passage through the wall, seemed an apt sound track for Ruth's dejection.

"If I lose Anton, I'll lose my mind," she said.

Juliet ignored this burst of self-pity. "Ruth, I think you'd better see something." Her soft, childish voice robbed the statement of any drama. Ruth looked up morosely. Juliet dug into her pocket and held out the handful of rosin.

"Smell it," she said.

"What?"

"Smell it." She squatted down and held her palm under Ruth's nose.

"It's rosin. The dancers use it to keep from slipping."

"Rosin and—?"

"And what?"

"Look at it. Touch it. It's rosin and talcum powder," said Juliet.

"Jesus!" Ruth rubbed a pinch between her fingers. "But how could that possibly be?"

"You tell me."

Ruth sniffed at the sample. "It isn't white."

"No, somebody went to the trouble of darkening it," said Juliet, straightening. "Mixed it with powdered pigment or pulverized eye shadow or something, I'd guess."

"Well, Jesus, Mary, and Joseph," said Ruth. "No wonder Anton slipped."

The piano music penetrating the wall changed to a new, brighter phrase, almost antic. Ruth dropped her head into her hands.

"I'd better go tell Greg," she said, without moving. "That rosin box has got to be cleaned immediately."

Juliet looked thoughtfully at the top of her friend's head. "Does this kind of thing happen often?"

Ruth raised her head. "Certainly not. In fact, I've never—well, no, I can't say I *never* heard of such a thing happening. Dance is hard. Most dancers never make it into a major company, and once they do, there's tremendous pressure to excel. Their performing lives are short. When they're finished, they're unprepared for anything else. They're always up against each other for parts. They get injured and no one cares as long as they keep dancing. Everyone assumes the men are gay. Whether they are or not, they have to cope with raging prejudice outside the dance world. The money isn't great. They have to take class every day. They have to keep their mouths shut and do as they're told. And all for what? Most of them never get out of the corps."

"So what have you heard of happening?"

"Oh, the usual stuff in a closed environment. Like in boarding schools. Petty thieving. Sucking up to management. Ganging up on people who suck up. Ostracizing weaklings." She paused, then added in a changed tone, "You know, Ryder Kensington just did a very weird thing to me. You know who he is?"

Juliet nodded.

"Well, when I came out of the locker room after the session, he was using the pay phone and I accidentally brushed against him. He jumped about a mile in the air, and then he glared at me as if I'd been raising a dagger to stab him in the back. You think he could be the mad powderer?"

"I don't know. Does he have any reason to dislike Anton Mohr?"

"What difference does that make? Anyone could have been injured."

"Maybe. Maybe not. Several people used that rosin box at the start of the last hour of your session today, and they didn't slip. I noticed."

"So you think the powder was put in late in the session?"

"Don't you?"

Ruth frowned. The sprightly piano phrase had ceased, and now the empty room reverberated only to their voices.

"Could someone have known that only Mohr was going to work in this studio after your session ended?" Juliet asked.

"God I'm hungry." Ruth rubbed her forehead wearily. "Yes, anyone could have known. There are schedules printed up for each day. They're distributed a day in advance. Here." She reached into the leather backpack she had been carrying when she returned from the locker room and pulled out a folded paper.

Juliet opened it. The schedule was very neatly done. Every studio was accounted for during each working hour, from class in the morning until the day ended. The name of each production was given, the dancer or dancers who were to be there, the choreographer or instructor working with them, sometimes even which act of a ballet was to be rehearsed.

"They all have to know," said Ruth, after Juliet had studied this for a few moments. "They have to know what shoes to bring and what to prepare and where to go . . ."

There was a long silence. Juliet went to the large purse she had left by her chair and returned with a plum, which she handed to Ruth.

"Thank you," said Ruth. She took an unhappy bite and added, as if conversationally, "I knew this project was cursed."

Juliet scratched her nose. It seemed to her that, for Ruth's sake if nothing else, a number of rather melodramatic questions needed to be addressed.

"Ruth," she began, "could Mohr have any—this sounds silly, but, any enemies? People in the company who might want him to fail?"

"I have no idea. Why should they? I mean, I really don't know him personally. I only worked with him once, in Germany. He seems quite likable to me."

"Then could anyone envy him—could someone else have wanted to dance his part?"

"Someone?" Ruth gave a dry laugh. "Try everyone. Every man, anyhow. And probably half the women. But that's ballet—there's only one Prince Charming."

"So might this have been done from envy?"

Ruth laughed again, shaking her head. "Look, dancers depend on each other. They have to. That's not a metaphor—I mean physically, they have to trust each other or they cannot dance. It's an intense bond. I'm not saying there's never any backstabbing, or that every member of the Jansch will pray tonight for Anton's swift recovery. But dancers just don't injure each other on purpose."

Juliet was silent a moment. She knew from experience that Ruth sometimes had clear, sharp insights into human behavior; without that, she would not have been the choreographer she was. But she also knew Ruth sometimes overlooked what was right in front of her face.

Presently, "Could anyone want you to fail?" she suggested. After all, she reflected, if Ruth often barked at the dancers the way she had at Lily today, resentment must accumulate.

"Do I have enemies, you mean?"

"I guess so, yes. It happened here. We have to consider who might want to hinder your production, don't you think?"

Ruth shook her head, nonplussed. "My brain just doesn't work that way. You know me, I'm a dancer. Plot is more your neck of the woods." She hesitated, then went on more slowly, "I suppose some people would be happy if I screwed this up. Actually, I did hear Victorine wanted to choreograph this ballet herself. She's done some choreography, but it hasn't been wildly successful."

"Does she like Anton Mohr?"

"Like him? I don't imagine they've ever spoken, except professionally. She's certainly polite with him. I know she thinks his classical training was inadequate. He's too modern for her, the way he moves."

"Hm. What about the dancers in *Great Ex*? Might any of them have a grudge against you?"

Ruth produced a sound midway between a sneeze and a laugh. "The dancers! Why should they?"

"Well, think about it. Perhaps because you embarrassed or slighted them in front of their peers? I doubt you're Lily Bediant's favorite person."

"Lily is much too sensitive. It's ridiculous, the way Victorine coddles her. All I did—"

Juliet cut her off firmly. "I'm not saying it was Lily. It could have been anyone with a grudge against the Jansch, I suppose. My point is simply that since the talcum powder was put in after your session ended, someone in this studio had to do it. And the people in this studio were connected with your production. Most of them dancers."

"Are you sure?"

"Unless you think the custodian did it. He came in to mop the floor. But he's the only outsider who was in here. I never left the room."

Ruth had finished her plum; now she gnawed at the stone with her small, sharp front teeth. "Maybe he did. Maybe he has a grievance with management."

"That's a little farfetched, don't you think?"

Ruth shrugged irritably. "I suppose. Anyway, I'd better go tell Greg." Slowly, she began to get to her feet. "Oh, my knees!" she exclaimed, halfway up.

"Injuries?"

"Degenerative arthritis. Not uncommon in dancers." She gave a tight, humorless grin. "All part of the fun."

Juliet guarded the rosin box while Ruth went to tell Gregory Fleetwood the story of the talcum powder. When the choreographer returned, her arms were full of yogurt containers, bottles of lemonade, and sandwiches, all of which she spread out on the floor.

"Sorry we can't go out for lunch. The next session starts at four." Ruth unwrapped a ham on rye and took a lusty bite. But an instant later, she stumbled again to her feet. "Oh God, I'm so rattled, I almost forgot," she muttered, plunging her hands into the depths of her backpack. She groped around, emerged with a sizable pink tablet and promptly downed it with a swig of lemonade. Then, with gingerly care, she lowered herself again to the floor.

"Vitamin?" Juliet asked curiously.

"No, Mistenflo. Cytotec." And, as the other continued to look confused, "It's a brand of misoprostol," Ruth went on. "Goodness, you are an outsider. Misoprostol keeps you from getting ulcers if you have to take antiinflammatory drugs all the time."

Juliet was silent a moment, then understood and exclaimed sympathetically, "Oh! Which you do because of your arthritis. Poor Ruth! You have paid a high price for your career."

Ruth sniffed briskly. "Beats getting black lung from mining coal. All occupations have hazards. Even you could get carpal tunnel syndrome, I guess. Or start to believe you're Jane Austen reincarnated."

Ruth, Juliet now remembered, did not care for pity unless she had specifically requested it. "Plenty of dancers are in my boat," she was going on. "Victorine takes the same medicines I do. In fact, she's a lot worse off. Anyway," she finished at last, pointedly changing the subject, "I talked to Greg."

"Oh good. And what's he going to do?"

"Jack shit."

"Really?"

"No, not quite." She drank again from the lemonade bottle. "He'll tell Anton what happened. And he'll tell him to keep it to himself. As for the rest, he'll send a flyer around the company saying a 'malicious incident' took place and anyone with information should contact him privately."

"'Malicious incident?' Isn't that a bit vague?"

Ruth shrugged. "He says he doesn't want to invite a copycat crime."

"Do you think he'll get any results?" Juliet asked doubtfully.

"No. But it might prevent a panic. To tell the truth, I think Greg's a lot more worried about morale among the dancers than any bit of localized mischief. Me, too. This kind of thing can give a company the galloping willies." She picked up a cup of blueberry yogurt and brandished it in Juliet's direction. "Eat, eat."

"Oh, that's okay, thanks. I'll have something when I get home."

"When you get home?" echoed Ruth. "You'll be starved by then."

For a moment, Juliet looked at her, puzzled. Then understanding dawned. "You don't mean for me to stay here the whole—?"

"Of course I do," interrupted Ruth. "You weren't planning to leave again?" she demanded, outraged. "There are three more hours of rehearsal left."

"But—"

"Juliet, you said that you would help me. You've already helped me. You can help me more. Today went infinitely better than any day I've had on *Great Ex* till now."

"Well, I do have a thought or two about that dinner scene. But I could call you—"

"And you'll have lots more thoughts," Ruth said firmly. "Let's be clear about this. You'll stay today and you'll come back tomorrow and—Juliet, you said we were going to whip this thing into shape."

Juliet did not remember having said quite that, though she did recall something about fixing it up. She put her hands over her face like a little girl who hopes to make herself invisible.

"You really shouldn't tempt me, Ruth," she said. "You know how I am with an excuse to duck work. Like an alcoholic with a bottle."

"You'll get the book done. You always do."

"Oh, wicked, wicked! Get thee behind me, Satan." Only last week, Juliet's editor, Portia Klein, had called to see how *London*

Quadrille was coming. Juliet had lied a little, omitting to mention that she was at a standstill as regarded Lady Porter's scheme, and adding two to the actual number of chapters already written.

"Write in the mornings," Ruth said. "I don't even start with the dancers till twelve. Come at one or two."

Juliet felt herself start to crumble. "After all," an inner voice coaxed seductively, "*London Quadrille* will come out all the better if you spend a little time away from it. Healthy distraction always refreshes the mind."

Besides, now there was this intriguing matter of the talcum powder. An image of Nancy Drew jumping gaily into her sporty roadster sprang into Juliet's head. Nancy Drew never had to sit alone in an office. Nancy Drew never had to make up stuff for imaginary people to say to each other. If someone wanted to sabotage Ruth, if someone had attacked Anton Mohr, wasn't that indeed a matter of plot? Plot and character? Perhaps she could talk to the dancers a bit, get to know them, find out a few things . . .

"I guess I could come for a few days," she said.

"Of course you can." Ruth shoved the yogurt container at her again. "Eat up. They'll be back here in ten minutes."

A few hours after Juliet got home from the Jansch, Ruth phoned to report on Anton. As Victorine had predicted, Dr. Keller found that his injury would not affect his back. On the other hand, he had sprained his ankle mildly and was not to dance for several days. This, Ruth went on, left her with a terrible dilemma, because she had scheduled a formal run-through of Act One for three o'clock on the coming Friday.

"A run-through?" asked Juliet, wondering what that meant and rather disinclined to learn just then. She had already gotten into her pajamas and had just sat down with the fourth volume of Anthony Powell's *A Dance to the Music of Time* when the telephone rang. In her opinion, her new job as sous-chef to Ruth Renswick's life was over for the day. "Can't you change the date? Or do it without Anton?"

"It's not that easy," said Ruth worriedly. A run-through, she explained, was an informal performance of a work-in-progress, in the studio, for a small, invited audience. It provided a chance for both dancers and choreographer to see and feel the work whole. Equally important, this run-through would be the first time the design team saw the piece in action, their first chance to refine and recalibrate the somewhat theoretical plans they had made for sets, costumes, and lights. It would also be the first official viewing of Ruth's progress by the administrators of the Jansch, who had so precipitously decided to stake their season on *Great Ex*. If they were pleased, money and attention would continue to flow. If they were displeased—well, Ruth didn't want to think about what would happen if they were displeased. In short, the run-through was vitally important, both on a practical and a ceremonial level, and to have it danced by the second cast did not suit her ideas at all.

On the other hand, she had already invited some two dozen extremely busy people (the costume designer and her staff, the set designer and his, the lighting designer, the American assistant to the composer), all of whom had made room in their schedules to come.

"So you'll change it and they'll make some more room," said Juliet, eyeing her Powell book longingly. Wistfully, she wondered how people qualified for that "extremely busy" label Ruth seemed to revere so much.

After considerable hand-wringing and why-don't-you yes-butting, Ruth finally agreed it must be postponed. They hung up at last and, the next day, Gretchen Manning was pressed into service to make the necessary, complicated web of calls and cross-calls. In the end, the run-through was rescheduled for Wednesday of the following week.

Meanwhile, rehearsals went on—
and, true to her word, Juliet went on attending them. The first thing
she did, on entering each afternoon, was to take a sniff at the rosin
box. So far, the outrage had not been repeated.

On the day following his injury, Anton Mohr, his left ankle
firmly wrapped with an elastic bandage, sat in his wonted place near
the piano and watched as Hart Hayden came to the fore, both literally
and figuratively. Partnering Elektra, Hayden gave himself unstint-
ingly to Ruth, while Kirsten Ahlswede, temporarily paired with the
dancer who was to be third Pip, a longtime soloist named Nicky
Sabatino, stood behind them and followed their lead. If Anton had
been shaken emotionally by his slip and the knowledge of its cause,
he did not show it. On the contrary, he seemed relaxed and attentive,
any professional threat he might feel from Hayden's taking his place
expertly erased from his features.

Hayden, Juliet noticed, while fully as diligent as Mohr had
been, fully as cooperative, had nevertheless quite a different manner
of working. Where Anton would grin or crack up in the midst of
devising a difficult lift, Hart was always serious, his face as impassive
as if he were meditating. He seemed to draw his energy from some
deep, interior well. At the same time, he frequently offered solutions
or even inventions to Ruth. And he danced delightfully. The inviting
charm Juliet had felt emanating from him when they first spoke was
concentrated now into a working essence that made Pip come alive
in gesture after gesture, movements infused with eagerness, innocence and longing.

Ruth spent the first part of the day correcting the choreography of the Christmas dinner ensemble scene in accordance with
Juliet's suggestions ("It's the humor! You're absolutely right!" she
had exclaimed almost joyfully, when Juliet gave her her critique).
Then she turned to polishing the duet for Pip and Estella that came
after the "Peeping Pip" pas de trois. Juliet watched, her eyes less on
Ruth and her progress than on the room as a whole. Though it worried her to leave Lady Porter and Lord Suffield in mid-conversation,

the Jansch had been much on her mind. She did not like the idea that someone might be out to undermine Ruth, and last night as she lay in bed, she had gone over and over what she could recall of the crowded scene at the end of yesterday's group rehearsal, the swirl of the dancers between Ruth's dismissal and the general departure, the various people she had noticed passing near the rosin box.

As Ruth polished the Pip–Estella pas de deux, Juliet looked on with quickened attention. The duet was a strange one, in which Pip had to dance out, by turns, his fear of Estella and his attraction to her, while Estella remained inscrutably haughty (hence its eventual nickname: the "Approach-Avoidance" duet). Juliet noticed Lily Bediant sitting in a corner, her knees drawn up to her chest, her violet eyes staring moodily as Hart Hayden and Elektra Andreades worked. Neither scene being addressed today included her. At the very least, Juliet surmised, she did not like having her time wasted.

It was while she was watching Hart Hayden experiment with various ways of lifting Elektra's right foot to his left shoulder that Juliet realized her own right foot had fallen asleep. She decided to creep out and wander around the building a bit. The slightly cooler air of the corridor came as a relief, and, pausing now and then to rotate her tingling foot, she climbed the stairs to the second floor.

Here, she poked around in the warren of little cubicles that served as offices for the dance instructors and stage crew. She stuck her head into a small room that housed a library of scores and notes on repertory. She scanned a number of bulletin boards where roles, schedules, and want ads were posted. She sat in a corner of the comfortable dancers' lounge, pretending to read the Times while eavesdropping as corps members gossiped and teased each other over cups of fat-free yogurt. Injuries were a staple of the chatter: who did what to which limb or joint, how long she or he would be out of commission, and what therapy had been prescribed. Anton's injury was mentioned. His claim that something external had caused the slip was noted and dismissed as the wishful thinking of a chagrined professional; apparently, he had so far obeyed Fleetwood's stipulation that he keep the truth to himself. From their tone and glances, Juliet got the idea Mohr was still considered an outsider by the corps. One member complained that he never took class with the rest of the company. But a tall, willowy woman immediately defended him, saying he lived in Brooklyn and that the class he went to was just quicker to get to. This bit of special pleading was met with a round of grins that caused the willowy girl to flush bright red, and Juliet knew then that probably half the women in the place were smitten with the German.

After injuries, complaints about colds dominated the conversation, along with jokes about blunders committed by company members during various rehearsals. One dancer, a compact man with a heavy Spanish accent, remarked that he'd heard Lily Bediant really "got it" from Ruth Renswick yesterday. But no one took him up on this opening gambit and the discussion moved on. Whether this fizzle was the result of a simple lack of interest on the part of the other dancers, or respect for Lily—or fear of her—Juliet could not tell. Meanwhile, without linking it to Anton's slip, the dancers began to discuss the "malicious incident" flyer they all had received; but as no one claimed any knowledge of what it could possibly refer to, this topic also was abandoned, in favor of last night's Letterman show.

Juliet stood and ambled away. In the women's locker room, she found a cardboard box with a sign soliciting worn-out pointe shoes to be donated to indigent aspiring ballerinas. Everywhere she went, people eyed her mistrustfully. Strangers were rare inside the Jansch, and stalkers (she later learned) not unheard of. Innocuous as Juliet thought she must look—a soft, somewhat shabby, no longer very youthful little person wearing a fixed, meaningless half-smile—her appearance seemed to waken all manner of suspicions here. Yet she did not, as yesterday, experience her dubious reception as the result of arrogance or snobbery but now saw in it the defensive clannishness of circus performers, even of freaks.

She had strolled restlessly up the stairs again and was absently coming down, musing on this epiphany, when she literally bumped into Hart Hayden.

"Excuse me!" she exclaimed fervently. The thought that she might bruise a dancer by knocking into him or stepping on his toe horrified her, like the idea of giving a singer strep throat. "I wasn't looking—"

"Takes two to collide." Hayden smiled. "I'm just going up to get a Dr Pepper. Come with me."

He swept his small, slim hand through the air, a gesture immensely, innately, involuntarily balletic, to invite her to turn and precede him. "Unless you're in a hurry."

"Oh, no." Juliet turned and trotted up ahead of him as gracefully as she could. She was surprised—and pleased—to find this great star of the company chose to be so friendly to her. He could so easily have scorned her, as most of his colleagues seemed to do.

"What were you daydreaming about?" he asked. "Got a hot date tonight?"

"Good God, no." She laughed. Hart led the way to the lounge and over to a sleek, automat-style, refrigerated machine that dispensed fresh fruit, juice, sodas, and other snacks. "Do you?"

"Me? I'm married to the dance. No kidding," he added, after Juliet laughed again. "If I sleep with anyone, I don't dance as well. So I don't sleep with anyone."

"Wow."

"I love dance," Hart Hayden said simply. He put some coins into the machine, pushed a button, waited while the selections revolved, then opened the door and plucked out his bottle in one neat motion. "It's hard, but there's nothing like it."

"I admire your dedication."

Dr Pepper in hand, he returned to the staircase and headed

back down. "I'm sure you feel the same way about writing," he went on, over his shoulder.

"I don't know. I'm not sure I like it enough to stay celibate."

"Oh, you would if you had to."

"I write better when I'm having sex," she said thoughtfully, wondering at the same time what kind of person (male? female?) Hart would have sex with if he did have any. Confusingly, she couldn't tell. "But I've never started an affair just to keep my sentences limber."

"Haven't you?" They had descended the stairs. Hayden's break would soon be over. "I would," he said seriously. Then, "Forgive me. I have to get back inside. Coming?"

"In a minute." Reluctant to reenter the steamy studio just yet, Juliet turned away and strolled down the corridor that led toward the locker rooms. A few yards along she stopped dead. Was that—? She sniffed. The odor was unexpected, yet decidedly familiar. She followed the scent down the hall to a heavy metal door with a red bar across it. ALARM WILL SOUND IF OPENED, the sign on it read.

The door opened, silently. A dancer pushed in, apologizing as he brushed past her. Juliet went out and found half a dozen corps members lounging on a rectangular metal platform that formed part of a fire escape, peacefully polluting the sunshine with burning cigarettes. It was a smoking parlor, obviously illegal, just as obviously well-attended.

"Hi," said Juliet, trying to hide her shock at finding dancers smoking. Especially the men, for whom weight was not so fraught an issue. But she soon reflected that since tobacco (chiefly in the form of Philip Morris) had been good to American dance—it had kept it alive almost single-handedly as troupes proliferated and audiences aged—it was only fitting that American dancers returned the favor.

Ruth must have granted the corps a longer break than the principals, because four or five of the dancers on the platform were in *Great Ex*. But Juliet knew the name of only one: Olympia Andreades,

Elektra's sister. Olympia said, "Hi" back—not very enthusiastically—
but the others greeted Juliet with the same hard glare she had experienced elsewhere. She persisted, pulling a worn pack of Winston's out
of her purse and asking if anyone had a match. Conversation had
stopped, but smokers' camaraderie began to work in her favor as a
male dancer held out a cheap lighter. Juliet smiled her thanks and lit
up. She was trying to think up an icebreaker for Olympia when the
other abruptly broke the silence herself.

"So, what do you think?" she asked.

"Pardon me?"

"How does it look to you?"

Olympia Andreades took in a deep lungful of smoke, then
exhaled mightily. She had her younger sister's dark eyes and hair, but
she was bigger and her features were on a larger, heavier scale. She
had olive skin, where Elektra's was ivory, and her lips were full, soft,
lush. "*Great Ex,*" she went on. "How does it look?"

"A little new," said Juliet guardedly. "But I think it will develop
nicely. What do you think?"

"Oh, we love it," Olympia answered promptly. "The music is
wonderful and the steps are more interesting than we usually get. We
the corps, I mean."

"I'm Juliet Bodine," said Juliet, since they hadn't been introduced. "You're Elektra Andreades' sister, aren't you?"

There was a pause.

Then, "Among my other achievements," Olympia drily agreed.

Juliet blushed and supposed it was not very entertaining to
dance in the corps while your little sister reveled in the limelight,
a treasured principal. She wondered how deep Olympia's resentment ran.

She smiled awkwardly. "How's Ruth to work with?" she asked,
hoping to change the subject.

Olympia shared a skeptical glance with her colleagues. "You're
her friend, aren't you?"

"Yes, but that doesn't mean I think she'd be easy to please. I'll bet she's hell to please."

No one answered.

Then, "They're all hell to please," said one of the men, a tall, dark-headed dancer with angular shoulders and hips. He had a foreign accent which Juliet tentatively identified as Russian. She looked at him.

"They?"

"All the choreographers. Choreographers everywhere. They play, and we are their puppets."

"You don't feel you are collaborating with them?"

"The corps?" He laughed, expelling smoke. "Maybe the principals do."

"Anton Mohr told me he felt Ruth allowed him to move in his own way."

To her surprise, this provoked a huge laugh from everyone.

"Anton Mohr moves his own way whoever he's with," said Olympia, with what Juliet could only think of as a snigger. The angular man sniggered in Russian, and Juliet saw a strange look pass between the two. Something about Anton Mohr was a company joke, something sexual.

Juliet's heart sank. Ruth had told her earlier today that, so far at least, no one had responded to Greg Fleetwood's wishy-washy flyer, either openly or anonymously. So Juliet was all the more inclined to keep an ear out for any useful bits of gossip. She was inquisitive by nature, and rather enjoyed poking her nose into things, especially for a good cause. But she did so hope sex would not be a central element in this little business. Not that she disliked sex—quite the contrary. It was just that she found the prospect of snooping around in other people's sex lives deeply embarrassing.

Nevertheless, she forced herself on. "Bit of a lady's man, is he?"

Again there was general laughter.

Then, "Oh, more than a bit, I'd say," Olympia Andreades

replied. She dipped her head knowingly, once more exchanging a glance and a grin with the angular Russian, then raised an expressive eyebrow. "And I think we'd have to say he's more than a bit of a man's man, too."

c h a p t e r

FOUR

Ballet dancers don't have a lot of
spare time, and what they do have is often devoted to soaking in hot
tubs or icing their knees or shellacking their pointe shoes (for
strength) or hammering at them (for flexibility). So it was that,
despite her eagerness to talk about writing, Teri Malone was unable
to accept an invitation to lunch at Juliet's apartment until the Sunday
following Anton's unfortunate fall.

By now, Juliet had realized that chatting with Teri would give
her a fine opportunity to get a little background dope on life at the
Jansch. Teri was a corps member and, as such, Juliet reasoned, more
likely to know of petty grievances among her colleagues than, say,
Hart, or Anton himself. In the three days since it had been circulated,
Greg Fleetwood's notice regarding the 'malicious incident' had still
achieved exactly nothing, nor was there any reason to think it would
do more in the future. No one had come forward, and by Saturday
the whole business seemed to have been forgotten. But the fact that
it remained unsolved and unpunished irked Juliet. If nothing else, it
offended her sense of her own mental acuity (a sense that often
verged on intellectual arrogance). And it worried her for Ruth.

Sunday had dawned dense with a heavy, noisy summer rain,
and the women were eating lunch in Juliet's dining room. The room
was lofty and long, and the table sat twelve, but Juliet thought the
kitchen, though convenient, lacked the appropriate sense of occa-

sion. The dining room was the one part of her apartment with which she had never felt quite satisfied. A thick Persian rug covered the floor, and the table was made of dark, highly polished oak. Hunter-green velvet curtains framed the two long windows, outside of which the steady rain now made a second curtain, veiling the river view. The effect should have been inviting and luxurious, yet the place always struck its owner as too stiff for the homely pleasure of eating. She never sat at this table without thinking about changing the decor.

With regard to the lunch, it would be more accurate to say that Juliet was eating, while Teri was sitting near food.

"You don't mind if I just . . . pick?" the dancer had asked apologetically, when Juliet sat her down before the lavish meal Ames had laid in before going home on Friday. "I got a notice from Max last week. Two pounds." The girl's cheeks crimsoned as she specified the shameful number, and she gave a nervous, unballerinalike giggle.

Juliet politely waved away any concern about how much or how little her guest consumed; but now, as she chewed squid salad, and as Teri watched her chew squid salad, Juliet could not help furtively eying the girl's figure and trying to guess which square inch of her would prove susceptible to reduction. She also could not help considering how she would have felt had Max Devijian told her to lose two pounds of body weight or risk losing her job.

". . . So then I thought of writing a book about Eau Claire, because hardly anyone ever sets a novel there, you know?" Teri was saying. "I actually wrote the beginning, almost a chapter. But then I started worrying, maybe there's a reason people don't write novels about Eau Claire, because maybe no one wants to read about Eau Claire. You know?"

The question appeared to be rhetorical, and Juliet contented herself with murmuring, "Mm." So far, Teri had needed no encouragement to talk about her aspirations as a novelist, nor had she asked for advice or information. She seemed to be on autopilot, and Juliet was inclined to let her talk herself out. Teri's small voice had a sort of whistle in it. Her vowels were distinctly Midwestern. The afternoon was a quiet one, with most people in Juliet's building out of town for the weekend, and Teri's voice flowed peaceably on, a bit like white noise.

Juliet had no plans after lunch, and she thought she might just spend a few hours at her desk, seeing as how she had played hooky at the Jansch three afternoons this week (she had gone in on Friday as well). She was just toying with the idea of a comical love scene set in the Pump Room at Bath when something Teri said caught her ear.

". . . but even if they didn't win the lawsuit, you know, it would so awful to have to go through it. And it isn't just the Jansch that could take me to court, any dancer who thought a character was based on him could sue me. A friend of my dad's is a lawyer, and he said it's not libel if it's not unflattering. But you can't write a novel and make all the characters friendly and good and nice, even I know that. You have to have conflict. Right?"

Juliet smiled vaguely. With mechanical precision, "The conflict between one good and another good is often the most interesting kind," she said. "But let me understand you. You think that if you write a novel based on your experiences in the Jansch, someone from the company might take you to court?"

"Don't you?"

The older woman pushed her chair back—it hadn't been much fun eating in front of her abstemious visitor anyhow—and absently ran a splayed hand through her curly blond hair. "Give me a f'r instance," she said.

"Well, f'r instance," Teri replied willingly, though her cheeks began to color again, "suppose one of the dancers in the novel stole another dancer's purse? Then everyone would think I meant Graham Barr. Even if he was different in other ways."

"Would they?"

"Well, I would. Graham stole three purses before they caught him and threw him out of the company."

"Hm. It seems to me, you'd be protected in that case by the Small Penis rule."

Teri giggled, but Juliet went on placidly, "The Small Penis rule states that, since a man is reluctant to come forward and announce that the character with the small penis was based on him, if you give someone a humiliating trait, you're likely to be safe. Anyhow, as I understand it, it's not libel if it's true. Have there been any thefts since he left?" As casually as she could, she added, "Could that be what Greg Fleetwood meant by a 'malicious incident' the other day?"

If Teri knew anything about the talcum powder, she hid it very well.

"I don't know what that was about," she said, looking very much as if she would have liked to know. "I don't think there've been any more thefts. But I mean—what if I just show a dancer who's really selfish, or someone with a very nasty temper? We have them," she said. "Or someone who sleeps around a lot, or a married dancer who's having an affair? There are so many reasons someone could get pissed off— Excuse me, could be offended and claim I've damaged their reputation."

"Do people sleep around a lot?" Juliet inquired, at the same time pretending great interest in the rainy view.

"Not everybody, of course, but sure, lots of people. I mean," she gave a shy smile, "maybe not lots, but people do have affairs."

"Oh. Like who?" asked Juliet, feeling wildly uncomfortable. 'Like who?' indeed. What a question.

To her credit, Teri Malone looked uneasy. "I'm not sure I should . . . " she mumbled.

"Anton Mohr, do you mean?" offered Juliet, thinking fondly of a good, long scrub in the shower. "I've heard about him."

Relieved, "I guess everyone knows about Anton by now," Teri said.

"I guess." Juliet grinned. At least, she tried for a grin.

Teri, unfortunately, continued silent. Juliet decided she would have to take a stab in the dark.

"I've heard he and Kirsten Ahlswede have been partners off stage," she hazarded, making her tone as insinuating as possible.

"You have?" Teri looked astounded. "That's one person I never— I'll have to tell Lily," she finished.

Hurriedly, "Maybe I got the names mixed up," Juliet corrected herself. "Could it have been Lily Bediant I mean?"

"Yeah, that makes much more sense." Teri, her guard down, nodded. "But that was almost a year ago, just after Anton joined the Jansch. Lily broke it off. She kind of—" The girl faltered, then went on with pleased embarrassment, "I guess Lily really likes me, because she kind of confides in me, you know?"

Juliet tried to imagine what would draw that taut, prickly creature to this teenaged mass of wistfulness. Probably, she judged, it was the combination of a sympathetic soul with an unthreatening body, a body incapable of competing with hers on the stage. Even at forty, Lily Bediant could literally dance rings around Teri Malone. Teri knew it herself. She had already told Juliet that she knew—even at twenty—that she would never get out of the corps. That was why she was so interested in writing. Juliet did not think writing a very good fallback plan for anyone, but she supposed it beat ballet.

"Anyway, Lily walked in on Anton one night in bed with—" Teri's wholesome cheeks went into full flush. "You do know—?"

"With a man?"

Teri's voice dropped as if a hushed tone would make her revelation more discreet. "Greg Fleetwood. Anton had told Lily they had a thing in Germany, but ages ago. The way he said it made Lily think it was all over."

"Maybe he thought it was," said Juliet charitably, at the same time wondering how long exactly "ages" could be, especially given Anton's youth.

"Maybe. But you really aren't supposed to sleep with the management. And Anton's been sleeping with everybody. Administrators and principals and soloists and even corps members— Olympia Andreades, you know her?"

"Yes, a little."

"Well, Anton slept with her, and with— But actually," Teri

broke off abruptly, "I'm not really sure I should be talking about all this."

Hearing in her voice a new note of wariness, "Of course," Juliet said demurely. "Let's change the subject." It would not do for Teri to feel she had been grilled.

"I just know I wouldn't like other people to talk about me that way," said Teri primly.

"Certainly not," Juliet agreed, though she wondered at the same time what kind of lurid past Teri could possibly have to be discreet about. Disappointed as a sleuth, but more relaxed as a person, Juliet stood and moved toward the kitchen. "Would you like some iced coffee? Tell me about how you think *Great Ex* is going. Don't you think Kirsten makes a wonderful Estella?"

Teri stood also and, picking up her pristine plate and silver, began to follow Juliet from the room. "Coffee would be terrific, thanks."

"And *Great Ex*?" Juliet persisted, beginning to move around the spacious kitchen. It still had the original glass-fronted cabinets, installed when the building went up in 1928, though a huge Sub-Zero covered up the dumbwaiter. Ames sometimes joked (at least, Juliet thought it was a joke; it was hard to tell with the dour Ames) about reconnecting the bells for the servants to the indicator box here.

"Kirsten's all right," Teri said.

"But?" prompted Juliet.

"But I think Lily would have been better."

Juliet's eyebrows shot up before she could rein them in. "Lily?"

"She would have been better," repeated the girl loyally. "And it's not just that we're friends. Victorine was furious when Ruth cast her as Miss Havisham."

"Was she?" Juliet busied herself at the refrigerator to avoid making eye contact with the girl at this delicate moment. "Why?"

"Lily's much too youthful to dance Miss Havisham," said Teri, with the nearest approach to passion Juliet had yet heard from her. "There's no reason on earth she should be cast in a character role like that. I mean, she's going to be Anton's Aurora in *Sleeping Beauty* this season, you know!"

"A character role?" Juliet echoed, perplexed. "What's that?"

"Oh, you know—the kind older dancers get, the kind where you don't dance much. The Princess's mother. The Bridegroom's father."

"Dear me. I hadn't thought of Miss Havisham as that kind of part," said Juliet. "I wonder if Ruth does. Was Lily upset herself?"

"Lily is much too professional to protest something like that officially. But between you and I, it did give her a jolt. She actually thought of refusing. But she's too professional for that, too."

"Between you and me," Juliet corrected the would-be writer, then, as the girl reddened, wished she hadn't. Know-it-allness was Juliet's besetting sin, one that annoyed friends and demolished intimacy. At the same time, another part of her brain noted that Lily had not been too professional to throw a tantrum during Wednesday's session. For a moment, a vivid image filled her mind: Lily Bediant as a sort of first wife, forced to watch and smile while the Jansch moved on to a second marriage with a younger lover.

Having now filled two glasses with ice and chilled coffee, Juliet smiled an invitation at Teri and led the way to her library. This was a place of modest proportions, with corner windows giving on both the river and Eighty-fourth Street below. Unlike the living room, which was lovely but inalterably grand, this was a cozy room, lined with books and filled with overstuffed furniture. A glass case in a far corner housed a small collection of Regency treasures: an ivory snuff box; a heart-shaped locket whose glass front enclosed a braided lock of reddish hair; a "moral" board game called "The Mirror of Truth" (its squares labeled Passion, Hypocrisy, Envy, Lying, Levity, and so on); a dueling pistol made by Manton himself; a cravat tied à la Byron; a mourning card, and other bric-à-brac.

Teri took a wordless glance at these, then sank gracefully into one of the two wide leather armchairs that flanked the bricked-in fireplace. Her loose, white sundress fell softly against her, revealing the tiny frame within, and Juliet wondered again how she could spare two pounds.

"Were other people disappointed by the casting?" Juliet asked lightly, settling herself in the opposite chair.

Teri shrugged. "You bet. Everyone in the company wanted to be in *Great Ex*. It's for sure the most interesting project we have going this year."

"I imagine the auditions were fierce."

"Oh, there weren't any auditions. Ruth just came into the studios and watched us work, and then she made her decisions."

"Really?" Juliet's surprise was genuine.

"Some people thought she should have had a trying-out period at least, to even up the playing field for people who didn't know her. Some of the soloists are really great, and for sure they could dance principal roles. But Ruth knew Anton from when she worked with him in Frankfurt, so— I don't want to say anything rude about her," she interrupted herself, abruptly turning prim. "I know you're friends." She flashed a practiced stage smile quite different from the bashful item she had been exhibiting till now. "And you are so nice to have me over."

That night, Juliet phoned Ruth to relay what scraps of information her lunch with Teri had yielded. Except for the fact that Anton's promiscuousness suggested a discarded lover as the culprit, however, they didn't seem to add up to much.

Ruth was not surprised to hear the casting of *Great Ex* had caused distress and grumbling among the dancers. Wanting roles and not getting them was a fact of the dancer's life, she said flatly. With regard to the business of Lily Bediant being young enough to dance Princess Aurora, and therefore too young for Miss Havisham, she suspected that pairing Lily with Anton Mohr had more to do with publicity than any exceptional youthfulness in Miss Bediant. Lily Bediant represented the old guard of the Jansch, the tradition of

American classical ballet. Anton carried the luster of the best of the new European companies. He was young, still new to the troupe, and relatively untried in the classics. Presenting him as Lily's partner in a favorite like *Sleeping Beauty* was just plain good marketing. People would be curious to see them paired, to see how Mohr handled the role of the Prince, and to watch the way he and Bediant—youth and age, innocence and experience—worked together.

As for Miss Havisham being a character role, said Ruth, Teri had probably misunderstood her older friend. Lily might be spoiled and temperamental, but she was smarter than that. Even if she hadn't realized initially that Miss Havisham would be a central character, she certainly knew it now. And so (for all her annoying over-protectiveness) did Victorine.

More intriguing to her was the fact that Anton Mohr had been carrying on with so many members of the company. It hardly startled her, Ruth said: Mohr had been known as a hedonist even when she met him in Germany, when he was barely seventeen. In her experience, she went on, some dancers went all ascetic, pouring their sensuality and sexuality into their work and living rather narrow lives offstage. Others threw themselves into the life of the body, exploring their capabilities, limits, and sensations in every possible way. Small wonder if a magnificent creature like Anton chose the latter path.

But the fact that Greg Fleetwood had been among his lovers might be significant. Of course Ruth had wanted Anton as her first Pip—anyone would be thrilled to have him—but when she and Greg had initially talked about casting, she also felt a distinct pressure from him to pick Mohr. This, perhaps, was the explanation. In any case, Juliet ought to try to nose out who else among the company might consider him- or herself spurned by Mohr, then review the pool for possible rosin vandals.

Juliet listened to all this meekly enough, apparently accepting Ruth's assessments and agreeing to continue what she called the "nosing out" of possible culprits. But she wondered privately if Ruth's frequent tone-deafness in the matter of human relations might not be playing her false. Even setting Lily aside as a special case, Juliet had seen the looks on the faces of the dancers when her friend clapped and corrected them, or gave them a tart reminder of some nuance stipulated yesterday but forgotten today. During the villagers' first scene, she had heard Ruth reprimand the corps for standing as if they were "waiting for the bus." And she had heard corps members quietly refer to Ruth as Ruthless. They might respect her, but they did not like her. Why shouldn't one of them want to rain a bit on her parade? Moreover, it crossed her mind that Ruth's very familiarity with the world of dance might blind her to circumstances an outsider would find suggestive. Later, she was to wish very much that she had paid more attention to this line of thought.

c h a p t e r

FIVE

On the next day, Monday, Dr. Keller pronounced Anton Mohr fit to return to work. During his few days off, he had developed a massive head cold; but that only made him one of many. Otherwise—providing he kept his ankle well bandaged—he was as good as new.

On Tuesday, Ruth asked Hart and Patrick to coach him on the newly devised lifts and leaps he had only been able to watch while his injury healed. The postponed run-through was scheduled for the following day, Wednesday, at three o'clock.

"And it's going to be a disaster," whispered Ruth to Juliet, when the latter arrived, late on Wednesday morning. She found Ruth already in the studio, about to start her first rehearsal hour. The full ensemble had been called and dancers were filing in all around them.

Ruth drew Juliet into a corner. "You watch," she went on fiercely. "Anton barely knows the new steps. I'm missing three transitions. Max is going to see what a mess I've made and change his mind about the gala. He'll hire a new choreographer. He'll— Let me see, what else can I think of to make myself totally crazy?"

Juliet took her hand. "It's going to be fine." She nodded hello to Teri Malone, who had come in and given her a quick, friendly smile, going on, "You're creating wonderful new work here. That's what Max will see."

"Right."

Juliet pushed her gently toward the dancers. "Go make a ballet." She seated herself near the front of the room, where she could quietly cheer Ruth on.

And cheering was needed. The first hour of the day did not go at all well. Even before Ruth could clap to bring the dancers to attention, Victorine Vaillancourt approached her, standing beside her at the front of the studio.

"The new lift you created yesterday for Miss Havisham," she said, quietly but loud enough for Juliet to hear, while all the dancers sat and watched. "When she raises and swings Estella."

"Yes?"

"Our ballerinas are not accustomed to such—such acrobatics. I am afraid you will have to change it."

Alarmed, Juliet sat up straighter. Even to her ear, the word "acrobatics" had an insulting ring. The dance mistress was probably only trying to protect her aging protégée. But Ruth would be sure to resent the term.

Yet Ruth, to her credit, kept her temper. "There is no reason why one woman can't lift another," she replied evenly. "The story requires it and I require it. If it is difficult for—for the Estellas, I can have Patrick coach them."

But Victorine glowered. "All the same," she said, "it will have to be changed."

"It will not be changed," Ruth answered. "But since that pas de deux is not part of this afternoon's run-through, may we set the matter aside for now?"

Victorine gave a graceful nod.

"So long as it will be changed," she murmured maddeningly, and sat down. Juliet noticed the conspiratorial glance she then sent to Lily Bediant, who had preserved an impassive silence throughout the altercation. Juliet felt a surge of dislike for Lily, who still allowed this aging protector to fight her battles.

Ruth raised her hands together to clap and was interrupted at once by the pianist, Luis Fortunato.

"Signorina. Measure six in the 'Peeping Pip.'"

Fortunato crossed the room to her, sheets of music in his hands.

"Sometimes you seem to want ta-ta-ta-TA, sometimes ta-TA, ta-TA." He shoved the pages toward her, scowled and beckoned her back to the piano. "The composer has written it ta-ta-ta-TA," he went on as, unwillingly, Ruth followed him. "But the steps you have now say ta-TA, ta-TA. Either way, I don't mind. But I must know what you want, and so must the dancers."

Ruth's face went grim with frustration. She needed every minute she could get to coax the production together around Anton before the guests arrived. But she dared not ignore such a problem if it really existed. Patrick joined her at the piano, and for ten minutes they went over that phrase and various others Fortunato claimed she'd been reading inconsistently, marking the steps and counting them out while the ensemble watched and waited.

And when, at last, the actual rehearsal began, things got worse. As Ruth had said, Anton Mohr had only an elementary grasp of the new steps, and he danced them without authority. He sneezed and sniffled and blew his nose. He made frequent mistakes in the choreography, and bungled one catch so badly that Kirsten spent a full minute doubled over before she could dance again. More than once, Ruth had to ask Hart to step in and show him how something was to be done. And although Anton picked it up quickly, it was clear even he was frustrated with his progress.

"Yesterday you did not say it so," he muttered darkly to Hart on one occasion when Ruth had summoned the latter to demonstrate a move.

Juliet saw the choreographer and her assistant exchange the same skeptical glance they had traded a week ago, when Anton claimed something had caused him to slip. Ruth, Juliet knew, had told no one about the talcum powder, not even Patrick.

"Did I say it more clearly today? I'm sorry," Hart answered mildly, and Juliet could not help but admire the generous, face-saving diplomacy of the reply. True, it left Anton still sullen; but he soon picked up the steps.

Ruth restarted the act from the top, and this time Anton danced the entire new sequence correctly, if not with spirit.

Gloomily, Ruth looked at the clock and thanked the dancers. "Take ten."

She turned to Juliet, but had time for no more than a despairing glance before Gretchen Manning came clicking in, hands full of lists, and carried her off. Rather relieved, Juliet spent the break on the fire escape with Olympia Andreades.

For better or worse, as of two days ago, Juliet had something in common with the ladies and gentlemen of the Jansch: a messy head cold of her own. Much as she loathed colds, this one had already had three beneficial effects. For one thing, it inspired her to give Fitzroy Cavendish a similar cold, which was helping immeasurably to create comedy in that love scene at Bath. It also provided a point of shared affliction to bemoan with members of the Jansch. She might not be able to execute a pirouette or launch a grand jeté but, by God, she could sneeze with the best of them. Finally—the good side of any cold—she did not need to smoke, her hyperosmia being sufficiently dampened by nature. But for the sake of picking up gossip, she had come out here anyway.

Olympia being a fellow sufferer, the two spent their first minutes on the little metal platform sharing Kleenex and heartily blowing their noses. For the moment, at least, they were alone. The weather had taken a sudden turn toward the sultry, and such sky as they could see from this pocket among the buildings was a curious yellowish gray. Truck horns sounded from Columbus Avenue, where a movie was being shot this afternoon. Remembering that Olympia had been among Anton's lovers, and also that she had been hovering near the rosin box just before his distressing slip, Juliet was determined to sound the ballerina out on the subject of her former beau.

Her sly remark that Mohr was a man's as well as a lady's man was also in Juliet's mind. It suggested some familiarity with the roster of her rivals (if she considered them to be rivals), a list Juliet would like to have.

After a little small talk, therefore, and the requisite Lighting of the Cigarettes, Juliet stretched out her arms, yawned and commenced lying.

"God I'm tired," she said, letting her head roll back across her shoulders. She emitted a soft, sensuous gasp.

Just as she had hoped, "Didn't you sleep last night?" Olympia asked. She smiled, her lush lips parting to reveal white, even teeth. She was beautiful, but for some reason she reminded Juliet of Amabel Edwards, a peripheral character in *Present Love*. Amabel had been rather spiteful, at one point deliberately clinging to a "friend" to prevent her from being alone with the object of her affections.

Juliet produced a sleepy grin. "Not enough. Seemed like a good idea at the time . . ." she added, as suggestively as she could. "You know how that is."

If she expected the other to respond with a detailed accounting of her own recent sexual activities, she was disappointed.

"Mm," was all Olympia said. She dragged on her cigarette, then released the smoke in two streams through her struggling nose. What a perfectly disgusting habit smoking was really, thought Juliet. Who would ever have dreamed it could become popular?

Silence, or what passes for silence in Manhattan, reigned.

At last, in desperation, "Anton Mohr seems to be picking up what he missed last week pretty quickly," she said.

"Oh, Anton can do anything," Olympia said carelessly, for once without double entendre. "He's sensational."

"I gather you know him pretty well?" Juliet hazarded.

Olympia shrugged and looked suddenly world-weary.

"He's not an easy person to know," said the dancer. She certainly didn't sound madly jealous, or cruelly betrayed—but, then, what would that sound like?

"I understand Lily Bediant had an affair with him at one time," Juliet ventured.

"Who didn't?" asked Olympia casually. But the look she gave Juliet made a change in tack seem prudent.

"I was in the studio that day when he fell," Juliet confided quickly. "It was awful. You don't realize—I mean, I didn't, while I was watching you all, how much gravity dancers are always fighting. But when he went down, boy, then I saw it."

"Mm," Olympia nodded.

Juliet had watched her narrowly throughout her little speech for any sign of glee or excessive distress, but the other was merely businesslike.

"I can't imagine what made him fall," Juliet added, still scrutinizing the dancer. "Nothing that I could see."

Olympia shrugged, her face blank. Then suddenly, "He was actually quite lucky," she said. "Ryder had a fall like that a couple of years ago. Wrenched his back and had to take three months off. He was livid."

"Oh, the poor man. It must be awful for a dancer to be immobilized."

Olympia raised an eyebrow. "Oh, he managed. Didn't stop him from giving Elektra a good belt now and then," she said blandly.

Juliet's mouth went dry. By now, she had recognized a perverse streak in Olympia: She was the kind of person who enjoys dropping provocative, unexpected information into a conversation. And clearly, her relationship with her sister was badly strained.

Still, Juliet was shocked. For all their problems, no question of physical abuse had ever arisen between her and Rob—between her and any man, for that matter.

"He hits her?" she asked.

Olympia shrugged again. "They fight. Whack away at each other. Believe me, she gives him good reason."

"Like what?" demanded Juliet, forgetting entirely for the moment her role as tactful investigator.

Olympia gave her a long look, her rich mouth twitching with amusement. "I don't know if you've noticed, but my talented sister can be a bit—trying? A bit aloof? A tad bit condescending? To mere mortals like Ryder and me, I mean."

In fact, Juliet hadn't noticed. Certainly, Elektra Andreades had not been as warm toward her as had Hart, her partner. But neither had she been anything but civil. Still, as Juliet now realized, that was probably the result of her privileged position at the Jansch—a friend of the choreographer, a personage to whom even Max Devijian and Gregory Fleetwood paid respectful attention. Calling the dancer's image to mind, especially in her interactions with her volatile, emotionally transparent husband, she could perceive in Elektra a cool haughtiness that would be extremely tiresome in a relative.

Not that such a thing would ever justify physical violence.

"You don't seem very concerned about her," she could not help saying.

Olympia shrugged again. "Elektra looks after herself. I've given up trying to play big sister to her. After all, she's a star. Whereas I—" She hesitated. "Whereas I have a sense of humor," she finished, and gave a barking laugh.

"Yet you're quite close to Ryder, aren't you?" Juliet asked.

"Ryder?" Olympia took a deep drag of her cigarette, then burst into a fit of coughing. Juliet was afraid she would lose her train of thought, but when she could speak, "I get along with him as well as anyone does," she said. "I guess. He's a moody bastard."

A moment later, she grinned and burst again into laughter, this time raucous laughter.

"And I'm a moody bitch!" she crowed, stubbing her cigarette out against the railing. "I'd better go back inside," she added, and waved cheerily. "Hope you get lucky again tonight! Bye!"

chapter

SIX

　　　　　　　　　　　　　Juliet wondered if something super-
natural could have happened to Anton Mohr during the break.

　　　　Having lingered on the fire escape before returning to what she
feared would be a scene of even greater tension, she instead entered
the studio to find the second hour of rehearsal off to a flying start. In
the middle of the floor, Mohr was dancing—but really dancing.
Somehow, he was now able to execute his steps not only accurately
but with persuasive feeling. He was Pip. Juliet watched in astonishment as he somehow became boyish, small, frail during the earlier
scenes, then grew into springy, sexually awkward adolescence in the
trio with Estella and Miss Havisham. Of his cold, there was no sign.
The steps seemed to flow out of him with organic ease as he alter-
nately cowered and floated, snatched unsuccessfully at the flying
oranges, hid, hungered for Estella's regard. With his performance as
context, Kirsten Ahlswede's icy beauty seemed all at once perverse,
twisted by the precepts of her wicked protectress. Lily Bediant's Miss
Havisham, previously stern but emotionally opaque, was now palpably grim with years of anger and pain. Suddenly, the ballet had life.

　　　　Juliet was not the only one caught up in amazement. The
whole ensemble felt the change and stared from every corner. For a
dancer, there is no audience like his colleagues. If he stumbles, they
will see it; if he flies, he will impress them most of all. The studio

was electric with a strange excitement. Even Ruth stopped taking notes. The nineteen minutes of Act One which she had thus far choreographed concluded with the Estella–Pip "Approach–Avoidance" pas de deux, so that the corps and soloists were again at leisure to watch. When the duet came to an end, the room rang with applause.

Winded and heaving, Mohr smiled but otherwise ignored the clapping. Kirsten and Lily shot satisfied glances at each other, and Ruth—also smiling, for once—commended and thanked all three. Prettily, Lily thanked her in return.

"How did he do that?" Juliet demanded of Patrick Wegweiser a few minutes later, when Ruth had given what notes she had, then dismissed everyone for lunch. Since the design team was coming in for the run-through, Ruth had made plans to get together with them ahead of time, along with the Jansch's stage manager, head carpenter, and others. Patrick, whom she usually commandeered during lunch hours for follow-up work and preparation, was therefore free.

Patrick's long face was full of pride, and his small blue eyes flashed with pleasure. "That's Anton," he said. "He's extraordinary. But you ain't seen nothing yet—wait till he has some time to develop the character."

"But he was the character," Juliet objected, repeating, "How did he do that? Before the break he could barely reproduce the steps."

Patrick knelt to put his things into a canvas dance bag. "He gave one interpretation of the character—a quick, easy interpretation," he said. "It's like . . . How do I explain it?" He paused, still kneeling. The fluorescent light darted short rays through his curly red hair. "It's like a master actor, you know? Once he has the lines, he starts to let his insight, his personality flow out through them. Anton has that gift. He's not a bravura performer, he doesn't make your heart stop with the height of his leaps. He has to work to get the steps; but that's just mechanical. It's the way he releases himself into the movement that's so unusual—that's unique. And it will get deeper and deeper. You'll see, he'll fill Cadwell Hall with Pip. He just has the ability to project himself that way. Most dancers can't. I never could," he went on, and his tone was suddenly almost bitter. "People who see Anton Mohr dance Pip will never forget it."

Juliet listened thoughtfully. Then, "Can Hart Hayden fill a hall?" she asked. "You started to say something once about him and Elektra, that they've been stars of the Jansch for years, but—but something. You didn't finish your sentence."

"Oh. Maybe that they'd never inspired the kind of creative ferment an Anton Mohr does? They're wonderful at what they do, but they only do what you tell them. At least, that's been Ruth's experience. Although I do think Hart's been quite inventive on *Great Ex*. But—what did you ask first? Oh, yes, projection. Yes, they can both project themselves marvelously. It's what leading dancers do."

Patrick stood, his canvas bag slung over his shoulder, and it occurred to Juliet this would be a good opportunity to check him out as a possible culprit. His fortunes rose and fell with Ruth's, so it wouldn't make much sense for him to try to sabotage her work; and he obviously worshiped Anton. But might he envy him even more than he admired him? And might he not secretly loath his boss?

Patrick worked like a dog for Ruth, coming in early, staying through lunches, leaving long after everyone else; yet he never received more than casual thanks from the dancers or (so far as Juliet could see) his employer. Whenever she choreographed, he copied her movements, committing them to memory at once so that he could repeat them for her to look at. Later, he replicated them, recorded them, taught them to the dancers. He placated Luis, he coaxed the corps. His diplomacy mended the holes left by Ruth's acid touch. He danced constantly, with Ruth, with the dancers, during rehearsals and during breaks. He was Ruth's interpreter, guardian, and shadow; yet when Juliet had asked Ruth how much she paid him, she was shocked to learn it was half what she gave her own marvelous—but strictly nine-to-five—Ames. Even in the reduced scale of dance salaries, she could not believe it was near enough. And how must it be to play the drudge while others frolicked in the limelight?

"Want to have lunch?" she asked. "I'll take you out wherever you like—my treat."

Patrick looked dubious. "Thanks, but I'll have a bite here. Ruth might need me."

"Can I join you?" Juliet raised a straw bag she had brought that morning and swung it enticingly. "I'll share my bologna sandwich."

Patrick smiled. "Promise not to and you've got yourself a deal," he said. "Meet me back here in ten minutes. I just have to go and beg the physical therapist to move my neck around."

He disappeared, and Juliet found herself alone in the studio. She let herself out into the empty corridor, empty now even of music, and began an idle wander along the halls. Usually, there were a few people at work in the studios even at lunch time, catching up on something with one of the ballet masters, or stretching and strengthening muscles. But today she saw no one, no one at all—until she reached the farthest end of a hall she had not explored before, where a tiny studio-cum-exercise room had been crammed in between a staircase and a storage room. Here she peered through the small window in the door and was surprised to see Hart Hayden alone. No music issued from the room, but Hayden was dancing like—like a madman, was the word that came to mind. Riveted, Juliet stared through the little pane. He was twitching. He twitched at the knees, then the shoulders and head. He grabbed his own hair and yanked his head back. He laced his fingers and grabbed his head, then knifed the air with upflung hands. Juliet found herself shaking her own head as if she were about to start twitching. There was something familiar about the movements, about the scene— Abruptly, he began to calm down, tugging at his clothes as if recovering his self-control. He smoothed his hair, straightened his cuffs. Soon he sat on a nearby chair and coolly mimed something—maybe filling a glass from a bottle.

Recollecting herself and fearing that he might observe her at any moment, Juliet scurried away back down the hall. He was only rehearsing a scene, surely; yet there was an intimacy about the moment that made her prefer not to be caught watching.

She hurried back to Studio Three, catching Patrick just as he returned.

"How's your neck?"

"Better," he said, rubbing it. "Come on. I have an idea where we can go."

Reversing their course of a week before, he led her through the maze of halls and staircases up to the top floor, where the Olympian administration kept itself clear of the sweat and groans in the building's lower reaches. He moved swiftly and Juliet scurried after him, feeling (as always at the Jansch) like a farm animal at a convention of gazelles. Finally, he turned into a small corner office.

"They gave this to Ruth to use while she's here," he explained over his shoulder, as he swung his own bag down onto a modest, tidy desk. The office was minuscule, uncarpeted, and unornamented, but it actually had a window. Patrick seated himself at the desk, allowing Juliet to draw up a chair opposite and look outside.

There was not much to see—just the large, elderly office building across the narrow courtyard—but the window was clean (unlike those in the studio), the day had brightened, and altogether, the place was pleasant enough. Juliet removed the lunch of poached asparagus and Tuscan white bean salad that Ames had packed for her and set it out where Patrick could help himself.

"Wine?" she inquired, producing plastic tumblers and a silver thermal flask.

Patrick laughed and declined. "Not that I couldn't use a glass," he said, unfolding the waxed paper around a tuna sandwich. "With the run-through coming up, Ruth's been absolutely wacko."

"I'll bet." Juliet poured herself a glass of Chardonnay and raised it in salute to Patrick's bottle of Diet 7-Up. "How do you manage with her? I love her, but she must be hell to work for."

Patrick shrugged. Juliet could not be sure, but a certain uneasiness seemed to creep into his long, lightly freckled face. "She is. But I don't take it personally. When she's really bad, I pretend she has brain damage, some kind of frontal lobe injury that makes her literally unable to be polite."

"What a good imagination you must have," said Juliet, laughing.

"Oh, I'm pretty resourceful."

"And forgiving, you must be."

Juliet had forgotten that Patrick was a starer, the sort of person who locks his gaze into yours during conversation and never looks away. She herself was a glancer—she took a look into her companion's eyes now and then, then let her own wander for a bit—and she never understood why some people locked eyes so steadily. Did they understand more of the human condition? Were they more bold in meeting the souls of their fellow men? Was it an invitation to commune, or was it a challenge? Whatever the point (if any), after a few minutes, the habit invariably made her wildly uncomfortable, distracting her from any discussion and making her wish she could leave the room. Having now reached this unhappy juncture with Patrick, she broke her gaze quite consciously and refreshed herself by blowing her nose with abandon.

She was thus in the unfortunate position of missing the look on his face when he more or less barked out something that sounded like, "Ppfff!"

She looked up from her tissue too late. "No?"

He smiled, or at least, he drew back his lips. "Oh, I can hold a grudge," he said lightly. "I guess anyone can."

Was it her imagination, or was he deliberately trying to soften his first response? His cheeks had certainly reddened. They almost matched his hair.

"Like what?" she asked bluntly. She tried to return his habitual stare in hopes of reading the truth in his eyes, but his concentrated gaze overpowered her will. Involuntarily, she rubbed at her nose again and glanced out the window behind him and into the building beyond, where a man and a woman in an office opposite were passionately necking.

"Oh, for example—" he began, and stopped.

Juliet made herself look at him. His cheeks had reddened even more.

"For example, two or three years ago now, Greg Fleetwood offered to give me some studio space for free when the season ended, because I"—Patrick paused again, faltering yet staring on, his cheeks flaming even more brightly—"because I did him a favor. I do a little choreographing myself, you know, and I wanted to work out a piece with a few friends. Studio time costs a fortune. Anyway, when I phoned six months later, he never even answered my calls. It was like he didn't know me. So even now, I find myself kind of scowling at him. That kind of thing."

Patrick's blush had begun to subside, but Juliet wondered: Could he resent Anton's favored position with Fleetwood, and would such a grudge be enough to make him want to injure the favorite? The trouble with people, she could not help thinking, was that you never knew; you never knew what the hell was going on in their hearts. It was always guesswork, and taking their word for things, and supposing their past behavior would predict their future. But for herself, she knew she lied all the time, tried to mislead people into thinking she liked them when she did not, or persuade them she was not angry when she was, or make them believe she'd never noticed a slight or oversight that in fact had outraged her, and that still rankled deeply. Was Patrick capable of plotting a secret and vicious revenge? Was he the sort of person who could nurse a growing hatred of his employer until it exploded in violence?

As Olympia Andreades might have said, who wasn't?

Across the courtyard, the couple who had been necking were now laughing uproariously. Juliet wondered which of them had made the joke, since they both seemed to be enjoying it equally. Perhaps something they had overheard.

"Oh, dear," she said aloud, adding innocently, "What was the favor?"

At this, Patrick's blush returned all over again. He looked down (at last!) at his hands and seemed to steady himself before he spoke. "It was just— Oh, for Chrissake, I took care of his gerbils while he was away, that's all."

"His gerbils?"

"Pet gerbils. You know, those jumpy little rodents? Greg keeps them—or he used to, I wouldn't know."

There was an element of injured dignity in Patrick's last few words that suddenly gave Juliet a flash of insight into his character. Patrick Wegweiser was not only a happy server. He was the kind of person who enjoys abasing himself. If he had worked in an office, he would have been the one who washed out everyone else's coffee mugs. At parties, no doubt, he took it upon himself to hang up coats, empty ashtrays. Perhaps it was a handy neurosis for a less than stellar dancer—perhaps for any dancer.

"People are swine," she said.

"Well," Patrick seemed determined to be fair, "they're better than rodents, anyway."

"Bigger than rodents," Juliet allowed. Then, "Why do you think Anton hurt himself that day?" she asked suddenly. "What made him fall?"

This time, even though her nose itched and the couple in the window behind him had gone back to groping each other madly, she was careful to keep her eyes on Patrick's face.

If he were covering guilty knowledge, he did it very well. "Dancers fall," he said informatively, once more the impassive tour guide in the world of ballet. "There's a lot of balance involved, and the steps Ruth creates are particularly odd sometimes."

"But he wasn't dancing Ruth's steps," Juliet objected.

Patrick only shrugged.

"He said he thought something made him slip," she persisted.

Patrick crumpled up his empty waxed paper and brushed

crumbs from his lips. "God knows I love Anton," he said, "and there's no dancer like him. But thinking isn't really his strong suit, if you get my drift. Look, I've got to go down to Ruth and see if she's looking for me. She's pretty jumpy about having all these people here." He stood, smiling. "Good to catch up with you. You know your way back to the studio?"

Juliet nodded and smiled. She had also finished her lunch, but she sat on for a few minutes anyhow, gazing absently at the couple across the way, who were now undressing each other while in offices all around them, their unwitting colleagues frowned at papers and snarled into phones. What an interesting way to spend the afternoon. And how extremely different from her own plans. Her thoughts returning to these, she began to pack away her flask and tumblers, at the same time mentally crossing Patrick off her list of suspects. Unless he suffered from multiple-personality disorder, he admired Anton far too much ever to do him harm.

In no particular order, that left Elektra Andreades, Olympia Andreades, Hart Hayden, Lily Bediant, Victorine Vaillancourt, Ryder Kensington—and anyone else of forty or so people she might have failed to notice near the rosin box at the crucial juncture, five unremarkable minutes at the end of last Wednesday's rehearsal when a full ensemble of dancers had stood and stretched and knelt and packed and crossed and crisscrossed and recrossed a vast studio before whisking themselves away in a dozen directions.

Juliet stood to leave Ruth's office and was somehow dismayed to notice that the busy couple, who had disappeared a moment before, could not be missed from this new height. They were rolling on the gray wall-to-wall industrial carpeting: clinched, half-dressed, and apparently either sobbing together or chortling at each other like maniacs.

c h a p t e r

SEVEN

Having literally bumped into him as she left Ruth's office after lunch, Juliet walked to the run-through in the company of Max Devijian.

The executive director had not neglected her during the week since she had first visited Ruth at the Jansch. Several times, he had stopped to fawn on her as they passed in the corridors. On each occasion, his dark eyes blazing energy, his thinning hair alive with purpose, he would grab her head in his hands like a melon and smooch either side of her face.

"Our good angel!" he would chortle, and smooch again before hurrying off.

One time, he had broached the idea of having her join the Jansch's board, and it was to this subject that he returned today. Juliet, who found the Authors Guild bureaucracy enough for her, knew she would never accept any such position. Healthy distraction was one thing; becoming enmeshed in an organization was quite another. She first tried gently to discourage him, then slowly realized gentle was not the way to go. By the time they had descended both flights of stairs, her stomach was knotted and she noticed with some embarrassment that her voice had grown quite shrill.

"No!" she heard herself shriek, then amended, "I mean, no thank you." They turned into the corridor that led to Studio Three. "I appreciate your faith in me, Max, but it's out of the question."

But shrill or reasoned, all her protests were for nought. Max raised a slender finger and wagged it playfully at her. "You're not off the hook, Miss Bodine," he said. He put a hand on the knob of the closed door to Studio Three and paused long enough to bus her soundly on the cheek. "I'll get you yet!"

As he opened the door, a wave of heat and noise swept into the corridor. Studio Three had been transformed, no longer a quiet atelier but an ad hoc cocktail lounge. A tangle of voices bounced off the walls. Bodies in street clothes milled at random. There was the unfamiliar smell of food.

Max dove into the fray, abandoning Juliet, who hovered near the door to survey the scene. Gregory Fleetwood, elegantly animated, was already holding court amidst a small cluster of designers and their assistants. Not only the invited guests but any member of the Jansch staff who could find an excuse to come had crowded into the room, where they chattered ferociously and muscled each other to get to a little buffet composed of cheese, grapes, and Champagne. It was even hotter than usual. Juliet noticed the Champagne was moving especially well.

This little cocktail hour had been Ruth's idea, a chance for the administrators of the Jansch to put faces to the names of her creative team (and vice versa) in a way she hoped would strengthen everyone's commitment to the project. Even she had mustered some semblance of social grace: Juliet saw her introducing a slight, youthful woman dressed all in red leather (the costume designer?) to a gaunt, gawky man of perhaps sixty. (Photographer? Press agent?) Dressed in a simple but stylish black shirt and her usual tights, Ruth was concealing her nervousness well, betraying it only now and then with a quick look at the clock. Patrick trailed around behind her, doubtless cleaning up the social gaffes she left behind.

Juliet sidled up to the buffet to pour herself a small glass of Champagne, then threaded her way back out through the mob to a chair in the corner near the piano, the last in a triple row of folding chairs set up along the front wall for the visiting dignitaries. A shyness that seldom afflicted her elsewhere came over her in sociable crowds. As she sat, she noticed Max reaching out to give Ruth a celebratory kiss, which Ruth tried to receive calmly. Ruth was afraid of Max, she had confided to Juliet. Greg Fleetwood was a dancer, and he had done some choreography himself. He knew how productions faltered and floundered as they were put together, then gradually came to cohere. But Max was no artist, and what he might or might not understand of the creative process Ruth did not know. She only knew that if he felt *Great Ex* was going wrong, it would be her head on the line, her comfort and authority undermined. The Jansch was still struggling to renew itself. The company had a lot riding on *Great Ex*, far more than Ruth liked. Rehearsal time cost them well in excess of one hundred thousand dollars a week. Competition with other New York ballet companies would be brutal this year: City Ballet was working on a major project with Mark Morris, Ballet Theater was producing a new full-length work by Lar Lubovitch. And the Kirov, the Royal Danish, and the Feld Ballet would all be in town for substantial runs. Max might want to give her her freedom, creatively speaking, but they both knew if *Great Ex* flopped, it would be a punishing blow for the company.

While the guests refreshed themselves, meanwhile, the ensemble waited, pushed deep toward the back of the studio, corps by the windows at the rear, soloists and principals chiefly on the sides. They did not have to be told to lay off the refreshments. Not one went near the little buffet. Instead, they behaved as always during unstructured time in the studio, stretching and toning their muscles, practicing bits and pieces of choreography, teasing one another, comparing notes on elusive steps. Juliet noticed Teri Malone wore pink tights and a dazzlingly white leotard; she sat some yards toward the back wall from the piano, wrestling (as it seemed) with a pointe shoe while glancing almost surreptitiously, ever and anon, toward Anton Mohr. In the farthest corner of the room, Olympia Andreades sat side by side with the angular Russian tobacco fiend. The two of them were looking intently through a magazine whose name Juliet could not read. Ryder

Kensington was working at the barre not far away, while his wife leaned back under the opposite barre, near the door, and serenely sewed ribbons onto a shoe. Beside her, Hart Hayden sat with legs splayed, bowing forward, then diving from side to side. In the middle of the room, Kirsten Ahlswede hunched over her feet, apparently stuffing shredded paper towels between her toes, yet somehow managing to look coldly autocratic anyway. Anton Mohr lay on his back almost under the piano, doing his ab-strengthening exercises and swigging between repetitions from a plastic bottle of Coke. Presently, Juliet dared to creep over to him and interrupt him.

"Anton?"

She crouched beside him, wishing her thighs were thinner.

Anton sat up and took a slug of soda.

"You were gorgeous to watch today." She smiled. "Even scary, in such an enclosed space. Kind of like seeing an eagle fly in a pet shop."

The handsome face darkened as Anton frowned and slightly shook his head. "The listening scene does not please me," he said. "There I am too—what would you say?" He made a slicing movement with his hand. "Thin? Flat? Not deep."

Juliet nodded as he conveyed his thought correctly, then worried he would interpret this to mean she agreed with him about the performance. She was about to address this when she felt someone coming up behind her. She turned her head to find Lily Bediant approaching; from the corner of her eye, she saw Anton's face quicken in response. Feeling hopelessly clumsy and uninteresting between these two fairy-tale creatures, Juliet straightened hurriedly, her knee almost knocking his Coke bottle over in her haste. It tottered, but Lily swooped in and neatly caught it. She looked up at Julie with a cold, violet glance that sent the latter clomping away.

After last session's star turn, Anton was even more a center of attention than usual, Juliet noticed, resuming her seat. Something of glamour that was ordinarily absent in the studio seemed to cling to him. Lily's delicate head bent to that of her ex-lover as she whispered what seemed to be a joke in his ear. When they laughed at the end, their heads gleamed together so brightly that Juliet would hardly have been surprised to see a shower of sparks stream from them. What could the joke have been? How many choreographers does it take to screw in a lightbulb? Whatever it was, Lily rose gracefully and left him.

But he was too magnetic today, it seemed, to be left alone. A minute or two later, Ryder Kensington sauntered across the room and squatted easily near him. From his gestures, Juliet gathered they were discussing some detail of their initial collision in Scene One. Moving the Coke away to have more room, Ryder stretched his long arms straight out from his chest and made the snatching gesture Ruth had devised for just after Magwitch's first near-collision with Pip. Anton abandoned his exercises and stood up with him. Experimentally, he turned his head away and created the flinching gesture with which Pip responded to Magwitch's grab, whereupon Ryder briefly adjusted the younger man's head as if to suggest an even more frightened cringe. As the men stood nodding, murmuring and comparing gestures together, Juliet thought of all the times she had watched ballets and wondered what were the real relations between the prince and princess, the Sugar Plum Fairy and her swain, the doll and the inventor. In all other forms—operas, plays, even modern dance—it seemed possible to her to read something of the performers' offstage feelings in their body language. But ballet was body language. Personal feeling seemed totally hidden.

And now, here she was, if not privy to the most personal moments of a company, then at least front and center while they were off guard. Hart Hayden had come up near Anton while the latter was still talking to Ryder Kensington. For a few minutes, Hayden waited quietly, first sitting on the soles of his feet, then stretching out his legs and leaning over, hands clamped to his toes, while the other two finished up. How must it be for Ryder to see his wife touching Hart every day, intimately joined in steps and rhythm, as interdependent as two trapeze artists swinging to each others' wrists? Juliet was still unsure of Hart's (shelved) sexual proclivity, though she was normally able to place this, and Hayden did not seem to be trying to hide it. He was one of those men who are most of all charming. An old-fashioned strength, perhaps, but all the more welcome for that, Juliet thought. It was not the heady charisma Greg Fleetwood exuded, nor the rather smarmy ooze emitted by Max, but rather a subtle kind of charm genuinely focused on setting another person at ease. It was oddly close to the princely air he had on stage—minus the noblesse oblige, luckily. As she watched, Ryder walked away and Hart knelt on the floor, setting the bottle of Coke on a nearby chair to get it out of the way. He leaned forward interrogatively to Anton, apparently singing a snatch of the score while counting it out on his fingers, then sketching a few of the gestures that punctuated it with his narrow hands.

The buzzing creative team, meanwhile, had reached that moment in a gathering when uneasiness wears off and unfeigned pleasure begins to set in. There was authentic laughter and a certain amount of friendly elbowing, and the champagne flowed as fast as Gretchen Manning's minions could open the bottles. Juliet saw Victorine detach herself from a pair of costume apprentices to move around on the floor among the dancers. She bent over Lily and stroked her cheek as she murmured some few words. She glided on to Teri Malone, to whom she showed her foot slightly askew, then perfectly straight, askew then straight, while Teri copied her, earnestly nodding. As Victorine moved on to Anton, Teri felt Juliet's eyes on her and smiled at her shyly.

Victorine, meanwhile, stooped with difficulty to speak to Anton. He rose respectfully to his feet, then gave her a broad smile. As they talked, Juliet was surprised by the affection she seemed to see in Anton's face. Not that he'd ever been unaffectionate to Victorine that she had noticed—only he'd never struck her as particularly demonstrative before.

Victorine glanced around, then gestured to Elektra Andreades, who had put away her needle and thread, to come over. Elektra obeyed. The dance mistress turned to her and tucked her own head down submissively, as Estella did in the pas de trois with Miss Havisham and Pip. Elektra did likewise and stood holding the pose while Victorine, dancing Miss Havisham, used Elektra to show Anton what she thought the pas de trois needed here. She wanted him to try to kneel and look up into Estella's face. But the idea did not seem to work out, and after a few minutes, Victorine threw up her hands, laughed briefly, and walked away. Behind her, Anton chugged from his Coke, then sat again on the floor and drew Elektra down beside him. Eyeing Mademoiselle as she crossed to the front of the room, Juliet had the curious thought that there was something malign in the expression on her tightly controlled, still beautiful, Gallic features. A moment later, however, glimpsing her as she slowly, carefully lowered herself into a chair, Juliet revised her opinion and decided that what she had seen in that handsome, haughty face was pain.

The sociable interval dragged on. Only the more prominent dancers dared to look irritated at being kept waiting. Finally, after some half an hour of playing hostess, Ruth withdrew from among her guests and summoned Luis Fortunato to the piano. Sitting beside him on the bench, she spoke to him forcefully about tempo (judging by her gestures), then waved at Patrick and brought him into the discussion as well. Greg Fleetwood, meanwhile, stole onto the studio floor and stooped briefly to have a word with the production's brightest star. Anton was slowly massaging his left foot. He looked up and greeted Fleetwood with a grin, murmured something to the older man as the latter knelt to examine his ankle, then shook his hand warmly. By now, Ruth, Luis, and Patrick had finally reached the point of nodding in unison. Ruth clapped for the attention of the dancers, at the same time alerting the audience that it was time to sit down. Slowly, regretfully, the knots of visitors resolved themselves into three neat rows of spectators seated expectantly on three rows of folding chairs. Fleetwood joined them, perching in the front row between Max Devijian and the woman in red leather.

Meanwhile, the dancers hastily thrust their bottles of water and soda into their bags, hitched their leotards down where it counted and assembled themselves facing front, individuality wiped from their expressions and replaced with the cool dancer's hauteur Juliet disliked so much.

Ruth Renswick faced them.

"From Act One, Scene One," she announced. "Anton? Ryder?"

The dancers thus summoned went to their opening positions. Luis Fortunato raised his hands over the keys. Ruth turned to her guests.

"We have about nineteen minutes of Act One, with a couple of transitions missing," she told them, "so we'll move through it with a few brief interruptions." She walked toward the side of the room so that she could address everyone more easily. "Luis is kindly going to play a piano arrangement of the overture," she went on more loudly, then continued by naming the leading dancers, both for the watchers' benefit and so that the performers could make their last preparations. Finally, like an acrophobe boarding a plane, she waved despairingly at Luis. He began to play. The run-through was out of Ruth's control, thought Juliet, as she watched her old friend reluctantly sit down, and out-of-control was not a feeling Ruth enjoyed.

The overture Ken Parisi had written was full of the cannons and gunshots that advertised Magwitch's escape, and the piano arrangement denoted these with heavy chords that crashed low on the keyboard. For fifteen or twenty seconds, the studio echoed with this clamor; then the guns gave way to a muscular, staccato tune in a minor key which Juliet recognized as Pip's theme. Gradually, this became intertwined with a haunting, sinuous melody evoking Miss Havisham and Estella. An all-purpose, Victorian bit of pomp-and-whalebone followed, then was pierced by a return of the guns. Suddenly, Ryder Kensington rushed to the center of the room, at first almost colliding with Anton, then snatching him up in his powerful arms.

For some ten minutes, the music bore the dancers swiftly along. In the first scene, Pip was repeatedly upended and tipped dizzily backward by the convict—as in the book. But he recovered from his fear to nuzzle timidly against Magwitch, winning the convict with the comfort of human warmth rather than (as in the book) the bringing of food. There were no chains and no question of a file. It interested Juliet to see how Kensington could soften in response to Pip's warmth. For the first time, she understood why Elektra would have married him: he was very lovely and moving when tender, as surly men unfortunately can be. Then the scene of Pip at home began, with a soloist named Maria Flor as the harsh (but no longer comic) Mrs. Joe. The oranges flew, Pip missed them, the soldiers arrived, and off they all went to hunt down the unfortunate convict.

Then everything came to a stop.

"No transition here," said Ruth, popping up and smiling in a way that was meant to be apologetic, though on her it looked pretty fierce. She raised one finger in the air and murmured, "Anton?"

Anton Mohr came forward to her. As he did, he could be seen for a moment almost to stagger. He was, however, grinning. Ruth looked up at him and stood on tiptoe to whisper furiously in his ear, while Anton, for whatever reason, slowly stroked her upper arm with a gentle hand.

Juliet guessed Ruth was asking if his injury had worsened again. He had been spellbinding in the opening scene, but even Juliet had noticed he lost momentum during the Christmas dinner. The choreography called for him to hop up on a chair to grab at the oranges, but he missed the mark and, stepping too close to the edge of the chair, almost brought it toppling down. He had recovered and finished, but with none of the brio he had shown earlier in the day. Could he have stage fright, Juliet wondered? It seemed unlikely. Now he was shaking his head at Ruth, smiling broadly, as if to say his ankle was fine. But Juliet could see his huge green eyes. They were shiny, and curiously unfocused.

The little conference finished, Ruth retired to her chair, nodded curtly at Luis and muttered to her guests, "We'll go on."

Luis began the "Peeping Pip" pas de trois.

Lily Bediant started bent over a crouching Kirsten, her arms encircling the younger woman, then slowly rising, as if she were conjuring an apparition. The two women moved together sensuously at first, then with increasing angularity and agitation. As Miss Havisham began to exert open control over her pupil, Anton stole onto the scene, creeping to a wooden frame that represented the French doors.

But there was something wrong. Instead of looking afraid of discovery—adolescent, awkward, timid—Anton Mohr wore the delighted grin of a child sitting ringside at a circus. What's more, he was moving around in ways Ruth had never told him to. He raised his arms and stretched them. He let his head roll back and forth. He pirouetted twice. When the steps called for him to echo at a distance those of the women, he instead went forward to them and danced as closely as if they were all at a wedding reception. Juliet, glancing questioningly at Ruth, saw her trying to catch the pianist's eye; but it was impossible. Luis rolled right on into the next bit, the "Approach–Avoidance" pas de deux for Pip and Estella, without a break.

Now Mohr's dancing became downright wild. Breaking entirely from the choreography, he caressed an astonished Kirsten Ahlswede, kissed her, carried her in a sailing sort of lift Juliet did not recall from rehearsal, then set her down and burst into a passionate cadenza entirely his own. The whole studio watched in amazement as he flew around it, now throwing himself down on the floor, now leaping and turning in giant circles. It was splendid, but it was terribly frightening for those who knew the piece. Ruth stood in her place with her mouth half open, torn between wanting to stop him and not daring to speak.

Anton Mohr seemed to be in a trance of some kind, like a sleepwalker who might fall if wakened. The music ended, but he danced on. It was no longer a performance. Evidently unaware of his surroundings, he moved like a child alone, without self-conscious-ness, in a joyful frenzy. Juliet thought suddenly of a documentary she had seen showing people who spoke in tongues, the glad, whole-hearted way they gave themselves over to an alien force. Anton was ecstatic, she realized with a shiver of horror. She had never been near a man in this state before.

Ruth was moving slowly toward the middle of the room, her dark face expressive of a dozen warring impulses, her body radioac-tive with emotion. She looked several times toward Greg Fleetwood, as if he might know how to explain Anton's conduct, but though he looked more angry than puzzled, he did not offer any help. With the German whirling behind her, the choreographer finally shrugged at her audience, a gesture that eloquently disowned all responsibility for this display. Not far from her, Victorine Vaillancourt also had risen and started to come forward; but she stopped, for once at a loss for what to do. All around the edges of the studio, dancers fell back and stared. A weird, scared silence filled the room, broken only by the frantic squeaking of Mohr's dance shoes on the floor.

Then he began to sing, or rather, to howl, his distorted German syllables interrupted by gasps. His singing was distracted, offhand, as if he were humming to himself. His gaze more and more inward, he skipped and swooped, leapt and minced, until at last—after what seemed hours but was, in fact, only four minutes—he suddenly sank to the floor as if fainting and lay there completely immobile.

In the first startled moments that followed, his collapse evoked more relief than alarm.

chapter

EIGHT

For a few minutes following Anton's fall, everything seemed to be happening at once. With considerable aplomb, Gregory Fleetwood swiftly evicted both guests and dancers. At the same time, Patrick used Juliet's cell phone to call 911. Amid the evacuating crowd of dancers and civilians, Victorine knelt protectively beside Anton. He lay unconscious, his skin a bizarre red. As the room emptied, Patrick obeyed a paramedic on the other end of the phone, kneeling across from Victorine and checking the patient's vital signs to see whether any life-saving measures should be taken. But since Anton was breathing—albeit barely—and the cause of his collapse was unknown, there was little to do until the ambulance came.

While they waited, Victorine held Anton's inert hand. Patrick and Ruth huddled together on the piano bench. Juliet paced around the room. From the corner of her eye, she saw Greg Fleetwood return from sending the outsiders on their way. He was itching to evict her as well. Deliberately, she avoided his glance.

The medics turned up surprisingly quickly, all heavy boots and health and equipment. Two uniformed police officers (summoned automatically by same the 911 dispatcher who sent the ambulance) lumbered in after them, looking for all the world as if they'd just stepped off the set of *Law and Order*. Momentarily disoriented, they stared around at the mirrored walls, the grimy windows, the sweat-worn barres, the limp figure in leotard and tights on the floor. One held a form on a clipboard on which he took down from Patrick Anton's name, age, and address. As they finished and Patrick rejoined Ruth, Juliet hesitantly came close to where the officer with the clipboard stood near the door. He was tall and young, with wispy brown hair and a sprinkle of freckles on his snub nose. She hesitated a few moments, then gently touched his arm.

"Officer—Officer Peltz," she murmured, reading the name from his name tag, "I think Mr. Mohr may have been drugged."

"No kidding," said Officer Peltz. The medics' ringing series of questions about Anton's behavior before he lost consciousness, coupled with Ruth's quiet, precise answers, had already made it clear the dancer had been in some kind of delirium.

"I mean," said Juliet evenly, reining in her temper, "drugged against his will."

"Oh yeah? What's your name?"

Juliet gave it. Peltz wrote it down on his pad, along with a short notation.

"Friend of Mr. Mohr?" asked the officer.

"Not really. Barely an acquaintance. But—will you be at the hospital? Will you make sure the doctors check for drugs?"

"Oh, they'll check for drugs," said his partner, a thickset man with pale hair and a bull neck, who had now strolled up. He gave a short laugh.

"This lady thinks someone slipped the guy a mickey," Peltz explained. "Any special reason you think he didn't take whatever he took on purpose?"

Juliet hesitated. It was obvious they were now considering whether she herself had secretly drugged Anton, then regretted it when she saw the catastrophic results.

"You see anything?" put in the partner, whose name was Roarke, as she still failed to answer.

Finally, she shook her head no. "I just don't think he'd do such a foolish thing. It would be like a pilot getting drunk on the runway just before takeoff. If it is a question of drugs, anyway."

The men exchanged glances. Pilots have been known to drink, their looks said. Juliet thought of arguing the point further and decided not to. Neither of these men struck her as particularly bright.

"Did you see him eat or drink anything?" Roarke prodded. "Someone monkey around with his food or anything?"

"No. That is—" Her soft, girlish voice halted and she blinked rapidly. "He did have a soda, but I didn't see anyone tamper with it, no."

Officer Peltz raised an eyebrow, then took her address and phone number. A few moments later, the medics carried their patient away, Victorine hurrying behind them to accompany him in the ambulance. The police went also. As they all left, Greg announced that he would go as well, in a cab.

And then, to Juliet's amazement, Ruth called the dancers back in to get on with choreographing the end of the first act. Naturally shaken, the dancers looked faintly astonished at being made to resume routine work. But there were two valuable rehearsal hours left in the day, two unreplaceable hours worth three or four thousand dollars in salaries. Ruth briskly announced that Anton was being "seen to" and began at once addressing various matters of timing and gesture she had found amiss during the run-through.

Juliet was just resuming her chair when she noticed, under the piano, Anton's dance bag and the Coke he had been drinking. Evidently, the police had not thought his things worth picking up. A little self-consciously, she collected them herself, finding the cap to the bottle in an outer pocket of the bag. She brought them back to the chair with her and sat down rather reluctantly. She both admired Ruth's discipline and thought she was out of her mind. No sane person could concentrate in the wake of such a scene. But Ruth was not entirely sane these days—at least, not about *Great Ex*. She was a woman obsessed, terrified of failure, and entirely unable to see beyond her cherished project.

The others seemed to react more normally. Patrick, though he obeyed Ruth, was pale and visibly distressed. Hart, who stood in for Anton, moved his body as he was told. But, as complete a professional as he was, he could put no feeling or fluidity into what he did, and his face was opaque with mixed emotions. Ruth had called on him to partner Kirsten Ahlswede, who was much too tall for him—five or six inches taller than he. Kirsten's ice-blue eyes were stony, perhaps with shock, perhaps with anger at Ruth's persistence, perhaps for some dancer's reason Juliet could not hope to divine. She caught a peculiar glance passing between Kirsten and Lily Bediant as they began to listen to Ruth's notes on the pas de trois. Apprehension was legible in Lily's face and in her every gesture, though she dutifully performed the steps Ruth required. Teri Malone, who stood with the corps waiting her turn for notes, looked as if she might run back to Eau Claire for good; near her, Olympia Andreades scowled and simmered. Elektra sat with her husband for once, against the wall under a barre, her small, lovely face pinched and frightened, his solemn but unreadable. The only relaxed expression Juliet saw belonged to Alexei Ostrovsky, the angular Russian, who seemed to be rather enjoying the discomfiture of everyone else. While Ruth was absorbed with Luis in yet another discussion of measures and beats, Alexei absolutely mimicked Anton's weird performance, whirling as if giddy and finishing by pretending to fall to the floor in a daze. His clowning earned a few uncertain smiles, but more eye-rolling and glares, and so even he subsided into decorous stillness.

When Ruth finally thanked and released the group, a palpable whoosh of relief passed over the room. The dancers departed, a hum of murmurs and mutters rising from them as they went. More than one sent a glance of disapproval in Ruth's direction; but she, of course, was oblivious.

Once the room was empty, Juliet offered to drive her to the hospital. But Ruth was exhausted and angry and said she saw no point in going there. Any news would be relayed to her by Greg or Victorine, probably sooner than she wanted to hear it, she said.

Out of patience for once with her difficult friend, Juliet left abruptly and alone. It was her creed that one took the bad with the good in those one loved; but Ruth's selfish myopia was wearing on her today. For her own part, she had found the scene of Anton's collapse extremely upsetting. She considered dropping his bag at the hospital but decided it could wait till tomorrow. Victorine and Greg would make sure he had anything necessary tonight.

Instead, she went home and phoned Molly Laurence, her oldest friend in the world and, of everyone she knew, Most Likely to Console. Five years ago, Molly had met a man, quit her job and left the city. Now she was marooned on Long Island, caught (on the hook of her three-year-old son's happiness) in an extremely unhappy marriage. But she was still Molly, and she had only to listen to Juliet for a few minutes before making her diagnosis.

"Sweetie, you had a very disturbing experience. No wonder you're feeling rattled. You need a warm bath and some Beethoven," Molly prescribed authoritatively. "Scented oil or salts in the bath and—um, I would say the String Quartet in C, Opus 59, Number 3. If you can't sit still long enough for the whole thing, just do the second movement."

Juliet obeyed. She soaked herself for nearly an hour, then had peanut butter and jelly on toasted white bread for dinner. Her equilibrium restored, she spent the remainder of the evening with Lady Porter, who was beginning to show surprising depths of cunning.

"Dead?"

Juliet sat up against the pillows, dropped the cordless, lost it under a pillow and found it again.

"What did you say?"

"Anton's dead," Ruth repeated. "He died about an hour ago, in the ICU. Greg just called me. He was overheated, way overheated, and they couldn't get his temperature down. I think he basically boiled to death."

"Good God." Juliet squinched her face up and tried to get her bearings. Her bedside clock said 6:12, and a white glow showed at the windows. "Did the doctors say he'd been drugged?"

" 'Been drugged?' " echoed Ruth, stressing the 'been.' "No. They said he'd taken Ecstasy."

"Taken what?"

"Ecstasy. Ek-stah-cee. It's a street drug, Juliet. What convent are you living in?"

Juliet sat up straighter. "Is it lethal? Did he overdose?"

"No, of course it's not lethal. It makes people feel fabulous." Ruth was quiet a moment, and when she spoke again her tone was more neutral. "And they don't think he overdosed. Greg says they don't know yet why he reacted so badly. He was dancing, and it was hot in the room, and he may have gotten dehydrated and—they don't know. He's just dead. Juliet, how could he? What am I going to do?"

Realizing a little belatedly that she was awake for the day, Juliet got out of bed and headed toward the kitchen. "Ruth," she asked, on her way down the stairs, "had you ever seen Anton on drugs before?"

"No. Why?"

"Do dancers even do drugs?"

"God, yes. All kinds. Especially speed and coke."

"Really?" Juliet was surprised. Those gorgeous bodies. She reached the kitchen, tucked the phone between her shoulder and ear and picked up the kettle. "Ruth, yesterday, during the run-through, you whispered something to Anton—just after the scene with the oranges. What did you say?"

"I don't know. I guess I asked him if his ankle was bothering him, and—

"Was it?" interrupted Juliet, pausing at the sink.

"No. He said he felt a little dizzy, but great. So I told him, in that case, get hold of yourself and quit fucking up."

"Yes, he was sort of fucking up," Juliet agreed. For the first time, the fact that Anton Mohr was dead, gone, began to come home to her. She felt tears start to her eyes and worked to check them. "Why did he smile at you and pat you?"

"I have no idea. Because he was high as a kite, presumably. How he could do this when—"

As Ruth took up her lament, Juliet put down the kettle and walked into the front hall just to reassure herself. Yes, Anton's dance bag was there.

"Juliet?" Ruth had started going on about some meeting. "Did you hear me? Can you come?"

"Sorry, what? Come where?"

"To the Jansch. Can you hold my hand at the Jansch at noon today? Greg is going to announce what happened, and I have to think about recasting. Well, not think about it, do it. Shit, I better get off the phone."

Ruth hung up before Juliet had even given her answer.

"Yes, I'll be there," she said into the dead receiver, then hung up, poured boiling water over a tea bag in a mug, and went upstairs to pee. At the same time, she wondered how and why Anton Mohr should have died so young. Her thoughts ranged from the elegiac to the pragmatic, with many stops in between. When she had complimented him in the studio, just after her lunch with Patrick yesterday, he had been perfectly sober, even a little grouchy—certainly not in a mood to grin or gambol. Her own experiments with illicit drugs had now faded into the mists of time, but she still remembered the strange interval between dropping the dose and feeling its effects: that heightened sense of waiting, of giddy, apprehensive attention to every interior sensation, the examination of each stray thought to see if it could herald the start of the high, the feeling of keeping a giggly secret from outsiders. She had seen nothing like this in Anton.

Early as it was, the day was already well under way. Sunlight painted the pebbled glass of the bathroom window a radiant white. Juliet splashed her face with water, combed her hair and went back down to the kitchen to sip tea in the unfamiliar light. Cupping her hands around the hot mug, she allowed her thoughts to return to her own affairs. With satisfaction, she recalled the six pages she had managed to turn out before falling into bed last night. Any day now, Lord Suffield would offer for Caroline Castlingham and after that, *London Quadrille* would practically write itself.

Thanks to her unwontedly early start, Juliet had already showered, dressed, and sat down at her desk by the time the doorman's buzzer sounded, some minutes after nine. Ames, who had just gone into her little office to type last night's six pages into the computer, answered the house phone, then came into the adjoining room, where Juliet was poring over the 1807 edition of *Lodge's Peerage* for names. She needed names for a dinner party Lady Porter was planning to give; anyway, a browse through Lodge was a good antidote for brooding over Anton Mohr's death.

"A Detective Murray Landis is in the lobby," said Ames, her intonation turning the statement into a question.

Juliet looked up, her head full of Augustas and Frederics and Jemimas. "Murray?" she repeated dubiously, as if Ames had been suggesting the name for a character in *London Quadrille.*

"Evidently he's from the precinct house on West Seventy-third Street," said Ames. "He wants to come up and see you."

"Oh! It must be about Anton Mohr." Juliet stood up and moved away from the desk, then stopped. "Murray Landis? I knew a Murray Landis at Radcliffe. I mean, he was a student at Harvard. An art student. Are you sure?"

"It may not be the same one, Dr. Bodine," said Ames, her large, plain face studiously blank as usual. Ames always insisted on calling Juliet Dr. Bodine, just as she always insisted on wearing a suit and stockings to her job. Juliet sometimes wondered what Ames had been like as a little girl. Exactly the same as fifty years later, she would have bet: tall, pale, contained, watchful, and absolutely competent. She had, no doubt, been the sort of child who decides early to keep her own counsel, the sort who delivers even her cleverest observations without cracking a smile. Jolly and effusive Ames was not and never would be; but Juliet had learned over the years that she had a brand of loyalty that was perhaps superior to mere easy friendship. She also had a certain subtle, dry—indeed, parched—kind of humor. In fact, she was probably laughing uproariously at her employer right now.

"Shall I have him sent up?" she asked.

"Yes, you'd better. Take him into the library. I'll see him there."

Juliet went down the stairs to her library, her thoughts chasing around in her brain like mice in a maze. Was it normal for a detective to come to one's house? Why should she be visited so soon rather than Max or Greg? Could the police really imagine she had doped Anton Mohr? What had ever become of Murray Landis, anyway? They had met when he started dating her roommate, Mona, during their sophomore year. She never saw Mona these days—Mona had married a diplomat and moved to Norway, last she heard—and she couldn't think—

"Miss Bodine?"

A tall, lanky man with dark eyes, a long, crooked nose and curiously flat cheekbones appeared at the door to the library. He had dark skin and short, curly hair, and his nose looked as if it had once been broken. Instinctively, Juliet backed away a step or two. It is one thing to see curling, discolored photographs of our parents, for example, and laugh at their funny clothes and fresh faces, the hilarious way their hair was combed. But to see a face we think of as young suddenly middle-aged is frightening. In the end (though habit spares us the worst of the special effects), we are all Dorian Gray.

Juliet stared at the tall policeman, dismay, confusion, and delight crowding into her soft face. As with most people, Murray Landis had both changed and grown more the same over the years. The slight stoop in his bony shoulders had been there in embryonic form even when he was nineteen. His olive skin had toughened, and his crisp, curly hair was flecked with gray. His nose seemed even more crooked now. But his small, dark eyes were as bright, as sharp, and he gave altogether the same effect of absolute maleness. His khaki slacks were deeply frayed at the cuffs, and his dark sports jacket was about to lose a button. But they hung on his lean frame well.

He had recognized her, too; she could see it in his eyes. As he came forward to shake her hand, Juliet remembered the scruffy art student he had once been. A sculptor, he was, always scrounging around for junked vehicles and toys, bits of furniture, silverware. He was restless and intense, almost electric with energy, the sort of boy (in those first years of college, she still thought of them as "boys") who constantly stirred the coins in his pocket or prowled the room or sat and maddeningly jiggled a hand or foot as he talked. Many nights, Juliet had cleared out of the dorm room to give him and Mona privacy; many nights, the two were asleep together when drowsiness drove Juliet back home. She couldn't remember what had made the pair break up. Jealousy? Some sexual mess? That was usually the careless, lustful Mona's downfall. Juliet had always remembered Murray (as one does remember people for such things) as the first person to quote to her E. M. Forster's complaint that you can't "face facts" because facts are like the walls of a room: face one and your back is to the other three. He had been like that: unusually open-minded, all-sided in his thinking, curious, full of strange enthusiasms and unexpected opinions. He was also kind, and sensitive, and patient—you had to be, to go out with Mona—and (Juliet had thought) quite talented. Looking at him now, she supposed there must be less likely candidates for the New York Police Department, but she couldn't think of one offhand.

"Juliet Bodine. I thought it had to be you," he said, in the strong Brooklyn accent she had forgotten. Jooliet. I thawdid hadda be you. Suddenly, she remembered: His father had been a cop, and maybe an uncle or two. He had been at Harvard on scholarship, and that, come to think of it, had been part of the trouble between Mona and him. He had a chip on his shoulder, a lurking suspicion that Mona, tooth-straightened, nose-jobbed only child of suburban wealth, was more interested in him as a socioeconomic curio than as a person.

"Okay if I sit down?" he asked now, as Juliet stood lost in recollection.

"Of course. Please."

She came back to the present, made him comfortable in one of the leather armchairs, offered coffee, asked how he'd been.

He nodded and smiled. "Been good. Been good. You look good. It's a long time," he said.

A horrified thought as to how she must have changed flitted through her head. "A long time," she echoed faintly.

"You've done well for yourself," he went on, indicating the prosperousness of her life with a quick glance around at the heavy curtains, the book-lined walls, the staircase to the second floor just visible through the doorway. Juliet's heart sank a notch at this seeming return to the theme where she had left him: money, prestige, who had it, who didn't.

"I've been lucky," she said. "My books sell."

"You're a writer?"

"Historical romances. Under a pen name."

"You always were smart."

"What happened to your art degree?"

"Oh, I still make art. I'm working with shadows right now. Light and shadows. I'll show you sometime if you want. It's hard to explain."

"I'd like that."

"You don't have to worry about the money thing, by the way," he said, with a flash of the uncanny sensitivity she remembered of old. "I kind of got over that."

"Good for you."

"Yeah, I married money." He laughed. "And then money and I got divorced."

"I'm sorry."

"It's a while ago. Listen, I'll tell you the reason I'm here."

He sat forward, his face growing serious. He had lost his old change-rattling nervousness, but none of his intensity, Juliet noticed. He also smelled the same. Ivory soap, coffee, Mennen deodorant, and above it all a super-layer of pure man smell. Pheromones it might be. It hit her powerfully, even with her cold. How nice it was to be with him again. Abruptly, she recalled a thrilling hour they had spent together waiting for Mona in the dorm room; nothing had happened, but the buzz of attraction between them had been intoxicatingly strong.

"This man who died this morning, Anton Mohr," he said. "He was a friend of yours?"

Juliet explained her connection to Anton, to the Jansch, to Ruth Renswick. She thought Landis might have known Ruth back at school, but he hadn't.

"And you think someone slipped some kind of drug to Mr. Mohr?" he took up. "That's what I read in the report."

"I don't know," said Juliet, noticing that formal "Mr." Mohr. It seemed odd coming from the boy she remembered. "It crossed my mind. I do have his things from yesterday, including the Coke he was drinking. I brought them home for him, thinking I'd bring them to him today." Tears prickled in her eyes at the reminder of what now seemed yesterday's innocence, but she forced them away.

At the same time, Murray's eyebrows rose. "This bag has been in your possession all night long?"

"Yes," said Juliet. His tone seemed faintly to suggest this had been foolish, even criminal. Did he think she'd meant to steal the bag?

"Ever heard of a chain of custody of evidence?" he asked.

"Not really, no," said Juliet. "Should I have?"

"Well, I sure wish you had, Juliet. What we call the chain of custody documents whoever had his hands on any piece of evidence and when. Now, if you had given this bag to Officer Peltz yesterday, I wouldn't have to wonder what happened to it in the last sixteen hours. See my point? So why didn't you give it to Officer Peltz?"

Juliet straightened herself in her chair. She knew she was not a very imposing figure even at the height of her dignity; but it couldn't hurt to sit up straight. What ailed the man? Didn't he remember how many nights she had stayed out of her own room so he could dally with Mona undisturbed? A moment ago, she had been so pleased to see him. But he seemed to have withdrawn into pure officialdom.

"Because I had no idea Anton was going to die," she said, as neutrally as possible. "It belonged to him. I was planning to give it to him. Anyway, why didn't Officer Peltz take it himself?" she went on, her tone gaining heat. "He's the policeman. I told him Anton had drunk a soda. He should have asked me where it was."

"Hmph," said Landis. "Let me understand this: Why exactly did you suggest to Peltz that Mr. Mohr's drink might have been spiked?"

"I didn't suggest that."

She heard the sharpness in her own voice, but really, it wasn't her fault. Landis was being positively peremptory.

Annoyed, she went on, "Look, I didn't have to come forward yesterday at all. I did it because I thought it was right. What I told Peltz was that Anton had been drinking a soda, but that I had not seen anyone tamper with it. And I tried to explain that Anton didn't seem to me the type to use recreational drugs. I certainly doubted, and I still doubt, whether he would have deliberately jeopardized an important performance. Maybe you don't understand just how important that run-through was."

In a few words, she explained the significance of yesterday's event, how many people crucial to the production's success had been seeing it for the first time and why this mattered so much. Prompted, she went on to describe Mohr's normal, self-possessed demeanor, his increasingly erratic behavior as the performance began, and the explosiveness of his breakdown.

For a while, Landis allowed her to run on. He had removed a small notebook from an inner pocket in which, at mysterious intervals, he marked a word or two down. At first, Juliet assumed he was recording the details she reported. But eventually, she guessed it was not so simple as that.

"And—pardon me, I still don't quite understand," Landis finally interrupted. "Did you have any actual reason to think anyone had a grudge against Mr. Mohr?"

He was leaning sharply toward her, his dark eyes narrowed. With a sense of physical shock, Juliet realized he was viewing her as a suspect, not a witness. What he had been writing down were probably questions about inconsistencies, possible motives, maybe her own involuntary body language.

At the same time, his question reminded her that he had no knowledge of the booby trap that had been set up in the rosin box a week before. No wonder he seemed so skeptical, so puzzled! Relieved, she hurried to clear things up.

"Oh, yes, I do have a reason," she said, smiling. "I'm sorry, I should have explained in the first place."

As succinctly as possible, she retailed the incident, described Anton's slip and temporary injury.

"I'm sure that powder was put in there at the very end of the ensemble session," she finished. "Anyone with a schedule would have known only he would be using the studio after that. So it must have been meant for him."

Detective Landis nodded. But, contrary to her expectations, he did not seem to relax.

"Talcum powder as a dangerous instrument," he said, and one of his nostrils twitched as if he were suppressing a smile. "That's a new one. But it's still felony assault. Did you mention this to Peltz?"

"No, it didn't occur to me."

"I see," Detective Landis said, rather portentously, she thought. "And what happened after you reported the talcum episode to the Jansch administration?"

Juliet explained the flyer Greg Fleetwood had sent around. Hearing her own words, it struck her as very odd that Fleetwood should have taken such a limp approach to a problem that had endangered his own protégé and former lover. Why hadn't he done better?

"And did anyone come forward?" asked Landis.

"No."

"No," agreed Landis, eyeing her narrowly. "Did Mohr suggest to Fleetwood any possible perpetrator?"

"I don't know," said Juliet, feeling obscurely defensive. "Ask Fleetwood. But the fact that no one did come forward is the reason I've been watching the *Great Ex* ensemble so closely myself," she added.

"Watching—?"

"Watching and listening," she added reluctantly. "And asking questions."

"Oh, you mean snooping. Playing private eye."

"I knew you were going to say that!"

"Did you know that in New York State, private investigators are required to have a license? Has Miss Renswick been paying you for your services at the Jansch?"

"Of course she hasn't," Juliet said stiffly. "And I really didn't think of what I was doing as playing private eye." She wondered if he would have taken this tone with her if she'd been a man. "Or playing anything," she added.

Landis's look was frankly skeptical. "By the way, while you were snooping around, you didn't happen to question Mohr about who he thought might have done it?" he asked.

"No, I didn't."

"No." He gazed at her as if this omission was proof positive of some sinister motive on her part. Yet the truth was, she had not felt it was her place even to let Anton know she was aware of the booby trap into which he had fallen. That had seemed to her an internal affair of the Jansch, about which she ought to keep her mouth shut even with the victim. Besides, concerned about their star's performance, Ruth and Greg had both wished to downplay any suggestion that Anton had been the chosen target.

Gazing back at Detective Landis, however, she didn't think he would be very impressed by this reasoning.

"And so your close involvement with the Jansch has been purely altruistic?" he asked at length.

Juliet lost patience. "Look, do you really think I had anything to do with making Anton Mohr slip?" she finally burst out indignantly. "Or causing his death?"

"From my point of view," Landis said, "you seem to be right in the middle of both events."

"Oh, for God's sake!" Who was Murray Landis to come around judging her? She hadn't even thought of him in years.

He scrutinized her a moment longer. Then, quite abruptly, he seemed to make a conscious decision to warm his manner toward her radically. Deliberately, he set aside his notebook, leaned back, crossed one long, lean leg over the other and smiled.

"So whadja learn?" he asked. His tone now was direct, friendly. "Who do you like for the bad guy? Assuming somebody had it in for Mohr."

Juliet hesitated. A minute ago, she thought she would have paid any amount to divert the detective's suspicions from herself. But she didn't trust this sudden about-face in his demeanor. And the prospect of implicating others was most unappealing.

"Okay, nobody likes to rat," he prodded, reading her face, "but tell me who you think. You been nosing around. You musta learned something. Who do you suspect? Give me something to go on."

Unhappily, Juliet shifted in her chair. "Well, I haven't come up with a suspect as such," she said, aware that she was mumbling. "I did learn Mohr had had affairs with several people."

"These being?" Landis prodded again.

"These being . . . a dancer named Olympia Andreades"—her color deepened to crimson as she gave the name—"and another named Lily Bediant, and Greg Fleetwood himself, and at least one other person, but I didn't learn who."

To her distress, Murray had begun to write each name down as she gave it. But when he looked up now she saw no particular interest in his face.

"Any of these folks married?" he asked.

"I don't think so. Not that I know of, anyway."

"Then they're not suspects," he said.

Juliet was about to argue when his next question diverted her attention.

"How about yourself?"

"Am I married?"

"Yes."

"No. You're not telling me you think I did it?"

"No, I'm asking. Did you?"

"Of course not. Why would—"

"You didn't dislike Mohr?"

"I didn't even know him."

"But you knew him well enough to think he's not the type to do recreational drugs?"

"He just didn't strike me that way," she repeated, her irritation mounting again. "Look, if I had been involved, what possible motive do you think I could have for approaching Officer Peltz yest—"

"How's the production been going?" Landis interrupted. "Any special tensions? How do the dancers like your friend Ruth?"

Over the past few years, due partly to luck of the draw, partly to the rich supply of museums, concert halls, and theaters within the confines of his precinct, suspicious deaths involving cultural institutions had become a kind of specialty for Detective Landis. He had worked on a case of homicide at the Museum of Natural History and another concerning a prominent curator of American folk art. He knew the personal mechanics of the New-York Historical Society, the security system at the Metropolitan Opera House, and the chain of command in several off-Broadway theaters. Ballet was new to him, but he was well aware that any kind of collective, creative endeavor brought friction.

"I guess they like her well enough," mumbled Juliet.

"Come on, 'fess up. I'm not going to charge her with murder just because you say she's hard to work with. More likely someone would murder her. How's it going? What's she like?"

Juliet gave a large sigh. In for a dime, in for a dollar, she told herself. If she wanted to clear this thing up, she would have to be completely honest.

"Well, she's awful," she began. "I mean, the dancers admire her work very much, they respect her, they're all crazy to dance for her in *Great Ex*, but she's—let me put it this way, when it comes to picking up the nuances in other people's attitudes toward herself, Ruth's got two left brains. She's brusque, demanding, driven, infuriating—I think I might have killed her myself."

"But you don't think someone killed Anton Mohr just to give her a headache, do you?"

"I don't think anyone meant to kill Anton. If all he took was Ecstasy, why should he die?"

Landis nodded, admitting the logic of this. "The M.E. doesn't know. She's doing an autopsy to see. But it can happen—it's happened a couple dozen times at raves in England, apparently. A person takes Ecstasy and dances for hours in a hot room, doesn't drink enough water—some of them overheat, some recover and some just don't. But that's dancing for hours. This—" He spread his hands. "This is a little different."

"Exactly. And what I'm thinking is maybe someone meant to make Ruth look like a fool by causing Anton to go haywire. This was Ruth's moment to prove her worth, to triumph. Instead, it was a fiasco. Now there's a dancer named—well, you already have her name, Lily Bediant. She apparently wanted to dance the role of Estella. Are you familiar with *Great Expectations*?"

"Yeah, sure."

"So instead, Ruth cast her as Miss Havisham."

"What, the crazy old lady?"

"Right. Crazy middle-aged lady, by modern standards. Anyway, Lily seems to be rather hot-tempered. And I understand she was quite annoyed."

"Hot-tempered like violent?"

"Oh, I don't know that. But prickly and—not a forgiving nature, that's for sure."

"And who told you she was peeved?"

Juliet explained.

"And you trust this Teri Malone person?"

"Yes."

"She doesn't have her own axe to grind?"

"Not that I know of."

"Tell me who else you trust. You trust Ruth?"

"Oh, absolutely. She's a mensch, a person. I don't mean to make her sound any less. She's just a—a little dense sometimes about human beings."

"And you like her? You wish her well?"

"Like her? I just told you, she's one of my dearest friends."

"You wouldn't want to put a spoke in her wheel professionally, by any chance?" he asked, smiling slyly. "Believe me, I understand. I'm an artist myself. You know what they say, it's not enough for you to succeed, you also need your friends to fail."

Juliet's resentment got away from her. "What the hell is the matter with you? Don't you believe anything I say?"

"Not particularly," he said calmly. He didn't appear to have taken offense. "I'm a police officer. I'm investigating a case."

"Well, you sure take your job seriously," she sputtered.

"You would like me to take a possible homicide frivolously?" he asked.

Quelled, Juliet conceded, "Of course not. I just don't quite get why you have to talk to me like I'm Jeffrey Dahmer."

Landis's nostril twitched again, but all he said was, "Maybe we should get back to the matter at hand. Who else can you tell me about? What about this Victoria, the woman who came with him into the E.R.?"

"Oh, Victorine. She's the chief dance instructor there." Juliet considered. "She's a pretty tough bird, but I doubt—Well, she was very angry about Lily Bediant," she amended. "So Teri said. Lily is her protégée."

"So that's a motive."

She shrugged. "Ruth did say Victorine wanted to choreograph this project herself. But I can't see her drugging Anton. She lives for dance, and he was a great dancer at the start of a great career. Anyway, she's not the felonious type."

"And who is?"

Juliet said nothing, but she felt uncomfortable. Evidently, her discomfort showed in her face. Landis uncrossed his legs and leaned forward again.

"Look, if you really think a crime was committed, if you really want it solved," he said bluntly, "you've got to help me, Juliet. There's going to be another crime come along that's fresher—some robbery, some rape—and I'm going to have to jump on that, that's the way it happens. Unfortunately, time is of the essence."

"All right. I don't know why he should wish Anton harm, or Ruth, but the Magwitch is a guy named Ryder Kensington," Juliet said reluctantly. "He's in the corps. He's married to Elektra Andreades, one of the principals—she dances Estella in the second cast. Olympia Andreades is her sister. Ryder's a big man, with kind of a savage look—and I don't know, there's something nasty about him. Olympia told me he's—" she hesitated, "moody, even brutal with his wife. Very hard to get along with. I can believe it."

"His sister-in-law told you this?"

"Yes. They seem close. They spend a lot of time together."

"You think they have something going on the side?"

"I have no idea. It never occurred to me."

"Really? What a sun-dappled forest clearing your mind must be. And who else? Anton was the star, right? So who's going to be the star now?"

"I don't know that either. Ruth is deciding this morning."

"And your guess—?"

"Well, the logical choice is Hart Hayden. He's the second Pip, the Pip in the second cast."

"Was he in the room when Mohr went down?"

"We all were. All these people were in the room."

"And this Hart Hayden, he's good?"

"He's marvelous."

"So why wasn't he the star in the first place?"

Juliet shook her head. "I hate to keep saying 'I don't know.' Ruth's assistant told me he doesn't have the look she wanted. Not grounded enough, too up in the air, I think he said."

"But you figure he'll get the part now?"

"I don't see who else."

"Was he pissed he didn't get it in the first place?"

Murray had sat back and crossed his legs once more. His left foot, balanced over his right knee, began to bounce. It occurred to Juliet he had probably retained his Brooklyn accent on purpose. It was disarming and doubtless useful for getting along with many people. And indeed, as she was later to learn, he was perfectly capable of dropping it and speaking unexceptionably at will. In the matter of accents, he was bilingual. He reminded Juliet of her Puerto Rican friend, Camila, who would sometimes slip from English to Spanish and back in mid-sentence.

His friendliness of the last few minutes seemed authentic. Yet she did not believe he'd stopped suspecting her. For the first time, it occurred to her that good acting skills were probably necessary to a good detective.

She shook her head again. "I really have no idea. He doesn't seem so. He has leading roles in several other ballets this season, I think. And he was a wonderful teacher with Anton."

"He taught Mohr?"

"Well, there were things Hart knew how to do that Anton didn't. Anton doesn't—didn't have as strong a classical training as Hart. And Hart is very smart about dance; he's unusually intelligent in general, I think. So at times, Ruth would have Hart show Anton things—how to handle a lift, how many steps to take where in a little transition."

"And he was good at this."

"Wonderful. Very patient and—delicate."

"Delicate which he needed to be because Anton was touchy."

"I think any artist is touchy who has to be shown how to do something, don't you? In public?"

Now Landis shrugged. "How did you like Anton?" he asked, leaning forward and staring into her eyes until Juliet felt impaled by his gaze.

"As I said, I barely knew him," she said, struggling to meet his look.

"You ever alone with him?"

"No. Yes," she corrected, "for a few minutes once, the first day I met him. He tried to flirt with me. At least, I think he was flirting."

"Oh yeah? How'd he do?"

Juliet gave an involuntary half-smile. "Considering we were alone for under two minutes, pretty well, I'd say."

"Sleep with him?"

At this, she broke eye contact and laughed outright. "Murray, it was two minutes alone in the studio. Less than that. And I had just met him."

"And that was the end of things?"

"That was the end of things. There were no 'things' to end."

"Mm." The detective sat back and nodded his head for a bit, as if putting all this information together. "Mm," he said. He looked at his watch, although a domed clock on the mantelpiece clearly showed it was 9:45. "Well, the M.E.'s doing the autopsy at ten-thirty. I'll go over there to watch now, then stop in at the studio and poke around—"

"Oh!" Juliet jumped to her feet. "Don't forget to take his things."

She hurried out to the front hall and returned with a small black canvas bag made in Germany.

"This is Anton's stuff," she said. "The Coke is in it. You should check it."

"You really think someone drugged him?"

"I don't see what else could have happened. He was fine when the session started."

"But he could have dropped the Ecstasy anytime, couldn't he? Even before he came into the studio?"

Juliet remained standing. "No, I don't think so," she said firmly. "He wasn't like that. He cared too much about his career. You ought to have this analyzed."

Murray snorted as if stifling a laugh. "You truly believe someone mickeyed the Coke."

Juliet's gaze went cold and hard. She had stopped enjoying her interview with Detective Landis.

"Until yesterday, I didn't even know the word 'mickeyed' was still in use in the English language," she said, as starchily as possible. "I'm a citizen, I'm a witness, and I think the Coke would be worth checking. Half a dozen people came within reach of it before the run-through, and I'm sure I saw at least three touch it."

"Oh yeah? Who?"

Without hesitation, "Lily Bediant, Ryder Kensington, and Hart Hayden," she reeled off. "And Elektra Andreades, Victorine Vaillancourt, and Gregory Fleetwood were near him too. Any one of them might have done it. I wasn't watching him every second."

"The ones who did touch it, you see any of them really take hold of it? Drop something in?"

Reluctantly, "No," Juliet answered. "They just moved it from here to there, so they wouldn't knock it over. I almost knocked it over myself, when I went to pay him a compliment."

Murray raised an eyebrow. "Oh," he said. "Did you?" He was silent a moment or two. Finally, "Listen, I understand they were serving Champagne at this shindig yesterday," he said. "You have any?"

"Excuse me?"

"I said, did you have any Champagne at the studio before the run-through yesterday?"

"I had a small glass."

He smiled tightly. "And what did you have for lunch? You weren't drinking on an empty stomach, were you?"

To her annoyance, Juliet felt her cheeks go red again. "I had lunch," she said stiffly.

"Have a beer with it?"

"A glass of Chardonnay. But it surely didn't affect my ability to observe what went on."

"Oh, surely not," said the detective, his intonation and the Brooklyn accent making a mockery of the words. Nevertheless, he bowed his head and picked up the dance bag. "I'll take this with me to the M.E.'s lab. You want prints, too?"

"Yes, I think that would be appropriate." Juliet struggled to beat down her blush and regain her dignity. "If they find that the Coke was spiked."

"Right." Casually, "Have you opened this at all since you closed it up at the studio?" he asked.

"Certainly not."

"Okay," he said, standing at last.

But Juliet felt he did not believe her. Giving in to an overwhelming impulse, she burst out suddenly: "Listen, Murray, you don't really think I tried to harm Anton Mohr, do you? Or tampered with possible evidence?"

"Oh, no," he said. "I keep an open mind. I never put anything past anyone."

"Thanks."

"You know, living in a fancy apartment doesn't automatically exclude a person from suspicion of murder," he said.

"Excuse me?" squawked Juliet. "If I may say so, I'm not sure you did get over that money thing."

Murray raised his eyebrows and laughed, not meanly, but as if at himself. "You could be right there," he agreed. "But take it easy. If I thought you were guilty, we wouldn't be chatting tête-à-tête in your cozy little pad. We'd be down at the station house with a tape recorder and a pal of mine having a formal interrogation."

He picked up the dance bag, ready to leave, and suddenly gave her a brilliant smile, all sparkling teeth and bright eyes. "Nice to see you," he added. "Now do me a favor, wouldja? Don't leave town."

chapter

TEN

After Murray Landis's departure,
Juliet sat alone in the cool of her library and thought about him for
a long time. No doubt she was as morally opaque to him as were the
denizens of the Jansch to her; no doubt it was his job to suspect all
equally. Yet she could not help feeling angry about his behavior.
Maybe he had forgotten that peculiarly charged hour in her silent
dorm room, when they had done no more than study side by side,
yet bristled, vibrated with mutual attraction. Still, for God's sake,
they had smoked hashish together! If that was not a sacred bond,
what was?

All the same, she reflected (as at last she slowly climbed the
stairs to her desk), it was interesting to fall asleep with a budding
sculptor across a dorm room from you and wake ten or twenty years
later to find him a New York City police detective. She must remember to reread Washington Irving.

Meanwhile, there was Lady Porter's guest list to arrange. In the
little office adjacent to Juliet's larger one, Ames was tactfully beaver-
ing away on fan mail. Juliet closed her own door and escaped from
the world of sudden death to the vast, elegant dining room of Ankle
House. She set her ladyship's long table with Sèvres, polished her
heavy silver and chose (from an 1816 cookbook) a six-course meal
commencing with lobster soup and culminating in gooseberry fool.

Her writing came easily today. When the guests sat down to dine, Caroline Castlingham was astonished to discover across from her at table a gentleman she'd not seen since both were children. On that occasion, they had sneaked into the supper room at a ball together and made off with a tankard of syllabub, with which they had then escaped to Caroline's schoolroom upstairs. They had made themselves rather drunk while playing endless rounds of Consequences.

("A lady and a gentleman meet during a dancing lesson," Caroline remembered beginning one round.

"In consequence whereof," her drinking companion had gone on, "the gentleman trips over the lady's foot."

"In consequence whereof, the lady hits the gentleman over the head," Caroline had added.

"In consequence whereof," her interlocutor had replied, "the gentleman falls to the floor, sobbing."

At the age of twelve or so, and in their deepening inebriation, this had struck them both as so hilarious they could hardly breathe for laughing.)

Meeting this old acquaintance now across Lady Porter's dining table, the twenty-year-old Caroline could not at first prevent herself from exclaiming with pleasure. However, the gentleman's reciprocal enthusiasm proving excessively effusive, she soon chose to quell him with a chilly and dignified look, then ignored him for the rest of the evening.

Before Juliet knew it, two hours had gone by and she was a little late to start for the Jansch. Still in her work clothes—blue jeans and a T-shirt—she sprinted down to the street and dashed to West End Avenue, where two taxis almost collided in an attempt to get to her first.

She dodged them both, chose the less aggressive one, got in and gave the address of the Jansch. As the driver pulled out into traffic, the cell phone in her purse rang.

"Hello?"

"Juliet, do you think Hart is up to dancing Pip? Oh, Jesus, I still can't believe this is happening."

"Of course he is," said Juliet mechanically, wondering at the same time what on earth could be on the mind of the driver of the red Chevy—Bounder, was it called? Blunder? No, a Blazer, a Chevy Blazer—straddling both lanes three or four cars ahead of them on West End. "You're lucky to have him. He'll be marvelous."

"But I don't see Pip that way, I never have. You know," insisted Ruth. "I see him as earthy and springy and—"

"I'm sure Hart can do earthy and springy." Juliet intended the words to soothe, but they somehow had the opposite effect.

"No he *can't*, that's exactly why I called. I need you to tell me it'll be all right with a balletic Pip, an ungrounded Pip. Will it? You know the character."

"Of course it will be all right. It will be better than all right, it will be unique, it will be wonderful in a new way." With dismay, Juliet realized she would need to surpass her ordinary supportiveness skills if she wanted to calm and fortify the frenzied Ruth. Resourcefully, she summoned in imagination the adroit Sir Hugh Legburne—a steadfast friend and a superb flatterer, as Chapter Four of *The Consul-General* amply demonstrated—and channeled him.

"Ruth, dear, you're creating a work of real depth and imagination," she said. "There isn't going to be only one way to dance Pip. Over the years, there will be all kinds of Pips, in all kinds of productions, and each will be valid and interesting in its own way. That's what it means to create art. You have to try to surrender control a little to the work itself. Trust yourself. Trust dance. Trust Dickens, at least."

There was a moment of silence. Juliet wondered what the cab driver might be making of her end of this conversation.

Finally, "You really think *Great Ex* has depth?" Ruth asked.

"Yes, I really do," crooned Juliet, and lied, "Listen, we're turning onto Amsterdam. I'd better run."

"Watch out for reporters," Ruth hastily warned. "They're already crawling around the building here, God knows how."

Juliet was replacing the phone in her purse when it went off in her hand.

"Detective Landis, for Juliet Bodine."

"Hi, Murray."

"Oh, Juliet." The deep voice lost some of its bark. "Listen, I'm calling from the M.E.'s office. There was a container of medicine in Mohr's bag—one of those seven-compartment, one-a-day plastic things. Monday and Tuesday were empty, Wednesday had one pill left in it and the others had three each. Did you see it?"

"I told you, I didn't look."

"Well, the pills are a prescription medication called Nardil, an antidepressant. The M.E. recognized them right off the bat."

"Really?"

"Did Mohr seem depressed to you?"

"Not at all."

"Well, he was." Landis's voice hardened. "The M.E. says shrinks don't start with Nardil—it's the MAO-inhibitor type, the type that's dangerous to mix with a long list of foods and medications. It does the trick, but it's so hard for people to keep away from cheese and beer and whatnot that doctors only prescribe it if the easier, newer antidepressants don't work. So Anton Mohr had to have been a tough case. I'll get the name of his doctor and see if he'll talk to me, but— Oh, by the way, that was the reason he died. Ecstasy and Nardil—bad combination. Poor putz, the shrink probably never warned him about illegal drugs."

Juliet was silent for a while. Then, "But don't you think if he had been taking—"

But Landis interrupted her.

"You figure anyone else at the company knew he was on an antidepressant?" he asked, as the Blazer finally lumbered off into the far reaches of West Seventy-fifth Street.

"I don't know."

"Well, think about it, 'cause if someone did, maybe they did mean to kill him. Listen, I'm going to be over at the studios a little later on. If we see each other there, quick eye contact and that's it, you hear? You don't show and you don't tell anyone that you've been talking to me. No one. Not even your friend Ruth, for now. You got that, Juliet?"

"Thank you, yes, that's quite clear."

"I left the Coke at the lab. But right now, everything is pointing toward accidental death. Even if the soda was doped, he probably doped it himself. Remember hash brownies and dropping acid in sugar cubes? Anyway, I'll call his family when we hang up, see what they know about this history of depression."

"Yes, about that," Juliet tried again, "how do you figure—"

"Gotta run, Jule. They're bringing another body in."

He hung up, the phone making a painful click in Juliet's ear. Jule?

As usual, rehearsal for Great Expec-*tations* was slated to start at noon in Studio Three. The call having been for the entire cast, and her arrival having been impeded by the crowd of reporters disrupting routine in the building lobby, Juliet entered to find the ensemble already in the room. Many had pink eyes. They clutched each other even more than ordinarily, around the waist or shoulders. Kleenex fluttered damply from their graceful fingers. Juliet was surprised to see Elektra Andreades holding onto her husband—mutely, for comfort, the way people do who have temporarily lost their bearings. Though it was clear that everyone knew Anton was dead—most of the dancers had come here two hours ago to start class—Greg Fleetwood sat them down, stood before them and made a formal speech.

Greg had obviously been up all night. His eyes were red, his spiky hair flat, his voice gravelly. Max, hovering near him, wore the strained, sharp-eyed look of a man determined to ride out a public relations disaster.

"You're probably all aware by now that Anton Mohr died last night," said Greg, tears instantly, disconcertingly welling in his exhausted eyes. "He died of hyperthermia after taking a—a drug that had an adverse effect. We don't have a lot more detail now, and I must ask you all to say no more than this to any reporter who contacts you. I'm sure that Anton would want us to go on with the productions that meant so much to him . . ."

Juliet, sleepy again after the early start to her day, listened with only one ear as he continued. Her attention was on the faces before her. Elektra Andreades had let go of her husband (so much larger than she) and now sat hunched on the floor with her knees against her chest. She looked stricken—more than stricken, maybe. Scared? Ryder sat with his long, powerful legs out straight before him, a hard, sober look in his dark eyes. Across the room, Elektra's partner, Hart, looked as distressed, as disoriented as she did, though in his case, shock rather than fear seemed uppermost. Lily Bediant's violet eyes gazed steadily at Greg, but her face was blank, closed. Juliet thought suddenly of Murray's question and wondered if Lily had known Anton was taking Nardil. A drug with so many restrictions would be hard to keep secret from an intimate. Near her, the frosty Kirsten Ahlswede was in tears. Alexei had lost his wiseguy style and sat with his hands covering his head, as if he did not want to know what had happened. Olympia Andreades's soft, full mouth had crumpled; her eyes were clouded and pink. Victorine, awake at the hospital most of the night, had not come in.

If any of those before her had had a hand in Anton Mohr's death, Juliet could not see the guilt in his or her expression. What did guilt look like, anyhow? She thought of her own behavior when she had something to hide. Not a murder or even a legal misdemeanor—any impulses she had had of this sort had always been foiled by her muscular superego—but a social lie, or even a lapse in neighborliness. Once, to evade an invitation from a particularly annoying

acquaintance, she had pretended that she would be out of the country that weekend on business. Then she ran into her would-be hostess at the fish counter at Zabar's. How had she acted? She tried to
recall, to imagine how she appeared that afternoon to her inquisitor.
She had prepared an appropriate story in advance, exactly in case of
such a mishap, and she thought now that she had probably been
overly energetic in telling it. She smiled more than usual—pulled her
lips back, anyway—cringed and fawned a bit, as if out of sheer, animal make-nice instinct before what might be an angry predator. Her
story was unnecessarily elaborate. She felt compelled to kiss her tor-
mentor before they parted, though she did not habitually do so. But
all that had happened only when she was actually confronted with
someone who knew her guilt. Before and after, she had felt nothing—nothing but satisfaction at escaping a tedious dinner party—
and had looked no particular way at all.

Juliet had lost the thread of Greg's remarks but was recalled to
the business at hand by the sound of Ruth starting to speak in his
place. She looked up to see Greg, all his habitual cockiness gone,
shrinking into a corner near Max. As both a lover and an administrator, wouldn't Greg have known about the Nardil? And he had hired
Anton. If the depression was of such long standing, surely he would
have wanted to know whether it was controlled. But the Jansch was
his company, its artists his livelihood, his reputation. What possible
motive could he have had?

Ruth was also hoarse and her eyes red-rimmed (though from
what mix of selfish and selfless motives she had been crying Juliet
preferred not to know). On Juliet's arrival, she had clutched briefly at
her hand and fervently whispered, "Thank you."

Now, her address to the dancers showed her better side.

"What we have to do today is brutal, almost inhuman," she
began. "If I could, I would go home and cry and sleep for a week,
and I know most of you would, too. But that isn't an option. We have
to go on, and we have to go on now, and we have to go on without
Anton. If we don't, we risk the project we've all worked so hard to

make a reality. So—Hart, I would like you to take the role of first Pip. Can you manage that along with your other responsibilities?"

Hart Hayden glanced at Greg, who nodded. Then, quietly, "Sure," he said. Beneath the well-schooled mask of his handsome face, some new feeling was working to make itself visible, Juliet saw; but his fine, scholarly features were too well trained to allow it to appear. It could have been pleasure at the promotion; it could equally well have been alarm at the greater work the promotion would mean, or a professional resolve to rise to the task, or even a poignant flash of renewed grief.

Meanwhile, Ruth was going on, "Kirsten, I'm afraid Elektra will have to dance with Hart. I simply can't pair you with him, unless you can shrink by half a foot." The little joke met with silence, and Ruth went on, "You'll continue to learn Estella with Nicky Sabatino, as second Estella and second Pip, and I hope you know how much I've appreciated your contributions—which I hope you'll continue to make. Elektra, I trust you can manage first Estella?"

Elektra nodded, then glanced apologetically at Kirsten. The latter assumed a mask of sublime indifference, at the same time blinking back a swell of tears.

"Lily, you'll remain as First Havisham. I'd like you to learn Estella, too. Nicky, can you handle second Pip?"

Nicky, a dark, curly-haired demigod Juliet sometimes saw out on the fire escape, said yes. And then Luis Fortunato sat at the piano and the rehearsal began.

Reminding herself that she did need to get back to Lady Porter's soirée, Juliet was just beginning to slink away when the door opened and Detective Murray Landis entered, another man at his side. The second man was also a detective—there needed no deerstalker hat to tell Juliet that. Later, she would learn he was Tom Fales of the Manhattan North homicide squad, Landis's partner on this case.

Fales was big-boned and thickset, with protuberant blue eyes on either side of a thin red nose, and he wore the same kind of casual

khaki slacks-and-dark sports jacket clothing that made Landis look
so suspiciously average. But he also had a subtle quality—Landis had
it too—that made him look exactly like a television police detective.
What was it? No doctor or lawyer (to say nothing of writers) that
Juliet knew looked so much like his video counterpart; nor did one
expect these professionals to behave like their simulacra. But for
some reason, the moment a real policeman swaggered into view,
supra-authentic images of fictional officers rose in the mind's eye.
Perhaps the cop shows were simply better done than the medical and
forensic ones? Perhaps police took their own cues from television?

Curious to watch her old acquaintance in action, Juliet
arrested herself in mid-slink and sat down on the floor a few feet
from the exit, as if this had been her intention in leaving her chair in
the first place. The two detectives had drawn Patrick's notice at once
(and the notice of everyone in the room, for that matter, except the
oblivious Ruth) and he hurried over to them. Juliet heard his startled,
"Oh!" no doubt in response to their identities, but could make out
only mutters and murmurs after that. From his gestures, he was
showing them where Anton had danced, where he had fallen and
how, where most of the people in the room had been and so on.

Presently, Ruth looked up for her assistant, found him busy
chatting with strangers and sharply called his name. This occasioned
a break in the proceedings, as Patrick brought the men over and
introduced them to her.

More buzzing and murmurs, more nodding and gestures
(while the ensemble traded glances and raised eyebrows at one
another), and then Murray and his colleague stationed themselves in
the front corner of the room farthest from Juliet, where they stood
watching as Ruth returned to choreographing Pip's youthful fistfight
with Herbert Pocket, Miss Havisham's gentlemanly young relative.
Murray had not so much as looked at Juliet, so far as she knew, and
he kept his eyes on Ruth and the dancers now.

Pocket was to be danced by Alexei Ostrovsky, who Juliet now
knew had been a rising soloist when he left the Kirov for the Jansch.

He had no intention of staying in the corps here, nor did Ruth think he long would.

"What you're telling Pip is literally, 'Come and fight,' " Ruth was explaining to him when Juliet focused on them again. " 'Come and fight.' You want to fight, you look forward to fighting. For you, fighting is a game. You're a rich boy who just earned his second belt at a karate training center on the Upper East Side. You know what a karate belt is?"

Alexei nodded. He was wearing purple tights and a black sort of vest that left a good deal of his chest bare. His chest was hairless and narrow, but beautifully defined. His habitual smirk had not quite left his otherwise handsome face, and Juliet supposed this reflexive, superior twitch was part of the reason Ruth wanted him for the role.

"You want to try all your moves, and now you've found a real live lunk to try them on, understand? And you," Ruth turned to Hart Hayden, who stood listening with his head slightly dropped, as if he could concentrate better by looking at the floor, "Dickens compares you here to a 'savage young wolf' or a 'wild beast.' " Hart looked sharply up. "He says you feel like a beast after you deck Pocket, not once but many times," Ruth went on, "because he keeps coming at you and he has no strength at all, for all his fancy skipping and jumping around. Plus, there's Estella between you. And Estella—come here, Elektra—Estella is watching you."

Elektra Andreades rose effortlessly from the floor and joined the little group at the front of the room. She moved mechanically, her thoughts clearly elsewhere. But she seemed able to force herself to listen, for she did what she was told. Juliet saw her give Hart a speaking look, a wordless appeal for help, support, kindness. It struck Juliet, as it had before, how very much closer Hart and Elektra seemed than Ryder and Elektra. They had almost the kind of communication you see in twins, as if moving together for so many years had given them a secret, silent language.

Ruth soon began to mold some tentative steps, like a sculptor warming clay in her hands. "More watching!" she said meditatively.

"Maybe we'll create a sort of parallel here to Pip watching the Havisham–Estella pas de deux, I don't know. Anyway, after the fight is over, Estella will say to Pip, 'You may kiss me if you like.' And of course, you will kiss her, Hart. On the cheek, as she turns it to you." Ruth brought Hart and Elektra together, turning Elektra's chin so that her cheek was presented to Hart's pale lips. Behind them, neglected by Ruth, Kirsten and Nicky Sabatino attempted the same gesture, while a soloist named Arturo Ruiz awaited further instructions as second Pocket.

"Okay?" Ruth went on. "But it's a contemptuous gift, a tip, like a couple of crumpled bucks you give the bellboy. And you must think of yourself as an animal, Hart. A wild animal, coarse and earthy and low. Not noble or uplifting, not enlightened, not princely—" She paused and glanced guiltily at Juliet, who glared back meaningfully. "I'm sure you understand," Ruth corrected herself hurriedly, rather awkwardly patting Hart's arm.

Juliet wondered why it would be rather awkward to pat Hart Hayden's arm. It certainly would, she thought, unless the patter was a fellow dancer accustomed to stylized caresses. There was something shiny about him that discouraged patting and petting, a cleanly, almost antiseptic quality that was both attractive and disconcerting. It was extremely difficult to imagine Hayden giggling, say, or hiccoughing—taking any involuntary action, allowing his body to relax. He was the sort of person for whom a bout of flatulence could have tragic repercussions. Control. Everything was controlled with Hayden. Yet he was so intelligent and had been so welcoming and easy with her. He was not, Juliet concluded, as easy to read as she had first supposed.

Whatever his inward feelings, he managed to give his body over to Ruth. She worked first with Alexei, devising a kind of capering sequence of steps that half-menaced, half-teased Pip. But even before she had turned to work with him, Hart had begun to feel out his response, beginning with an almost apelike swinging of one arm, a confused hunch of the shoulders. Juliet was gratified to see that she had been (however fortuitously) correct about his ability to become an earthier Pip. Ruth eagerly soaked up his tentative movements and began to work them into a pattern to complement Pocket's.

"Lovely!" Ruth exclaimed, at a seemingly off-balance spin Hart improvised.

Juliet recognized the genuine enthusiasm in her voice and felt free to let her gaze wander away from the work, to Landis. She was startled to find him looking at her. The moment their eyes met, his cut away to the door, and he raised an index finger. "Go out the door and wait," she understood this to mean, and obeyed, ignoring Ruth's quick, reproachful glance as she crept away. The corridor was empty, except for the echoey swells of piano music from other studios on the floor.

Landis and Fales joined her a few minutes later. The former provided introductions.

"Anywhere quiet we can talk for a few minutes?"

Juliet, anticipating the question, had already checked the next studio down the hall and found it unoccupied. She led them in. Landis drew her to a spot away from the door, where they could not be seen through the little window.

"Cops and robbers," she remarked, with an uneasy laugh.

"Cops and murderers, according to you," said Landis, who seemed determined to keep her at arm's length. Which was fine with her, she had begun to think. "You mind letting me borrow your cell phone? I'll call the lab now, see what they found."

"The city doesn't give you guys cell phones?" Juliet asked, handing him the phone.

Landis laughed. "We still write our reports on typewriters," he said. "Meantime, why don't you help Detective Fales here make a diagram of Studio Three?"

Juliet obliged, identifying the main landmarks (mirrors, barres, rosin box) while Fales sketched swiftly in a spiral notebook. Landis went into a corner alone and muttered into the phone for a bit. Juliet could not help smiling a little at how uncomfortable and out of place he and Fales looked here. She supposed she must look equally incongruous and silly to the dancers.

Soon Landis folded the phone and returned to the others, his dark face thoughtful.

"You were right," he announced, handing Juliet the phone. He turned to Fales. "The Coke was heavily laced with Ecstasy."

"And the prints?" she asked hopefully.

He shook his head. "We'll check what we found, but they're not likely to prove much. Anyone could have taken an innocent swig from the bottle or handed it to him. You could have marked it when you opened the bag at home—"

Annoyed, "I told you, I never opened the bag at home," Juliet interrupted.

"It could have prints from the vendor who sold it," Landis went on, "or a delivery boy—"

"It came out of a machine," said Juliet.

"How do you know?"

She was quiet a moment. "I guess I don't know," she corrected herself. "I just assumed it came from the machine in the dancers' lounge, because it's the same kind of bottle."

"We'll check on that. We'll see if anyone saw him buying it. And when. If it was purchased inside and someone doped it, we'll have to check out who was near him—or it—from the time he acquired it. Can just anyone walk into this place?"

She shook her head. Next door, she heard Luis Fortunato playing the "Peeping Pip" trio and knew, with a sinking sensation, that Ruth was moving backwards. "You have to go past the receptionist. There's no other way in."

"And out?"

"You can go out quite a few ways. There's a fire escape and a couple of other doors that lead to the building stairwell."

"I'll need a list of everyone who was here yesterday."

"That shouldn't be any problem. Every day, there's a schedule written out, telling who goes where and when."

"Support staff? Visitors?"

"You'd better ask Gayle. She's the apricot blonde in front. Murray, did you talk to Anton's family? What did they say?"

Landis glanced at Fales before answering. Fales raised and lowered his furry eyebrows as if to say the irregularity did not trouble him if Landis thought it okay.

"Well, of course they're distraught," he began. "And I had to use an interpreter, they don't speak much English. But I gathered young Anton had a very rocky adolescence," he went on. His Brooklyn accent mysteriously faded as his voice unexpectedly gained warmth and his expression sympathy. "Up and down, up and down, shrinks, guidance counselors, lots of problems. A few collisions with the law, mostly about drug use." He paused and looked at her meaningly. She compressed her lips. "I have to tell you, they sounded shocked, but they didn't sound too surprised. I think they knew this could happen some day."

"They knew their son could be murdered?"

"They knew he could commit suicide. Recklessly, inadvertently, in a fit of despair, whatever. What they said, though they didn't say it outright, wasn't so much, 'This can't be.' It was more like, 'So, this is how it finally happened.'"

"But he had everything to live for!" Juliet protested. "He had just become a principal in a highly regarded company. He could have danced anywhere in the world. And he was physically splendid, the most splendid example of a human being I've ever seen."

"Yeah, I saw him too," said Murray and Juliet, about to argue, realized a moment later that he meant at the autopsy. "That makes it sad. It doesn't make it murder."

"But why would he put a drug in his Coke rather than simply drop a pill?" she demanded. "Why would anyone?"

"Ambivalence?" suggested Detective Landis. "Playing a little game with himself? Some people do sprinkle Ecstasy on food or take it in a beverage. And look at it the other way," he added. "Ecstasy has a discernable taste, a slightly bitter taste. If Mohr wasn't expecting it, why didn't he notice the Coke tasted funny?"

Juliet frowned but could think of no answer. Somehow, she had assumed MDMA was tasteless. But if—

"Oh!" she burst out suddenly. "Because he had a cold! They all did. I do. He'd have thought it tasted strange because he had a cold."

Landis glanced at Fales, who nodded.

"Could be," Landis acknowledged.

"Sure it could. It had to be," insisted Juliet. "Listen, I swear to you, Anton Mohr absolutely would not have—"

But Landis interrupted. "Keep your pants on." The Brooklyn in his English had returned. "I'm going to investigate. I'll question every dancer in the company, if I have to. And the staff." He turned to Fales. "Let's go out to his place this afternoon. He lived in Park Slope. You want to dump his phone?"

The other man nodded and Landis turned again to Juliet. "Dump his phone, that means check the records to see who he's been talking to. We'll look into it, we will. But you have to realize" ("buh you hafta realoize"—Landis was pouring the Brooklyn on now, maybe for Fales's benefit) "the guy was a known user of recreational drugs, he had a long history of clinical depression—it doesn't look particularly like homicide."

Fales shook his heavy head in agreement. For some reason, Juliet wanted to strangle him.

"Now, why don't you come back with us and peek in the window and tell us a little who's who, okay?" Landis went on. "I'll keep an eye out for anyone passing by."

Juliet did not move and he came close enough to put an arm lightly around her shoulders. "It's very rough, it's rough, I realize that," he said. "It's a terrible thing to see a human being come apart. I'm truly sorry. I'll help you. Now, come with me."

Gently but inexorably, he began to walk her toward the door to the hallway. His Doc Martens thumped on the floor. Fales's loafers scuffled behind them. Intellectually, Juliet appreciated Landis's sympathetic words, but in her stomach, she wished he would take his arm away from her shoulders. She didn't feel like being mollified. She felt like screaming—screaming bloody murder.

"Boy, I sure wish you hadn't taken that bottle home with you last night." Murray sighed as he turned the doorknob with his free hand. "It's not going to be much use as official evidence, I'm afraid. Oh yeah, and that reminds me, Jule," he added casually, letting Fales hold the door for them as he walked her out, "have you ever been fingerprinted?"

chapter

ELEVEN

Murray Landis had never enjoyed examining the residence of a homicide victim. If the body was there, you wanted to run away. But you had to go close instead. You wanted to cover it up. But you had to observe and probe.

Still, for him, it was even worse if the victim had died somewhere else. Especially if it was someone who lived alone. You unlocked the door and there was the box of Total still out on the table. There was the bowl in the sink, the last flakes dried in the last drops of milk. There was the *Daily News*, opened to whatever, an ad for a car, a sports column. Maybe you'd find a note scribbled in the margin: "Buy light bulbs." Everything screamed, "This guy woke up, went out the door and fell off the edge of the earth." Murray thought he would rather watch three autopsies than enter the dwelling of one dead guy who lived by himself.

However, police work was not a series of options. It was a series of imperatives: You had to see the guy cut up, you had to go into his place. In the beginning, he had enjoyed having people's private affairs be his business. He was an inquisitive person and this gave him a reason to ask lots of questions. But in the past few years, the answers had started to bother him. Did you know this lady you raped? Did you know it's illegal to enter the playground without a child? Are you aware of the laws regarding firearms in this state? What kind of answers could you expect to questions like that?

This shadow series he had started, a lot of it had to do with crime and criminals. The dark side of people, what they tried to hide. But he preferred to think about it as an aesthetic development, kind of a joke about form and content. Also about the surface, the illusion of depth, the two-dimensionality of painting. And about materials. And monetary value, collectibility. It was playful, but the shadow pieces were also sometimes really evocative. They grabbed your eye and baffled it, made you uneasy, made you think about how your brain wants to decipher meaning from an image. At least they made him think of that. He was experimenting now with multiple light sources, so some shadows were darker than others.

There weren't any shadows to speak of in Anton Mohr's apartment the afternoon he and Fales walked in. The place had only two smallish windows facing a dark courtyard. Anyway, the day was hot, sultry, and the sky overcast. It would probably rain in an hour or two.

Mohr might be the king of ballet, but he had been renting a one-room apartment on the third floor of a five-story walk-up, the same place another dancer from the Jansch used to live. A Jansch administrator named Anita Perez had gotten Mohr's immigration papers in order and helped him settle down in New York, and had known this place was about to be vacant. She had probably never seen it, Landis figured. She probably only knew it was in a decent neighborhood and charged reasonable rent. It was not the kind of place you would recommend to a person with a history of depression, or any person you wished well. It was small. The floor was cheap linoleum and the ceiling lower than average. The kitchenette was supposed to be hidden behind folding, slatted wooden doors, but half of one door had sustained an accident that left a dozen or so slats missing. The windows were obscured by businesslike, black antiburglar gates. The air was as hot and still as if no one had been in here in months. Murray couldn't help comparing it to the last apartment he'd visited, Bodine's place. Boy, was she sitting pretty.

Roaches scattered as Fales flicked on the glaring overhead light.

At least Mohr had done what he could to perk up his dwelling place. A four-poster double bed, set so that it angled out on a diagonal from one corner, formed the centerpiece of the room. It was covered with black-and-white sheets and a satiny black quilt. Sheepskin rugs were scattered around it, and framed ballet posters (some featuring Mohr) hung on the walls. A small wall unit held a handful of books about dance and fitness, an answering machine, a small television set and a stereo system, plus a sizable collection of jazz and classical CDs. A black lacquered Chinese folding screen created a small alcove Mohr had used for exercise: there were a set of weights, some mats and some rather exotic gizmos for stretching and the like. Near the kitchenette was a single table that served, by the look of it, as coffee table, desk, and dining table. Though most of the place was tidy enough (the inevitable cereal bowl sat upside down in a dishrack beside the sink), this table was covered with piles of paper, much of it unopened mail.

The light on the answering machine was flashing and Fales, with a nod at Landis, went to play back the messages. There was the usual whirr and click, then the mechanical announcement: "Three messages."

The first confirmed a dental appointment scheduled for next Monday.

"Jeez I hate dead guys," said Landis, a ridiculous comment but one he could not help making. Why did their ends have to be so abrupt?

"Next message," said the mechanical voice.

"Anton, it's Frank. Listen, I have something I think would interest you. Give me a call if you're up for it."

The detectives exchanged glances. Murray had worked with Fales before on two or three homicides. He was lazy—he never did anything Murray didn't specifically ask him to do—but he was smart.

"Dope dealer?" Murray asked.

"Ten to one," Fales agreed.

Meanwhile, a woman's voice had replaced Frank the dealer's.

"Hi Anton, this is Amanda," she began (or, more accurately, "Hi Anton, this is Amanda?"). "A friend of mine, Courtney? We're going to Club Paradiso this Saturday night, about midnight." ("About midnight?") "Want to come? I thought maybe we could all three have some fun together." Her voice dissolved into giggles as she finally made the statement, then conveniently left her number. When she hung up, the phone clattered for a while, as if she had missed the cradle.

"At least he didn't let his depression keep him home at night," observed Fales, after the two men had traded glances again.

"Look, Tom, what do you say you take his outside life and I do the ballet company?" Murray suggested, starting to paw through the papers (bills, letters, ballet programs) on the single table. "You talk to Amanda there, and the dope dealer, assuming that's who Frank is, and I'll start bringing the dancers down to the station."

"You're not going to investigate this?" Fales asked.

"Yeah, I am. I'll start, anyway. Put a day or two in." Landis' accent was thick as he said this, his voice blunt as a hammer. He didn't want Fales to think he was willing to jump however high Juliet Bodine said to. But he didn't believe she was at all likely to be involved in any wrongdoing. And he did, in fact, have a certain respect for her opinion. Though he'd seldom thought of her since college, he remembered her clearly. Indeed, a lush, tantalizing wave of interest had swept through him at first sight of her. It came back to him that, in college, if he had not been involved with Mona, he'd have tried to get involved with her. She had that kind of soft, well-cared-for beauty that always got to him, that smell of sheltered abundance. Murray had always, God help him, been drawn to the daughters of affluence.

And invariably resented them, too.

In any case, Juliet Bodine always had been smart. And she had been right about the Coke for sure. "If there's nothing there, we'll drop it," he added now. "I just don't want to go too fast and miss something. You know what I mean?"

Fales's eyebrows twitched and Landis could see that he wanted to say No, I do not know what you mean. But he didn't say anything. That was another good thing about Fales.

"I'm going back to the studio, get a couple of lists, maybe talk to a couple of people," Landis went on. "You'll sift through this crap?" He held up a handful of Jansch schedules and junk mail. "And get the phone records and follow up. I'll check his locker over at the Jansch. I want to call the I.N.S. too, see if they know something, maybe even get them on to Interpol, what the heck. For a nineteen-year-old, the guy traveled a lot. Oh, and I'll try his shrink."

"Good luck," said Fales, rolling his eyes. He had tried to get shrinks to talk three or four times, but no way. Patient confidentiality. Civil rights, thought Fales disgustedly, sitting down on the bed to read.

There were sixty-three dancers in the Jansch Repertory Ballet Troupe, plus four ballet mistresses, two ballet masters, four company pianists, the press director and her three underlings, the production manager and his staff of twenty electricians, carpenters, wardrobe assistants, and so on; the artistic director, the executive director, the part-time physical therapist and her massage therapist, the receptionist, the bookkeeper and a dozen or so assorted secretaries, administrative assistants, and gophers. Not every single one of these people had been on the premises on Wednesday, July 14, but the list of those who had topped a hundred. And that was not to mention the day's visitors: a couple of board members, a couple of messenger boys, three volunteer fund-raisers who came in to make calls, a writer from *Dance* magazine who had interviewed Max Devijian, an air-conditioning repair man and his crew of two, a woman who said she was the wife of one of the soloists but turned out to be an incensed girlfriend, the vendor who stocked the food-and-drinks machine (Landis made a tick against his name), all the guests for the run-through, and Juliet Bodine.

Landis had no problem with interviewing all hundred-whatever of them, but he wished he felt more convinced there was something to interview them about. He sat at his desk for a moment, thinking, then picked up the phone and called the Jansch.

"This is Detective Murray Landis. Public relations, please."

When Gretchen Manning herself came on the line, "Listen, could you put together copies of whatever press files you maintain for the company members?" asked Landis. "PR, features, brochures, whatever. I know it's a lot of copying, but it would help."

Manning eagerly answered that she would be thrilled to messenger any number of photocopies to Detective Landis, immediately or sooner. Landis was pretty sure she would also have named her firstborn after him, or flown him to Tahiti, or done any other little favor likely to keep him happy and quiet about the case. It was after four P.M. by the time he phoned her, and the press was all over this story. Dozens of messages from the P.D. press office regarding calls from various media outlets had been sitting on his desk when he got back. Some bright spark from the *Post* had even managed to get out to Mohr's apartment and waylay Landis when he left Fales there. Manning and her organization were taking the line that Mohr's death was the result of a bad drug interaction, but that any further details were private and up to his family to release. Now she told Landis she'd spoken to Herr Heinrich Mohr, Anton's father, who assured her that no information would be forthcoming from their end. The Jansch was hoping the whole thing would be a non-story by the time (inevitably, she supposed) the facts became public, she added. And didn't Detective Landis think that would be for the best?

Landis had met Manning earlier in the day, when he had returned to the studio to take a second look around. He had met Max Devijian too, and Fleetwood and a couple of others. He didn't think much of Fleetwood. The guy was too much pose and not enough substance. His dimwit flyer about the 'malicious incident' looked pretty damn half-hearted to Murray, the kind of thing bureaucracies do so they can say they did something. Plus it turned out he never had told Mohr about the talcum powder after all—didn't want to "unbalance" him, he claimed, didn't want to "burden" him. Landis would look into that. But he had liked Manning, appreciated her obvious dedication to her job—though he thought she was being a wee bit optimistic about the press. Devijian was a type he knew well, both from his experience as an investigator at various theaters and museums and from his own career in the arts: slick but soulful, phony but sincere, high class but (since he was always asking for money) not. Which was not to say Landis didn't approve of raising money for the arts. Noble profession.

Mohr's locker, when they had unlocked it for him, had not turned up much of interest. More Nardil, this time in the pharmacy bottle with the doctor's name on it. Landis already had a man on that, who had learned an hour ago that the prescribing doctor was a psychopharmacologist who had only met Mohr twice. She had supplied the name of the therapist who referred Mohr to her and Landis had left a message on the guy's machine a few minutes ago. Landis wondered which of them was responsible for failing to warn Mohr about interactions with illegal drugs. He supposed the prescribing doctor was the one who was legally liable, but who knew? This was America. Anyone could sue anyone—give it a shot, anyhow.

He wrote up his report for the day, took care of the press calls, divided the Jansch list into four sections, handed them out and went home. Mohr had died just a few minutes too late to make the tabloids' morning finals. As Murray left the subway and walked through a light rain past a newsstand on Broadway, he imagined the fun they would have with the story tomorrow. Would they go with PAS DE DEATH? Or, BALLET STAR IN FINAL SPIN?

c h a p t e r

TWELVE

To Juliet's vexation, Murray Landis allowed nearly four days to go by before contacting her again.

Her distress had several causes. First, she was curious to know what, if anything, he was learning. Next, after their somewhat friendlier encounter at the Jansch, she had thought he might begin to consider her in the light of a helper. Finally, and minimally, she hoped he would stop suspecting her of murder.

Oh, all right, and it would have been polite of him to find he could think of nothing except her strange beauty and magnetic personality.

She might have called him, of course, but something made her hesitate. To her irritation, she had to acknowledge this had partly to do with being "the girl." The girl did not call the boy; the boy called the girl. The ancient taboo, deeply impressed upon her in childhood by Maggie, the nanny who brought her up, had never lost its force. On a more sensible level, there was the issue of their formal roles, his official status as investigating officer, hers as witness (or, as she feared, suspect). That was for him, not her, to abridge or jettison if he chose.

And anyhow, why *was* he able to think of anything but her strange beauty?

In any case, she had her own pursuits to attend to during the intervening days. Ruth had asked her to come to rehearsal again—the Jansch rehearsed Tuesdays through Saturdays—but Juliet, though tempted, pled her health and stayed home. Fed up with the apparently inextinguishable cold she had contracted in Studio Three, on the Friday morning she had asked Ames to run down to the Mid-Manhattan Library and borrow whatever books she could find on parlor games of the 1800s and the etiquette of duels. She needed to consult the parlor game books about a round of Speculation she had written into Chapter Eight. The duels were of interest because it looked as if Lord Morecambe really was going to challenge Sir Edward Rice. She might as well be prepared in case Rice accepted.

Meanwhile, she tucked herself firmly into bed, where she remained the entire weekend, learning, among other bits of information, how to write a "cartel," or challenge (be brief, avoid strong language, give the cause of offense and the reason it is considered a duty to notice the matter, name a friend, and request the appointing of a time and place). She also observed with interest the similarities between Speculation—a game of property development—and the modern game of Monopoly. After the brief rain, the weather had turned brutally hot, so staying indoors was no sacrifice. By Sunday night, to her great satisfaction, her cold was a sniffle of its former self. On the minus side, however, she was—was she?—a bit raw about the netherbones. On Monday morning, she was definitely itchy. Yeast infection, she diagnosed. She ate a container of yogurt for breakfast and another for lunch, then crossed her fingers. And legs.

Meanwhile, the *Times* had run an obituary of Anton Mohr on Friday. It was poignant and very painful to read. The official formula, "due to an adverse drug interaction, according to a Jansch Company spokesman," only magnified the terrible sentence that followed: "He was nineteen." The list of his accomplishments was long, as was the roster of family members who survived him. Juliet made herself turn away from it and read the Weekend section movie reviews instead, but on Saturday they reprinted it, as they did sometimes with obituaries, and she stumbled on it again. There was also a short essay by a dance critic about how risky and high-pressured young dancers' lives could be; the writer cited a number of anorexia-related fatalities among ballerinas and several suicides, clearly implying that Anton had been one of the latter. Sometimes, Juliet thought she was better off in the nineteenth century, where the dead had been dead a good long time.

Ruth called her several times each day. The crowd of paparazzi and reporters lurking in the lobby of the Jansch building had only grown larger on Friday, and that evening, one of the latter managed to trail the choreographer to her apartment. Another somehow got hold of her unlisted phone number and a third snapped her picture as she entered a cab Saturday morning. The Internet gossip columns were evidently gripped by a happy frenzy of rumor and innuendo, and Ruth was beside herself: The title *Great Expectations* was being printed again and again, each time gaining notoriety and losing (she feared) any chance of ever being judged as a work of art. Despite the circus surrounding her, however, she reported making serious headway on the choreography. Then, on Sunday morning, when she finally had a moment to relax, Murray Landis showed up at her place.

"At ten a.m.," she complained to Juliet, phoning her as soon as he'd left. "Unannounced. Don't you think he could have called first?"

Juliet, who was still enjoined from telling Ruth that Murray was an old acquaintance, brushed this objection aside. "What did he want? Did he tell you anything?"

"Tell? No. Just asked. Asked about Anton, about the talcum powder thing, why did I cast him, who liked him, was he upset about anything, what did Greg say when I told him about the rosin, you name it." Ruth yawned. "God, I hadn't even finished my coffee." She yawned again, mightily. "Oh, did I tell you the Jansch is planning a memorial service for Anton? His body is being flown home."

"No, I didn't know."

"They're going to dance, some of them. It'll be at Cadwell Hall, a week from Monday."

"That should be interesting," Juliet said distractedly. Why didn't Landis visit *her*? Did she really seem so sinister? "And how is Hart working out?"

"Oh, he's a demon." Ruth's whole voice leaped up a few pitches. "He's really quite wonderful. I never dreamed he had so much in him. He actually seems almost"—Ruth paused, then found the word she was looking for—"almost possessed."

"Really! How wonderful," echoed Juliet automatically, although something about Ruth's words had struck her as strange. She tried to refocus her attention, but the impression receded as she went on, "And Elektra?"

Now Ruth's voice dropped into its usual register and lost the unwonted enthusiasm. "Elektra seems—I don't know. Distracted. She's cooperative enough, but I don't get the feeling her full attention is with me."

"Hm. That's a shame," said Juliet, still distracted herself. Politely, she asked about several of the others—Ryder, Lily, Victorine, Olympia. But Ruth now had eyes only for her stars, and thoughts only for *Great Ex.*

"They're all right, I guess. They just seem normal. Not that anything is truly normal over there. A ballet company is like a—I guess like a giant family, almost. An event like Anton's death knocks the spirit out of it for a while. Life goes on, but nobody's quite got the heart. If you came in yourself this week, you could see," she pointed out.

But Juliet did not promise. It sounded as if Ruth's work was moving forward nicely, and she had work of her own to do. She had enjoyed her weekend of research—she always enjoyed doing research—and for once was looking forward to applying some of it at her desk tomorrow. As for the mystery surrounding Anton's death, the police were on the case. Though she still felt stung by Landis' use of the words "playing private eye," Juliet judged she would be wisest to go back to being simply Angelica Kestrel-Haven once again.

Landis finally resumed contact with Juliet that Monday night at about nine p.m, though not by phoning. Instead, he turned up at her apartment unannounced, just as he had done with Ruth. Juliet had lightly dismissed her friend's squawks of protest about his lack of ceremony, but she had to confess it was inconvenient when it happened to oneself.

Especially since she had gotten into her pajamas at seven o'clock that evening. This was a luxury she often enjoyed. She was dreamily eating peach ice cream on the terrace, looking across the river and thinking about the thousands of mysterious lives being lived in the silent, twinkling habitations of New Jersey, when the house phone buzzed. She dropped her spoon.

"Go away," she snarled aloud on her way to the intercom. Life wasn't chockablock with sensual perks for single women, but surely private snacks en deshabille ought to be among them.

"Murray Landis is here to see you," the doorman—Marco, from the sound of his voice—blandly informed her. His tone suggested she must be expecting him, a circumstance so far from the truth that she almost blurted back, "So what?"

Instead, she took a moment to dither, acutely aware of how far short of gravitas her sleeveless, pink-and-white striped cotton PJs fell. In movies—old black-and-white movies, anyway—the heroine always had some fabulous peignoir to slip on, with feathers and a flowing sash. Never mind movies; during the Regency, boudoir apparel was a genus unto itself. Juliet's robe, on the other hand, was made of lavender terrycloth, and when she tied the thick cord around her waist, she had roughly the silhouette of a not particularly athletic koala.

"Ask him to give me a minute before he comes up," she finally told Marco, then resentfully hurried down the stairs to change.

It was with a perverse feeling of satisfaction that she opened the front door to him a few minutes later wearing an especially ragged pair of cut-off jeans and a National Writers Union sweatshirt. If he wanted fancy, he should have given her some notice.

"Not getting you at a bad time, I hope," said Murray mechanically—probably his standard alternative greeting to "Police! Freeze!" Juliet thought.

She smiled politely. "Come up to the terrace."

He followed her up the stairs, but since she held the terrace door open for him, it was he who first observed the pint of Häagen-Dazs now melting on the restraining wall. Muttering, she whisked it off around the corner of the wraparound terrace and chucked it into the narrow, north-facing side, where she stored her gardening things.

Returning, "Can I get you a drink?" she offered.

Murray declined, admired the view, then sat down at the very end of a chaise longue. "I thought you'd be interested in knowing what we've found out so far about Anton Mohr," he said.

Suppressing an impulse to reply, "Oh yeah? What took you?" Juliet seated herself uncomfortably on a wrought-iron loveseat she had long regretted owning. If he wasn't particularly chummy, at least Landis didn't seem to regard her as public enemy number one.

"First of all," he briskly announced, "it turns out Mohr had a drug connection right inside the company itself. A member of the corps named Frank Endicott, do you know him? He deals to beef up his income. I gather the dancers don't make very much."

"A member of the Jansch corps deals drugs?" Juliet was shocked all over again at this evidence of the dancers' human frailty. "Maybe I know his face. I don't recognize the name."

"He's not in *Great Expectations*, so you might not. He shares a two-bedroom with Hart Hayden—platonic, so they say. He also claims Hayden's not one of his customers. Endicott's a big, tall guy, very skinny? Long head, pale blond hair, those white kind of eyebrows and eyelashes you can hardly see. He wears a couple of silver rings in one ear."

Juliet nodded as a face appeared in her mind's eye. She had seen him several times, in the lobby mostly, hanging out and chatting with Gayle.

"He's pretty small potatoes as a dealer," Landis went on, "but he kept Anton supplied with grass and hash."

"Oh. But not—"

"And Ecstasy," added Landis. "Endicott says he sold him a dozen hits early in the spring. And Mohr's recent phone records show frequent calls between them," he added. His voice warmed. "I'm sorry, Jule, I know you didn't think he was the type, and I know you don't like this ending to the story, but there's every good reason to think Mohr was responsible for his own death. His therapist wouldn't say much, but he did tell me Mohr had tried suicide once before. I mean, tried it once," he amended, as Juliet opened her mouth to object. "Still, this probably was an accident. The Nardil was working, but he'd only been on it a couple of months, and it seems neither the therapist nor the psychopharmacologist who officially prescribed it thought to warn him off illegal substances."

Juliet said nothing. For the first time, she entertained the possibility that she was wrong altogether. She did not like to be wrong. And, in fact, she was not very often wrong. But maybe the powder in the rosin had been intended for someone else. Or maybe it had been aimed at Anton but unconnected to the fatal Ecstasy.

"What about his soda? Any useful prints on it?"

He shook his head. "The good news about the Coke is that we found someone who saw Mohr buy it, and that person stayed with him all the way from point of purchase to inside the studio. You were right, it came from the vending machine in the lounge. So if anything happened to it, it happened in Studio Three."

"Who saw him?"

"Your friend Teri Malone. We were lucky, she was one of the first ones we interviewed. You don't think there's any reason to doubt her word, by the way, do you?"

Juliet shook her head.

"Didn't think so. She seems to have climbed out from inside an ear of corn. Those wide open eyes—whew! Powerful vacuum.

"Anyway, she had lunch in the lounge that day and she happened to be sitting near the machine when Mohr came in. She remembers it because he'd never talked to her before, and that day he asked to borrow a quarter. She was thrilled, she doesn't try to hide it. He took the quarter and bought the Coke and she walked with him to Studio Three, apparently delivering a little lecture as they went about how Coke is a diuretic and not a good choice for a dancer about to go to work. That reception or whatever it was that your friend Ruth had arranged was under way when they got there, and Malone says Mohr sat right down and started stretching and never left till the run-through started. She remembers that because she was excited about finally having made contact with him. She positioned herself within easy view and was hoping he'd say more to her. But he didn't. I wouldn't be surprised if she'd planned never to wash the fingers he brushed when he took the quarter. Anton Mohr may have been screwed up, but he sure must have had charisma. Anyway, Malone says she had her eye on him all the time."

A faint, contradictory recollection niggled at Juliet's consciousness, but she only said, "I see. And—?"

"And that's about it."

Juliet was silent a moment. From a balcony a few stories down, a burst of laughter and a smell of lighter fluid drifted into the night. "And the prints—?"

He shrugged. "Do you have a bottle I can use?"

Juliet went indoors. There was a little fridge and a wet-bar the previous owner had installed in an upstairs closet. Ames used it to keep her lunch in. Juliet took out a bottle of Perrier and returned with it to the terrace.

Landis stood up and set it on the painted table to demonstrate how you could hold a bottle without leaving prints.

"You just take it like this." He put the web between his thumb and index finger up against the glass threading, where the metal top screwed on. Squeezing gently, he lifted the bottle. "No prints," he said, setting it down. "All we found on the bottle were his, yours, and a few useless smudges."

Juliet looked glum.

"Prints are really hard anyway," said Landis consolingly. "I've probably seen prints come in as real evidence maybe two or three times out of a hundred. Anyway, a person could just drop the stuff in—a capsule or powder or whatever form they chose—right into the open top. So I'm not saying it couldn't happen. I'm just saying everything points the other way. Unless—"

He hesitated. "Unless?" Juliet prompted.

"Unless you were trying to frame someone. See, if you put the E in there yourself, maybe later, you could make it look like—"

"Excuse me, do you mean unless 'you,' as in 'anyone,' was trying to frame someone?" she interrupted. "Or do you mean unless 'you,' i.e. me, was trying to frame someone?"

"Just what I said." He seemed puzzled. "Unless you were trying to—"

"I had hoped you meant unless *one* was trying to frame someone," she snapped. "You can't really think I had anything to do with this crime, can you? Still?"

He shrugged. "No. But I don't really think there was a crime," he said. "That's what I really don't think."

She was silent for a minute, remembering facts and the four walls of a room. Of all the stupid possibilities to keep an open mind about . . .

Finally, "What did Greg Fleetwood say about the powder?" she asked. "Did Anton have any idea who had done it?"

"Fleetwood never told him about it," Landis answered bluntly. Addressing Juliet's look of surprise, "Did he have a motive?" he went on. "Sure. He didn't want to upset his star. Or, if we're to follow your theory, maybe Fleetwood rigged it himself and didn't want to inform his own victim. We're pursuing it, trust me." He shrugged. "He seemed pretty miserable about the whole thing. To my eye, at least."

Juliet frowned. "This Frank Endicott," she said. "Are there other dancers he supplies as well?"

"Oh, yes. He wasn't crazy about giving up names, but he mentioned a few. We told him we wouldn't go after them. That guy Ryder you don't care for, he's a customer. But he likes mostly speed. Frank didn't remember him buying Ecstasy. And Olympia Andreada—"

"Andreades."

"Right, she buys a lot of pot. There are six or seven others, but they're not in *Great Ex,* so they're probably beside the point. Unless more than one person is in it. But anyone can score a drug like Ecstasy anywhere, it isn't much of a trick. Frank Endicott didn't even necessarily supply the dose that killed Mohr. The point is, unless we can find an eyewitness who actually saw the perpetrator drop something into that Coke bottle, we don't have a prayer of getting a conviction. Or even an arrest. And quite honestly . . . Well, I already said that." His words faded away and he looked again at the river, the sparkling bridge, the twinkly Jersey shore.

"Quite honestly, you don't think there's anyone to arrest," Juliet filled in.

He nodded.

"Teri saw nothing?" she asked, but not very hopefully. "You said she had her eye on Anton the whole time. If that's true, she must have seen him drop the Ecstasy into the Coke, at least."

"Yeah, I asked her about that, too," he said, shrugging again. "She didn't see that either. But obviously, it must have happened— he dropped it in or someone else did. Of course, there's always the chance that she slipped it in herself—"

"Oh, forget it," said Juliet impatiently.

"Yeah, I am forgetting it. More or less. Unless Malone's the best actress since Bernhardt, she's leveling with us. What happened is probably what happens lots of times; people think they're watching something closely, but really they often turn their eyes away. She did mention the same folks as you as going near him then."

"As a matter of fact," Juliet said, suddenly remembering the contradictory detail that had been troubling her, "at one point during that interval, Victorine showed Teri how to do a step. So she couldn't have been watching every second."

She pressed her lips together as a wave of irrational dislike of Teri Malone swept over her. The truth was, she herself thought she had been watching fairly closely—and what had she seen?

"We will keep asking," Landis was going on. "We'll keep asking everyone. We've already gotten through forty or so interviews, and now that we've narrowed it down to people who were in Studio Three for the run-through, we only have maybe thirty left to go. But so far, no one noticed anyone acting strange around that Coke bottle.

"We have learned some interesting things though," he went on, as Juliet said nothing. "There's a former car thief in the company, and a convicted hooker. The Jansch has an illegal immigrant on staff, and there are a couple of people on the creative team that the Department of Motor Vehicles is very sorry they ever gave licenses to. And I can tell you, Anton Mohr got around—"

"I already knew that."

"—but he wasn't universally loved. Some people found him cold and arrogant, hard to talk to—in fact, maybe most people did. Gretchen Manning told me he gave her a giant headache—wouldn't talk to this magazine, wouldn't shut up with that one. Several of the soloists admitted they resented his coming in as a principal, over their heads. I mean, the guy was only nineteen. Hart Hayden, he said straight out he didn't think much of Mohr as a person at all. But you can see they're pretty different types—and Hayden admits he wouldn't have minded being cast for the leading Pip himself. I respect a person who can be truthful like that with a police officer," he added. "You'd be amazed the lies people tell."

"And what did Ryder Kensington say?"

"I haven't called him in yet. I'll get to him eventually."

All the frustration and disappointment that had been building in Juliet over the last quarter of an hour suddenly exploded.

"But he's the one I think is most—"

"I know, he's the one you like best for the killer. That's why I'm saving him for last," said Landis calmly. "The ones you suspect, those are the ones you leave to stew a little. Right now, Kensington knows all his pals have been called and he's thinking how come he hasn't. He's ripening." Landis smiled. "Anyway, you call these guys early, they lawyer up before you know what questions you want to ask them."

" 'Lawyer up?' "

"Sorry, hire a lawyer. You call, they tell you to ask their attorney, and then where are you? Don't worry, I know who's on your list."

"Hart Hayden was also with Anton right before the run-through," said Juliet rather sullenly, looking down at the terrace's stone floor.

"I know that."

"And Lily Bediant, and Elektra Andreades, and—"

"And Greg Fleetwood and Victoria Vaillancourt. Victorine," he corrected himself. "Juliet, I'm on top of it. Trust me. I had the Jansch send me over a tape of Mohr dancing. He was terrific. If somebody offed him, believe me, I want to know about it."

Juliet looked up. Landis was smiling at her in an unmistakably friendly way. Belatedly, it occurred to her that almost everything he was doing or had arranged to have done in the matter Anton Mohr's death—the lab analysis and fingerprint check on the Coke bottle, dozens of interviews, the search for the dealer, scores of background checks—everything had been done for her, done because of her claim that Anton Mohr (a person she barely knew) would not have risked screwing up a run-through by deliberately taking a recreational drug. She doubted whether any other officer in the NYPD would have taken a tenth of the trouble—and he was not done yet, he said.

"I'm sorry," she said contritely. "I really appreciate what you're doing."

"You know our motto." He smiled his bright, white smile. "'Courtesy, Professionalism, Respect.'"

Yet two days later, barely a week after Anton Mohr's collapse, the police investigation into his death was over. Every possible witness had been interviewed. No one had seen a thing. Given the psychological history of the deceased (as Landis's partner, Fales, kept referring to Mohr during a final courtesy visit to Juliet), there was every reason to conclude that he had doctored the Coke himself and died accidentally. He lived high, he sank low. He took risks and he miscalculated. The medical examiner officially classified the death as an accident. The case was closed.

chapter

THIRTEEN

The creation of a work of art, or even a work of artifice, typically involves such extremes of despair, elation, self-blame, doubt, frustration, embarrassment, dread, grandiosity, and exhaustion as few people would voluntarily endure for any other purpose except, perhaps, to raise a child. Young people often invoke the longstanding link between madness and art with approval, even impatient anticipation; but actually to be mad is not fun.

However, like the rearing of a child, most artistic work is started in a state of hopefulness that fades only when it is too late to turn back. Happy the artist who does not come, sooner or later, to fear and hate the work he has in hand. Even a mediocre play, painting, film, or symphony will likely exact a grueling toll on its maker. In fact, the law of averages alone suggests that more hearts have ached over the mediocre than the masterful.

In this respect, ambition (so highly regarded by guidance counselors and management consultants) is particularly dangerous. While the humbler artisan may pleasantly surprise himself now and then with a result that exceeds his own expectations, great ambition seems to spawn great struggle. An artist truly seized by the need to realize an ideal vision lives in a grip of a compulsion so strong—a dream so tempting and lovely—that family demands, love affairs, financial responsibilities, common kindness, even morality fall aside and are left behind.

Juliet stayed away from the Jansch for a whole week, Monday through Friday, before she felt she had made enough progress on *London Quadrille* to allow herself to go back for a visit. All in all, she was now feeling quite satisfied with her manuscript. An entirely unexpected chapter had cropped up in which Fitzroy Cavendish challenged a professional pugilist in hopes of inflaming Caroline Castlingham's desire. The poor boy ended up with nothing to show for his pluck except a broken nose, to which his mother insisted on applying hot, wet cloths to minimize the consequent bruising.

On her return to the Jansch, that Saturday afternoon, Juliet saw at once that Ruth also had made much progress in her work during the preceding week—though at what cost was equally visible, both in her face and in the bodies of the dancers she used as raw material. A number of the men sported back braces: wide, tight elastic bands worn around their waists to relieve strain on their vertebrae. The physical therapist and her massage therapist were kept busy repairing, soothing, and restoring mobility to "*Great Ex* Necks"; they had never seen such a rash of neck-muscle strains with any other project, the Marlboro-smoking massage therapist confided to Juliet on the fire escape.

Even more, though, a visible grimness had come into the faces of most of the dancers. This was partly accounted for by the music, which acquired an arhythmic, complex dissonance in this phase of the narrative arc (Ruth had arrived at Pip's rise in London, his growing snobbery, and was building to the discovery of his benefactor's identity) and, besides being unlovely, was hell to count out and dance to. It also had to do, no doubt, with their continuing grief and shock about Anton Mohr. Victorine, usually so austere and meticulous in her appearance, was now almost unkempt, her face haggard, her bun askew. An equally important factor in the changed look of Studio Three, Juliet thought, was Ruth's own grimness. As her deadline approached, she was terrified, almost petrified, about failing in her effort. And although she tried to keep her fear to herself, the dancers were surely too sensitive to body language not to see it.

She absolutely threw herself upon Juliet when she arrived—for Ruth, an unprecedented display of grateful affection. Juliet, who had been watching through the window in the door until the choreographer declared the statutory break, now gently detached herself from her sweaty, clinging friend and congratulated her on the new passages she had just been rehearsing.

"Do you think?" asked Ruth plaintively, her hard, dark face unwontedly appealing.

"Absolutely, it's brilliant," said Juliet, and meant it. Ruth had fashioned an exciting, disturbing interlude in which Pip swirled in and out of the two worlds he inhabited, the refined world of London and Miss Havisham's house, and the homey, coarse world into which he had been born. Hart Hayden's steps and gestures eloquently conveyed a growing sense of being torn between the two milieux, his movements literally low when he visited Joe and Biddy, his whole body rising as he aspired to the elegant heights of his great expectations. She could see now why Ruth had described Hart as possessed. He did dance as if some overwhelming inner force had hold of him. His concentration was fierce, his bearing no longer princely but human, vulnerable. Elektra, with a much smaller role in this section, performed coolly but unremarkably. It was Hart you couldn't take your eyes off.

"You must not leave me like that again," Ruth now scolded Juliet. "A whole week! You deserted me! You have to stay today, and come tomorrow and the next day, too. I need you."

"Obviously not," she said, adding, "Hi," in response to a smile and wave from Teri Malone, who passed them on her way out of the studio along with several other corps members.

"You have no idea how hard it was—"

"It's always hard, isn't it?"

Ruth frowned. "Don't punish me with my own accomplishment," she said, abandoning the play for sympathy and reverting to the imperative mood so much more natural to her. "Any minute now, I'm going to come up against a wall again and you won't know how to help me, because you haven't been around. I'm getting to the part of the book where—"

She would have gone on arguing, but thankfully, Juliet noticed Patrick trying to get his boss's attention and was able to interrupt her. A woman Juliet dimly remembered as having something to do with costumes was with him; Ruth went to them and a vigorous round of note-consulting, head-shaking, and note-making ensued.

"Fittings," Ruth muttered to Juliet, returning at length when the conference was finished. "They weren't supposed to start till next week, but there's some snafu at the costume makers. A show being mounted for Broadway changed designers or something, and now we have to change *our* schedule." Her resentment was bitter, wholehearted, and had the welcome effect of rerouting her thoughts from Juliet's alleged desertion and responsibilities. Soon, rehearsal recommenced and Juliet was able to fade first to the sidelines, then completely out of the room. In her own opinion, what Ruth had created without her was the most difficult part of the book to render in dance—the portion in which Pip's character only gradually changed. If Ruth could do that on her own, she could surely handle the rest. Whereas (as she sternly reminded herself) *London Quadrille* needed Angelica Kestrel-Haven.

Still, it was Saturday, and Juliet always gave herself Saturdays off. She lingered a while, gazing through the window in the door. After a time, Max Devijian materialized beside her.

He stood there, watching briefly and listening through the door to the piano accompaniment before remarking with surprising indiscretion, "That dissonant music would kill me to listen to over and over." Remembering himself, he added swiftly, "Although I do think it captures the development of the story perfectly. It's really quite extraordinary."

Juliet gave him a gently skeptical glance.

"Ow!" he added, peering through the window as Hart Hayden

executed a brutal drop to the knees. "I'm amazed Victorine is allowing that move. Hart's cartilage is shot."

"What do you mean?"

The executive director lowered his voice to a confidential murmur. "Don't tell anyone, but Hart Hayden will be forced to retire from performing after this season. The doctors say he can't afford another knee surgery. He won't dance again."

"Jesus. How old is he?"

Max shrugged. "Thirty-three?" He did not sound especially sympathetic.

"And what will he do?"

"What do any of them do?"

The cynicism of this answer caused Juliet to turn at last and take a good, careful look at Max. His large eyes were circled in gray and the corners of his mouth slumped. He seemed to have aged five years. Juliet had never seen him so dejected—never seen him dejected in any degree.

"How is the Jansch doing now?" she asked. "Will you bring another star in to replace Anton Mohr?"

He shook his head. "Too late for this year. There isn't another Anton Mohr, anyway."

"I guess you took quite a hit, public relations–wise," Juliet said. For the first time since their acquaintance, she felt sorry for Max Devijian. Despite Gretchen Manning's valiant efforts at containment—and Detective Landis's cooperative discretion—Anton's death had wound up filling the scandal sheets and local TV and radio news for days on end. High culture, recreational drug use, antidepressants, giant egos, AIDS, anorexia: the facts and attendant fantasies were all too juicy to leave alone. Reporters had haunted the Jansch's building endlessly, badgering dancers and staff (and dozens of people coming and going from other premises in the building as well) for information, hints, quotes. Close-ups of Anton's splendid face and full-length shots of his glorious body found their way into national magazines, accompanied by the inevitable reminiscences of "close friends" and insights from nameless "sources familiar with the ballet world." By the time bomb-making equipment was discovered in the basement of a transient hotel in midtown Manhattan, Ruth was ready to send a thank you note to the would-be terrorists for getting the media off her back.

"Well, I can't say it was the kind of press that funders like to see," Max now agreed. After a pause, he asked with unusual candor, "You think this piece will go?"

Juliet blinked in surprise. "*Great Ex?*"

He nodded.

"You bet."

He looked at her, meeting her blue eyes with his large brown ones. His were bleary and apprehensive.

"Of course you would," he said. "She's your friend."

"Even if she weren't. Didn't you like what you saw at the run-through? Ruth told me you said you were pleased."

Max flinched. "I didn't want to alarm her, of course, but the truth is, I've found it a bit hard to remember it with any clarity," he said.

Impatiently, "All right," said Juliet, "but haven't you watched it at all since then?"

"I've poked my head in now and then."

"Well, you ought to go in and sit down for a while. It's terrific. Take another look in there."

On the other side of the door, Ruth was working out a spectacular spinning lift with Hart and Elektra. It started as Elektra fell backwards into Hart's arms, as if not deigning to look at him. He then lifted her by the hips and twirled her rather roughly around. After two revolutions, he sank down and knelt, bringing Elektra with him slowly to the floor, where she glided away while Hayden lay prostrate, reaching out to her retreating, insouciant back. The pair finished executing all this, then discussed with Ruth the difficulties they were having. From their gestures, Elektra apparently felt she was slipping out of Hart's grasp. Hart thought he might need to hitch her up higher and hold her more across the hips in order to keep his balance. How much strength it must take for Hart to balance Elektra's weight on his chest and abdomen as he sank gradually—gradually!—to the floor Juliet could hardly imagine, not to mention how Elektra maintained a rigid posture with legs straight before her and feet pointed precisely together. Dissected like this, the lift did seem no different than an acrobatic feat, a circus trick performed by athletes—equally difficult, equally amazing, but hardly a matter of aesthetics. Still, it was gorgeous to look at, or would be once the two got the details worked out. No wonder Martha Graham had called dancers "athletes of God."

"One quarter of our entire budget this season is riding on Ruth Renswick's shoulders," was all Max said, removing his gaze from the window and turning again to Juliet. "And I hear from our production manager that we'll probably need more, unless the set designer can simplify what he and Ruth had in mind. I can't dip into the endowment. I can't take it out of the other productions. And it's hard, you know, to go to the board or a donor and say, 'Well, we lost our star, but don't worry, it'll still be fabulous. Just give us more money.'"

He sighed. Juliet hesitated. Then, "Max, I've never seen you like this," she ventured. Generally, it was her policy to ask a question only if she really wanted to know the answer; but she was human, and Max seemed so wretched. "Are you all right?"

"Don't mind me." He gave her a quick, sad smile. "My worries about *Great Ex* are a bit of a smoke screen anyhow. The truth is—" He broke off, then resumed, "Well, I might as well tell you. It will be public in a couple of weeks anyhow. Though I'd rather you not repeat it till it's announced."

"Certainly. Till what's announced?" asked Juliet, at the same time marveling (as she often did) at the compulsion people feel to confide what they want kept quiet.

Max's voice dropped and he drew her away from the door as if someone might have an ear pressed to its other side.

"It's Greg," he whispered. "He's leaving the company."

"He is? And going where?"

Max leaned even closer, bending his head to hers. Juliet could see the individual strands of dark hair combed back from his receding hairline. "Washington. He's going to give away money for the government."

"You mean the National Endowment?" Juliet whispered back.

"Can you imagine? Now *I* have to ask *him* for money."

"But he—" Juliet's words faltered as her mind tried to move in several directions at once. "But has he been planning to leave for a while?" she asked finally.

Devijian shrugged. "He's been talking with them since before the summer rehearsals started, but he just made up his mind to accept last week."

"You mean they just offered it to him last week?"

"No, a month ago almost. He's been toying with it all this time, if you can picture what that's been like for me. Trying to get better terms, I guess, although he claimed he wasn't sure if he wanted to go." He shook his head. "God knows he's done a great job, but I don't think he was really happy here. He feels undervalued. I probably didn't stroke his ego enough."

Max's tone was sardonic, but Juliet remembered his reputation for indifference to his subordinates and thought this likely enough.

At the same time, he was going on, "He's a dancer, he likes to be in the spotlight. Here, he had to put other people into the spotlight and stand back. Well, people will certainly kiss his ass when he starts handing out grants."

There was in his voice a bitterness like that of a jilted lover. Juliet patted his arm mechanically. "When you say he decided last week," she asked, trying to make the question seem natural, "do you mean before Anton died?"

He looked at her strangely (and small wonder, she reflected). "No. As a matter of fact, a day or two after. Why?"

"Oh, I just— I was just thinking, that's a lot of bad news for you at once. No wonder you're feeling low. But I'm sure you'll get a fine replacement."

His gaze was bleak. "You have any suggestions?"

Juliet promised to think about it. Devijian reminded her to keep the news to herself and smiled a half-hearted smile.

"I guess it's not the end of the world," he said.

"Not at all."

"Just feels like it." He smiled again and meandered away down the corridor, the set of his shoulders somehow a little less hopeless than when he had arrived.

That evening, Ruth and Juliet met for a bite at a café on Amsterdam Avenue. They sat at a table on the sidewalk, sipping Campari-and-sodas in the simmering twilight and watching dogs pee on a NO PARKING sign some few feet away. Roosting buses snored beside them, then roared away as the light at Eighty-first Street turned green; panhandlers thrust their arms over the cheerful striped-canvas barriers the café had set out to discourage panhandlers; giant teenaged boys lolloped by, thumping one another as their oversized jeans slipped indiscreetly from the pale flesh of their hips. Radios blared from cars, dwarfing the gabble of conversation. Lone men walking past leered at handsome young women; lone women fastened melancholy eyes on even passable young men. A husband strolling by sent Juliet a desperate S.O.S. over the heads of his wife and child.

"Nice to be out of doors," Juliet remarked to Ruth, at the same time returning a glance she hoped would remind this man of his marriage vows. If she had ever believed in such a thing as innocent flirtation, Rob had changed her mind.

She lit a cigarette. The smell of the pavement (dirt, urine, spilled soft drinks, emulsifying garbage) mingled with the mists of exhaust from the avenue and the aromas of the dishes set before the café's customers to form a pungent, decadent bouquet. Juliet dragged deeply on the cigarette, leaned back, and sent her own smoky breath out to join the general tumult.

"Now you can't let anyone know you know this," she began, and went on to repeat what Max had said that afternoon about Greg Fleetwood's impending departure.

"Jeez. Washington. What do you think made him decide to go?" Ruth asked.

"Exactly my question. Tell me if you find this too farfetched. We know Greg and Anton were lovers in Germany. We know Greg brought Anton to the Jansch. So could it be that Greg expected him, as his protégé, to continue to be his lover?"

Ruth blinked and shrugged. "Could," she allowed.

"But instead, Anton dumped him. You can see why. In Germany, Anton was young and unproven, while Greg must have seemed immensely glamorous and powerful. But once he got over here, Anton was the star. Greg would suddenly look old to him, a has-been who expected Anton to be grateful to him. Which all by itself is not an attractive trait. So Anton took another lover, and another. A woman, a man—"

"Greg himself, on at least one occasion," Ruth put in.

"Greg too," agreed Juliet. "But maybe only that once. Ruth, does Greg have a romantic partner?"

"No. Not unless it's a deep secret, or a new development."

"That's what I thought. So assuming there's no big significant other—and even if there were—a person as vain and arrogant as Greg Fleetwood would not take rejection lightly."

Ruth was silent for some moments. Finally, "You're assuming a lot," she said.

"Greg was the one who sent around that useless 'malicious incident' flyer about the talcum powder. And he lied to you when he said he would tell Anton about it."

"He may not have been lying. Maybe he just had second thoughts."

Juliet ignored this. "Greg was also in the studio twice the day the rosin was rigged," she went on. "Once very near the end of the ensemble session."

"Did you see him go near the box?"

"I wasn't watching. He went here and there around the room—that's all I remember. Till now, I never seriously thought that he could be involved. The idea that he would deliberately injure a star of the Jansch was so farfetched. But if he had turned against Anton for personal reasons, and since he's leaving the Jansch . . ."

Juliet took another drag on her cigarette and stubbed it out.

"We have to remember," she went on, "whoever booby-trapped the rosin probably only wanted to make Anton look ridiculous. Ditto whoever spiked his Coke. It was a strong dose, but nothing close to overdose level. Murray tells me it would take about thirty times what was in there to kill someone." (Murray Landis had released her from her vow of secrecy days ago, and she had promptly told Ruth of their former acquaintance.) "No one could have realized it would be lethal," she finished.

"Oh, really? Surely Greg would know Anton was using Nardil, if anyone did," Ruth observed.

"Yeah, that occurred to me, too. But even if he did, would he have known that Nardil and Ecstasy can be so dangerous taken together?" Juliet asked. "Maybe Greg is running away from a spiteful act gone disastrously wrong."

"On the other hand, maybe since Anton died, there's simply nothing to keep Greg here," Ruth argued in return. She leaned forward, her bare arms pressed to the white cloth clipped onto both sides of the table. "I'm the one who told him about the talcum powder, remember, and he looked absolutely stunned. He was very upset for Anton. So maybe he feels guilty now that he didn't do more to protect him. Maybe the only reason he's been staying in a job he didn't like very much in the first place was because Anton *was* here, because he loved Anton. Maybe the prospect of being here now, being reminded of him daily, is too painful."

Juliet's mouth twitched. She had to admit Ruth's speculations were no less plausible than her own.

"Okay," she said presently, "let's review the others. Motive, means, and opportunity. Isn't that what the lawyers say?

"Now in the talcum powder incident," she went on, "anyone had the means, and dozens of people had the opportunity. The Ecstasy—that's a bit more limited. But not much. So let's look at the possible motives. Don't you think Ryder Kensington could have done it?"

"Done which?"

"Both, maybe. Powdered the rosin. Doped the Coke."

"But why?"

"Well, he's a pretty volatile guy. Olympia tells me he's hit Elektra."

"Really?" Ruth seemed more interested than shocked. "Does she let him, I wonder?"

Juliet shrugged. "Remember the way Ryder jumped when you passed him at the phone booth that day, just when the rosin made Anton slip? And he and Olympia are weirdly tight, don't you think? She had an affair with Anton. Maybe Ryder didn't like that."

Ruth stirred the watery remains of her drink with a slow finger. "Possibly," she conceded.

"He was certainly in the right place at the right time—both times."

"True," said Ruth. "But I have a simpler idea. Maybe Olympia did it herself."

"Because Anton ditched her?"

"Could be."

"Could." Juliet frowned and began to look around for their waiter, a sunny young man with a head of thick, blond curls. "But she seemed awfully jolly about his fickle nature when I talked to her about him. And I don't recall seeing her near him that day before the run-through. If we're entertaining ex-lovers as suspects, I'd say Lily Bediant was more likely. After all, he two-timed her."

"A year before?"

"Lily doesn't seem to me the sort to forget. And she might have wanted to give you a little grief, too." Juliet spotted their waiter some half dozen tables away, chatting with a couple of young women over the canvas barrier. She began to perform semaphore.

Ruth had straightened. "Me?" she bristled. "Why?"

"Because you cast her as an old maid."

"Miss Havisham's a great role," Ruth protested indignantly. "Besides, she's only in her fifties. Just because Teri Malone said—"

"Teri does seem to be in Lily's confidence," observed Juliet, vigorously crossing and uncrossing her arms over her head. "And speaking of crazy old maids, I've sometimes wondered if Victorine could be so far gone that she would abet her precious Lily in an attack on you."

"And screw up *Great Ex*? And injure Anton?"

Juliet shrugged. "He wasn't the only one who looked like a fool that day," she pointed out. When she had raised this possibility with Landis, he hadn't seemed to make much of the idea. But it still seemed to her worth consideration. "That run-through was your chance to shine. You needed to shine. And instead . . ."

She left the sentence unfinished as the waiter at last noticed her flailing arms and sauntered over to them.

"Everything all right, ladies?"

"I believe we asked for some food from you earlier this evening," Juliet said politely. "It was this evening, wasn't it, Ruth? About forty-five minutes ago? So—please, sir, may we have some food? We're quite hungry now."

The waiter gave her the pitying smile the laid-back reserve for the highly strung. "I'll go check in the kitchen," he said, as if this were a favor undertaken strictly from kindness.

When he had sauntered away again, Juliet went on. "Besides, didn't you tell me Victorine wanted to choreograph *Great Expectations* herself?"

Ruth's narrow forehead wrinkled. She sat quietly for some moments. Meanwhile, Juliet counted on her fingers.

"Let's see, there were six people I know talked to Anton before the run-through: Greg Fleetwood, Ryder, Lily, Elektra, Victorine and—who are we leaving out. Oh, Hart Hayden! What about Hart? Could he have slept with Anton?"

"I suppose. Although I have heard Hart is more or less celibate."

"Yes, he told me that himself."

"Could he have been jealous about not being the first Pip?"

"He could have," Ruth said dubiously. "On the other hand, Anton could have been jealous of him, because in this season's *Giselle*, Hart is the first Albrecht and Anton was the second. You see, the trouble is—" She leaned forward and spoke more earnestly. "The trouble with all your suspects is, Juliet, that they're all dancers. Every one of them has spent years of his or her life—has spent his or her life, period—struggling and suffering and sacrificing for dance. Every one of them has lost parts they coveted. And dance is a communal art. Every one of these people stands to lose if *Great Ex* flops. It isn't only me. It's the whole company, even Greg."

"Well, somebody did it."

"Not necessarily."

"Oh, Ruth, don't tell me you're joining Landis' camp! You think Anton took that dope on purpose? Why would he put it in his Coke, if he meant to take it? Why not just pop a pill?"

"I don't know."

"I refuse to believe he sabotaged himself."

"He was depressed," Ruth pointed out.

"No, he *wasn't* depressed. He was being successfully treated for depression." Juliet, who had struggled through depression herself, heard the anger in her voice and tried to calm down. "Murray Landis may have been depressed. You may have been depressed. But the one person in all of this we can be sure was not depressed—at least, not depressed in his behavior—was Anton. Anyway," she went on, after a rather sullen pause, "you don't think he made himself slip with the talcum powder, do you?"

"Of course not."

"So someone didn't mind hurting him."

"Granted. But Juliet—" Ruth began and faltered. "Sweetie, don't jump down my throat, but don't you think you're a little bit biased in favor of thinking this was a murder?"

"Biased?"

"Well, yes. Murray Landis thinks it was suicide, and Murray Landis hurt your feelings. Now you're angry at him, and as a result, determined to think he's wrong. Therefore it had to be homicide."

"Murray Landis hurt my feelings?"

"Now, don't get angry at me."

"Angry?"

"Juliet, I know you. When you start repeating what I say, you're getting mad. You are biased, and you were hurt, because you thought Landis should have treated you as a friend, not a suspect. He was only doing his job, but you took it personally."

Juliet picked up a fork with her left hand and started to rub its tines with her right. "I'm capable of being a little more grown up than that, don't you think?" she said.

"For a short while, maybe. But ultimately? No."

"Ruth!"

"I'm sorry, I don't really think any of us is more grown up than that. I think it's very painful when someone we like and trust doesn't like and trust us back. Even if it's that other person's responsibility not to trust us. But look at it from Murray's point of view. He probably did enjoy running into you again. He probably wanted to shmooze and catch up and reminisce and the whole thing. It wasn't easy for him to keep his distance, but he had to do it and he did it. It was his job. So don't begrudge him that."

"If he wanted to shmooze so much, why hasn't he called since the case was dropped?"

"See? You are hurt. But it really was quite admirable of him to maintain that distance, I think," Ruth went on. "It means he takes his work seriously. Which is something we like in a person. Isn't it?"

Juliet was beginning to see her point, but she did not feel quite ready to admit it. It bothered her that Ruth—Ruth, of all people!—could know her better than she knew herself.

"Sorry, I think you've lost me a bit here," she equivocated. "Do you really think my—" She paused, searching for a dignified word, then resumed, "—do you really think my disappointment with Murray's attitude could cloud my judgment of the facts?"

"Well, certainly. You're human. Don't you believe all thought is influenced by emotion?" Ruth asked. "Don't you think our wishes always influence our logic?"

"Not at all," Juliet objected, gladly leaping to the firmer ground of abstract argument. "Action is rooted in emotion, that I'll grant you. But thought—no. And by definition, certainly not logic."

And from here, the two launched into a prolonged discussion in which Ruth maintained that emotion influenced even which "facts" were so identified, while Juliet insisted that a baseline of objective reality underlay any thought that deserved the name. This pleasant dispute took them through their dinners (when these were finally brought by the waiter, who placed them on the table as if indulging two children's silly whims) and on to coffee and blueberry pie. Nothing more was said between them as to how Anton had died, or whether Juliet had judged Murray Landis too harshly. All the same, the matter was on Juliet's mind after they finally parted. On her way home, she decided she would get in touch with him. Maybe she would invite him to the memorial for Mohr.

If it is true that there are two kinds of people in the world (as one kind of person, at least, perennially asserts), then one of the divides is surely between those who can speak wittily, eloquently, and movingly of the recently dead and those who—cannot. Whatever mechanism of thought permits certain mourners to celebrate aloud the life of a vanished loved one (for example, to remind a gathered assembly of the off-color jokes Mom used to tell late at night, or the time Cousin Pete walked all the way to Pine Creek in a snowstorm just to be sure Uncle Jim had enough food) and by doing so, moreover, to bring the departed back to life for a moment in affectionate memory *and* at the same time help begin the healing of those surviving the loss—that gift or skill or mechanism of thought is surely provided for by some chromosome present in certain human beings and simply not present in others.

Juliet, who belonged to the latter group—the group of people who cannot put two sentences together for months when overtaken by grief, let alone fluently articulate what she had cherished in them a few days later—was astonished by the memorial service mounted by Jansch members and others for Anton Mohr. For one thing, despite its immense size, Cadwell Hall was three-quarters filled with mourners: fellow dancers, dance teachers, dance buffs, dance writers, dance underwriters, dance-shoe ribbon manufacturers, for all Juliet knew, streamed in through the Hall's heavy, old-fashioned doors and took their seats amid an uncertain murmur of hushed greetings and shared condolences.

With an alacrity she found gratifying, Murray Landis had agreed to accompany her there. They met a few minutes before seven at Columbus Circle and walked over in the increasingly pink light of late afternoon. Mindful of Ruth's belief that she had been blaming him for doing his job well, Juliet had been prepared to greet him warmly, as a friend. But, spotting her first, he came up with a hand formally extended to shake hers. Forced to reciprocate, she heard her "Hello" come out uncertain, ambiguous.

Now, amid the respectful buzz of the gathering audience, they picked their way single file to seats toward the back of the orchestra. Juliet, who had imagined this emotionally loaded occasion as an opportunity to spot the guilt-stricken face of the culprit (if culprit there was, which even she had begun to doubt) found herself thwarted by both the size of the crowd and the astounding polish of the program. She looked around as best she could, but the Jansch members were spread throughout the auditorium, their faces glimpsable now and then but mostly too far away or too absorbed in conversation to be read. Ryder and Elektra sat together in a box in the mezzanine; Victorine had Lily Bediant on one side, Teri on the other, a few rows up from the front of the orchestra. On the way in, Juliet had caught sight of Hart, but he disappeared down a side aisle and she couldn't spot him after that.

The program was brief but powerful. A chamber music group had been assembled and supplied with music to which three numbers were danced, the first two choreographed by Twyla Tharp and William Forsythe respectively and performed by members of various contemporary troupes. Both were pieces with which Anton Mohr had been closely identified, and both were full of vigor and enthusiasm, far from melancholy. It was clear a decision had been made to lean in this direction, and the short orations that followed (by Greg and Victorine for the Jansch and by several other luminaries of the American and European dance worlds) reflected this. For Juliet, the most moving part of the service was the last, the third dance, which Kirsten Ahlswede (as Anton's last partner) performed solo to what Murray whispered was one of the courtly dances from Benjamin Britten's *Gloriana*.

"Are you a Britten aficionado?" Juliet whispered back, momentarily distracted by what seemed a remarkable feat of musicology.

He shrugged. Still curious, she turned her eyes back to the stage. The choreography, whoever had created it, was somewhere between ballet and modern dance, with repeated gestures of slowly bent head, slowly bowed back, slowly bent knee. It was more a tribute than an elegy. Without being maudlin, it spoke of both loss and recovery, anger at death, and acceptance. Later, Juliet learned that Ruth herself had choreographed it some years ago, after the death of a former lover.

There was an uneasy silence when Kirsten's performance came to an end. It seemed strange not to clap, but equally incongruous to applaud at a memorial. The curtain fell and a few long seconds went by before Greg took the stage again.

"That concludes the service," he said. He had lost the look of utter exhaustion and shock he had worn just after Anton's death and now had almost his habitual panache. Juliet thought again of his decision not to tell Anton about the talcum powder, of his sudden resignation, which had yet to be made public. "Thank you for coming. Good night."

Pensive and sober, the audience rustled gradually to its feet, filing into the aisles and out of the auditorium almost in silence. The program had been very lively and beautiful, yet it left an impression of solemnity that was not much like Anton Mohr. On the sidewalk in front of the hall, a number of people lingered in pairs and clusters, murmuring about the program, trying to avoid anything that sounded like a review, unsure what to do with themselves now that it was over. Murray and Juliet were among these, trying to decide whether to go have a bite together, when Ruth, who had been backstage to prepare Kirsten, came out of a side door.

She was alone and apparently not in the mood for conversation. She gave Juliet a stiff little wave and Landis a barely perceptible nod, then barreled away in the direction of Seventh Avenue.

"I thought she was a good friend of yours," said Murray, smiling in the way people do when startled by some sudden rudeness.

"Oh, yes." Juliet had also been disconcerted, but recognized Ruth's abruptness for what it was: sheer obliviousness of the feelings of others. "If I call her tomorrow and tell her that she was rude, she won't remember having done it—but she'll apologize anyway," she assured him. "So—"

They returned to their former impasse, which secretly had more to do with each guessing whether the other cared to prolong the evening than whether either or both wanted to go and eat. They wanted to go and eat. And they wanted to prolong the evening. But Juliet made Murray nervous. She was too soft, too conventional, too sheltered, too prosperous for him. She wrote genre novels; he made cutting-edge art. His family was blue collar, hers—well, diamond collar, probably. Since his divorce, he had concluded it was unwise to see women who differed from him on such basic matters. He could not imagine Juliet Bodine knocking back Rolling Rocks at gallery openings in Greenpoint, or camping out on the mattress in his fourth-floor walk-up, or grabbing a burger at the Irish Harp with a couple of guys from the station—not to mention noshing on gefilte fish with his folks in Sheepshead Bay. Eve, his ex-wife, had glittered in the moneyed, sunny world where she worked for an auction house, but wilted and sulked whenever he took her to his turf. That had been enough of that.

For her part, Juliet saw in Landis precisely the sort of man who would resent her success. In fairness, she had learned that almost any man would do that who was not more successful, in worldly terms, than she. But Landis would surely suffer from it—and he would make her suffer. She had had enough of that during her marriage. When they met, Rob Ambrosetti had been a clever, up-and-coming off-Broadway director. When his career sagged and languished and hers soared, he had taken his frustration out on her.

She had seen in Landis's eyes by now that he did, indeed, remember that sweet, erotic hour of careful inaction they had shared, and that he still felt the pull toward her that he had felt then. That was mutual. But they were both too old to imagine they could simply indulge the sexual charge between them without creating an emotional mess. Still, the question remained, could they at least have a meal together?

Finally, "It's such a lovely evening. I'm heading north. Will you walk with me?" said Juliet.

"Yes, let's walk," Murray answered, with evident relief.

The rhythm of walking, the soft warmth of the night, the growing distance between them and the sad impressions of the ceremony, plus the constant necessity of evading other pedestrians, gradually distracted them from their awkwardness and allowed them to speak naturally again. Indeed, the need to release at least some of the painful energy each felt after the service soon led them to take an almost giddy tone.

"I always think there should be a verb that means 'to pass,' but with regard to walking," remarked Juliet, as they neared the outskirts of Lincoln Center. "The way you pass in a car, only on foot. I've thought 'skibble' might do it. As in, 'These tourists ahead of us are so slow. Let's skibble.' "

"Skibble," repeated Murray reflectively. "Nice. What about circumambulate?"

"Oh, that's good, I like that. That's really a word, isn't it? 'Shall we circumambulate?' Could it be transitive, do you think?"

" 'Let's circumambulate them?' I don't think so."

"How about 'peristep'?"

"Or 'pedipass'?"

" 'What's your hurry? Why did you pedipass that family?' " Juliet tried it out. "Yes, that could work."

It was almost eight o'clock, but because it was a Monday, Lincoln Center was closed. The Met, the Newhouse, Avery Fisher were blank-faced, dark, almost ominously so. Yet scores of people, many of them young, hung around the plaza for no apparent reason, evidently simply enjoying the night, the colorful banners billowing toward Broadway, the coolness of the fountain.

"Thanks for inviting me," Landis said as they crossed the complicated intersection at Sixty-fifth Street.

"Thanks for coming."

"I've never had much time for ballet per se, but I like modern dance quite a lot. Dance is the musical equivalent of sculpture, I always think. Music you can see."

"I like sculpture because when you walk around it, it seems to move," Juliet said. "Hey, how did you recognize that Benjamin Britten piece?"

"Just an old favorite of mine. I'm a bit of an opera buff."

"Are you?"

"You don't have to sound shocked. Cops can enjoy opera, you know."

"I'm sorry—"

"In fact, we have a policeman's amateur opera company. 'CopOpera,' it's called."

"Really?"

"No, not really." Murray burst out laughing—not very politely, Juliet thought. "Oh, I loved the look on your face!" Calming himself, he went on, "But there is a Visual Arts Softball League. I'm captain of the Sculptors."

"Now I know you're joking."

"Not at all. We play every Wednesday night at eight, Field Four in Riverside Park. Come and watch us. We'll be there this week."

"Where's Field Four?"

While Murray told her, Juliet returned in her thoughts to what Ruth had said about him the other night at the sidewalk café. On the whole, she now believed Ruth was right. Murray's attitude toward her during the official investigation of Anton's death had been no more nor less than professionally appropriate, and she had wronged him by taking it personally. Moreover, she suspected he had been rather offended by her own attitude, which (she recognized too late) had been quite mistrustful of him. Quite prejudiced, in fact. She shook herself mentally.

"What I'd really like to see is your work," she told him.

"That could be arranged. My studio—"

"Oh look, we're at Planet Sushi," she cried, interrupting him. "Let's eat here on the porch."

At dinner, Murray introduced Juliet to edamame—steamed, salted soy beans. Juliet introduced Murray to smoked eel and sea urchin. They discussed the old days in Cambridge and current mayoral politics in New York. Treading carefully to keep the fact marooned in history, Murray revealed that he and Mona had once had a memorable fight because Mona thought he was attracted to Juliet (true, he admitted). Equally carefully, Juliet confessed she had found Murray attractive in those long-ago days as well. As for Mona's current life, Murray had last heard from her a couple of years before. Her husband had left the diplomatic service and entered a

Buddhist monastery. Mona was back in Cherry Hill, living with her parents.

It wasn't until their table had been cleared and red bean ice cream set before them that Juliet returned to the idea of arranging to see his work.

"Oh yeah, for sure," Murray said. "I'd like that. Maybe next week?" He poured her a little more sake, then took the last of it himself. "I'll give you a call and we'll make some plans."

The conversation flagged. There was a bad moment over the ice cream when they looked each other in the eyes. Definitely, Juliet thought, it would take some effort to keep the brakes on here. After dinner, when Murray offered to walk her home, she said she'd take a cab. Then she jumped into one before he could talk her out of it. He stood on the curb as she waved good-bye through the open window.

chapter

FOURTEEN

After the memorial service and her
dinner with Landis on Monday night, Juliet decided to make herself
stay away from the Jansch again for at least a couple of weeks. None
of this was really her business, anyway. And it was clear that Ruth
was quite able now to move forward on the choreography on her
own. Whereas *London Quadrille* would not grow a page longer (she
reminded herself severely) unless she herself sat down and wrote it.

"'For the world, which seems to lie before us like a land of
dreams,'" she quoted aloud the next morning, as she put herself on a
forced march up the stairs to her desk, "'so various, so beautiful, so
new,' is really just there to make us crazy and distract us from our
work," she finished, veering sharply off from Matthew Arnold as the
rough, spicy smell of Murray Landis's skin returned to her, and that
bad moment of gazing at one another.

"No, no, no," she loudly declared.

As to the business of Anton Mohr's death, though she could
not quite relinquish the notion that something other than accident
had at least contributed to it, she could think of nothing Landis had
failed to do by way of investigation. If he had turned up nothing,
there must be nothing to turn up. She was being morbid, clinging to
the idea that there was more to the story despite all the evidence (or
lack thereof). Certainly, the memorial service had provided no clue of

anything untoward. It had been respectful, ceremonious, and properly sad. Now it was time to move on, and the best way to accomplish that was to keep herself at her desk.

Unless, she added, arriving at that desk, something interesting happened.

*It was not Juliet's fault that some*thing interesting happened just one day later, on the following morning, in the form of an urgent phone call from Victorine Vaillancourt. Ames knocked to report it just as the author was sitting down with Sir Edward to consider Lord Morecambe's challenge. Naturally, he would have to accept it; but should he choose pistols or swords? And who could he ask to be his second? The obvious man was—

It was at this point that Ames softly rapped and put her head in to announce the "urgent" call.

Juliet was annoyed. What could possibly be more urgent than choosing a second?

"I'm sorry. She sounds very anxious," said Ames. "Is she old?"

Juliet sighed, her mind reluctantly returning to New York and the present century. "I don't know. Yes, she probably is quite old. Thank you, Ames. I'll pick up in here."

Victorine was extremely, ornately apologetic. She knew Juliet had her work; she herself hated to be disturbed when at work, and yet—

It was true that her voice sounded shaky. She was so severe and formidable in person, one forgot that she really was elderly (at least, one forgot until seeing her stand up or sit down, which she never did without careful attention to her worn, obviously painful joints). Juliet automatically sought to soothe her by assuring her that she had interrupted nothing of note.

"What can I do for you?" she asked.

"I'm afraid it's your friend Ruth," said Victorine, her accent thicker than usual. "She phoned me last night after the memorial service. Now that I come to the studios, I find she evidently phoned many dancers in *Great Expectations*. I don't know quite what she said to them, but to me, I think the word is—harangue?" she finished tentatively.

Juliet hesitated. "There is such a word as harangue in English," she conceded cautiously. "Berate, it means. Scold."

"Perhaps the word I am looking for is harass?" Victorine suggested.

"I don't know." Juliet sighed again. "Maybe you'd better tell me exactly what she's been saying."

"Oh, thank you. I wonder, is there any chance at all you could come here to discuss this? I wouldn't ask, except that—" Her voice broke off and she was silent for a few moments. "It's quite difficult for me to travel even a short distance. I try not to display my infirmities, but . . . You will do me a very great favor."

Juliet was beginning to understand why the dancers so adored Victorine. She had a side that was very winning. Her presence was naturally powerful, almost forbidding; but when she revealed her frailty, it was impossible not to want to do your best to help her. Some people were like that; Juliet had met them before. In fact, she had created a similar character in *Cousin Cecilia*, her third book. Lady Sophia—what had her name been? Oglethorpe? Rattray. King of Siam syndrome, you could call it, she supposed.

Which, for the moment, made her Anna.

"I can be there in half an hour," she said now, literally pushing her manuscript aside.

"I am grateful to you." In Victorine's voice, with her manner, it was as if she had paid Juliet a rare, long dreamed-of compliment.

Twenty minutes after they hung up, Juliet was seated on an uncomfortable metal chair opposite Victorine's desk.

As senior dance mistress, Victorine Vaillancourt had been given a somewhat larger office than the common run of cubicles on the second floor. It was midway down a long corridor, just next to the library of scores Juliet had once visited. She had summoned Victorine from this office on the day of the talcum powder attack, and she had passed it many times since on her way to the ladies' room (the ladies' room on the first floor was also the women's locker room, where Juliet felt hopelessly out of place). But the dance mistress seemed to spend little time here. The desk had on it only a few notebooks and oversized loose-leaf volumes, a mug full of pencils and pens, and a sheaf of unopened letters.

At Victorine's request, Juliet had closed the door, yet the dance mistress pitched her voice very low as she started to explain. Juliet remembered that, passing along the hall, she had often heard voices and sounds from inside the cubicles on this floor; the walls were probably nothing more than Sheetrock.

"I don't wish to involve you in intrigues," Victorine began, giving a wisp of a smile, "let alone put you in an uncomfortable position vis-à-vis your friend. But the truth is, Miss Renswick seems to have gone a bit over the line last night. She complains to me that the dancers are not concentrating enough on their characters. She seems to feel they are shortchanging her production and giving their best elsewhere. This is not true. I tried to explain to her—although she certainly ought to know for herself—that the dancers cannot be expected to polish their characters, to develop their precise manner, and so on—while they are still learning, *enfin*, while she is still creating the steps! Dancers do not study acting—"

"They don't?" Juliet had not meant to interrupt, but she was so surprised by this assertion that she did so anyway.

"No, they do not. Chinese dancers, perhaps, receive such training. Perhaps some few other schools. But for us, no. Nor is acting per se a part of the dancer's art, I believe. Dance is dance, acting is acting. In any case, to demand that my people create characters like—" Victorine had lost her soft, imploring tone and spoke with energetic indignation, "—like instant rice, like instant, what do you say here, mashed potatoes, *non. Ça, non!*"

Juliet did not quite know what to say. "I can see this is very troubling for you," she murmured. That seemed safe enough.

Victorine clearly realized she had become carried away in an unseemly fashion. Much more quietly, "Yes, indeed," she answered. "Very troubling to me and for the dancers, no help at all. To work with dancers is a delicate task." She frowned. "I don't know if your Miss Renswick comprehends this. Lily Bediant was in tears when she came in today," she said, pronouncing the surname Bay-dee-ahn, as if it had been a French word. "She has worked her toes to the bone for Root. And they are all still row from the loss of Anton Mohr." Juliet realized after a moment she meant all the dancers were still emotionally "raw." "It is too much. A dancer responds to strictness, to discipline, yes, but she is not to be—*tyrannisée. Tyranniser*, how do you say it?"

"Tyrannized? Not to be bullied?"

"*Précisément*. You speak French."

"A little," said Juliet, with a false modesty she was later to reflect bitterly ought to have been authentic. "I was fluent once, but that was many years ago."

Victorine gave a sudden, surprisingly deep laugh. "Wait a few decades before you start speaking of 'many years ago,' that is my counsel," she said. "Treasure your yout."

Victorine's accent was back in force, and her syntax was going fast. Juliet wondered whether the real trouble was simply that Ruth had made her favorite protégée cry, or if the harm was truly more widespread.

"On the phone, I understood you to say that Ruth had spoken to several people—?" she prompted.

"Oh yes, indeed. They do not all cry, but two or three come to me very angry, and I hear there were others. And I heard her myself, she have take me to task as well. This is not done, Mademoiselle Bodine. In ballet, not done at all."

Juliet's discomfort must have showed in her expression, because although she paused, Victorine did not wait for her to answer.

"However, I do not invite you here so you can soot my feelings. My feelings are still pretty tough, thank God, whatever else has happened to me. I ask you here because I think perhaps you can save your friend from herself. She will do her ballet no good by such tactics, and she must be told. I have discussed this with Grégoire, but he thinks, and I agree, you are the better one to have a word with her. If she hears it from him, she will think he is displeased with her work and become even more—*déboussolée*, what is the word?"

"Unglued? Disoriented? Unhinged?"

"Unhinged. Dear God, thirty years in New York and still I must ask. *En tout cas*, if I speak to her, she will imagine Grégoire does not support me. I have not his authority. *Alors, enfin*, we appeal to you. As a friend of Miss Renswick and as a friend of the Jansch. She needs you. It's clear she is worried, she is *sous pression*, it is a difficult job, no one doubts this. I myself once drove an automobile into the Seine while choreographing a new version of *Giselle*—"

"You did?"

"Oh, yes," said Victorine, her tone implying she saw no reason why Juliet should doubt it. "Dance is hard. Dancers' lives are full of difficulty. Fathers lose sight of their children, children allow their mothers to die unattended, husbands get fed up with their dancing wives and fall by the sideway—"

"Wayside," Juliet corrected automatically.

"The wayside, bones break, people roar at each other, all sorts of unattractive behavior is normal in a field that is so demanding. *Enfin*, I am not angry at Miss Renswick, nor is Grégoire. We all understand what she suffers. But can you calm her? She was much, much calmer in the days when you were in the studio, Mademoiselle, and the dancers cannot work without calm.

"Of course, if you say no," she added with a Gallic twitch of her upper lip, "we will understand."

But of course, Juliet said yes. Ames raised her eyebrows when she called to say she would probably be at the Jansch the whole afternoon (Juliet could hear her raise her eyebrows, even over the phone) but work was not everything, Juliet told herself. Friendship was more. And so began her second vigil at the bedside of Terpsichore.

When Ruth came in at 11:30 that morning, Juliet intercepted her and chatted with her until, inevitably, Ruth herself referred to her frenzied phone calls of the night before. Juliet then gently suggested that you catch more flies with honey than et cetera. Ruth was too glad to see her to argue.

Later in the day, pretending she had just heard of the dancers' reaction to the phone calls while eavesdropping in the lounge, Juliet managed to persuade Ruth to apologize in person to those she had phoned, expressing her confidence in their abilities and blaming her own frayed nerves for the contretemps. Ruth meekly obeyed, with the result that by three o'clock, when she began working with the full ensemble for the first time that day, the atmosphere in the studio was reasonably congenial.

It was during the break in this session, at 3:45, that Juliet left the room to find a quiet corner from which to call Ames. Apparently, her brain had already been engaged enough with the manuscript when she left her desk that morning that it was continuing to work on Lord Morecambe's duel even without her conscious attention. Several bright ideas had come into her imagination unbidden while she watched Ruth walk the corps (now transformed from villagers into Londoners) through a complex scene just before Act Two ended. If would be most helpful to her if Ames could locate certain notes she had made five or six years ago about the layout and landmarks of Hampstead Heath.

Many of the dancers also left the studio at the break, some to smoke, some to pee, some, no doubt, just to escape from the room. In the next studio over, a rising young Mexican soloist named Rafael Paredes was rehearsing a bit of bravura dancing from *Don Quixote,* and several of the *Great Ex*-ers, especially men, crowded around the windowed door to watch. Juliet noticed Ryder Kensington and Nicky Sabatino among them. Hart had also come out and was strolling down the corridor, exchanging a few words with a corps member Juliet believed was named Kip, or Skip. Lily Bediant was making a beeline for the dancers' lounge, Elektra ditto, a few steps behind her.

The few pay phones at the Jansch were always engaged, and Juliet thought it in poor taste to blather cryptically into one's cell phone in a public place. She was starting to head up to Ruth's little office to call Ames when the idea of borrowing Victorine's more centrally located cubicle crossed her mind. Victorine was still in Studio Three, and surely she would understand if—

But as she neared Victorine's office, she found the door was not, as usual, wide open but only very slightly ajar. She had come near and was about to peek in when the sound of a drawer being opened and closed inside arrested her. Then another drawer— opened, shut. She hesitated, confused. The idea that someone else might share the little office with Victorine occurred to her. Or perhaps a junior staff member had been sent to fetch some notes. In either case, it was an inopportune moment to borrow the office, and she was just turning away to climb the staircase up to Ruth's after all when a familiar, but temporarily unidentifiable, rattling sound from within met her ears. It ended at once and another drawer slid shut. Slowly, Juliet resumed her retreat down the hall to the staircase. Something faintly disturbing about her impressions continued to tickle the edge of her thoughts, but without penetrating them enough to take definite form.

In any case, she wanted her thoughts to herself. Along with the Hampstead Heath setting, a few other small revisions and new ideas had occurred to her, and she hurried up to the quiet of Ruth's office, whence she could call Ames and ask her to write them all safely down.

She found her assistant in an unprecedented tizzy. Evidently, the mail had come and Ames had inadvertently opened what she then discovered was a private letter. As far as Juliet could tell, no harm whatever had been done, but Ames had never made such a mistake before (she had almost never made any mistake before) and she was in an agony of remorse.

"I didn't want to call you on the cell phone during the rehearsal, Dr. Bodine," she kept explaining, "because I didn't know what I might be interrupting. I thought it was wiser to wait, but I am so glad you called. Dr. Bodine, I don't know how I'll sleep tonight—"

"Ames, dear, for heaven's sake, it really doesn't matter. Who was it from?"

"Oh, I hate to even tell you—"

"Ames!"

"It's from Mr. Ambrosetti, I think. He just signs it 'Rob.' And there wasn't any name at all on the envelope or, as I say, I would never in the world have—"

"Rob?"

Juliet's voice had changed entirely. More than five years after the divorce, word from Rob still had the power to stir in her a stinging mixture of longing, anger, pain, and remorse that could drain her body of pleasure in a moment. Like radioactive waste, she sometimes reflected, these sorrowful byproducts had half-lives much longer than that of the happiness that long ago spawned them.

With an effort, she worked to regain her composure. "What did he want?"

"Please, I really would rather not read it out loud unless it's absolutely—" began Ames, in such evident anguish that Juliet temporarily set aside her own distress.

"Never mind. I just wondered if it was business or—" She faltered. Or what? Or funny business. Forcing herself to focus, "Listen, there are a couple of things I need you to take care of for me," she said.

She had been standing all this while, facing Ruth's window

and idly looking across the courtyard at the woman in the office opposite (it was her office, evidently), who today appeared to be engaged in composing something on her computer. Juliet supposed it could be passionate e-mail, but the woman's expression suggested a managerial report or a legal brief. She herself now rounded Ruth's desk, sat down in Ruth's chair, and allowed her gaze to wander over the desktop for the first time.

"What I need most," she continued to Ames, "if you can find it— Oh!"

"Excuse me?"

"Oh, just a minute. Nothing." With an new effort of will, Juliet made herself remember and repeat her list of requests. But what she had just seen had broken her train of thought, made her forget even the waiting letter from Rob. Lying on Ruth's desk was a note written with a black felt pen in block capitals on a torn sheet of plain white paper:

LIGHTEN UP ON
THE DANCERS
OR ELSE

was all it said.

Juliet returned to Studio Three a bit late and found Ruth already at work again with the corps, trying to get them to dance out to music the steps she had walked them through earlier—slowly if necessary, but at least to dance, so that she could see the effect. The scene was the one that immediately followed Pip's discovery that his secret benefactor was the coarse convict, Magwitch, rather than the refined Miss Havisham. Ruth's idea was to make it a sort of nightmarish companion piece, a dark twin to the scene she had worked on yesterday in which Pip swirled excitedly between his low start in life and genteel society. She had worked on it with Patrick all through the weekend, as she had told Juliet, and she was introducing for the purpose a new lexicon of movement, a set of steps and gestures intended to be leering, looming, menacing, like figures distorted by a wavy funhouse mirror.

Juliet discovered her in the midst of a tense, but at least not insulting, address to the corps.

"Don't forget, you'll have lighting to help you," she was saying, "so it won't look as bald as it might feel here. But I do need you to try to imagine yourselves as sinister figures, grotesques. Fingers re-ee-eally long and crooked, necks re-ee-eally stretched, backs ve-e-ry fluid, like you were moving against water, in water. Knees *bent*. Ankles *flexed*. Can you all do me a favor please and please bend your knees? Please." She turned to the pianist. "Ray, very slowly, please. From the first measure. I'll give you four. *One* and *two* and *three* and *four*—"

The music began and the dancers, with no apparent difficulty, reproduced the long, intricate series of movements they had first been shown only an hour before. This time, the London characters and those from the Essex marshes wove in and out of each other's worlds, their groups mingling and reforming, oozing, almost, across the stage, their shoulders often hunched inward, their feet almost pigeon-toed. Pip, meanwhile, lay downstage across a trio of chairs standing in for his bed, eyes shut, body writhing as he struggled (thematically speaking) to wake. Parisi's music for this section was agitated and even more discordant than its earlier twin. Despite the fact that there was only the homely piano to represent all the instruments of the orchestra, Juliet thought the whole thing was pretty damned effective.

Ruth did not.

"Thank you," she mumbled to the dancers as the music ended and they more or less collapsed, worn out by the unaccustomed motions and the effort of remembering and performing them all. "That was horrible. Not you," she hastened to add, turning again to the panting dancers. "Me. Jesus God," her voice suddenly rose to a howl, "those steps! For Chrissake, it looks like Bob Fosse!"

Literally beating herself on the head with her small, clenched fists, she looked up at the clock and found there were ten minutes left until the end of the session.

"Go," she said to the dancers. "Save yourselves. You're young. Leave me here. Corps members, I'll see you tomorrow. Soloists and principals, come back at five."

She sank to the floor, a bony, gray-haired wreck. As the corps members collected their things, she looked up again and called out, "You were wonderful, really. Thank you."

Juliet noticed Victorine—as usual, erect at her post on a chair at the front of the room—nodding a sort of benison to the weary dancers. She reminded Juliet of a mother who wordlessly smiles understanding and sympathy at children who have just witnessed an upsetting outburst from Dad. Meanwhile, Patrick was warning off those departing dancers who thought they might try to comfort Ruth.

"It's better just to leave her," Juliet heard him hiss to Hart, who seemed disposed to have a quick word with the crumpled chore-ographer. "Trust me."

Patrick rolled his eyes and Hart moved on, flashing a com-radely smile at Juliet herself as he went.

As for Juliet, eager as she was to discuss with Ruth the note she had found, she realized it would be better to take care of aes-thetics first. She let her friend have a chance to drink some water, cool off, and collect herself a bit, then got her to sit down on a chair in the now empty studio. She drew a chair up opposite and sat with her knees almost touching Ruth's. Ruth had picked up one of the small oranges used for the Christmas dinner scene and was slowly peeling it.

"What about a pas de deux?" Juliet began.

"You mean, throw out the whole—" Ruth said, and stopped peeling.

"It's always seemed to me an obvious place for a pas de deux," Juliet went on. "From the first time I read your synopsis. Pip and Magwitch, so different in their ideas and feelings about their relationship—talk about a companion piece to an earlier scene, think of their first meeting, how you can use that collision and that family of steps and gestures now! The music will fit perfectly and the scene— well, not to be rude, but I think it would carry the audience forward much better than any scene with the corps. Narratively, I mean."

Ruth was silent for a few moments. In her head, Juliet guessed, she was replaying what she had created of Act Two, trying to see the flow of movement and how such a change would affect it.

She resumed peeling the orange. "So then when Drummle and Estella begin their waltz afterwards—"

"—you don't have to worry about getting the whole corps off the stage," Juliet finished. (Ruth's synopsis, and Parisi's score, provided a waltz for Estella and her haughty fiancé, Bentley Drummle, with Miss Havisham a brooding third.)

Ruth considered this. "On the other hand, I do have to worry about getting them on somewhere. People expect the corps to be part of a ballet. They can't be on for just two minutes out of twenty."

"That's why I think you need to include them in the waltz scene. Then it looks like a celebration and makes it clearer that Drummle and Estella are engaged."

"More costumes mean more expense," Ruth muttered. She had removed the whole peel now and sat with the scraps balanced on one knee while she thoughtfully detached an orange section. "Max won't like that."

"Put ribbons and sashes on them, that's all. You don't imagine nineteenth century English villagers kept formal evening wear, do you?"

"So the corps is on stage, and then—" Ruth put an orange section into her mouth.

"Pip appears, watches, maybe cuts in and has a little turn

around the room with Estella. Then Drummle snaps her away, takes her offstage, the corps follows and Miss Havisham is alone—"

"—for her Remorse Solo," Ruth took up. "End of Act Two. Oh God, maybe it would work."

"I think it would."

"It means Pip is dancing constantly for—I don't know, ten minutes maybe."

"Give the bulk of the duet to Magwitch."

"Ryder?" said Ruth doubtfully, the word muffled by another mouthful of orange.

"You don't think he can pull it off?"

"No. I mean yes, he probably could. He's actually very good." She chewed and swallowed. "I wouldn't be surprised if he becomes a soloist next year. I think Greg has overlooked him. He has a lot of strengths."

Mention of Ryder and strength reminded Juliet of the note on Ruth's desk upstairs. She was about to broach the topic when Ruth handed her both peels and orange and stood up as if in a trance. She went to the center of the room and began moving experimentally.

"Tah-tum! Tah-tah-tum!" she sang, or rather muttered, to herself, obviously starting to create a second Magwitch–Pip pas de deux. Juliet watched, hoping she would sit down after a minute or two.

Instead, "Find Patrick and get him in here, would you?" Ruth called out, not even slowing down.

Reluctant but resigned, Juliet tossed the remains of the orange into the wastebasket and left the studio. Patrick, she discovered after a little wandering about, was in the dancers' lounge, leaning against the same machine that had supplied Anton with the fatal Coke and drinking deeply from a bottle of lemonade.

"Her nibs is looking for you," she said, and Patrick, groaning, went off. Juliet hesitated, then decided to sit in the lounge and have a break herself. The note on Ruth's desk would have to wait.

c h a p t e r

FIFTEEN

Juliet had read enough about goril-
las to know that they did not reveal their secrets all at once.

Primatologists insinuated themselves among them and patiently
watched for months before discerning the subtle hierarchies in their
ranks. And so it was no surprise to find that she herself could now
pick out groupings among the Jansch dancers that had been invisible
to her on her first arrival.

In the dancers' lounge that Tuesday afternoon, Olympia Andreades was lying full length on a sofa, her head propped up against
one arm, her long legs draped across the contiguous laps of Alexei
Ostrovsky and Skip (or Kip) Whoever-he-was. The three seemed to
be playing some sort of word game, like Geography, except that the
words each contributed were the names of celebrities, not place
names, and did not bear any orthographic relationship to each other
that Juliet could discern. Across the way, Lily Bediant and Teri Malone shared an oversized armchair, Teri massaging Lily's upper arms
for her while they whispered to each other, smiling occasionally as if
at an interesting secret. Hart and Elektra also sat side by side, on a
sofa under the windows. As Juliet watched, Hart fed his partner from
a box of raisins—one raisin, a second raisin, a third—each leaving
his delicate fingers singly and disappearing as it was nibbled in by
her equally delicate lips. Framed and glowingly backlit as the two

were by the window behind them, each raisin (thought Juliet) could almost be traced as it reappeared, a nearly visible lumplet passing along the ballerina's slender neck. The very sight of such gastronomical restraint made her yearn for a cheeseburger to sink her teeth into, a cheeseburger dripping blood onto a plate of fries. Then Elektra suddenly raised her hands and lowered her head. She sneezed mightily, twice. Juliet had forgotten the poor woman had a cold; what on earth could she even taste of those pitiful, lingeringly ingested ex-grapes?

In her early days at the Jansch, Juliet remarked to herself as she looked away to survey the other dozen or so dancers in the lounge, all she would have been able to make of these groupings was that, by and large, the principals kept to themselves, the corps and soloists likewise. Nicky Sabatino and Jon Trapp, a longtime principal who was to star in *Blood Wedding* this season, sat at a table in the middle of the room arguing vehemently about the Yankees' chances for the World Series. At another table, four corps members shared a vending-machine-sized package of pretzels as they collaborated on a crossword puzzle. Such a pairing as Lily and Teri, still buzzing softly in their armchair, was most unusual, and even in the early days, Juliet would no doubt have solemnly recorded the aberration in her field notes for later study.

But she now understood that other groups existed within (and sometimes traversed) the basic tripartite hierarchy. One clan of dancers was . . . racier, was the word that came to mind, than the others. They laughed louder, teased each other more harshly, and gave an impression of wildness that the others did not. Olympia and Ryder were of this set, which Juliet suspected also indulged in drugs. Another subgroup was pursuing second careers that would take them away from dance. You rarely saw a dancer reading a book for pleasure, but there was a coterie that could be glimpsed in the lounge dutifully highlighting lines in a psychology or physiology text. There were cults who gathered around particular dancers, devotees of a specific principal or pair. There were dancers who hardly socialized within the company—not very many, but a few. Some dancers drew together because they all had children. Russians stuck mainly with Russians; Latino and Asian dancers were more dispersed. (There was only one African-American dancer, even in this day and age, who could therefore neither cluster nor disperse.) Some dancers sucked up to the administrators more (or more blatantly, or more success-fully) than others. A few were trying to choreograph new works, hoping the Jansch would allow them to create something on the company one day.

And there were romances: gay romances, straight romances, overt romances, surreptitious romances. The only rule of thumb Juliet had discovered in this realm was that open physical contact between dancers was no indication of sexual attachment. Unlike most human beings, dancers stroked and rubbed and grabbed and nuzzled and jumped on one another all day long without intending anything either as an overture or a claim. She wondered what sort of extreme explicit-ness would be necessary, in the circumstances, to signal sexual inter-est. Perhaps they put it in writing? Or waited until they were actually in bed together before concluding this was sex? On the other hand, there might be layers and layers of communication among them (glances? gestures? moans?) that she had not yet learned to distinguish. What-ever it was, she did not think it could be scent. Much of the time, they reeked either of sweat (each perspiring his or her own unique, quite identifiable smell, she had noticed) or force-ten perfumes.

Juliet's musings were interrupted, like many a primatologist's, no doubt, by a sudden, mass movement of the subjects of her study. As if at an inaudible signal (eventually, she realized it was the large wall clock pointing at one minute before five) nearly all the dancers rose to their feet and headed down the stairs in a body.

Later, she was to think with astonishment of what had taken place right before her eyes.

———

The most obviously dramatic event
of the afternoon occurred just after 6:30, down in Studio Three,
where Ruth was working on a second Pip–Estella–Havisham pas de
trois—dubbed the "Love Her, Love Her" trio, after Miss Havisham's
orders to Pip—that came midway through Act Two. Ruth would have
preferred to work on the new Pip–Magwitch pas de deux—soon to be
known as the Recognition Duet—but she had not requested the Magwitches, and she did have her Estellas and Havishams, so she was
forced to stick to her original plans.

Although the pas de trois occurred before the scene she had
tried and scrapped earlier that day, Ruth had not yet made much
headway with it. Juliet watched as she slowly worked through the
measures of the music, which was grave, hypnotic, and extremely
beautiful. The beginning was fixed: In an allusion to his having been
hired to entertain her, Pip bent and loaded Miss Havisham up onto
his shoulders, then straightened and carried her a few steps before
gently allowing her to slide down and onto her feet. But after that,
the trio was pretty much up for grabs. Ruth felt her way along, draw-
ing heavily on the contributions of her leading dancers, especially
Lily (Juliet was surprised to see), who seemed of the three the most
focused this afternoon. Elektra was plagued with sneezing fits and
complained, as the session wore on, that she didn't feel quite well.
Hart seemed uncharacteristically distracted. But Lily Bediant was full
of ideas, even suggesting steps for the other two that would express
Pip's ardent admiration and the languid sufferance Estella returns.
Behind her, the second Havisham, Mary Christie, worked hard to
keep up, while Kirsten Ahlswede and Nicky Sabatino longed for
Ruth's attention in vain.

At a certain point, working with Lily and Patrick, Ruth devised
a lift in which Pip was to seize Estella by the waist, lower her almost
to the ground as if he would ravish her, then turn with her still in his
hands and raise her high above himself, so that he looked up at her
as if in worship instead. Estella was to remain rigid throughout this,
indifferent, emotionally beyond reach. It was a typically Renswickian

reversal, a sequence of moves that created momentum for the dancers as well as an expectation in the audience, then turned everything on its head. Ruth had created several like it in *Wuthering Heights*. But they had not been easy to work out and this one promised to be a lulu. There were a dozen different physical conundrums to solve: how Pip should hold Estella at each moment, how he could handle the load of her weight as he slowly raised her above him; how Estella could cheat by imperceptibly helping to propel herself up, then position herself so that his hands would help keep her body rigid, how her weight could be distributed to take the least toll on Pip. There was intricate footwork, too, lest they step on or trip each other, and precise timing vis-à-vis the music. Juliet watched, torn between amazement and absolute boredom, as each instant of the maneuver was painstakingly planned, practiced, retooled, retried. Elektra was gleaming with sweat and (throwing away delicacy) had taken to grunting loudly whenever Hart grabbed her, lifted her up, or set her down. By the time Ruth was satisfied enough to move on, Hart, too, was drenched with perspiration and breathing in hard, short gasps.

So it should not, perhaps, have come as such a complete surprise when, having been asked by Ruth to return to the start of the pas de trois and do the whole thing, to music, so that she could see the new lift in context, Hart began the scene as required by lifting Lily Bediant to his shoulders, straightened, carried her some steps away, then lost his grip and dumped her onto the floor behind him.

There ensued what Juliet now learned was the usual pandemonium following a dancer's fall. Victorine (who had been at work with some Wilis in the studio next door) was summoned, as was the physical therapist, who happened to be on site that day. Lily had broken her fall with her hands, but her chin had banged on the floor and the underside of her jaw was bleeding a little. Still, she kept saying she was okay and could everyone just please go on working without her? Juliet thought her quite valiant. At the least, falling head first from a height of five feet or so must shake a person up. Hart, meanwhile, was beside himself with mortification and regret. To drop a partner, while far from unheard of, was a violation of the most basic kind of trust.

"I don't know what happened, I had her and then I just—" he kept sputtering, while those around him tried not to look at him as if he were a criminal.

"It happens," Patrick told him repeatedly, putting an arm around him, patting his shoulder.

"Not to me. I've never dropped anyone."

"It happens, buddy."

Ruth, though dismayed, professed herself relieved that the fall had not been worse. Lily would have to go see Dr. Keller. But the bleeding had stopped almost at once and she seemed to be more or less herself.

"They do get dropped," Ruth whispered to Juliet. "If you looked under the chins of ten ballerinas, you'd probably see scars on five. She's lucky, considering."

The physical therapist had arrived and had sat Lily down to examine her. Hart knelt beside her chair. When the therapist had given his opinion that nothing too awful had happened, he breathed a sigh of relief that was audible throughout the studio.

"Lily, I am so sorry—"

Lily shook her glossy platinum mane, which today was only loosely bound with a ribbon. "Stop. It was an accident."

Juliet's estimation of Lily rocketed skyward. Hitherto, all she had seen of the prima ballerina was peevishness, tantrums, and vanity; here, finally, was part of what had enabled her to become great. Patrick was calling for a car to take her to the doctor.

"Let me go with you?" Hart said.

"It's really not necessary."

"Please. Unless you can't stand me."

Lily smiled, an act of kindness that had the unfortunate effect of causing her chin to bleed again. "If it makes you feel better," she said. She stood, wobbled, and quickly sat again.

"Let him go with you," ordered Victorine, who had been glowering at Hayden but saw that he would make a more useful escort than she would. She produced a handkerchief from within the long sleeve of her leotard and handed it solemnly to her favorite.

Looking as pale as his victim, Hart knelt beside her while Patrick fetched Lily's purse and some street clothes for her to slip on. By the time she limped out on Hayden's arm, it was past seven and all the studios were emptying out. Dancers could be heard in the corridors; doors opened and shut all over the building.

"Be very careful with her," Victorine warned, as Lily moved cautiously away. Victorine watched them down the corridor, then said good night and herself went slowly out the door, her back as straight as ever, her steps visibly hesitant, almost trembling.

Meanwhile, predictably no doubt, Ruth had had a few further thoughts about the new lift that she wanted to try out with Patrick. Juliet watched, ready to leave but determined to have a quiet word about the threatening note upstairs before she went.

Ruth had begun to trace out a new pattern of footwork with her assistant when she suddenly exclaimed, "Oh, damn! I meant to see if I could have the Pips and Magwitches tomorrow between three and four to get started on that new . . ." She broke off for a moment, then resumed, "Juliet, do you know who Amy Egan is? The woman who does the schedules, do you know her office?"

"Yes."

Amy Egan was a middle-aged former dancer who spent most of her day trying to reconcile the conflicting needs of some eighty-odd dancers and dance masters. She and Juliet had introduced themselves to each other one day in the second floor ladies' room when Amy was looking desperately for a tampon, which Juliet was able to supply.

"Would you mind very much running up there to see if she's

left or not?" Ruth asked. "If she's there, could you ask her? If I could just have Hart and Ryder, even that would be okay. Three to four is our lunch break tomorrow," she went on to the exhausted but always stoical Patrick, "but we can work right through."

Patrick's blue eyes widened briefly, but he said nothing and Juliet left on her errand. Amy Egan was not in her office—indeed, the whole second floor was silent and seemed to be empty—but Juliet took a photocopy of the next day's schedule from a stack always kept on her desk. At least Ruth could see where Ryder and Hart were expected during that hour. She was passing back along the corridor to the stairs when a voice caught her ear. It was Victorine.

"*Mais comment cela se peut-il?*" she said; or at least, that was what Juliet thought she said. The door to her office was closed, but Victorine's voice was loud and quite clear.

There was no answering voice, and Juliet surmised that she was talking to herself. That same sound of a drawer being opened and shut which she had heard in the afternoon was now repeated, and the voice went on distractedly. "*Mais—où sont-ils, mes misten-flûtes?*" it said.

"How wonderful my French really is!" exclaimed Juliet to herself, pausing in the hall to preen herself on this fresh evidence of her brain's superior powers. She had minored in French at Radcliffe, a circumstance that had come in handy while researching *The Parisian Gentleman*, which Angelica K-H had written some seven or eight years ago. She clearly recalled encountering "*misten-flûte*" in the *Mémoires d'un Officier de l'Armée de Napoléon*. "To remember that, after all this time!" she now marveled. Silently, she translated the whole of Victorine's spoken thoughts: " 'But how can that be? But—where are they, my thingamajigs?' I wonder what she's missing. Maybe *I* could help her," she reflected, with a final touch of vanitas.

However, she decided on reflection that the even nobler thing to do was to move tactfully away, leaving Mademoiselle her illusion of privacy.

She went back downstairs and was about to enter Studio Three when a slender figure in street clothes darted up beside her.

"Miss Kestrel-Haven?"

Juliet looked around to find Teri Malone's brown eyes fixed beseechingly on her.

She laughed. "Please, call me Juliet."

"Of course." Teri's apple-cheeks began to flush. "I'm so sorry—I mean, I hope you won't mind—" She bent her head and started to burrow into a large leather bag slung over her shoulder. "If you don't want to look at it, of course I completely understand."

She looked up again, holding out perhaps twenty sheets of paper clipped together.

"It's only a rough draft, of course. But it's Chapter One, and I hoped . . ." She lost courage and her voice faded away.

"I'd be delighted," Juliet lied, taking the proffered pages. "I'll let you know as soon as I've read it."

"Oh, you are so— Thank you!" breathed Teri, and scampered away.

Juliet tucked the chapter under her arm and reentered the studio. Ruth had finally stopped torturing Patrick, she found, and let him go home. Now she had gathered up her own things and was on her way out the door.

"You were absolutely right about that nightmare scene with the corps," she greeted Juliet, taking her arm and moving her back out the door, then swiftly down the corridor toward the locker rooms. "This pas de deux is going to add so much depth to the Pip–Magwitch relationship, and when you think about it, that's the pivot of the whole story in some ways, isn't it? How brilliant of you to see it. I'm starting to think we'll have to cosign this ballet. Did you find Amy?"

Juliet shook her head and handed Ruth the schedule. Pleasant as it was to be fulsomely thanked, she did not want to wait another second before raising the matter of the mysterious note.

"Ruth, have you been up to your office today? Did you see what's on your desk?"

Sweaty and newly aware of a hundred aches, Ruth did not slow down but continued to hurry along the hall, bringing Juliet with her. "Why, what's on my desk?" she asked.

"Then you haven't seen it."

"Haven't seen what?"

"Well, I hate to tell you, especially when you've got your creative juices flowing again, but—" The two women now entered the locker room, which gave every sign of being deserted. Still, Juliet circled the double bank of lockers in the middle and stuck her head into the shower room before going on in a low tone, "There's a handwritten note on your desk that says 'Lighten up on the dancers or else.' No signature, of course."

Ruth started to laugh.

"What's funny?"

Ruth only laughed more, then hugged Juliet. "I wrote that, you dope, after you lectured me this morning," she said. "It's a reminder from me to me."

*Juliet decided not to read Rob's let-*ter—or Teri's chapter—until she had had dinner and a chance to rest. Sitting all day in a rehearsal studio full of people was very trying to her, never mind the various tensions and tasks she was there to try to address. In the ordinary course of things, she was alone most of her waking hours, albeit with Ames often in the next room. And this, as a rule, was all the company she liked. Whatever Rob had to say, she would receive it better when she was more refreshed.

She had stopped on her way home from the Jansch at a Korean market, where she collected a small mountain of lettuces, bell peppers, mushrooms, avocados, and other oddments. The sight of Elektra Andreades piteously savoring her little raisins lingered in her memory, and she tossed a packet of raw cashews, some croutons, half a dozen kiwis, and a cantaloupe into her basket as well. For a few moments, she hovered by a flat brimming with Bing cherries, dark and firm and almost intolerably tempting. But "pesticides, pesticides," she admonished herself, hardening her will by envisioning a fresh squirt of toxic chemicals glistening on each luscious mouthful. She would ask Ames to call Whole Foods and find out if they had organic cherries. Forbidden fruit, indeed.

It was now almost the end of July, and the summer had been ripening beautifully. The sultry heat of a few weeks ago had been replaced by a less humid, more genial warmth. The equinox was far enough behind that the evenings were noticeably shorter, but there was still plenty of light at eight o'clock when she took her salad (now washed, cut up, dressed and tumbled into a gigantic porcelain bowl) up to the terrace and sat down to look at the river and eat.

Reading at dinner was a habit she tried to avoid, since it took away half the taste of the meal. Instead, she let her eyes rest, now on the fresh, gleaming salad, now on the rosy horizon and violet water. She marveled, as she often did, at the variety of food, its fantastic shapes and colors, its pleasantness to the mouth. She marveled likewise at the beauty of the river and the horizon, wondering why it should be that a vista of trees, river, and sky could so deeply comfort the soul. Not long ago, in the lobby of the Met, between the second and third acts of *La Traviata,* she had overheard a young woman remark to her companion, "Nature is the screen saver of life." Now she remembered this and sighed. She supposed nature really had become the screen saver of life—and life, for many, the screen saver of television.

As she peeled a kiwi, her mood became gradually less philosophical. She could not shake off a guilty sense of having leapt a little too gladly to Ruth's aid today. She really was like an alcoholic; whenever the slightest excuse arose, she abandoned her desk. Poor Sir Edward Rice was still sitting alone in his study contemplating Lord Morecambe's insolent challenge. Books, she reproved herself, do not write themselves. And when she had come home this evening, she found a note from Ames saying that the cover illustration for *London Quadrille* had been posted that morning on her fan club's Web site. Juliet wished the publisher would not release those covers in advance. They seemed to create such pressure. She sighed again. She would work six hours tomorrow, no matter what. She could go to the Jansch afterward. She would have Ames call Victorine and let her know when to expect her.

She finished her meal, started to stand up, then wriggled around uncomfortably. That itch. It had been so long since she had a yeast infection. Perhaps another yogurt for dessert? She had even heard of women applying plain yogurt directly . . . Maybe she should check for natural cures on the Internet.

At about 9:30, feeling that she must read Rob's letter, she went to her office and found it on top of the pile of correspondence Ames had left her. It was folded, and a yellow Post-it was stuck to the outside, with the message, "I'm so sorry!" in Ames's psychotically neat print. Juliet thought a moment, then decided it would be best to read it at her desk, where she usually felt her most confident. Perhaps Rob had had a practical reason for writing, something Juliet could help him with. Maybe he needed an organ transplant, or had mistakenly become the target of a nationwide FBI manhunt. She opened the letter. But the matter was nothing so simple.

When Rob and Juliet's marriage had exploded, the ostensible cause, the catalyst, was an affair Rob had been having for four months with an aspiring young actress named Elise. The marriage had had plenty of problems that Juliet was aware of before then, but she had no inkling of this business until he brought it to her attention. Then she was as hurt by the accumulation of lies Rob had told her during the secret liaison as by his revelation. Declaring that he could no longer live stifled and under Juliet's "thumb," Rob had packed up his belongings and moved with his inamorata to Toronto. Three weeks after she signed the final divorce papers, Juliet had received an announcement of the marriage of Robert

Vincent Ambrosetti to Elise Maria Craig. Six months later came a second announcement: the birth of their daughter, Jemima Rose Ambrosetti.

Rob's friends and Juliet's had never quite mixed, and Juliet had not known a baby was in the works. She had reached a sort of emotional equilibrium before Jemima's arrival, but the birth announcement set off a period of distress, almost despair, hardly less painful than the initial breakup. Still, she pulled out of it. By the time, two years later, when a mutual acquaintance informed her that Elise and Rob also had divorced, Juliet had put Rob and her marriage well into the past.

Unfortunately, since his second divorce, Rob had been writing to her with increasing affection and ever greater frequency. At first the letters were penitent and pleading, then sober and weighty, then merely wistful. But finally (and much more intelligently), they became entertaining. Rob was in the theater, after all. He could be very amusing. Juliet had asked him not to write; it upset and confused her. But though he would abstain for a month or two, eventually a missive always came. He was dying to leave Toronto, he told her, but Elise had settled in. Moving back to New York would mean giving up his visits with Jemima, at least until he had enough money to fly back and forth. Rob could be very funny when he was unhappy, and he was quite hilarious on the subject of Canada in general and Toronto in particular. Juliet felt herself twisted with every letter she received.

This letter was a particularly funny one. She read it, set it down with tears in her eyes—tears from laughing and from crying—and mentally drafted the short, measured reply she would send back tomorrow. For now, she picked up Teri's opening chapter, which comprised a description of life in a large family in Eau Claire, Wisconsin, in 1902, and carried it off to read in bed. It was not, she found with pleasure, half bad.

The following morning, Sir Edward
Rice chose Francis Sneed, his cousin, as his second. Juliet, sitting
dutifully at her desk with a pitcher of iced tea to sustain her, was surprised by the choice—but she had to concede that although Charles
Dalrymple might be Sir Edward's closest friend, Dalrymple was also
a Derbyshire neighbor of Lord Morecambe. Naturally, Sir Edward
would not wish to force him into an awkward position. (Actually,
Morecambe was Dalrymple's neighbour, Angelica K-H always favour-
ing the English style of spelling.)

Usually, the first half hour or so of work was the hardest, Juliet
found. Once she had made herself go to her desk and sit there for a
while, things began to take on a momentum of their own and she
worked quite happily. The redoubtable Ames had already located the
requested notes on Hampstead Heath, so after arranging the matter
of Sir Edward's second, Juliet spent a happy couple of hours ram-
bling there, refreshing her knowledge of landmarks and locating a
likely retreat where a duel could be fought unobserved early one
April morning. It was a wrench to look up from a description of the
bill of fare at Jack Straw's Castle in 1817 and find it was 4:15 in New
York. Hastily, she snatched up Teri's chapter (now embellished with
an admiring, and mostly sincere, note on a yellow Post-It), a few
essentials and sped out the door.

As the season of preparation continued and the season of performance approached, Juliet had noticed a growing sense of purpose
and efficiency at the Jansch. Anton Mohr's death had not been forgotten, but the memorial for him seemed to have succeeded in brack-
eting off the trauma somewhat, making it part of the past so that the
company could look forward and the requisite work go on.

Peering into the studios that day (after leaving the chapter in
Teri's mailbox, behind the bandbox lobby), she saw in each room a
competent little machine busy at work: dancers settling into their
roles, instructors starting to make familiar jokes about persistent fail-
ings, projects beginning to gel. Even Studio Three had lost some of
the ambience of sustained emergency that so often pervaded it,

although it had not yet achieved the calm Victorine thought essential. Still, Patrick actually came to the door to usher Juliet in while Ruth managed to work on without him. Ruth had not been able to get hold of Ryder and Hart for the hour between three o'clock and four, Patrick explained to Juliet in a whisper; but between one o'clock and three she had had Elektra, Hart, and Lily, and they had gotten a very good distance in that time toward completing the four-minute "Love Her, Love Her" pas de trois. She had them again now and was hoping to finish the thing before going home that evening. At six, the whole ensemble was scheduled to come to Studio Three and she planned to try a run-through then of all she had choreographed so far of Act Two.

"How is Lily?" Juliet whispered back. "What did the doctor say?"

Ruth was working with the injured star just at the moment, going over with her a maneuver that required her to wave her arm as if performing some evil act of magic. The ballerina was listening attentively and looked quite as usual. The only sign Juliet could see of yesterday's mishap was a bluish bruise under her jaw.

"He said it was nothing," Patrick replied. "Just a bump. And she says her head feels okay now."

"Well, that's good luck." Juliet gazed a moment longer at Lily, then glanced around the room. Hart was holding onto the barre, performing some sort of leg-stretching exercise. Elektra, some yards away, was standing unnaturally still, her head dropped forward, her shoulders uncharacteristically hunched. She looked peaky, strange, a bit less anorexic than usual somehow, but very unhappy.

Juliet pointed this out to Patrick.

"I know," he said. "She must have a stomach bug. You can see she's green around the gills."

Juliet nodded. She wished Ruth would notice and let Elektra go home. It was painful to watch someone so obviously miserable trying to act normal.

And try Elektra did. Soon, Ruth turned back to her and asked her to dance the whole sequence up to the measure she was now working on. And Elektra danced—not "full out," as the dancers called it, but not merely "marking" it either. As she had yesterday, she grunted often, especially when Hart lifted her or set her down. When at last Ruth declared a break, the two sat down together near the piano, not far from Juliet.

Ruth was busy with Patrick and sat scribbling notes with him for a while, so Juliet was at liberty to eavesdrop. Indeed, it would have been hard not to.

"God, I am so sick!" Elektra more or less yelled. "Ouch! Help me!"

Hayden gave her what seemed to Juliet a peculiar look, but all he said was, "Maybe you're hungry. You haven't been eating very much."

"How could I be hungry?" she answered irritably. "You've been feeding me those fucking raisins for two days. I feel like I'm going to puke them out every time I go up or down in the air." She lowered her voice. "I wish she'd get off that damned 'Madonna/Whore Lift.'" (Such was the name Ruth had given to the tricky raising-and-lowering bit of business she had devised yesterday.) "My ribs feel like shit. Not that that's your fault," she added, then lay down flat on the floor.

"Sorry. I'm pretty whipped, too," Hart said, and he did in fact look terrible. His yellow hair hung in damp clumps; his lean, handsome face was pale and strained. He even had a sort of twitch at the corner of one eye, Juliet noticed. Patrick had told her it was simply not done for the dancers to complain to the choreographer, no matter how worn out they were or how much pain they suffered. Listening to these two, Juliet thought it a ridiculous and perfectly inhumane system. As if Ruth were some kind of god whose creative throes were so extraordinary and precious that they must be allowed to toss and tumble the lives of everyone around her!

The break came to an end and the difficult, tedious rehearsal session began once more. Lily Bediant, who had gone out of the room, came back in with a full, new bottle of water and an expression of serene martyrdom. Mary Christie, Nicky Sabatino, and Kirsten Ahlswede, who had spent their ten minutes of freedom stretching and hopping by the barre, resumed their places toward the back of the room, apparently resigned to another hour of trying to copy what the first cast was doing (and being utterly ignored). Elektra dragged herself to her feet and placed herself at Ruth's mercy, while Hart went back to carting her and Lily from (as Anton Mohr might have put it) here to there, there to here. Victorine sat on, upright and vigilant. Luis Fortunato uncomplainingly played the same notes over and over and over.

And then Elektra fainted.

She was dancing by herself just before she fell, watching herself in the mirror as she practiced a sort of run-and-spin step from the second act, while Hart and Lily once again tried the early lift in the "Love Her" section. She made a little sound, almost inaudible under the heavy piano notes, and sort of toppled woozily over. Then she lay on her side in a semi-fetal crouch, eyes half open but rolled back, arms limp and askew, skin clammy and pale.

"I'll get an ammonia capsule," said Patrick, rushing from the room.

"It's probably hunger," Hart suggested, still gasping from his exertions. "She hasn't been eating."

Victorine cast a look of disgust at Ruth. "Exhaustion, more likely."

"Maybe the heat?" suggested Juliet, who was always appalled by the greenhouse temperatures of the studio.

"Oh, look!"

An expression of horror on her face, Kirsten Ahlswede was pointing to her fallen colleague. At first, standing on the other side of the room, Juliet, Ruth and Victorine could not see what she meant. Then it spread.

A scarlet stain had begun to seep from between the unconscious woman's legs. It was turning rapidly into a red, red puddle.

SIXTEEN

Ryder Kensington did not seem to Juliet the sort of man to lose his head in a crisis. Yet, twenty minutes after hearing that his wife had been rushed to the hospital, he appeared to have fallen apart completely.

"You stay here," Juliet said, sitting him down in a molded plastic chair in the emergency room waiting area at St Luke's–Roosevelt. "I'll find out where she is."

An hour ago, in a scene creepily reminiscent of Anton's removal two weeks before, medics and police officers had clomped into Studio Three. (Juliet now knew police were automatically dispatched whenever the city sent an ambulance.) They asked questions, then vanished with Elektra on a stretcher. At least she had recovered consciousness and could answer some of the questions herself. But her husband was not to be found. Greg went with the ambulance, while Juliet and Patrick searched for Ryder in vain, chasing grimly up and down the corridors of the Jansch while trying not to create an appearance of alarm. The schedule showed he had not been called to any rehearsal during that hour, but he should have shown up for Ruth's full-cast second act run-through at six.

He didn't.

It was past 6:30 when Amy Egan got out of the subway at Astor Place and found that her pager had been beeped. Ryder had gone downtown to the costume-makers for an emergency fitting, she told Gayle, the receptionist, an urgent matter on account of which (as Amy had taken care to inform the second Magwitch) he had been granted a late arrival for the six o'clock call. Gayle relayed the message and phoned the costumiers; but they said Ryder had left the workshop some time ago.

And indeed, he ambled into the sleek little lobby just as Gayle hung up. Looking strangely ordinary in a red tank top and jeans, he was mouthing the words to something on his Walkman and did not at first realize that the little knot of worried people in the lobby had anything to do with him.

"Elektra?" he said, after Patrick explained, his tone seeming to suggest (Juliet thought) that among his many wives, Elektra was the one he would least have expected to have a medical emergency.

But after this equivocal eruption, he seemed to lose his wits altogether. Juliet told him she had a car already waiting for him downstairs, then escorted—or rather, ushered—him to it. Seeing his blank face as he climbed in, she also climbed in and sat down beside him. (Patrick, naturally, had to go back and help Ruth, who had no intention of giving up her last hour of work for the day.) And so they arrived at St. Luke's together, where the emergency room waiting area teemed with coughing children, bleeding teenagers, groaning seniors—the usual crowd of New Yorkers having an unexpectedly trying day. Juliet squeezed Ryder's muscular shoulder firmly before marching off to tackle the triage desk.

She soon learned Elektra had been taken in immediately and was now being treated in some recess she was not to penetrate. The moment her informant turned away, however, Juliet swept smoothly through a pair of doors marked "DO NOT ENTER" and found Greg Fleetwood leaning against a column in the middle of a maze of curtained cubicles.

"She's in there," Greg said, pointing to a cubicle so full of people that its curtain kept billowing out as they hurried around inside.

"Do you know—?"

"Nothing at all."

Remembering that Greg had recently spent hours at this very hospital with Anton, Juliet took pity on him and sent him out to stay with Ryder while she kept watch in his place. Behind the cubicle's curtain, legs encased in green scrubs were visible from the knee down. They bustled from this side of the bed to that, then that to this. Occasionally, a person emerged or dashed in, far too intent on the business at hand for Juliet to dare to ask a question. Machines beeped. Voices muttered unintelligibly. After what seemed a long time, a slight, very young woman came out, identified herself as Dr. Chen and asked if Juliet were the next of kin.

She felt herself blanch at the sinister question. "No. Her husband is in the waiting room."

"I'll come with you," said Dr. Chen, and led the way.

They found Ryder alone, Greg having escaped to go across the street and fetch a couple of iced coffees.

"Come, please," said the doctor, waving Ryder through a door behind the triage desk that Juliet had not noticed before. She tried to get Ryder to meet her eyes, so that she could excuse herself, but he wouldn't look up.

"I'll wait for you out—" she began; but Dr. Chen gestured at her to come and she followed. The door led to a labyrinthine set of tiny examining rooms. Finding an empty one, Dr. Chen bade them sit down. Ryder taking the only chair, Juliet perched on the examining table.

"I'm afraid your wife has lost the baby," Dr. Chen said gently, but without preface.

"The—"

So far as Juliet knew, it was Ryder's first word since he had blurted out his wife's name back in the lobby of the Jansch. He said it and stopped, looking absolutely flummoxed.

Juliet, too, felt dumbfounded. Elektra, pregnant! No wonder she'd been green.

"The good news is, she's doing well and should make a full

recovery," the doctor went on reassuringly. "There's no reason why she can't conceive soon again. She did lose quite a bit of blood. But I expect she'll be herself in a few days. Only—" she looked sympathetically at Ryder, "without the baby. I'm so sorry."

Ryder sat as if paralyzed. Finally, "Without what baby?" he brought out.

There was a pause. Juliet felt her own heart thumping in her chest. Then, "Didn't you know?" asked Dr. Chen. "Your wife was pregnant."

"Elektra Andreades? Do you have the right patient?"

Dr. Chen consulted a manilla file in her hand. "Yes, that's right, Mr. Andreades," she said. "She was more than three months pregnant. Thirteen weeks."

"My wife couldn't have been three months pregnant," Ryder said, his heavy eyebrows lowered, his voice full of scorn for this doctor who did not know the basic facts of life. "First of all, my wife has partially occluded Fallopian tubes that make it extremely problematic for her to conceive. Second, we haven't even had sex since—"

Juliet felt herself start to blush. Seeing the flaw in his logic, Ryder suddenly shut up. There was an awful silence in the room. The fluorescent lights buzzed. Down the hall, a nurse's ringing voice asked, "And has your nose always slanted to the left, Mrs. Lester?"

Finally, "They are bringing her up to the fourth floor," Dr. Chen said, her eyes fleeing to Juliet's for comfort. "Take any elevator from the lobby and the floor nurse at the station will tell you which room number to go to."

Clutching her folder to her thin chest in an oddly schoolgirlish way, Dr. Chen gave a faint, melancholy half-smile, bobbed her head, and left the room. Just past the doorway, she stopped and remembered to shoo her visitors out with her. As the door to the examining rooms swung shut, the doctor dematerialized, leaving Juliet alone with Ryder in the waiting area once more.

Ryder was almost a foot taller than Juliet, and she could not see his face well unless she stood back a little and looked slightly up. She was reluctant to do this—she was afraid to do it—yet she was aware that a sort of electric storm seemed to be passing through his strong, handsome features. His dark eyes flinched and glowered, his eyebrows twitched, his mouth and jaw rippled. Nor was it only his face; Juliet had the impression that she could feel energy rising off his skin like steam. Scalding steam. She looked hopefully around for Greg. But they had only been gone a couple of minutes. He was probably still on line at some Starbucks. Lucky Greg.

"Do you want—" she began.

"I'll go up to her now," Ryder broke in. "Thanks for—"

"I'll go with you," Juliet interrupted, as an image of the helpless Elektra receiving him alone flashed in her mind.

"That won't be necessary," Ryder said.

"I'd like to see her." Juliet hurried beside him into the lobby. To her relief, Ryder didn't argue. She felt very small next to him and supposed he might have decided that, like a cat or a housefly, she was too insignificant to worry about. They waited in silence for the elevator, then got in together.

On the fourth floor, a nurse sent them down the corridor to Room 418. Ryder stalked off, Juliet scurrying behind. Four-eighteen was a semi-private room, but the bed near the door was empty. In the bed by the window, Elektra lay with her eyes closed, still pale but less frighteningly so than a couple of hours ago. Her dark hair, sweaty and damp, spread out in a tangle on the pillow behind her. Even at such a moment, she was extremely beautiful, Juliet thought.

Ryder went up to her bedside and touched her shoulder. Her eyes flew open.

"Hi," he said.

"Hi."

Juliet hovered in the doorway. She wasn't sure if either of them was even aware of her, but she was ready to summon a nurse at Ryder's first sudden move.

But he didn't make a move. Instead, "Who knocked you up?" he asked, almost conversationally.

His wife's eyes closed again. "Anton Mohr."

"Well, son of a bitch," said Ryder, his hands clenched at his sides. Juliet noticed his wedding ring winking in the harsh electric light. As she had grown toward middle age, she had begun to marvel at marriage, which seemed to her (when sustained long enough, at least) a mysterious and confusing institution. From the acorn of romance grew an oak of reality that no more resembled that dear, exciting, cherished little seed than—well, than an oak resembles an acorn. She had sometimes wondered what a wedding ring would look like that metamorphosed as much as the relationship it symbolized.

"When were you going to tell me?" Ryder asked.

Opening her eyes once more, Elektra began to cry. "Get out," she said. "I feel shitty enough as it is."

She sat up a little to reach for a tissue from the bedside table and, for the first time, noticed Juliet.

"What the fuck are you doing here?" she asked.

Caught off guard, "I just wanted to make sure . . ." Juliet began, then could not finish the sentence. What the fuck was she doing here? It was obvious that there were wheels within wheels at work in the Jansch she could never understand. Nor (probably) did she have any good reason to try. She had distinctly understood Teri Malone to say that Olympia Andreades had been Anton's lover. Yet now her sister . . .

Juliet shook her head. "I'm sorry," she said. "I just brought Ryder over. I'll go now."

She went.

It was now almost nine o'clock on Wednesday night. Juliet took a cab straight up to Riverside and One

Hundred Sixth Street and (trying to pretend she was packing heat or knew jujitsu) walked briskly into the shadowy park. The Sculptors were playing the Conceptual Artists tonight, she found. And, apparently, creaming them.

When she arrived, the Sculptors were just taking the field. Under the tall electric lights, sky-blue "Sculptors Do It In Three Dimensions" T-shirts distinguished them from their adversaries. (The Conceptual Artists wore white T-shirts with a likeness of Ludwig Wittgenstein silkscreened on the back.) Murray went out to right field, and Juliet soon saw why. The first Conceptual Artist up sent a high fly his way. Murray plucked it from the air and whipped it to the Sculptor at second. Two outs. The next batter, underfed and nearsighted, with a buzz-cut, and a totem pole tattooed down his left arm, peered, swung, peered, swung, wiped his glasses and peered and swung again, but without hitting anything. The Sculptors were up again.

In the shuffle of changing sides, Juliet managed to catch hold of Murray.

"Hey, Jule!" He looked down at her, surprised and—she couldn't be mistaken—pleased. "You came!"

"I need to talk to you," she said, with more composure than she felt. The scene at the hospital had been extremely disturbing. She wanted to discuss it with someone who knew the dynamics involved, and it couldn't be Ruth, because Ruth would be appalled to learn Elektra had been pregnant and delighted she miscarried—she was bound to, since it meant her leading Estella could dance.

"Great. We'll be done in a half hour or so. Take a seat. You can be our fan," said Murray.

With a valedictory nod, he turned away again to hoot encouragement at Jennifer, a weedy young blonde in miniskirt, pierced nose, and Reeboks who had trotted up to home plate.

She had already let two balls and two strikes go by without taking a swing. Apparently, the Visual Arts League frowned on catcalls and heckling, but there was plenty of shouting and whistling in support of each team's own players.

Juliet sat on the Sculptors' bench, apparently the lone spectator. Murray certainly looked good in a mitt. She made herself turn her eyes elsewhere and recognized, at first base, the captain of the Conceptual Artists, who had recently created a work involving the Flatiron building and a large quantity of Oxford shirts. The *New York Observer* had run an enthusiastic review.

By the time the game ended, Juliet was in a better mood than when she had arrived.

Winded and sweaty, Murray plunked himself down beside her on the bench. "Want to have a drink?" He nodded toward the café set up for the summer on the concrete terrace above the sandy volleyball courts.

"Sure."

She waited while he assembled the team's softballs, bats, and other paraphernalia, then walked alongside him over the dim, slightly sloping paths. Even in the uneven electric light, she could see beads of sweat glistening in his curly hair.

"You guys certainly mopped the field with those Conceptual Artists," she said, feeling suddenly unwilling to explain what had brought her here.

Murray shrugged. "They were at a disadvantage. Their pitcher is doing a piece where he's on display in a stall in the meat district all week. You should come next Wednesday. We're playing the Color Field Painters. They really stink."

They sat down at a table beside the railing dividing the café from the courts and playing fields below. Beyond these lay the busy highway and beyond that, the gleaming Hudson.

"So what's the matter?" asked Murray. "You didn't come here to pick up fielding tips."

Juliet told him.

"Anton. Jeez," Murray said, when she got to the scene in Elektra's room. "Imagine the baby those two would have had."

Juliet nodded. She did not think Ruth would have spared a thought for that.

"The whole thing shook me up," she said.

"No wonder. What did Greg Fleetwood say?"

"Greg!" Juliet stared at him, stricken. "I totally forgot him."

Landis laughed, more merrily than Juliet thought necessary. "I'm sure he's figured out where she is by now," he said.

She dropped her head to the small table. A waiter came and she heard Murray order a gin gimlet. Grunts and thumps arose from a team of volleyballers on a court below.

Looking up, "I'll have a gin gimlet too," Juliet said. As the waiter left, she went on, "Listen, I'm worried for Elektra. That's what I want to talk to you about. It isn't my business, of course, but I really think Ryder may do some violence to her. Olympia told me he beats her, and now she's just lying there, like a sitting duck—lying duck—waiting for when he chooses to come back. I mean, he's her husband. The nurses are certainly going to let him in."

"Did he try to hit her just now?"

Juliet shook her head. "Not while I was there. But I keep thinking . . . I know it probably sounds silly."

"It does seem unlikely he'd attack in cold blood, since he didn't in the first heat of passion."

"I don't know. He took it so strangely. Almost like he wasn't surprised. I just feel it's irresponsible to do nothing. Except for the two of them, I'm the only one who knows what went on in that room tonight."

"When you say that Kensington didn't seem surprised, are you suggesting he already knew Anton Mohr had been his wife's lover?"

It was a policeman's question, and it made Juliet uneasy to have to answer it before she could weigh the implications of her reply.

"I'm not sure. He definitely was surprised when the doctor told him she had been pregnant. He almost fell off his chair. But he hardly batted an eye when Elektra said it was Anton's."

"What did he ask her, exactly?"

"He said, 'Who knocked you up?' or, 'So, who knocked you up?' Something like that."

"And when she said 'It was Anton'—"

"He said, 'Holy shit.' No, 'Son of a bitch,' he said. And he asked her when she was planning to let him know."

Their drinks arrived. Murray held his to his sweating forehead. "Knowing your wife is having an affair makes a hell of a good motive for whacking her lover," he said.

"I know. On the other hand—" Juliet paused and fell silent.

"Yeah? Go on, say it."

"On the other hand, if Elektra told Anton she was pregnant and he didn't jump up and down with joy, maybe she decided to punish him herself."

"By powdering the rosin," Murray added.

"Or spiking the Coke. And/or."

Murray considered, chewing on his slice of lime. "Just now in the hospital, did she look scared of Kensington?" he asked finally.

Juliet shook her head. "She looked too tired to be scared. Too sad."

"If you're concerned, why don't you go back and ask her tomorrow?"

"You think I should?"

"If you're worried about her. Go first thing in the morning."

Now Juliet was silent. First thing in the morning, she was supposed to bandage Sir Edward Rice's wounded leg and sneak him back into Lady Porter's house. Of course, Elektra had the claim that she was real on her side of the balance.

"I don't think she particularly likes me," she remarked. "You wouldn't want to drop in on her instead, would you?"

Landis merely raised his eyebrows.

"Oh, all right," Juliet said. "I'll go."

———

Visiting hours at St. Luke's–
Roosevelt (Juliet was glad to learn after Murray kindly put her into a
cab and gave the driver her home address) did not begin until eleven
in the morning. For a few happy minutes after hanging up on the
recording, therefore, she thought she would be able to spend a little
time, at least, with Sir Edward in the morning after all.

But then she realized Ryder (if he were as angry as she feared)
might not wait until the officially sanctioned hour. So she arose two
hours before she would normally have done, drank her coffee hastily,
went out, and hailed a taxi on Broadway.

The day was still pale but already uncomfortably warm. Cabs
were abundant and ordinary traffic sparse, as happens in the city in
summertime. Juliet arrived at St. Luke's well before eight o'clock
and found it was no trouble at all to slip up to the fourth floor. There
were plenty of civilians milling through the hospital: relatives waiting for patients in surgery, visitors to outpatient clinics, the usual
hapless caught up in the usual emergencies. Once upstairs, she simply ignored the nurses' station and walked purposefully down
the halls to Room 418. There were advantages to having a soft,
innocuous face and a smile that suggested bewilderment. What she
would have done if she had bumped into Ryder on the way she had
no idea.

She found Elektra alone and awake, her hair somewhat more
orderly, her frightening pallor gone. If her husband had beaten her
last night, it had not been on her face. Her complexion was smooth
and unbruised as she lay with her eyes closed and listened to the
Today show, which flickered on the television mounted high on the
opposite wall. At the sound of Juliet's footsteps, her eyes flew open
and she sat up a little. She appeared startled but not displeased to
discover Juliet.

"Am I disturbing you?"

Elektra reached for the remote and clicked the TV off.

"No. I thought you were the nurse's aide." Her feet moved restlessly under the sheet. Juliet supposed it must be strange for her to

rest in bed when movement and exertion were the constants of her life. "I asked to have somebody wash my hair."

"How do you feel today?"

"Pretty crappy. I lost my baby, you know." Tears swam in her eyes.

"I'm so sorry. It's a horrible thing. I—" Juliet paused, then, without quite meaning to, added, "I lost a baby myself once. It's awful."

Elektra's dark eyes were filled with tears, but she did not allow them to spill over. "Did you have another?"

"No." That, too, had been part of the trouble between Juliet and Rob, part of the reason the birth of his daughter, Jemima, had hit Juliet so hard.

Juliet's own eyes grew tearful and Elektra started to cry. Juliet moved forward and, not liking to sit on the bed, awkwardly stroked her hand while standing beside her.

"But I was older than you," she lied. "You have lots more time."

"Maybe." Elektra was silent a moment, then burst out again, "I don't understand what happened. I saw my obstetrician just two days ago. Everything was fine. And now . . ."

"Miscarriages are much more common than most people realize," Juliet said quietly, though doubtful whether this fact could be of any comfort. "They actually occur in as many as a fifth of pregnancies. Just a lot of them happen before people know they're pregnant."

Elektra said nothing. With a struggle, she worked to get hold of herself. She took her hand from Juliet and grabbed a tissue to wipe her eyes. She blew her nose and ran her fingers through her thick, dark hair. In less than a minute, she had recovered a large measure of her habitual composure. Her breathing slowed, her beautiful features resumed their usual expression—power at rest, Juliet supposed you would call it. If she had not seen the transformation herself, she would have said it was not possible for a woman in a hospital bed—

in a hospital gown!—to have so much poise, so much dignity. Inwardly, Juliet also tried to gather herself together. It was not easy to address the Firebird in a spirit of womanly solidarity.

"Listen, I hope you'll forgive me if I'm way off base here, but I couldn't help worrying after I left you yesterday. Your husband—I've gotten the idea he can be—" Her words broke off again, but really, what other way was there of putting it? "Violent," she finished at last. "I wondered if you were scared."

Elektra gave a small, sad smile. "Scared of Ryder?"

With a flash of insight, Juliet saw her meaning: After the death of her lover and the loss of their baby, what could she have to fear from an angry husband? So what if he hit her? As long as he didn't kill her . . . And maybe even that didn't seem to her such a terrible threat just now.

After a moment, Elektra went on. "Since you've asked, Ryder has taken a swing at me now and then. He's a fucked-up, self-pitying, ambitious, frustrated, big, small man. But he never hit me where it would show; that would be unprofessional. And I've always given him his own back." She gave the tight little smile again. "Sometimes, I thumped him first. And to be honest, I felt a little sorry for him last night. He always wanted to have a kid while he was still young himself. We tried for a long time, years. Dancing is great, but it's not forever. We wanted a family, even if it took me off stage for a while. But it was no good, we never got anywhere. So last night was kind of a kick in teeth for him that way."

Juliet would have thought it was a kick in the teeth to learn one's wife had a lover at all, but Elektra didn't mention this. Perhaps it was understood between them that fidelity was no longer expected.

Or perhaps not.

After a moment, thinking of Landis, she steeled herself and asked.

"I'm confused. Did Ryder already know about you and Anton?"

Was it her imagination, or did Elektra give a little look of fear before she jumped onto her high horse?

"Look, I know you're a friend of Ruth's and a donor to the Jansch and everything," the ballerina answered, once more as lofty as any snow maiden, "and I appreciate your coming over to see if I'm okay. But I really don't care to discuss my marriage further with you."

"Of course not. I'm so sorry."

For a moment, Juliet was appalled by her own behavior. Then she remembered that if someone had killed Anton Mohr—if Ryder had—that would be far more appalling.

"Listen, if you speak to Ruth," Elektra went on, her tone brisk, "could you please let her know I was planning to tell her about the baby at the end of this week? I wouldn't have let her choreograph the whole ballet on me and Hart. I was just waiting to make sure I didn't—" Elektra's tears welled up again and she blinked hard against them, "—didn't miscarry," she finished.

The timely arrival of a nurse's aide with a basin and a bottle of shampoo spared both the women another round of tears. Juliet wished Elektra good luck and swiftly headed home.

When Juliet got back to her apartment, she found three messages from Ruth on her answering machine, all sputtering and fuming about Elektra's having kept her pregnancy secret, all demanding to know where Juliet was and why she didn't pick up the phone.

Cravenly, Juliet had not phoned Ruth last night, hoping instead that Greg Fleetwood would get the honor of conveying the news of Elektra's miscarriage to her. It was a relief to find this had, in fact, happened. Unfortunately, though, Ruth did not seem to have calmed down much since then.

"When was she going to tell me?" Ruth shrieked, when Juliet

called her back. "Greg says she was three months pregnant! Was she waiting till opening night?"

Juliet relayed the ballerina's message on this point.

"Is she crazy? Five weeks to opening and she thinks that would have been time enough to recast?"

"Would you have had to recast?"

"Are *you* crazy? A pregnant Estella? That would be nice for the kiddies."

"Oh," said Juliet, considering. It was true; surely Elektra could not have gone on much longer without showing. "Well, at least you'd only have had to replace Estella," she observed, hoping to calm Ruth. "You'd still have had your Pip."

"Juliet, who do you think could dance this role with Hart except Elektra? He's six inches shorter than Kirsten Ahlswede—make that ten inches when she's on pointe. And she probably weighs as much as he does. How's he supposed to lug that around? I would have had to start all over again using—using God knows who. Kirsten and Nicky Sabatino, I guess. Jeez!"

"When does the doctor think she'll be back?" Juliet asked, trying to guide Ruth away from the disaster that might have been.

"She'll probably come home tomorrow," Ruth said grudgingly, apparently reluctant to stop complaining. "As long as she rests through the weekend, she's supposed to be okay by Wednesday. And by the way, her husband asked me a couple of days ago if he could miss rehearsal this Saturday," she added, seizing on another hardship.

"What for?"

"Didn't say. Just asked for a 'personal day.' I guess now he can spend it with her."

Juliet had said nothing as yet about the identity of the lost baby's father, and she did not intend to. That was a secret she had stumbled on entirely by chance. True, it added a bit to her ideas about the identity of the talcum powderer. But if either Ryder or Elektra were guilty, it was over and done with now. Maybe after *Great Expectations* opened, Juliet would share the information with Ruth. Till then, it could only distract her, the last thing she needed now. Juliet promised to come to rehearsal late that afternoon and after a few more minutes, the two women said good-bye.

chapter SEVENTEEN

"But the whole point of ambition,"
Ruth was saying, "is that it's deeply personal." Her spoon rattled restlessly in the porcelain cup that held her last, melting lump of ice cream. "It's an irresistible inner drive to achieve excellence, to be as great or even greater than the people who inspired you. That's ambition, that's what it means."

It was the last Sunday in August, and Ruth and Juliet were having lunch in the latter's kitchen. A month had gone by since Elektra's miscarriage and, to her own astonishment, Ruth had finished Act Three of *Great Expectations* two days ahead of schedule. She explained the miracle by saying the act was shorter than the first two and drew heavily on the vocabulary of movements she had already created for them. But Juliet believed that, like many artists, Ruth simply worked better in adverse circumstances than so-called optimal ones. The stress of events surrounding *Great Ex* actually helped. Look at Elektra Andreades: Her catastrophic loss and week-long absence had clearly concentrated her energies; after her return, she applied herself with a fierceness, and danced Estella with a proud, angry coldness, that Juliet could only chalk up to a broken heart.

And so Ruth Renswick's *Great Expectations* was now complete. All that lay ahead was letting the dancers learn how to move through the whole thing at once and working with them as they developed and deepened their characterizations. Then tech rehearsals, dress rehearsals and—surviving the premiere. The lunch in Juliet's kitchen (the women had been driven indoors by an ozone alert) was, in a small way, a kind of victory meal. Juliet having also (nearly) finished *London Quadrille*, the two were contentedly gorging themselves on a banquet of crûdités, hummus, tapenades, smoked trout, Portuguese rolls, ginger ice cream, and the kind of argument they liked best: theoretical, insoluble, and in no way intended to change each other's ideas.

"I don't think so," Juliet replied. "I think that's part of ambition, but it's a narrow view." She poured milk into her coffee. "I think most ambitious people, or many people, at least, are pushed by a need for social recognition, a need to have their value authenticated, or—what do I mean?—publicly labeled by other people."

Savoring the dispute, Ruth suspended her spoon above the table. "Other people they respect?" she asked.

"Any people. People they fear, people they admire, their mother and father, even people for whom they have utter contempt." Juliet stood and went to the fridge to put the remains of the trout away. "It's an alarming business, ambition. Think of a person who— I don't know, who writes advertising copy. He wants to hoodwink his audience into buying things they don't even need. Does he admire them? No. Does he feel a yearning to manipulate them, to vanquish them, to make them line up in droves? Yes."

"That person feels a need to buy a second home in the Hamptons," Ruth objected. "That's not ambition. Nobody's driven to write advertising copy."

"I disagree. I think that's exactly what does happen. People get in a job and they're given a challenge and—by God, that becomes the way they show their worth. They'll sell more paperclips than anyone else in the world, or issue more parking violations, or wash more lepers' feet, whatever it is. The house in the Hamptons is part of it, but it isn't the whole picture, not at all. Do you want more coffee?"

"I'm fine. Do you feel that way about Angelica Kestrel-Haven? Is writing her books the way you show your worth?" Ruth asked.

"Hardly," said Juliet. "If anything, I write them in spite of the way they make most people I know perceive me. Do you have any idea the contempt I get at dinner parties? How many people call my books 'bodice rippers' and 'Gothics' and ask me how long it takes me to 'grind one out'? I don't feel driven to be Angelica Kestrel-Haven at all. I just enjoy writing."

"You do?" Ruth asked, apparently shocked.

Juliet, sitting down again, answered, "Yes. Why are you so surprised?"

"Well, for one thing, you seem to be willing to use pretty near any excuse to get out of it."

Juliet, who had just returned from giving her lecture at the Association of University Departments of Folklore and Mythology annual meeting in Boston, laughed. The lecture was a good example of a junket she had said yes to just because it provided a dignified reason to desert her desk. "I didn't say it was easy," she answered. "I said I enjoy it. I do get—" Her voice dropped. "You know, I do get . . . the B word."

"Bored?"

"Blocked," Juliet whispered.

In retrospect, *London Quadrille* hadn't gone so badly—only a few weeks here and there spent at the Jansch to interrupt it, a few days of playing—oh, might as well say it, playing Nancy Drew. And she had only two more chapters to go. During *The Parisian Gentleman*, she had actually learned to program in HTML.

"But I usually like it," she took up again. "Most of the time, it's fun. Whereas being ambitious is not. Being driven to achieve is not fun."

There was a silence while Ruth took this in. Finally, "So?" she said.

"So doesn't it make sense to do something you enjoy?"

"Make sense?" Ruth repeated dubiously.

"Since you only live once? If you have the choice—not that most people do, but if you do—shouldn't you do the things that bring you pleasure?"

"Since you only live once, you should make it count," Ruth said firmly. "You should work your hardest and give your all. You should strive to be the best whatever-you-are that you can be. Give back to the field you love. Before you die, make the finest contribution you possibly can to whatever you care about. That's what you should do."

"No matter the personal cost? I don't see that."

"No matter."

Juliet shook her head. "You've spent too much time in ballet studios," she said, then instantly regretted it. It had been a relief to discuss something other than dance with Ruth.

"If people weren't driven, there would be no dance," Ruth said.

"Sure there would. It would just be different. Different kinds of dance. Like folk dance. You'd have that."

"There certainly wouldn't be any ballet."

"Sure there would. Or could. It just wouldn't be so insanely perfect."

Now Ruth shook her head. "Ballet is perfect. That's its nature. It's extreme, and it requires extreme effort. In your world, there would be no ballet, no *ballets*, no brain surgery—at least, no successful brain surgery—no rocket science, no hunger strikers, no—"

"No supermodels, no Green Berets, no religious fanatics, no burnout—" Juliet broke in.

"No achievement—"

"No uncomfortable achievement."

"No striving—"

"No unhappy striving—"

"It just wouldn't *work*," Ruth erupted in frustration, as Juliet rose and took the dregs of their ice cream away.

"Wouldn't work because—?"

"Because people *are* ambitious," said Ruth, "that's the way people are. They want to make their mark in the world, they want to shine, they want to be remembered. They want to make something worth making. *And* they want everybody to say, 'You made that? That is valuable! I couldn't have made that.' That's what people want, and they want it more than they want to be happy or comfortable or good or loved or any other thing. That's what I think."

"In other words, they want recognition."

"That's a piece of it. But it's mainly the thing itself."

"Some people."

"Some people, of course," Ruth allowed. "A lot of people would be happy to get by with whatever drivel gets a rise from other people. Of course not everyone is driven to excel. But for those who are, there is no choice but to do it. To try and work and push and claw and try some more until you drop. That's the way."

Juliet poured herself a fresh cup of coffee. "That's the way because we define it as the way," she said. "If our children were brought up differently, if society placed a greater value on happiness and less on achievement—"

"Then you'd have Polynesia," said Ruth scornfully.

"And what's wrong with Polynesia?"

"If every place were Polynesia, no one would know there was a Polynesia. There would be no one to find it. No explorers, no clipper ships, no astrolabes, no maps . . ."

Juliet shrugged. A scarcity of astrolabes did not trouble her.

"You shrug now, but you'd be crying when your period came and no one had invented Tylenol."

Juliet laughed. "Oh, that reminds me. What's the name of that medication people use for a yeast infection? It used to be prescription only?"

"Monistat?"

"That's it. Thank you. I've been so . . ." Juliet wriggled demonstratively. In the past four weeks, she must have gone through three gallons of yogurt, but it had only dampened, not eradicated the itch.

"Speaking of"—Ruth stopped and wriggled in imitation—"how's your love life?"

"Love life?" Juliet echoed, as if the concept were unfamiliar.

"You ever see Murray Landis again?"

"You know, I'm kind of pissed off at Murray Landis," Juliet said, with sudden energy. She had phoned him right after her second visit to Elektra at the hospital, left him a voice-mail message summarizing what she'd learned. But she'd never heard back from him. She didn't think he disliked her, so she had concluded he was afraid to see her. That didn't raise him in her estimation.

"Still?"

"No, again. A month ago, he said he'd call me and have me over to see his sculpture, but he didn't. I think there's something wrong with that guy."

"There usually is." Ruth laughed. "You know that old definition, that a novel is a work of fiction of a certain length with something wrong with it? Could we say that a man is a boy of a certain age with something wrong with him? Or is that horribly sexist?"

Juliet was about to suggest all adults were grown children with something amiss when the phone rang.

"I'll let the machine get it," she said. The machine was in the kitchen, noisy and impossible to ignore, and they sat waiting in silence through three rings till it clicked on.

Juliet's businesslike voice regretted her inability to get to the phone and invited the caller to leave a message.

Another click.

A bit of masculine throat-clearing.

Then, "Jule?"

Juliet jumped.

Except for the health-destroying ozone level, it was a perfect summer evening, the heat of the day peacefully rising as the twilight gently fell. Juliet entered Central Park as part of a gathering stream of playgoers flowing eastward between the tall, lush-leafed arcade of trees.

When he had phoned earlier that day, Murray explained that a friend of his who worked the park had just given him a pair of tickets to *Macbeth* for the evening at the Delacorte. He wondered if Juliet would like to come.

"I'd be delighted," Juliet said, wondering hard why the invitation had come now.

"Great," said Landis. "Unfortunately, I can't meet you ahead of time. I caught a murder yesterday. I'm going to have to work."

"That's no problem."

"Look for me at the Delacorte box office just before eight, okay?"

"Sure," said Juliet, and hung up.

"Catching" a murder, she took it, was a term of art meaning that a homicide had taken place in the precinct and it was a particular detective's turn to investigate it. She had dined on a slice of pizza on a bench near the Planetarium before strolling into the park.

In the Diana Ross Playground, near the entrance, a few children still squealed as they dashed through the sprinkling fountain in the dusk. A handful of cut flowers marked the site of the brutal attack, years before, on a young woman pianist. Tired dog owners, nannies, elderly strollers, quarreling couples lolled on the benches along the path to the theater. Farther in, hundreds of bicyclists and in line skaters zipped along the park drive, forcing the accumulating throng of pedestrians to wait for a red light at the crosswalk near Belvedere Castle, then scurry over ASAP, lest some velocity-delirious rollerblader run them over. Juliet, scurrying with them, caught herself wishing she could politely hitch her underpants down. Tomorrow, absolutely, she would give in and buy a box of Monistat.

And then she was there, where the fantastic gray stone blocks loom over the little lake, where Romeo and Juliet, a bronze tangle of lean, adolescent limbs, keep watch for Shakespeare. A hum of theatrical excitement mingled with the burble of cicadas. No one here had paid for a ticket: they were all free, given away to those (and only those) who had stood in line this afternoon, two tickets per customer, no more. It was as democratic, as pure a cultural event as the city affords, and the feeling among those gathered was correspondingly heady.

Landis rushed up to the box office a minute or two late, wearing a rancid sweatshirt and an expression of exhausted satisfaction. Juliet stood on tiptoe, meaning to peck at his cheek. At the same instant, he put out his hand to shake hers. There followed a moment of living cubism, a dizzying macedoine of hands and lips in closeup. Finally, Juliet grazed Landis's sweaty cheek with her temple, while he clutched a handful of her forearm.

They stepped back and smiled at each other, both a little pink.

"How's your case?" Juliet asked.

"Got him. Vicious little punk."

"Congratulations."

Murray carefully took her arm and guided her toward one of the theater's entrances. "It was a pleasure," he said. "Piece of crap took a knife to his sister because she was making it with a member of a rival gang."

"He killed her?"

"No, the boy she was making it with. But he carved her up pretty well. She'll be sleeping alone for a while."

Juliet was silent a moment. Then, "How did you find him so fast?" she asked. "How did you know it was him?"

"Talked to the victim's mother. She couldn't be more than thirty herself. The killer's fourteen. The mother was scared to say anything, of course, because they will come after her. But I never went to her place, so hopefully . . ."

Murray's words trailed off as he gave the tickets to an usher and was led to their seats. Juliet followed behind.

"How lucky that you were able to get him so quickly," she said, as they settled in. Their seats were ten rows back and dead center—suspiciously good. Juliet began to wonder if Murray's friend, being a police officer, had gotten special treatment after all.

Murray shrugged. "Most homicide cases, if they're going to be solved, you're going to make an arrest within forty-eight hours," he said. "After that, unless a new lead happens to come up, the case kind of gets shoved aside. You run with the fresh homicide, that's the rule. It probably shouldn't be that way, but—"

Murray shrugged again and Juliet knew he was thinking of Anton Mohr. It crossed her mind, as it had once or twice before, that she had never really thanked him for the exhaustive care with which he had conducted his investigation. She didn't want him to think she faulted his technique or zeal. Indeed, in the last month or so, even she had stopped believing that someone had committed murder.

But the lights were going down (and the moon coming up) and they hadn't even had a chance to look at their programs. She opened hers to glance at the cast list. Duncan, Macbeth, Lady Macbeth . . . And in a flash, that strange, intense, rage-filled little dance she had seen Hart Hayden perform so many weeks ago alone in the tiny rehearsal room returned to her vividly. Then, she had known it was familiar but couldn't place it. Now, suddenly, she recognized it: It was Iago's first-act solo in Lubovitch's *Othello*, a dance of furious frustration, thwarted ambition, and lethal envy.

Juliet returned her attention to the program, her mind relieved by this answered question, then puzzled all over again a moment later. *Othello* wasn't being danced by the Jansch this season.

Macbeth is not a very romantic play, and it wasn't particularly hard for Juliet and Murray to make their way home from it without surrendering to lust. The performance had been good and they had plenty to talk about.

Landis insisted on walking Juliet through the park and all the way to the door of her building. Then he stopped about five feet short of the awning, his arms folded against his lean chest, his strong hands tucked under his arms. He stood almost dancing with unease, nodding and smiling and saying, "Great to see you!" and "Thanks for coming on such short notice!" and eyeing the doorman as if terrified Juliet might throw her arms around him and smooch him good night. Juliet thought she might have been able to take him down by flinging herself at his ankles, but she certainly saw no way to get near his face.

Though she had been listening all evening for an explanation, nothing he had said tonight even hinted at why he had thought to offer her the extra ticket to *Macbeth* today, why he had called her now and not before. She didn't care to ask. His demeanor had been friendly, a bit more casual than before, perhaps, but otherwise unremarkable.

Keeping her distance, "Hey, when are you going to let me see your work?" she asked.

"Oh, God, sorry about that. I meant to call you and then I just . . . just never . . . just forgot, I guess . . ."

His words trailed off and Juliet thought he was not, perhaps, such a very good actor after all. He might have mixed feelings about letting her see his work, but he certainly hadn't forgotten to call her. Her idea that he was afraid to be alone with her was confirmed.

And, probably, with good reason. It had already occurred to her to offer him a drink; but a quick recollection of the heady thrill his gaze could elicit in her had made her think again. Better to follow his lead. The truth was, it had been so long since she had been strongly attracted to a man, just the smell, the shiver of sexual possibility in the air had been a pleasure. She thanked him again, waved, and went inside.

In the elevator, it occurred to her that a chaste, prudish man might make for an interesting Regency hero. Very interesting. Letting herself into her quiet apartment, she trotted up to her desk and jotted the thought down on an index card for her "future ideas" file. As she stood up to leave, she automatically hitched down her underpants. Clearly, she now had a raging yeast infection.

Yet, uncomfortable as the infection was, as vivid as *Macbeth* had been, as curious as she was about Murray Landis, she went to bed with her head full of the idea of a priggish Regency hero. Oh, yes, that would be fun! She lay awake for nearly an hour weaving a plot around the notion before she fell asleep.

In the morning, even before Ames arrived, Juliet called the pharmacy and asked them to deliver some Monistat ASAP. Then she made some tea and went to her study, where her reference section included an invaluable layman's guide to pharmacology. Did you have to use Monistat only at night? She seemed to remember some such requirement. Perversely, with the cure so close, the itch seemed worse now than ever. She didn't think she could stand to wait sixteen more hours. Maybe she could use it and work lying down?

Finding the book, she sat down with it in one of the leather armchairs and flipped through the pages. Librium, Lopressor, Luvox, Macrodantin, Mexitil, Mistenflo, Micronor, Modicon—

Mistenflo? For a brief, strange moment, the word seemed to hover in the air like a magic bird—a living thing that promised miraculous understanding.

Her breath quickened as she turned the pages back.

Like Cytotec, a brand of misoprostol. Inhibits production of stomach acid, protecting the lining. . . . Patients who must take nonsteroidal anti-inflammatory drugs, such as those with acute, chronic arthritis, may use Mistenflo to avoid development of ulcers. . . . Contraindications: Because it can induce miscarriage, Mistenflo MUST NOT BE TAKEN DURING PREGNANCY.

Mistenflo, you conceited fool. Juliet dropped the book into her lap, her itch forgotten. Not *mistenflûte*. Anyway, now that she thought of it, '*mistenflûte*' meant a person, like 'so-and-so.' Moreover, it had proved to be archaic. 'Truc,' 'machin,' that's what you said for 'thingamajig.'

For a long time, she sat immobile, thinking. Slowly, as if the past two months were a large, much-folded map she could only now lay flat and study whole, she began to see the flow and pattern of events. Observations she had scarcely acknowledged heretofore joined with words she had heard Ruth say only yesterday—words she herself had said—and knitted together to make a simple story. She stood and, almost as if in a dream, went up the stairs to her desk, where she turned the computer on and went to Medline.

"Misoprostol," she typed.

Up it popped, along with dozens of other abstracts: "The Brazilian Experience with Cytotec."

Juliet read. "In Brazil, where abortion is illegal, the synthetic prostaglandin misoprostol has been used, with and without medical supervision, since the early 1980s to induce abortion quietly and inexpensively . . ."

Brazil. Her mind raced back to the first day she had visited the Jansch. How could she have been such a dolt as not to have seen it before? Still, she would have to ask Elektra Andreades one question—no, two—just to be absolutely sure.

chapter

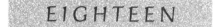

EIGHTEEN

It was 9:50 in the morning when Juliet phoned the Jansch.

"Gayle, I'm hoping to put together a little first-night celebration for Ruth," she improvised, when the receptionist answered. "Is there any chance I could talk to Elektra Andreades for a minute?"

As she had hoped, Elektra was there and class had not yet begun. Soon, she was on the line.

"Listen, I'm sorry to bother you," Juliet began, "and I'm really sorry to seem to be sticking my nose into your business, but . . ."

She asked. The answers were as she expected. Promising to explain later, she hung up and dialed Landis, home number first. His machine picked up. She left a message and tried him at work.

"Detective Landis is out," said a hurried voice.

"Do you expect him back today?"

"I got no idea."

She left a message there, too, carefully saying it had to do with official business, then decided it wouldn't hurt to do a little library research until he got back to her. Four or five years ago, when she was writing *Marianne, or, The Actor's Stratagem*, about a governess hired by a great lady of the Regency stage, she had done some research on Sarah Siddons in the theater collection of the Public Library for the Performing Arts at Lincoln Center. There, she had noticed other researchers leafing through thick files of clippings on living actors. Another phone call informed her that there was indeed a dance collection of such files, too; an hour later (pausing only long enough to use an applicatorful of the newly delivered Monistat, and the hell with whether you were supposed to stay horizontal), she had filled out a little slip of paper and handed it to the librarian.

In return, she received a fat sheaf of reviews, features, programs, photographs, and press releases collected by farsighted New York Public Library employees over the past fifteen years. The early photographs among these documents showed a small, rather scrawny youth with pale, lank hair around a heavily airbrushed face, a youth who (the accompanying texts explained) had grown up in Fort Pillow, Tennessee.

Slowly, Juliet leafed through the clippings, studying the bits of frail newsprint as closely as if they had been relics of a forgotten civilization. There was no native-son-makes-good piece that she could find from the Nashville *Courier*, or even the Fort Pillow *Star*. There were no interviews with proud parents or siblings either, and only a brief word from a retired, former ballet teacher in Memphis. So that was that. Juliet looked up to find herself gazing into the eyes of a bust of Nijinsky. She shivered a little in the library's air-conditioned air.

Yet even as she worked out the details—even as, in her mind, she explained it all to Murray—she was aware that no court would consider the evidence she had in hand proof of anything, let alone felony assault, manslaughter two, and (if her memory served, at least) murder. She handed the file back to the incurious clerk behind the window and headed home, as Angelica K-H might have put it, plunged in thought. The weather had turned breezy and the ozone alert had been lifted at dawn, so she decided to walk. Her cell phone rang just as she entered Riverside Park.

She sat down to answer on a bench not far from where a man lay stretched out asleep in the shade of a giant oak. From another tree, a bold squirrel squarely eyed her, evidently mistaking her for some human friend of his.

"Murray, it was Hart," she said into the phone. "Hart Hayden killed Anton Mohr."

He said he would meet her in ten minutes on the top of Mount Tom, the rocky outcrop at the corner of Eighty-third Street and Riverside Drive that Edgar Allan Poe, in his "Raven"-writing days, was said to have climbed in order to gaze at the Hudson River. Glad she was wearing sneakers, Juliet walked the remaining half mile, then picked her way up the mount (called by locals "Rat Hill," for good reason) over broken glass, empty potato-chip bags, and spent condoms.

The wind sighed voluptuously through the leaf-laden trees, dusty now at the end of summer and thick with a worn heaviness. Murray, looking un-coplike in black Levis and a white T-shirt, was already waiting at the peak of the hill. Their eyes met, then skidded away; as if by tacit, mutual consent, neither tried to greet the other with anything more personal than a spoken "Hi." Murray had spread a denim jacket out over the rough, dirty schist, and he gestured to Juliet to sit here, then seated himself cross-legged on the bare rock a few feet away. Below them, the strip of trees sighed and the highway hummed. A red tug pulled a laden barge up the churning river.

"So spill it," Murray said.

"Okay." She closed her eyes, then fixed them on the barge as she tried to get her thoughts in order. "As motives for murder go," she started, still gazing at the river, "it was rather a noble one. And so simple, it was hard to spot.

"I just visited the Library for the Performing Arts. Hart Hayden grew up in rural Tennessee, the youngest of six kids on the family chicken farm. He was short, he was scrawny, and he had a case of acne bad enough to scar his face forever. His real name, if you'll believe it, was George Washington. His sexuality was, I imagine, ambiguous. And he adored ballet. You can guess what his adolescence must have been like.

"But he had grit. He got himself to a local dancing school and he got himself out of Tennessee. On scholarship at a prestigious arts academy in North Carolina, he met Elektra Andreades, a girl petite enough to make him look tall. He changed his name, invented Hart Hayden. With ambition and talent, he and Elektra made themselves stars of American ballet. Elektra married, but Hayden lived for dance, setting aside his sexual life, his personal life, aspiring to nothing more. His height was a disadvantage, but, thanks to Elektra, he coped with it well. There was only one lack in his career: No choreographer ever found him inspiring, no one ever created a dance on him, for him. When he retired, he would leave behind no permanent mark. And that prospect, after all he'd done, all he'd given up, haunted him painfully.

"Enter Ruth Renswick. A few years ago, she came to the Jansch and remounted an old piece of hers called *Cycles*. Hayden had just the look she wanted, and she used him prominently. He was great. Flash forward a couple of years. The Jansch commissions Ruth to create a full-length *Great Expectations*. Now Hayden's prayers are answered: who would Renswick cast for Pip but him? For once, his size and slightness were on his side. He was Pip. He even came from a similar background. And he knew Ruth liked him."

Juliet paused and stole a look at Murray to see if he seemed interested. He was frowning at the promenade, apparently watching a couple of kids on bikes there, his dark face, with the strange, flat cheekbones, unreadable.

Juliet made herself go on, switching to the present tense in hopes it would liven things up. "But when the time comes," she recommenced, "Ruth announces the first Pip will be Anton Mohr. Hayden is stunned. But he's a scrapper, and he makes up his mind to show her her mistake. He does have the part of second Pip, and luckily, she's choreographing with both casts. From the start, he extends himself for her, works tirelessly, offers inventions, solutions. But she doesn't see it. Weeks go by, and Anton—despite his relative ineptness as a classical ballet partner—is still her darling.

"So Hayden gets a bright idea—a bright, nasty idea. He buys some powdered pigment or grinds up some brown cosmetic, eyeshadow probably, and mixes it with talcum powder. This he takes to the Jansch. He waits for his moment. It arrives when Anton is scheduled to dance alone in Studio Three just after a full ensemble session. During the changeover, Hayden dumps the powder into the rosin box. Mohr takes his fall, injures himself and—voilà, Hayden's chance to shine.

"Again, he works his tail off for Ruth. He even takes the trouble to cultivate me, her friend and advisor, to get me to like him. But Ruth still doesn't get the picture. Anton is her star, and as soon as he's healed, she not only reinstates him, she makes Hayden teach him what he missed—the very steps Hayden himself devised. He's seething, but he does it. He also thinks up a second plan.

"Now it's the day of the run-through. Good news for Hart at the start of rehearsals: Mohr knows the steps, but he stinks. Hope springs. Maybe Ruth will ask Hayden to dance Pip in the run-through after all? But after the break, Anton suddenly catches fire. He gives a magnificent performance; everyone in the studio stops and stares. Ruth is delighted. At the lunch hour, Hayden goes off to the farthest little studio alone and, writhing with envy, relieves himself by dancing Iago's first act solo from *Othello*.

"He also makes up his mind to set in motion his second plan, his ace in the hole. Just before the run-through, he'll slip a hit of Ecstasy to Mohr. Where did he get it? No problem: his roommate is the company drug dealer. Hayden can't just hand a pill to Mohr, so he's brought it in powdered or capsule form. During the little reception, he finds a pretext to get near Mohr and nimbly, surreptitiously drops the drug into his habitual Coca-Cola. Slipping the stuff in quietly is child's play for Hart, a famously graceful dancer whose current job is to leap up and down from tables, pretend to catch oranges, actually catch flying women—dancers are deft, agile, they're practically jugglers. So now, Mohr will wreck the run-through and Ruth will finally see the error of her ways. But instead—"

"Hold on a second." Landis had been looking impatient for several minutes, and now he burst out at last. "I specifically asked Ruth about competition among the dancers. She says, and it stands to reason, that dancers are disappointed all the time. They're always competing. And Hayden himself admitted to me it bothered him not to be cast as first Pip. He was perfectly upfront about it. That type of frustration is their way of life. Ruth said so, and I have to believe her."

"Yes, but that's where Ruth's very familiarity with the dance world played her false. Because what she didn't know is that, after this year, Hart Hayden will never dance professionally again. Max Devijian told me, in confidence, that his knees have had it. Another season could cripple him for life.

"And Hayden is one of those artists who truly are dedicated to their art. It wasn't only personal ambition that motivated him; it was devotion to ballet itself. The way he saw it, he could create a better Pip than Anton Mohr. He knew Pip, he understood him, and he believed it would be an irretrievable loss to ballet if he didn't define Pip in dance forever. Hart committed his crimes in the very name of dance. That's what was so misleading. I kept thinking dancers don't kill for a part, as you say. But one might—if his art was his life.

"I misjudged Hart. Maybe you did too. He's very smart and charming and controlled, but inside, he's one of those coiled-up people whose drive springs from horror of their own roots. He grew up an outcast, a weirdo isolated from his peers. He had transformed himself, but the core of rage he built up as a child never left him. In other words, he's a much, much more extreme personality than the persona he created for himself."

Murray looked more interested than he had previously. "So talk," he said, gesturing impatiently.

"Okay. So unfortunately, Anton dies. It's nothing Hart meant to happen, and it makes him plenty nervous. But what's done is done, and he didn't come all this way to lose his nerve now. Finally—finally!—Ruth makes him the first Pip. He throws himself into the part passionately, dances as if possessed, to quote Ruth. And everything is peachy. Until, hardly more than a week later, Elektra tells him she's three months pregnant."

"She told him?"

Juliet nodded. "I called her this morning to ask. He's the only one she did tell. They're closer than brother and sister, I think, and she thought he deserved a heads-up. Oh, and by the way, I also asked her whether Ryder was auditioning for another company. I had a hunch that's why he was so secretive and jumpy. And he is; in the spring, he'll be moving to L.A. They had already agreed to divorce.

"Anyway, naturally, Hart tried to talk Elektra into an abortion. He said it was a mistake to have a baby with Ryder at this point, it wouldn't save their marriage, it would ruin her career and so on—Elektra didn't tell him Ryder wasn't the father—but she had already made up her mind.

"So Hayden looks ahead. Elektra was barely showing, if she was showing at all; but if she was already thirteen weeks along, by the time the season got under way, she'd be more than four months. No way could she dance Estella. And—this is important—no way could he dance with anyone else. Kirsten Ahlswede is half a foot taller than he is. Even if she could find one, Ruth's not going to start with a new Estella, and Hayden knows it. If Elektra doesn't dance, he doesn't dance. And Anton would have died for no reason. Hayden is like our friend Macbeth now—'stepped so far in blood that, should he wade no more, returning were as tedious as go o'er.' "

"But what can he do?" asked Landis. "Black magic?"

"Ah, now that's the clever part. You see, Hart has danced with the Ballet Rio. I knew he had some connection to them, because he was wearing a Ballet Rio T-shirt the first time I met him. When I looked him up at the library just now, I found he was a guest artist there three years ago. And in Brazil, a drug called misoprostol, a synthetic prostaglandin, is commonly used as an abortifacient. It's a well-known resource; he could easily have learned about it from any of the dancers.

"Now, misoprostol, which is known in this country by the brand-names Cytotec and Mistenflo, is used here to prevent the development of ulcers. It's quite commonly prescribed and widely available—unlike, for example, RU-486. No doubt Hart would have tried that if he could have gotten hold of some. But misoprostol is far less high-profile. Elderly people with chronic arthritis often take it, because the medication they need for the arthritis tends to cause ulcers."

"And dancers tend to get arthritis," Landis filled in.

"Precisely. In this case, it was Victorine Vaillancourt—"

Juliet faltered momentarily. During most of her recital, she had kept her eyes on the river, the park, the sky. But she had just felt Landis's eyes on her and had taken another glance at him. The look on his face now showed keen, pure, appreciative admiration. It was very pleasant to her.

A moment passed before she could look away again and finish, "Victorine Vaillancourt takes Mistenflo."

"And how did you know that?"

"Ruth happened to mention it to me the day of the talcum powder incident."

"And how would Hayden have known?" Landis's eyes, too, were once more on the scenery.

"Why shouldn't he? He's worked with Victorine for years and years. And Mistenflo is taken with meals. He must have seen her take it dozens of times, maybe hundreds. All he had to do was steal a couple of pills from her. Which I happened to hear him doing."

Juliet described the afternoon some five weeks before when she had gone to Victorine's door planning to make use of the privacy of her office. The familiar rattling inside, she now knew, had been the sound of the pills spilling out of the bottle. And she had smelled Hayden, too, though she hadn't stopped then to analyze the sensation.

"Paco Rabanne, Neutrogena, and his particular sweat," she told Murray. "That was him."

"Can you really tell that?"

Juliet closed her eyes and sniffed. "Ivory soap," she said, "Mennen deodorant. And . . . what are you wearing that's made of leather, new leather? Shoes?" She opened her eyes.

"It's a new wallet," said Murray, producing it, half incredulous. He shook his head. "Amazing. And how did you know that the rattling pills were Mistenflo?"

"Oh, that." Juliet was annoyed to feel herself blush at this reminder of her error and her fatuous self-congratulation about it. "Later that afternoon, I happened to hear Victorine muttering to herself in French as I went down the hall past her door. I thought she was saying, 'Now where are my thingamajigs?' But I made a little translation mistake." Her blush deepened. "What she really said was, 'Where are my Mistenflos?' "

"Hm," said Murray. He sounded less than convinced.

"You can easily ask her if any were missing," Juliet pointed out. "Anyway, now Hayden had to get the Mistenflo into Elektra's system. And there he was lucky again. He has a routine of feeding his partner little bits of food. That first day I met them, I saw him give her something—it looked like a Rice Krispie or a sunflower seed, something tiny. Evidently, he broke up the Mistenflo and put the fragments into raisins, because that's what I saw him feeding her in the dancers' lounge later that day. And that's what she complained the next day he'd been forcing her to eat. She had a cold, too, don't forget.

"By the way, all this took a toll on Hayden's nerves. The day he stole the pills, he actually dropped Lily Bediant. Anyhow, by the end of the next afternoon, the medicine had done its work. Elektra miscarried."

Landis gazed at the rock, his expression thoughtful. "According to the most recent court decisions, killing a fetus is legally considered murder, you know," he said.

"Yes, I thought I remembered reading that."

There was a longish silence.

"And that's it?" Landis finally asked.

"What's what?"

"That's your theory, that's why you phoned me today?"

Juliet felt a stirring of anger and forced it down. "Yes," she said evenly.

Landis finally raised his eyes and looked at her directly. "Well, it's an interesting story," he said, his accent dropping into Brooklynese, "an ingenious story, an elegant story, and you tell it very well. That stuff about the Brazilian abortion pills was especially entertaining."

Juliet was immediately outraged by his choice of the word 'entertaining,' but even more to hear him deliberately pronounce the preceding word 'ekspecially.' A Harvard graduate! Really, that was taking folksiness too far.

Meantime, he was going on, "But Jule, I gotta say, what you've got here is mainly guesswork. Women miscarry. Elektra could have lost the baby on her own. Anton could have taken the E himself. Practically anyone could have rigged the rosin box."

"I realize that, but who could have done all three? Who would have?" She struggled to keep her tone neutral, dispassionate. "That's what made me see it. It's like three transparencies. If you lay all three down, one over the next, the only suspect whose trajectory, whose storyline, hits the mark all three times is Hart Hayden."

But Landis only shrugged.

"Look," he said, "your brainwork is impressive. But the key to making a charge stick is evidence, okay? If you're right, the Mistenflo ought to have shown up in Elektra's blood tests. I'll check with the doctor at St. Luke's. I'll ask Victorine Whosy if she lost some pills. I doubt Frank Endicott would even notice a couple of missing hits of

Ecstasy, but I can try him, too. Assuming anything turns up positive, I can call Hayden in, give him a little extra going over. But I have to tell you, without some kind of physical evidence, you don't have a case. Are you ready to swear out a written statement? Face him in court?"

Juliet had not quite considered this consequence before. It was one thing to work matters out intellectually and tell Landis about it, another to become a formal witness in criminal proceedings. She thought of Ruth, who had asked her for help with *Great Expectations*, not to derail it at the last moment by demanding the arrest of her leading man.

Then she remembered Elektra, inert, the pool of blood spreading around her.

"Yes," she said, "I am."

Landis called her that evening, at about seven p.m. There was no hope any trace of Mistenflo would have shown up in the samples of Elektra's blood taken at the hospital, he reported: Not only would a routine screening have failed to show such a thing, Dr. Chen had explained that the only lab she knew of that could even test for it was in Montreal. Besides, the substance would have been entirely metabolized within about two hours of Elektra's ingesting it.

Victorine Vaillancourt did remember wondering, one afternoon a month or so ago, if she'd somehow misplaced a couple of Mistenflo tablets. But she had later decided she must have transferred them to the pill-case she carried in her purse. She kept quite a bit of Mistenflo about her, at home, in her office, in several pocketbooks she used, because she needed it so regularly. She certainly could not swear at this late date that even one pill had been stolen.

As for Frank Endicott, he had actually laughed when Landis asked him about a missing hit or two of Ecstasy. Then, remembering he was talking to the law, he had explained more soberly that (in those old, old days when he had dealt in illicit drugs), he did not keep such detailed inventories of his stock.

And that was that.

"I'm sorry to say it, Jule, 'cause I like your theory, I really admire the way you put it together," said Murray. "You could even be right. But what you got is what we police call bupkis. Anyway, even if Victorine knew she lost some pills, I never heard of a smell-witness."

"Yes, that's very amusing."

"Don't take it out on me, sweetheart. I'd grill the guy all night if we had a smidge of real evidence. If you had gotten that dunce Peltz to take the dance bag with him, we'd of had a clear chain of evidence and, who knows, maybe we could of used what we found there to—"

"But I never tampered with anything—"

Landis had ignored the interruption and was continuing, "—to build a case. But as it is, it could be tainted evidence, and I got no cause to pursue him. I'm sorry, Jule," he said. "Sometimes the bad guys win."

c h a p t e r

NINETEEN

On the morning of Tuesday, Sep-
tember seventh, the day of the gala opening of the Jansch Repertory
Ballet Troupe's sixty-second season in New York, Juliet sent Ruth a
dozen roses and a card wishing her triumph on a Dickensian scale.

Ruth called just before noon. "Thanks for the flowers. Do you
know what projectile vomiting is?"

"Why?"

"Because that's the point I'm about to reach. I'm so nervous I
could—I don't know what. So nervous I could scream."

"Why don't you?"

There was a pause. Then, "Hold the phone away from your
ear," Ruth instructed.

Juliet obeyed just in time to save herself from receiving the full
force of an ear-piercing shriek.

"Holy cats!" she said, when the line had stopped reverberat-
ing. "Do you feel better?"

"Yes, actually, I do."

"Great. Now go enjoy tonight."

"Thank you, Juliet."

Juliet had invited Murray to attend
the premiere of *Great Expectations* with her as a sort of olive branch,

a handsome, generous gesture intended to show she had no hard feelings about his refusal to act further on her theory about Hart Hayden.

A week had passed since that day on Mount Tom, and though she still believed she was right—and still hoped that somehow, the truth could be made to come to light—she actually had forgiven Landis quite a bit. Even that stupid crack about the smell-witness. (Anyway, the phrase would be "nose-witness," wouldn't it?) After a certain amount of fuming and indignation, she had concluded that, once again, he was only doing his professional best. If Murray said the law needed more to go on, it must be so. All the same, she had Caroline Castlingham dump a pitcher of milk punch onto the Earl of Suffield's head.

Inviting him to join her, it had not occurred to her that he would wear a tuxedo. Murray Landis in a tuxedo was a sight for which she had not prepared herself. But when he came to the door to fetch her, there he was in living black-and-white, looking lean and streetwise and hard and elegant and just generally as if he had walked out of a print ad for the male gender. Any remaining grudge she harbored against him disappeared like smoke as she silently thanked whatever impulse had made her put on her slinkiest dress (her only slinky dress, more accurately), the silver one with the sheer, beaded bolero and a long slit up the side of the embroidered skirt. One of the nicest things about staying away from the Jansch this last little while had been the gradual healing of her self-image. She felt soft and fragrant and pretty, and nothing she saw in Landis's face made her feel otherwise.

"Brawcha an awkid," he announced, bringing forward a clear plastic box of a kind Juliet had not seen since high school. Inside was a deep violet orchid fixed artfully to a pale lavender ribbon. Keeping his body a minimum of three feet from hers at all times, Murray opened the box, reached out his arms and tied the corsage to her wrist. It was a somewhat delicate operation, requiring her to turn her wrist up and submit to being tickled slightly by the accidental brushing of his calloused but dexterous artist's fingers.

A curious pleasure tingled through her. Obviously, he had understood the spirit in which she had invited him. And the orchid, with its associations to a long-gone world, made her feel shy and tender. It was just like Landis, in a way, to bring something at once so innocent and so layered with cultural meaning. Finding herself a little lost for words, she could only smile her thanks at him. He smiled back, apparently equally pleased by her response.

Juliet moved away to fetch a pashmina shawl from the front hall closet. The weather was still warm and summery during the days, but the evenings could get cool, and Cadwell Hall, as she recalled, could be positively frigid.

"Dr. Bodine?"

Ames had clumped in suddenly from the direction of the kitchen, a towering heap of long-stemmed stargazer lilies in her arms. In Juliet's absence, she would be in charge of overseeing the activities of the caterer, the florist, and the half dozen other professionals who had already begun to prepare the apartment for the party set to begin past midnight. "Did you want these in the glass vases or the tall baskets?"

"Oh, the baskets, I think, but see what the florist says," Juliet replied. She turned back to Murray, intending to introduce him properly to Ames, and saw that his face had gone abruptly dark and angry, as if something had offended him. It was the huge sheaf of lilies, she realized an instant later, which he read as dwarfing his wrist corsage. A flash of reciprocal anger surged through her at what seemed to her his willful obtuseness, his self-centered childishness— as if her having purchased flowers in bulk meant she could not be touched by his single bloom. She had told him she was planning an after-the-show party for the *Great Ex* ensemble. (She had decided early last week to make this impromptu lie to Gayle a reality after all.) Did he imagine she would offer them popcorn and beer in a room strung with crêpe paper streamers?

She felt her own jaw clench and took hold of his arm rather roughly. "We should go now," she muttered. "Ames, I'll be reachable by voice mail on the cell phone."

For the next half-hour, conversation between the bristling pair wilted. Neither cared to acknowledge the disappointment each had experienced; neither could put it out of his mind. But the sight of Cadwell Hall filled to its topmost tier with glittering, excited balletomanes (and an acknowledgment in Ruth's notes in the program of the "irreplaceable aid and comfort" Juliet Bodine had provided during the creation of this *Great Expectations*) did something to lift Juliet's spirits, at least, and once the performance began, both left their personal concerns behind and plunged willingly into a sustained, thrilling act of imagination.

It was extraordinary, Juliet thought, watching from the first row of the mezzanine, how the orchestral music, the flow of the narrative, the scenery and grandeur of the stage, even the electricity of the audience infused the scenes she had watched so often with new life. In the time since she had last been in the studio, the dancers had subtly adjusted their movements and expressions to create real characters, so that the drama Ruth had choreographed into each interaction was increased tenfold. Pip's initial encounter with the desperate convict, Magwitch, was as vertiginous as the scene in Dickens itself. A vivid concatenation of lighting, projections, and quasi-grotesque choreography created the fire that burned Miss Havisham; later, parallel effects in fluid greens and blues engulfed the stage as Magwitch and his nemesis, Compeyson, struggled underwater. Again and again, the audience could be felt to stiffen, gasp, relax as a mass. The humor Ruth had incorporated, most of it in Act One, evoked the sorts of smiles that almost but not quite rise to audible laughter. The music, rehearsed in the last few days under the supervision of the composer himself, was superbly played.

And the dancing was vigorous, passionate, exquisite. Ryder made a darkly complex Magwitch, Lily a chilling Havisham. Best of all were Elektra and Hart, she a girl imprisoned by her own inflexible, heartless pride, he a revelation of (by turns) youthful naïveté, yearning, foolish romanticism, brutal ambition and, finally, strength.

Watching them, Juliet's consciousness oscillated weirdly, flickering from the perception of Hart as a dancer to Hart as killer. Art and morality, indeed. (Or artistry and height!) But she could not think long about even that, so absorbed was she by the work Ruth had made, and so happy for her.

The applause at the end of the first two acts was enthusiastic, and the milling crowds that wandered the Hall at intermission were palpably excited, but nothing prepared Juliet for the response to the final curtain. The audience roared and shot to their feet en masse, beating their hands together with that peculiar communal rapture people sometimes achieve at a successful premiere. As the dancers came out for their bows, the audience yelled bravo and brava and bravi with lusty pleasure—bravi for the corps, bravi for the soloists, brava for Lily Bediant (a lavish bouquet was handed up to her from the orchestra), and for Elektra Andreades (ditto).

As Pip, Hart was, of course, the last to take his bow. The house went wild at the sight of him. Later, people would agree he had never danced so brilliantly, so viscerally; it was the singular sort of performance one never forgets. He took a shallow, rather Victorian bow at first, then another, then finally, as the applause thundered on, a deep, theatrical one. His pale hair soaked with sweat, his face glistening, he looked up to the highest tier and around the house, held his hand to his heart, smiled and bowed again, then took Elektra's hand and drew her forward with him. Finally, he dropped to one knee beside her and kissed her fingertips. As he stood again, Juliet (like everyone else in the place, still standing as well) thought she saw an almost feverish glittering in his eyes. A trick of the light, she supposed.

The curtain dropped and rose again, and then began the parade of behind-the-scene players onto the stage: the conductor, the composer, Greg Fleetwood, and, finally, Ruth, looking small and unlike herself in a formal gown. She grimaced, unable to come any closer to the gracious, grateful smile she should have produced, then gave a bow that reminded everyone she also had been a great dancer. Max Devijian walked out on stage with a gigantic bouquet for her and, finally, the curtain fell for the last time.

All their former constraint washed away by the past three hours, Juliet and Landis dawdled at their seats, gazing down at the tops of the heads of those decamping from the orchestra and comparing notes on what they had heard and seen. Occasionally, someone Juliet knew interrupted them and she performed an offhand introduction. Once, Murray nodded coolly to an acquaintance of his own. He showed himself to be more adroit at the required, meaningless meeting-and-greeting than Juliet would have expected, though she did notice his Brooklyn accent was at its peak.

The Jansch had arranged a Champagne reception for the company and a select (but large) set of patrons, donors, and board members to take place on the stage the moment the house was cleared—the sort of event that kept contributions coming in—but Juliet felt she had better skip this and get home to prepare for her own celebration. The only person she really wanted to see anyway was Ruth, and Ruth would be swamped here with admirers bent on claiming a moment of her triumph.

"You'll come with me, won't you?" Juliet asked Landis as, at last, they began to make their way downstairs to the lobby.

Murray made a doubtful face. "I don't know. You gotta remember, I interviewed a lot of these folks officially. I might make them uncomfortable."

"So what?"

"So it's their party, isn't it? Wouldn't my turning up sort of— dampen things?"

For a moment, she could think of nothing to say. It was a point, she supposed. But an irritating point. And she could not help but suspect it had more to do with his general skittishness about her than any great sensitivity to the feelings of the dancers.

"Oh, fine," she muttered, at length. In silence, they worked their way across the crowded lobby and out the heavy doors. By arrangement, Ames had sent a car from the service Juliet used, and as they emerged into the clear, still-warm night, she spotted it duly waiting a dozen feet away.

"Can I give you a lift somewhere, at least?" she asked. "Or are you afraid that will dampen something, too?"

Murray shook his head. "I'm just trying to make sure your party is fun," he said.

"For whom?" He opened the car door for her. She allowed herself to look full in his eyes for a moment. "I would like you to be there."

He gave a small smile. "Then I'll come later on. After things get going."

He helped her into the car, waiting while she tucked a fold of her long skirt safely inside the frame.

He leaned down. "You look very beautiful tonight," he said, then slammed the door.

Teri Malone, Juliet later learned, had spread the word among her colleagues that Ruth's friend Miss Bodine lived in a sort of urban Taj Mahal no one among them could afford to miss. It was partly to this, partly to the dancers' general inclination to party, that she owed the massive attendance at her celebration. The dancers began arriving at about twelve-thirty a.m., corps members first (these being the least sought-after at the official do), then soloists (complaining bitterly of having to chat up the donors right after having had to perform), second cast, Patrick, Lily Bediant, and, finally—one on each of Ruth's arms—Elektra and Hart themselves.

Juliet had already experienced that heady hostess' liftoff that makes local geography swirl and derails any sense of time. People were wandering about on both floors and the terrace of her home, in and out of her living and dining room, up in the sitting room outside her office and—with loud exclamations at the sparkling view—out of doors. Surprisingly, but rather usefully, she found that Teri Malone had set herself up as a sort of junior hostess. Teri had observed and remembered much more of the apartment than Juliet would have thought, and every few minutes, the dancer's small, whistly voice could be heard advising a newcomer on the location of a drink, a bathroom, or phone. Juliet began to see how Teri had won Lily Bediant's confidence. She was deferential in a most agreeable, dignified way, and even if you knew she was trying to catch at your coattails a bit (Juliet suspected she wanted an introduction to Portia Klein), she was not at all unpleasant to have around.

After considerable thought, Juliet had decided on a menu of Gershwin and Cole Porter for the music upstairs, Billie Holiday and Fats Waller for the floor below. The caterers were offering a cold but very substantial meal in the dining room; a full bar had been set up there and another upstairs. Ames, formidable in a dark silk suit and operating from the kitchen, had the staff well in hand. Juliet's only complaint was the smell of the flowers, which she had asked the florist to try to limit, but which was quite overwhelming. She had just decided to run up for a smoke on the terrace when Ruth and her two leading dancers arrived.

"Sweetie!" Ruth threw her arms around Juliet with rare exuberance, kissing her on both cheeks. "You're a genius! I'm a genius!" She gestured to Hart and Elektra to follow her inside. "And here are two more geniuses. Weren't they fabulous?"

Juliet embraced her friend with a deep sense of satisfaction. Yet, at the same moment, the sight of Hart Hayden crossing her threshold unsettled her badly, scared her in fact, she found. She felt her palms go cold and damp. How could she have failed to anticipate this? She believed he had murdered, twice. Must she now make him comfortable, let him roam freely in her apartment?

As Ruth came inside, first one, then another of the company who chanced to be near the front hall caught sight of her and began to applaud. Drawn by the sound, others appeared from the library and the living room, also clapping and cheering. As Juliet escorted Ruth past them and into the dining room, a sort of corridor of cheering dancers formed around them. Ruth laughed and bowed, as loose and happy as Juliet had ever seen her. But pleased as she was for her friend, Juliet's thoughts were still with Hart. He had stepped back and clapped with the rest of them, as had Elektra; but his blue, intelligent eyes struck Juliet as strange, freighted with a swaggering, bellicose, reckless triumph.

Ryder had come out from the dining room and saluted his wife with a calm, congratulatory kiss on the cheek, a far friendlier greeting than Juliet had seen in the past. She supposed his imminent move to Los Angeles had lessened the tension between them.

In the dining room, the applause at last died down and was replaced by ordinary party chatter.

"Oh, my God, I am so relieved!" Ruth whispered to Juliet as the others went back to enjoying themselves. "I wouldn't do this again for a million dollars. Where's the vodka?"

Juliet hastened to fetch food and drink, but her glance kept shifting uneasily to Hart, now standing by the bar with a newly poured highball in his hand. A moment ago, he had given her a quick, friendly smile, and she had tried to return it naturally, reminding herself that he could not possibly know her suspicions.

And yet . . . She wondered if Landis might be anywhere she could reach him by phone. She didn't know him well enough to guess what he would do to kill an hour or two in midtown in the middle of the night. She comforted herself with the fact that it was already well past one. If he was coming at all—and he'd said he was—surely it would be soon.

Before she went up for her longed-for smoke, it crossed her mind to enlist Teri's help with the cake she planned to serve at two. She had had it made specially, with sagging tiers and spun-sugar cobwebs, to resemble Miss Havisham's wedding cake. The bakery had done a spectacular job. She would gather everyone in the living room and make a little toast to Ruth before cutting it. But it would not be easy to round up the guests. After a brief search, she found Teri, conveniently already in the kitchen, where she had gone to alert Ames that the ice supply was running out upstairs. The three of them conferred as to the best way to herd the masses down into one room. Then, finally, Juliet went up to the terrace.

Once there, she found that some clever soul had located her Motown collection and substituted them for the CDs she'd left in the stereo. The terrace was flooded with Marvin Gaye's "Going to a Go-Go," and the dancers (she recognized Olympia, Lily, Nick Sabatino, Alexei, Ryder, and others among them) were bumping and grinding at each other for all they were worth. Juliet, cigarette lit, leaned against the concrete wall and watched for a while, surprised at how down and dirty their dancing was. She supposed that even now, she had only a superficial understanding of the world of ballet.

"Care to cut a rug?"

It was Patrick, thoughtful and self-sacrificing to the last, who had taken pity and invited her merely mortal self onto the floor. She had finished her cigarette and for some time, her hips and shoulders had been twitching. She was longing to dance; but now that the possibility offered, she felt quite unnerved.

"It's all right, no one will watch you," he encouraged. He leaned over to whisper in her ear, "They only watch themselves. Look at the way they linger by their reflections in the glass door. They can't help it; it's instinctive."

Seeing he was right, Juliet smiled, slipped out of her shoes and allowed herself to move forward with him. In her devotion to Motown, Juliet Bodine held herself second to no man, and soon she was part of the gyrating mass, happily howling along with The Temptations. The embroidered skirt was not ideal for dancing, but at least the slit allowed for a certain freedom of movement, and she thoroughly enjoyed herself through the better part of a girl-groups compilation. Two a.m. was approaching when she finally retired, sweaty and joyful, from the floor. With the idea of fetching a couple of extra chairs (people had started to sit on the ground by the dance floor, their glasses perilously at their feet), she left the populated part of the terrace and went, still shoeless, around to the north-facing side of the wraparound.

This part of the terrace was a mere four feet wide. It was not lit. Juliet chiefly used it for storing extra chaise longues and garden supplies. Just by the far wall, on the other side of which was her neighbor's terrace, she kept a half-dozen spare occasional tables and chairs. Enjoying the respite from the loud music ("You Haven't Done Nothing" was not nearly so audible here as she would have expected—maybe she would not incur the wrath of all her neighbors?), she went along the narrow corridor between the side of the building and the waist-high concrete wall to disentangle two spindly chairs from the rest. She was awkwardly starting back with them when a short, slender figure appeared in front of her, coming from the main terrace. It stopped, silhouetted against the light. Her mood of exhilaration promptly evaporated and a shiver of dread forked through her chest like lightning. She set down the chairs. She had been wondering where he was.

"Hart?" She noticed the quiver in her own voice and hoped that he would not.

The figure came toward her in silence.

"Hart, is that you?"

She had an impulse to yell for help. Instead, she backed away a few steps toward the restraining wall. She ordered herself to be calm, be a grown up. He could not know her thoughts, even though they seemed to her to announce themselves like the telltale heart.

Yet in fact, when he spoke it was only to say, "Miss Bodine, I've been wanting a word with you." He smiled. "I want to thank you for helping Ruth get through all that."

He came closer to her and again, she instinctively took another step back, only to feel her tailbone smack the restraining wall. His

Southern accent was unusually strong, almost a drawl. A reek of rum came off him, accompanied by fragrances of cologne and shampoo.

He brought his pale, ascetic face near to hers, so near she could feel his warm breath. "I know *Great Ex* wouldn't be half so fine except for your contribution."

"Well, thank you, but I'm sure Ruth would have managed," said Juliet, striving to remove her uneasiness from her tone. But she, too, had been drinking, and her mind was not at its clearest. She tried to move forward as if casually, toward the lighted end of the narrow terrace. "I was just going down—"

But Hayden had planted himself in front of her. He cut off her words. "Will you allow me to kiss your hand?" he asked, still smiling. His white teeth gleamed amid the shadows.

"That's not necessary."

"Oh, but it would give me such pleasure."

He made a little bow, a very courtly, balletic little bow, and reached out for her left hand with his right.

Try as she might, Juliet could not stop herself from flinching away. It was only a slight gesture, just the tiniest hesitation before she let him take hold of her hand. But he saw it. She knew at once that he had.

His strong fingers wrapped around her wrist, Hart was suddenly very still. He looked questioningly at her. His smile faded.

"Now, what—?" he began.

Too late, Juliet realized that though he could not read her thoughts, English was not his native language anyway. Body was. He spoke the language of the body fluently; it was his life. He could read every breath and tremble in her, every shift in posture, to the last flutter of her eyelid.

He adjusted his hold on her wrist to make it firmer. Juliet thought of him lifting Elektra into the Madonna pose and a new thrill of fear ran through her.

"You're very nervous," he observed, gazing straight into her eyes. "Now, what could be troubling you?"

Juliet felt her fear visible on her face. She tried to will it away, tried to smile as she answered, "Oh, it's the party, I guess. I just want it to go well. You know, hostess jitters."

"Is that so?" drawled Hayden slowly, musingly. "Why, you're as jumpy as a jackrabbit."

Around the corner, even as he spoke, the Stevie Wonder song wound down to silence. Suddenly, blessedly, Juliet heard Teri's whistly voice call over the ensuing quiet, "Everybody downstairs for cake, please! Everybody down to the living room! No more music till after the cake is cut!"

Juliet's tight chest loosened as there followed a murmur of voices, some complaining, others celebratory, and a general shuffling of feet. "Listen, I have to go inside now," she said. "I'm going to make a toast to Ruth."

"She'll wait. Tell me what's on your mind."

"I really think I should—"

Again, she tried to move past him. His fingers tightened around her wrist, crushing the orchid in her old-fashioned corsage.

"She'll wait," he repeated. "Right now, you are going to tell me exactly, *exactly* what is in your mind. What have you been busy at, Miss Bodine?"

His shrewd, drink-reddened eyes narrowed as he peered at her, and she seemed to see behind them his sharp mind whirring, sorting, piecing things together. "You know," he said deliberately, "my room-mate Frank told me a policeman phoned him just a week ago to ask if he had missed some drugs. Did you know that?"

A second went by, then another. Juliet only stared at him, her heart thumping. "Let go of me," she finally said, her voice dry, hoarse.

"I think you did know that," he went on, ignoring her. "I think that was the same policeman you sat next to at Anton's memorial."

Juliet felt herself go paler. She remembered glimpsing Hart there, but had not realized he had seen her.

"That man interviewed me," he said. "Victorine mentioned he

phoned her last week, too, to ask if she was missing some medicine. I think you've been giving that detective ideas. Now, haven't you?"

His grasp on her wrist tightened yet more. Then he twisted her arm up and, frighteningly, bent it behind her.

"Let me go." Her voice came out as no more than a whisper, her mouth dry, her throat clenched. "I want to go inside now."

"I don't think so."

Somehow, with some dancer's art Juliet would never be able to explain, Hart caught hold of her waist with his free hand and lifted her up. Before she knew it, she was sitting unsteadily on the wall, both her arms bent painfully behind her back, Hart's fingers clamped around each of her wrists. He was so close to her that she could feel the tense rise and fall of his chest in her own.

"You've been waiting, haven't you?" he said. "You know something. Or you think you do. But you've been waiting till the show opened, so you wouldn't wreck it for your friend. What is it?"

He leaned even closer to her, leaned so that she was tipped back, began to lose her balance. If he let go suddenly, she thought, she might topple backward. She thought of what Murray had said about letting a suspect stew, about how long Hart had been alone with his guilt, dreading discovery (and maybe hoping for it, too?), suspecting every odd glance from his friends and colleagues.

It occurred to her to raise her legs and slam her feet into his chest, but without even her high heels to spike into him, she might only succeed in catapulting herself backwards. Her heart seemed to thud in her ears as loudly as if it were inside her skull. A sort of cloud descended in front of her eyes and she began to feel dizzy. But here, now, that could be disastrous—

"Hart?"

The voice was a woman's. Elektra, Juliet realized a moment later, her heart calming slightly. She was coming toward them, alone.

"I was looking for you, there's a cake downstairs," Elektra said. But her tone was distracted, her mind not on her words, and her small face, Juliet saw as her sight cleared and her momentary vertigo abated, was alive with puzzlement.

She came a few steps closer and stopped, peering at Hayden through the gloom.

"Hart, what are you doing?"

"Nothing, just having a talk," he said. "Why don't you go downstairs ahead of me?"

"A talk? Is that Juliet Bodine? Why are you holding her like that? What's the matter with you?"

She stood staring at her partner of so many years, her attention gradually more focused, her eyes increasingly serious. Hayden had still not released the pressure on Juliet's wrists, had not stopped tilting her backward. Juliet wanted to speak but, as in a nightmare, now seemed unable to make a sound.

"Lek, there's no reason for you to be a part of this. Please go downstairs. Now."

Hayden was becoming increasingly agitated and, no doubt without his realizing it, his voice had gotten louder. Elektra had come nearly halfway down the narrow terrace. Several yards behind her, Juliet suddenly saw a neat blond head appear around the corner from the main terrace, then disappear almost at once. Hart, who evidently had not seen it, renewed his grip on Juliet and spread her arms apart, raising them as if preparing to force her finally over the side. Juliet began to pray. How surprised God must be to hear from her after all this while.

Yet He must have remembered who she was, because in the very next moment, she found her voice.

"Hart killed your baby, Elektra," she said, her already aching arms stretched like wings behind her. "He caused your miscarriage. Those raisins he fed you that day had medicine in them, an abortion drug—"

Hayden, enraged, gave her arms a sudden jerk. Juliet squawked in terror. Elektra leapt forward and grabbed her partner by the elbows, pulling him back. She couldn't make him let go of Juliet, but she changed the balance, hampering him. Upper-body strength, thought Juliet, teetering on the wall but still alive. The ballerinas had been working out.

Elektra, grunting with effort, demanded, "Hart, is that true? Did you do that?"

In their strange relation to each other, Elektra facing his back, her hands clenched around his arms, his hands clutching Juliet, they all seemed to be rehearsing some unusual new step.

"No, I didn't."

"He killed Anton, too," said Juliet. "He doped his Coke, just before the run-through."

"I didn't. It's all a lie."

"If it's a lie," gasped Elektra, "why are you threatening her? Let go of her, Hart."

"Go downstairs."

Except to brace herself by putting a foot up against the wall, Elektra did not move. Years of physical intimacy of this kind must have taught her exactly how to hold Hart, Juliet thought, exactly how to anticipate his moves.

"You're afraid of her," Elektra said. "You were questioning her, or threatening her, and I interrupted you. Or were you planning to kill her? For God's sake, Hart. I *knew* Anton wouldn't have taken Ecstasy in the studio. I think you did give it to him. But why?"

She began to cry, but—Juliet saw, with gratitude and admiration—without loosening her hold on him.

"Was it ambition? Just for the part, to be the one who made Pip?" She panted, grunted, gasped. "Jesus, Hart, have you lost your mind?"

"Elektra," he tried again, his voice almost at a shout, "go away. Go down now. I don't want you involved in this."

"You shouldn't kill her, you should kill me," she sobbed. "You have killed me. You killed my baby—"

Hart's voice was harsh. He twisted sideways, still clutching Juliet's arms but no longer pushing at her.

"What good would it have done you to start a family with Ryder now?" he demanded. "Why didn't you listen to me? It would have wrecked—"

"It wasn't Ryder's baby. It was Anton's."

Hart's surprise was so powerful that he took a step back and at last slightly slackened his grip on Juliet. She was calculating whether she could twist her wrists out of his hands now, and if so, how best to slide and dart around him when she heard a woman shout, "Halt in the name of the law!"

All eyes looked to the corner of the terrace. There, Ames's solid, unmistakable bulk stood out against the night. Before her, in both hands, she held a large, heavy pistol, aimed directly at Hart Hayden.

At this second shock, Hart finally, suddenly let go of Juliet. She scrambled off the wall, dashed around him. Grabbing hold of Elektra as she passed, she pulled the ballerina toward Ames and safety. At the same moment, a dark, narrow blur raced around the corner and darted the other way into the narrow alley of the side terrace.

"Police, freeze!"

Landis had arrived at last. Gun drawn, he paused for an instant, then strode halfway down the length of the terrace. With a sobbing Elektra in tow, Juliet ran past him and collapsed on Ames, who gladly allowed the antique Manton pistol (innocent of ammunition for the past hundred years) to drop to her side.

"Miss Malone fetched me, Dr. Bodine. She saw you with Mr. Hayden," Ames murmured by way of explanation. "I took the liberty of unlocking your Regency display to provide myself with a weapon."

Meantime, Landis had begun a slow advance on Hart. At first, Hayden merely eyed him warily. But when the detective had come within two yards, the dancer sprang lightly up onto the waist-high wall.

Murray stopped walking and holstered his gun.

"Hayden, think a minute," he said, his voice reasonable, coaxing. "Take it easy. Talk to me now."

On the terrace wall, Hart pivoted, came up on one leg and raised his graceful arms in a beautiful arc.

"Everything will be fine. No one's going to hurt you." Landis's voice was a soothing river. "We can resolve all of this if you just relax and come down—"

Hayden gave a quick, desperate glance at Elektra, then faced the night again. He arched his back and bent his knee.

"No!" Juliet yelled. "It's not—"

But it was too late. Hart Hayden had leapt from the terrace into the darkness below.

chapter

TWENTY

"I must say I liked detective work as an excuse for not writing," Juliet admitted wistfully, offering Ruth a Fuji apple and a block of New York cheddar cheese.

It was late September and local Fujis had just begun to appear at the greenmarket. The women, bundled in fleece sweatshirts and blue jeans, were enjoying lunch in the crisp, breezy air on Juliet's terrace. Across the street, in Riverside Park, a few trees had already gone bright yellow. Others showed here and there a hint of the more garish colors of fall.

"All the fun of research and much better company," Juliet went on, starting to peel an apple.

The Andersons' was only a little balcony, but it was well located, two floors below Juliet's terrace and exactly under the spot from which Hart Hayden had jumped. Leaping from any other point, he would have sailed out into space and died instantly. As it was, a tearing sound (the Andersons' awning), then a sickening thud told the onlookers he had not gone far.

He had broken three bones—not counting ribs—and suffered extensive cuts and contusions. But quite enough of him remained intact to face a charge of the attempted homicide of Juliet Bodine. The doctors expected to release him from the hospital sometime in October.

"Speaking of company, are you seeing Murray Landis at all?" Ruth asked, slicing from the cheddar block a wafer of cheese thin enough to be translucent. This she laid atop a sliver of apple and slid into her mouth.

Ruth had been busy in the past few weeks, giving interviews, tightening up the production of *Great Ex*, sifting through newly offered commissions. For a while, she had been frantic about the loss of her leading dancer—a person she had liked as well as admired professionally. But after six or seven successful performances with the second and third casts, she had calmed down. It was sad for her that the splendid notices *Great Ex* had received ("Stunning!" "Magical!" "Moving!") had been overshadowed almost at once by the gory drama of Hart Hayden's "fall" (as his lawyer insisted on calling it) and the resurrection in the press of the lurid story of Anton's death. But Nick Sabatino and Kirsten had proven exceptional, and Lily Bediant, dancing Estella with Alexei Ostrovsky as Pip in the third cast, had pleased the sentimental crowds more than Elektra could ever have done. Ruth would gladly have allowed Elektra to dance, pairing her with Nick. But the death of her lover, the loss of her pregnancy, her impending divorce, her partner's betrayal, and his near-fatal jump had all combined to unbalance her thoroughly. She had dropped out for the season and was spending a month with friends in London.

Juliet sighed. "Well, in the ocular sense, yes," she replied. "I did see Murray Landis, a couple of weeks ago. He finally invited me to his studio to look at his sculpture. You ought to see it some time. It's pretty fascinating—strange, but not for the sake of strangeness."

She did not add how disappointed she had been, when at last the promised hour had arrived, to find that Murray had invited another visitor as well. This was an elderly collector, insistently courtly and maddeningly intrusive, who called Juliet "darling" and would not hear of leaving without her.

"But if you meant are we 'seeing each other' seeing each other," Juliet went on, "no. Or—I don't know, maybe I should say that all we have done is see."

She sighed again, a long sigh. Several times in the last month or so, she had dreamt of Murray Landis. Langorous, sensual dreams that clung deliciously to her waking consciousness for hours. During the studio visit, she had been disturbed repeatedly by an impulse to hop into his lap and bury her nose in the curve of his neck. When she had left him at Cadwell Hall just after the premiere, his reserve had unmistakably been breaking down. "You look very beautiful tonight," he had said—and there had been the orchid.

But alas, the evening's subsequent drama had given him plenty of time to retreat to his usual distance. Since then, he had been friendly, courteous, but no more. Juliet had to admit she still couldn't imagine a happy ending for a romantic relationship between them. But every day, she was less interested in such wise foresight and more drawn by short-term gratification. True, it was easier to stay out than to get out. But what was the point of living if you couldn't make a mistake now and then?

However, Murray showed no sign of any reciprocal recklessness.

Ruth shrugged sympathetically. "Men," she said, and the conversation turned to other matters.

Half an hour later, lunch eaten and coffee drunk, Ruth went off to Cadwell Hall to prepare for the evening's performance. After her departure, Juliet stood alone on the terrace for a long while, looking into the stiffening breeze off the river and thinking about the vanished summer. On September 15, on time to the day, she had given the completed manuscript of *London Quadrille* to Portia Klein. The editor read it overnight and pronounced it vintage Kestrel-Haven. Juliet had also given her Teri Malone's first chapter, which Portia, somewhat surprisingly, also simply adored. The dancer was planning to write through the winter break, then see where she was. Perhaps she would even quit the Jansch in the spring.

So Juliet felt satisfied with her summer's work. There was, moreover, the new book, the one with the chaste hero, which looked like lots of fun.

But the summer had also been hard, sad, shot through with

death and destruction, and it left behind more than a whiff of regret. A few days after her visit to his studio, Murray had phoned her from the station. The department had just gotten word as to legal plans for Hart Hayden's prosecution. In conjunction with his behavior at Juliet's party, the D.A. might have tried to nail him for Anton Mohr's death. But because Officer Peltz had not confiscated and analyzed the Coke at once, they did not believe there was adequate intact physical evidence to make it stick. Nor did they think a charge of his having caused Elektra's miscarriage with an untraced and untraceable substance would fly. As for the talcum powder, Murray had already gently intimated to Juliet it would be just as well if that matter were not examined too closely. He seemed to feel Greg Fleetwood could be found criminally negligent for his weak response and his failure to inform the victim. The result was that her own attempted homicide was the only charge Hart would face. Murray believed they would get a conviction; but without a record, Hayden would probably get no more than probation.

Juliet had immediately suffered a spasm of bitter frustration. Fate had seen to it that Hart Hayden would never dance again—indeed, would be lucky to walk again. But in the courts of men, he would literally get away with murder. If only she had forced Peltz to take that Coke bottle with him. If only she had not made such a foolish error in her French. The latter mistake had been due to sheer intellectual arrogance, a grimly familiar personal fault—in fact, the bête noir that roamed her inner landscape. When she blurted out the gist of her self-reproach to Murray, he heartily concurred.

"Yeah," he said. "And another thing, it was incredibly stupid to try to act as a P.I. That can be very dangerous. Don't do that next time, Jule."

"I certainly wasn't very good at it," she said ruefully, overlooking that curious 'next time' till much later.

"Now, there I don't agree with you. You were very good at it. You figured it out."

"But Anton is dead. And the baby he would have left is—"

"Hey, don't go all lofty on me. You think anyone but God could have second-guessed that lunatic?"

"But if I had made Peltz take the bag—"

"Oh, can it, Jule. You're smarter than that. Do you really believe Officer Bonehead Peltz would ever have had that soda pop analyzed? He took you for a hysterical broad. He'd probably have chugged what was left himself. And wouldn't that have taught him a lesson?" Murray paused to laugh, then resumed, "You ought to feel good about yourself, Jule. A lot of times, evil wins. At least this time, the guy was caught. You have any idea how many murders in this town go undetected?"

"No," said Juliet, intrigued.

"Well, neither do I. 'Cause they go undetected." Landis gave another laugh, as if he had told a good riddle, then went on, "The person who really fucked up in this case was me. I shouldn't have gone to that memorial with you. It's true the file was closed by then—but I'm usually smarter than that. And I should have realized those questions about the Mistenflo and the E could get back to Hayden. I put you in danger."

Juliet considered this. Then, "At least you also came to rescue me," she said.

She hung up feeling comforted. It was one of the growing number of things she liked Landis for.

Now she slowly turned her eyes from the river and roused herself to work. She had pooh-poohed Ruth's offer to help her with the dishes, and these consequently remained on the painted table in all their sorry disarray. Carrying the first load down to the kitchen, she noticed a light flashing on her answering machine.

She rewound it.

"Jule? Murray Landis."

("Dope," Juliet couldn't help thinking. How many Murrays did he think she knew? Meantime, his voice was going on.)

"Listen, I got a problem. Somebody clobbered a talking head up at the Karp Foundation's think tank—that's over near you, on

West End Avenue. They kind of specialize in those windy Bill Buck-ley–style types up there, you know what I mean, professional pontif-icators, gasbags, Ph.D. Which you'd think would make them trip themselves up if they talked long enough in an interrogation room. But in fact, I'm having a heck of a time making out which of these damned jokers is lying through his teeth. So . . . I feel kind of funny asking, but do you think I could come over your place, run it by you, maybe pick your brain? Maybe you could even go over there with me sometime, take a look around."

As the machine clicked off, the phrase at last returned to Juliet's memory. "Next time." So that was what he had meant. Her new business card materialized in the air before her:

JULIET BODINE

ROMANCE NOVELS
PRIVATE INVESTIGATIONS

She liked it. Maybe she'd get a P.I.'s license while avoiding her next book?

Cheerfully, she picked up the phone.

ACKNOWLEDGMENTS

This book was written with the help of many people. Among those who generously shared their expertise, their literary insights, and their encouragement are Dr. Alan Astrow, Ann Banks, Professor Robert J. Castelli, Ellen Chuse, Lieutenant Vincent DiDonato, Waverly Fitzgerald, Louisa Geswaldo, Dr. Alan Gribetz, Jessica Gribetz, Carol Hill, Caryn James, Gara LaMarche, Miriam Miller, Madeleine Monette, Brian Morton, Jill Nathanson, Dr. Gale Organist, Mary Pope Osborne, Dr. David B. Pall, Lieutenant Regina Rogers, Debbie Sankey, Sean Savoye, Lynne Sharon Schwartz, Laura Shapiro, Ellen Walker, and Lawrence Weschler. Mary Evans, who represented this book, and Hope Dellon, who edited it, are brilliant exemplars of their respective professions. Thank you.